THE GHOST WHISPERER'S GAMBIT

ROBIN T. POPP

LARKSPUR LANE PUBLISHING, LLC

CONTENTS

PROLOGUE

THE FULL MOON HUNG low in the sky, casting a pale glow over the *Rio Maldito*. Under the silvery orb, the river's surface sparkled with dancing shadows and light. The gentle lapping of the water against the shore provided a soothing soundtrack for the late-night audience gathered at Murphy's RV park. While most of the residents in Las Palomas had long since retreated to their air-conditioned homes, the guests at Murphy's RV park remained awake, drawn by the promise of something otherworldly.

At one table, two young boys, ages four and six, fidgeted as their weary parents tried to keep them still. Nearby, a young couple whispered softly to each other, lost in their own world. The kindly old man who had earlier played catch with the boys now sat at another table, puffing contentedly on his pipe. Nearby, the artist and his wife sat in chairs outside their trailer, still skeptical but unable to resist the curiosity that had brought them here.

As midnight drew near, a gasp from one boy captured everyone's attention. Across the river a woman had appeared, her features blurred and distorted like a fuzzy image on an old television set.

An apparition?

The ghostly figure moved with a sense of purpose along the riverbank, her long pale gown billowing and swirling around her legs, caught in a breeze that only she seemed to feel.

The onlookers, mesmerized by her ghostly appearance, held their breath as she passed by.

Moments passed, and just when it seemed she would disappear without a glance in their direction, she halted and turned towards them. Her eyes were twin orbs of glowing yellow light, radiating an unsettling intensity that sent shivers down the spines of those watching.

Some onlookers slowly rose to their feet, feeling a mix of fascination and fear. They instinctively huddled together, seeking comfort and protection in each other's presence as they watched the apparition draw nearer.

With a suddenness that startled them all, the woman rose in the air and gave an inhuman shriek that pierced the night, drawing terrified screams from the women and children. Then she flew across the river towards them, her arms outstretched with sheets of mist trailing behind her like a majestic cape.

With a deafening rush of air, she swooped past the now fleeing group—and simply vanished, leaving behind only the lingering echoes of her haunting scream.

CHAPTER ONE

AT 9:00 P.M., DANE Wolfe pushed open the doors to Kathy's Café and a wall of noise and warmth greeted him. Despite the late hour, the place was packed.

As he made his way to a table in the back, Dane couldn't help but notice that most of the patrons were locals, though there were a few tourists scattered among them.

Las Palomas was a small town nestled in the southern region of Texas, its population too insignificant to warrant much attention on maps. Yet that didn't stop a steady stream of visitors from coming each year. They didn't come for the flat, sparsely forested scenery or for a leisurely float trip down the muddy *Rio Maldito*. No, they came for the ghosts.

Especially lately.

"Evening, Chief." A middle-aged woman dressed in a blue and white checkered waitress uniform emerged from between the tables, balancing an empty mug in one hand and a carafe of hot coffee in the other.

"Hey, Linda," Dane greeted her with a tired smile. "And it's Acting Chief, let's not forget that. How're you doing?"

"As well as can be expected, I suppose," she replied with a weary sigh, setting the mug down before him. A stray strand of dark blonde hair had escaped her ponytail, and she impatiently tucked it behind her ear as she poured the steaming liquid into his mug. "Coffee's fresh. Just brewed it."

"Thanks." He took a sip eagerly, feeling the hot liquid sear its way down his throat but not caring. "I can't tell you how much I need this."

Linda's smile lit up her tired face and took years off her worn appearance. "I bet. When are you expecting Sam back?"

Dane had been the acting police chief for the past four months, ever since Samantha Hunter, the actual police chief, was wounded during a dangerous drug bust. The weight of responsibility and concern for his injured friend weighed heavily on his shoulders. "Not for a while," he said, his voice weary with exhaustion. "But I spoke to her yesterday, and she sounded good."

"I'm glad to hear that." Linda's warm smile offered a small glimmer of comfort amid chaos. "Can I bring you something to eat? Apple pie, maybe? Annie made it fresh this afternoon."

"Just coffee for now, thanks."

"All right. Holler if you need anything." Linda gracefully set the carafe on the table and walked away, her long ponytail swaying with each step.

As he sat there, savoring the rich and bitter taste of the coffee, Dane studied the room. Kathy, the owner of the café, was standing at the mayor's table, talking to him and his wife. Other familiar faces sat at most of the tables in the room, save two, which were occupied by tourists.

One group of tourists rose from their table and made their way towards the door. Dane's gaze followed them across the room until Linda reappeared, setting a plate down in front of him.

"What's this?" he asked in surprise. "A brownie—with ice cream?"

"Wow—it's like I'm standing next to Sherlock Holmes," she replied sarcastically, but with a smile. "It's impressive, really. How do you do it?"

He rolled his eyes. "You know what I mean. I didn't order this."

She shrugged. "You looked tired. I figured you might need a little sugar to go with your caffeine. It's on me."

He gave her a pointed look. "So it has nothing to do with me tearing up that ticket for you yesterday?"

Her cheeks flushed slightly as she admitted, "Maybe a little. Thanks again."

"No problem." He'd only wanted to get his point across that she couldn't leave her car double-parked in the street, no matter how quick the errand or how sparse the traffic. Picking up his fork, he gestured to the brownie. "And thanks for this."

"You bet."

Just then, the remaining table of tourists caught his attention, and Dane looked over to see that a man had his hand raised in the universal gesture for "bring me the bill." Linda waved back to let him know she'd seen him.

"About damn time," she muttered under her breath before hurrying back to the front counter where she retrieved the customer's tab. She took it over to him and a few minutes later, the group, having paid for their meal, headed out the door as Linda held it open for them.

"Have a great evening," she called with a smile as they left.

When they were gone, she closed the door, then locked it. Flipping the sign so that it now read "Sorry, we're closed," she turned around to meet the stares of those still sitting in the diner.

"Well? What are you waiting for?" she demanded.

At this, several people got up and hurried over to the windows, where they lowered and closed the blinds. As they worked, Mayor Garcia headed to the front counter. He waited until everyone had returned to their seats before pulling out a gavel and rapping it on the countertop.

"I call this emergency town council meeting to order. Our first order of business," he pulled a folded piece of paper from his front jacket pocket and waved it in the air for all to see. "We have a schedule, people. Who the hell didn't follow it?"

Dane scanned the room for a guilty face and noticed, with some disappointment, that everyone else was doing the same.

"Speak up," Mayor Garcia urged, anger creeping into his tone. "Who's responsible for *La Llorona* showing up at Murphy's last night? You scared those people half to death. One family didn't even stick around until morning before they packed their trailer and left."

"Somebody owes me money," Bill Murphy complained, "'cause I had to refund their entire two-night stay to make things right. I can't afford to do that again. Besides, the ghosts shouldn't be attacking the guests. It's not good for business."

Mayor Garcia studied the crowd for a long moment before heaving a sigh. "I know impersonating ghosts is new to everyone. And we agreed the Events Team, Dylan and a few of the other high school seniors, would do most of the impersonations. When they can't do it, members of the town council will fill in. That's why we have a schedule; so there are no... misunderstandings."

Dylan raised his hand. "It wasn't us, sir. I swear. My team was at the Double R Ranch last night just like the schedule says."

"That's true," Diego Juarez agreed. He was sitting next to his wife, Elise. "*El Muerto* made his ride just after midnight. We saw him, along with several of our guests."

Dane was pretty sure the boy was telling the truth, and he could tell from the mayor's expression that he thought so, too.

"So, if it wasn't the Events Team, then who? Anyone care to step forward and take responsibility?" Mayor Garcia asked.

Dane looked around to see if anyone raised their hand. Not that he intended to arrest anyone for pretending to be a ghost. Hell, if he did that, he'd have to arrest the entire room of people.

The idea to do the impersonations had come from Elise Juarez, who ran the Double R Ranch with her husband. They had taken over the ranch after Elise's father, Roy Richard-son, had been killed. Elise, who'd been living in New York at the time, had returned to Las Palomas to bury her father and then got involved with finding his killer. It was during that investigation that she learned that half of the *El Muerto* ghost sightings were actually ranch hands in disguise. It had been Roy's idea in order to attract more guests to the ranch. And it had worked.

When the town hired Elise to do their marketing, she'd suggested the town do similar impersonations of its more notable ghosts to attract more tourists. Las Palomas was legitimately haunted, but to account for the unreliable na-ture of ghosts, the idea was to provide an understudy, to use a theatrical term. If the ghost failed to appear on a moonlit night, then the understudy would fill in. Because it was important to keep the impersonations secret, only the town council members and a select group of high school seniors knew about it.

"There is another possibility," Zelda Zahn suggested, breaking the silence that had fallen over the room. Her jet-black hair was piled on her head with lengths of it falling down about her shoulders in thick, corkscrew curls. To Dane, she looked like a gypsy, though she didn't tell fortunes. Her "special talent" was detecting "auras," or, in more scientific terms, the energy patterns and colors given off by living things. Dane had once asked Zelda to explain how her talent worked and ended up getting a lecture in thermodynamics that he'd struggled to follow. In the end, he decided he didn't need to understand to know her talent was legitimate. Several times, she'd helped Las Palomas PD solve a crime by matching trace energy left behind at the crime scene to a suspect. Finding hard evidence was much easier once the police knew who had committed the crime.

"What other possibility, Zelda?" Mayor Garcia asked.

"The ghost at the park could have been the real *Llorona*."

Her statement met with a moment of stunned silence.

"Of course it's possible," Mayor Garcia conceded slowly. "But why would she start attacking the tourists now?"

"Perhaps she's troubled," Ruth Dorset, a member of the Events Team, suggested. "Like, more than usual for a ghost," she quickly amended when Dylan, sitting next to her, muttered, "Obviously."

"I think we need to find out," Zelda urged.

Mayor Garcia turned to address a grandmotherly figure. "Troubled spirits fall in your area, I believe?"

Sylvia Winters stood and her perfectly coiffed white hair shone like a halo beneath the fluorescent lights. Tonight, she wore a creamy saffron colored dress and looked like she'd just come from church. Then again, Dane couldn't remember a time she hadn't looked like that.

She greeted everyone with a warm smile and when she spoke in her slow, genteel Southern drawl, her words flowed over the group like molasses on a warm day. "Good evening. As soon as I learned of the trouble at Mr. Murphy's park, I gathered the Circle for an emergency session hoping to contact *Llorona*."

Sylvia was the chair of the Saturday Séance Circle and Dane mentally rolled his eyes at the image of six elderly women huddled around the Ouija board. He'd attended more meetings than he wanted to admit—at Sylvia's insistence—and it seemed to him the women spent more time drinking whiskey-spiked tea and gossiping than actually contacting the spirit world.

"Henri," she pronounced it *awn-ree*, "who is, as you know, my spirit guide, was unable to connect with *Llorona*."

"So where does that leave us?" Linda asked.

"I believe we need to bring in an expert. Someone whose expertise is summoning and talking to ghosts."

"You're kidding, right?" Dane sat dumbfounded. "A ghost psychologist? Are there really people like that? I mean, someone legitimate?"

Sylvia gave him a sympathetic look. "Of course, dear. Only they call themselves 'ghost whisperers.'"

"Like Jennifer Love Hewitt on that TV show," Ruth said excitedly.

Sylvia gave the girl an affectionate smile. "Exactly so."

Even though he lived in Las Palomas surrounded by individuals with actual para-psychic abilities, Dane couldn't help being suspicious of anyone who made their living counseling the dead. That wasn't his biggest concern, though.

"Assuming we bring in a ghost whisperer who's legit, aren't we taking a big risk?" he asked. "If they discover our Events Team activities, it'll destroy our town."

There was a general murmuring in the crowd.

"We could suspend all performances while the ghost whisperer is in town," Zelda suggested.

Several people in the diner agreed.

Mayor Garcia looked at Dane. "I don't see a problem with that, do you?"

"No, but I have one more question. If the ghost whisperer is successful in soothing *Llorona*, might she cross over? She's one of the town's biggest draws. Is that a risk we're willing to take?" Dane knew their revenue would take a big hit if they lost the famous wailing woman in white.

Hank Wells, the bank president, spoke from across the room. "I think we have to. I know we all agreed to only impersonate ghosts who actually haunt Las Palomas, and while the loss of *Llorona* would be impactful, it will be worse if we do nothing, and she continues to drive the tourists away."

His comment caused another stir, and the murmurings in the room grew louder until Mayor Garcia rapped his gavel on the counter again, drawing everyone's attention. "Let's put it to a vote. All those in favor of bringing in a ghost whisperer, raise your hand." He paused as nearly every hand in the room shot up. "Those opposed." Only a couple of hands went up. He turned to Sylvia. "Any recommendations?"

She smiled. "Madame Yolanda comes highly recommended. I called her manager earlier today, and she is available, for a fee, of course."

"How much?" the mayor asked.

"Twenty-five thousand dollars."

Loud gasps filled the room. Dane choked on the coffee he was sipping.

"Are you crazy?" He used his napkin to wipe off his chin. "Twenty-five thousand dollars for telling a dead woman everything's going to be okay? That's insane."

"She comes highly recommended," Sylvia protested.

"By whom?" Dane demanded. "And please don't tell me Henri." Sylvia snapped her mouth shut, leaving her abrupt silence to answer his question. "God Almighty, Sylvia. Please tell me you've got a more reputable source."

She gave him an admonishing look. "Mark Allen's *Spirit Guide* endorses her."

Dane had heard both Zelda and Sylvia talk before about Mark Allen's *Spirit Guide*. According to them, Mark Allen—whoever the hell he was—was *the* authority on all things spiritual.

"How much money do we have in the town's discretionary fund?" Mayor Garcia asked Hank Wells.

"Unfortunately, the repairs to the school used most of our funds, so we're down to forty thousand dollars, but half of that is earmarked for the town beautification project."

There was a general murmur of voices as they considered the news.

"Is there someone else we could consider who isn't as expensive?" Nita Garcia asked.

All eyes turned to Sylvia, and the room fell silent.

"It's not like there are a lot of ghost whisperers to choose from," Sylvia complained. "One does not train to be a ghost whisperer; one must be born with the ability to see and speak to the dead."

"We understand," Nita said patiently. "Surely there is more than one, though."

Sylvia pursed her lips as she seemed to think about it, then she opened her purse and pulled out a well-used booklet. She leafed through the pages, stopping when she found what she was looking for.

"I suppose we could try Gina Castillo," she said, looking up to meet Nita's gaze. "There is an article about her in the most recent edition of the *Spirit Guide.* She's relatively young but, according to the article, has enjoyed several successes. I could email her to get a quote, though I expect her rates will also be high."

"How high?" Dane asked. "Could you give us a rough estimate?"

"Maybe ten to fifteen thousand dollars?"

There was a general murmur throughout the room. Mayor Garcia rapped his gavel on the countertop to quiet the crowd. "I don't know. It's still a lot of money," he said.

"And completely unnecessary." Across the room, Peggy Olson stood.

Dane automatically cringed. Her arrogant tone grated on his nerves. Every town, he supposed, had their own Peggy Olson; an over-controlling, over-bearing busybody who thought they were better and more deserving than everyone else.

"Have you forgotten? I am a high functioning sensitive." She raised her chin a little, daring anyone to refute the claim.

"You are?" The mayor couldn't hide his skepticism. He shot Dane a quick glance, but Dane could only shrug. He had no idea if Peggy Olson had legitimate para-psychic abilities.

Peggy frowned, clearly not happy at being doubted. "Yes, I am. And while I am very busy with the town's beautification project, I suppose I can take time out of my schedule to contact *Llorona.*" She shot Sylvia a scathing look. "I won't charge the town twenty-five thousand dollars, either. I should think ten thousand would be more than sufficient for my time and effort."

The offer was met with silence.

It was Sylvia who finally broke that silence. "Gina Castillo will guarantee her work. If she can't communicate with the ghost, we won't have to pay her. Are you willing to extend us the same deal?"

Everyone looked at Peggy, who pursed her lips, clearly not happy. "It is inconceivable to think I would not be successful."

"Then guaranteeing your work shouldn't be a problem," Zelda pointed out.

Peggy's mouth twisted like she'd just bitten into a lemon. "Of course, I guarantee my work. On the very remote possibility that I cannot connect with *Llorona*, I will not accept payment despite the personal cost to myself."

"Then it's settled," the mayor announced. "Peggy, we accept your offer. Can you go out tomorrow night? Hopefully, we can resolve this quickly."

"And if Peggy's efforts are unsuccessful?" Sylvia asked the mayor.

"Then I suppose we won't have any choice but to hire this Gina Castillo."

Chapter Two

Gina Castillo moved about the musty attic with careful steps, mindful of not disturbing the piles of forgotten relics of earlier times. The area was fraught with history, each item a tangible reminder of lives once lived. Old newspapers, boxes of clothing and toys, reels of 8 mm film—all held secrets and stories waiting to be uncovered. As she navigated her way through the cluttered space, the thick layer of dust coating every surface tickled her nose, causing her to sneeze.

"Is he here?" Lydia Calhoun Jones whispered from the doorway, her voice barely audible in the attic's stillness. She was referring to the spirit of her late father, whose presence supposedly lingered in the old family home.

"Not yet," Gina replied, scanning the room for any signs of supernatural activity. A beam of light filtering through a small window caught her attention, highlighting swirling dust mites in its path. Was it her imagination, or did they seem thicker than normal? "David Calhoun, are you with us?" she whispered, almost reverently.

"This place gives me the creeps," Lydia muttered, breaking the solemn atmosphere. "I was the one who found his body. Did I tell you that? Found him dead in his old chair, eyes still open like he was watching TV."

"I can only imagine how difficult that must have been," Gina said kindly.

"Yeah. Did you know that when you die, your bladder empties?" Lydia rambled on, unaware of Gina's discomfort. "I really liked that chair, but we couldn't keep it after that. Had to burn it 'cause it's not like we could sell it. I mean, who wants a chair that someone died and then peed in, you know?"

Gina paused in her examination of the attic's contents and turned to face Lydia. Everyone had a different way of coping with loss and grief. Some mourned openly, while others hid their emotions and dealt with their pain in private. Lydia was clearly in a category of her own.

"Were you and your father close?" she asked gently, curious about their relationship.

Lydia gave a nonchalant shrug, her shoulders rising and falling dismissively. "He wasn't exactly the warm and fuzzy type, but we were close enough," she said with a hint of bitterness in her tone. "I don't have any siblings and my mom passed away about ten years ago, so it was just me and Dad—and Max, my husband."

Her words hung heavy in the air as Gina felt a wave of empathy wash over her. She knew the pain of losing a parent all too well. "I'm sorry," she said sympathetically. "I lost my mother—"

"How much longer do you think this will take?" Lydia interrupted, glancing at her wristwatch. "I have a hair appointment in thirty minutes."

Gina masked her irritation and maintained a professional demeanor. "We can begin now. Your father is here."

Lydia's eyes widened in surprise as she instinctively backed away from the doorway, scanning the space around Gina with an eager gaze. "He is? Where?"

Gina gestured to her left, where a faint beam of light flickered in the dim room.

"I don't see him." Lydia frowned, switching her focus back to Gina. "How do I know you're not just making all this up so you can take my money?"

Gina expected this question and calmly responded, "Ask your father a question that only you and he would know the answer to. I'll repeat his response for you."

"Okay." A spark of excitement lit up Lydia's face at the suggestion. Gina watched as she furrowed her brows in deep thought, almost looking pained by the effort. After two full minutes, her features relaxed into a smooth expression. "Alright, what was his favorite football team?"

Gina listened intently to the familiar buzzing in her ear before repeating the answer. "Houston Texans."

Lydia's face registered surprise, her eyebrows shooting up towards her hairline. "That's right." Then her brow furrowed in suspicion. "Wait a second. You could have guessed that since we live in Houston."

Gina resisted the urge to roll her eyes. She had encountered many people like this throughout her career as a ghost whisperer, and there were days like today when she preferred the company of the dead over the living.

"How about his favorite color?" Lydia continued, oblivious to Gina's internal frustration. "I think it was blue, but you could ask him and see."

I see stupid people, Gina silently parodied the line from *The Sixth Sense* movie. *They're everywhere and they don't even know they're stupid.*

Despite her thoughts, she maintained a polite smile. "Perhaps we should start with a question you already know the answer to—such as what did his favorite shirt look like or what was his favorite food? Maybe he had a special nickname for you?"

Lydia furrowed her brows in concentration, studying the floor as if searching for the answers there. Finally, she looked back up at Gina. "I didn't have a nickname, but my dad did when he was younger. What was it?"

Even a blind squirrel is bound to find an acorn now and then, Gina thought wryly.

Turning her attention to the space next to her, Gina directed her question to David Calhoun's spirit. "David, your daughter needs proof that you are with us. Can you answer her question?"

She listened closely for the answer, feeling a slight twinge of annoyance when all she heard was a ringing in her ear. Ignoring it, she turned to Lydia.

"His nickname was 'Boo'."

Lydia's eyes widened in surprise and disbelief; her mouth slightly agape. "That's right," she exclaimed, her voice tinged with wonder and nostalgia. "He got it when he was only four years old. It was his first time going trick-or-treating, and he had the time of his life scaring everyone. For months afterwards, he would go around trying to spook anyone he could, shouting 'Boo' at the top of his lungs." Lydia turned her gaze towards the spot where David Calhoun's ghost was "standing," a mixture of wonder and incredulity on her face. "Hi, Daddy," she breathed, her voice barely above a whisper. "This is incredible. I can't believe you're really here."

Lydia fell silent and Gina smiled sympathetically, understanding the emotional impact of the moment. This was why she was a ghost whisperer—for moments like these.

"Lydia, if there is anything you want to say to your father, now is the time," she gently prompted.

Still watching Lydia's face, Gina noticed a slight narrowing of Lydia's eyes—her only warning.

"Daddy," the woman suddenly snapped, her tone harsh and biting. "Where the hell did you hide your treasure? You always talked about it. Me and Max need it now that we don't get your social security checks anymore."

You had to admire the love of a close family, Gina thought facetiously. Given a chance to talk to her own mother again, Gina would have told her mother how much she loved and missed her—but her mother's ghost had never appeared to her.

The weight of Lydia's intense glare snapped Gina back to reality.

"Well?" Lydia demanded impatiently. "Is he telling you where he hid the money?"

Gina, suddenly feeling tired, listened for the buzzing in her ear. It directed her to an old suitcase hidden beneath a pile of clothes.

"Did you look in here?"

Lydia stepped into the room far enough to see around a stack of boxes that otherwise blocked her view. "Yeah. I think so."

"Maybe we should look again."

The lure of money proved greater than her fear of ghosts because Lydia released her hold on the door frame and went to stand beside Gina. Together, they gazed at the old suitcase for a few moments before Lydia dropped to her knees and fiddled with the rusty latch. After a brief struggle, the lid finally creaked open.

Inside, they found an assortment of dusty old books, trinkets and keepsakes, including a faded second place ribbon from a track meet and several loose photographs. Lydia wasted no time sifting through the contents, tossing items aside until she found a bundle of fifty-dollar bills. Quickly she counted it.

"A lousy thousand bucks?" she moaned.

Gina bent down next to Lydia, peering at the stack of papers Lydia had shoved aside. She reached out to touch the photograph on top—a young girl with bright blonde pigtails, laughing joyfully at the man standing next to her.

"Is that you and your father?" Gina asked, her voice filled with curiosity.

Lydia's expression turned solemn as she glanced at the photo and nodded. "Yeah," she mumbled, taking the picture from Gina's grasp and holding it gingerly between her fingers. "He was so handsome." A small smile tugged at the corners of her mouth. "I must have been around five or six in that picture." She picked up another photograph, this one an older portrait of a young couple. "These are my parents."

Then Lydia put the photos back and finished digging through the suitcase. "There's no more money here," she complained, disappointment evident in her tone. "Nothing but junk and pictures." She shot Gina a frustrated look. "He must have hidden his treasure somewhere else."

Gina silently cursed Lydia's foolishness. "I believe the contents of this suitcase—these family photographs—represent your father's treasure," she said coolly. "Lydia, *you* were his treasure."

She gave a wan smile. "I know, but I kind of was hoping for money, you know? This won't even cover the two thousand dollars we paid you."

Two thousand dollars? Hmmm.

"Before your father leaves, is there anything else you'd like to say to him?"

Impatiently, Gina watched as Lydia struggled to stuff all the photographs back into the suitcase.

"What?" Lydia asked, confused. "Oh, right. Um, yeah."

Finally, Gina thought as she braced herself for what was sure to be an emotional scene.

"Is there any more money hidden around here?"

Gina was too stunned to say a word. In that moment, she didn't know who she hated more: Uncle Victor, her manager, for getting her this assignment or Lydia, for being a selfish, ego-centric idiot, too stupid to appreciate her last contact with family.

"I'm sorry," she said calmly, but with a hint of irritation. "Your father's spirit has departed."

"Oh well," Lydia muttered, begrudgingly. "I suppose this will have to do."

Gina maintained her professional demeanor, careful not to let her emotions show. "Excellent," she said with forced enthusiasm. "Then I think we're finished here. I'll see myself out." Her words dripped with sarcasm as she turned on her heel and walked away, eager to leave this toxic environment behind.

Gina was proud of herself. She didn't race down the two flights of stairs and out the front door to get as far away from Lydia as she could. She walked purposefully but unhurriedly.

At the sidewalk, she turned left and continued down the street, counting the houses as she went. One. Two. Three. Four.

Reaching her car parked at the curb, she climbed in and glanced over at her passenger. A handsome man in his fifties, with neatly cut dark hair showing hints of gray at the temples. His trim salt-and-pepper mustache and beard gave him a Sean Connery appearance.

"All done?" he asked, turning to greet her.

"Yes, but I need a minute to calm down," she growled.

"I can see you're upset," Uncle Victor said in his infuriatingly calm tone, his phone clutched in his hand. "Tell me what's troubling you."

"You lied to me!" Her voice rose with each word. "To me!" She emphasized, feeling betrayal course through her veins.

Uncle Victor looked offended. "A misunderstanding, I'm sure. But perhaps you could clarify what exactly we are discussing?"

"You told me you charged Lydia five hundred dollars."

He pursed his lips in thought before responding. "Actually, I believe I said I was considering charging her five hundred dollars. However, after dealing with her insufferable attitude, I changed my mind when it came time to complete the deal. Surely you don't object? Besides, we gave a thousand of it back when I broke into their house earlier and hid it in that suitcase."

With his refined speech and polished demeanor, Uncle Victor seemed more like a member of Britain's aristocracy than the native Texan that he was.

It was hard to stay angry with him, especially considering she *hadn't* liked Lydia.

"I guess not," she admitted, her voice heavy with fatigue. "But a heads up would have been nice." She reached up and removed the small transmitter from her ear, feeling a sense of relief wash over her. "All things considered, I thought it went well, didn't you? Except when you took that phone call and forgot to turn off your mic."

"I apologize, but you did great on your own." He reached up and removed his own ear bud. "Good job, by the way.

Getting her to ask you for her father's nickname was a stroke of genius."

She shrugged. "Yeah, well, news flash—I don't think Lydia is exactly the sharpest tool in the shed. Getting her to ask the right question wasn't hard."

"Yes, but how'd you know the answer?"

A sly smile played on her lips as she revealed her secret. "I looked up the online obituary this morning and read the blog posts." She altered her voice and recited a few of the comments she had memorized. "'We'll miss Uncle Boo. He was the best.' 'Boo's gone, but not forgotten. His spirit will stay with us.'"

He returned her smile with one of his own. "Never underestimate the value of good research."

"It was one of the first lessons you taught me," Gina agreed. Then she started the engine, and they drove away.

Forty minutes later, they pulled into the garage of their Sugarland home. As they walked inside, Gina noticed her uncle was still moving stiffly. She'd first noticed it that morning but they'd been in a hurry, so she hadn't commented on it. Now, she was growing concerned.

"Are you feeling okay?"

"I'm fine," he assured her.

He clearly didn't want to talk about it, so she followed him through the house and into the study, where she sat in one of the chairs facing the desk. Uncle Victor took his seat behind the desk and studied her carefully. "You look exhausted. Have I been pushing you too hard?"

She shrugged. "It seems like we've been crazy busy, lately," she said. "Everyone's got a dearly departed they want me to talk to."

"Business is good," he agreed, causing her to glower at him.

"Do you even remember the conversation we had two weeks ago?"

"Of course, dear. You wanted to take a break."

"No!" she snapped. "I don't want a break. I want to stop. I don't like lying to people. The reason I look exhausted is because I lie awake at night, consumed with guilt."

"We're not hurting anyone," he challenged. "Our fees are reasonable, and I don't accept an assignment from anyone I think can't afford us."

She sighed. "It's not about the money."

"You give grieving people the closure they need," he reminded her.

"Except that I'm not really talking to spirits. Not like Mom did."

"You've got something your mother never had, intuition. You're so intuitive; you're practically psychic."

She rolled her eyes. "Please, spare me the accolades. Have you thought of an exit strategy yet? One that won't get us into trouble?" She heaved out a breath. "I still don't know why we can't tell people I'm burned out. It's the truth."

It was his turn to sigh. "I know."

They both fell quiet until Gina broke the silence a few minutes later. "I'm glad you charged her more. Lydia, that is. Let's use the extra money to take a vacation, like normal people do."

He raised an eyebrow at her comment about "normal people," but she hadn't lived a life that could be considered normal. Gina had been six years old when her mother passed away from cancer, leaving Gina in the care of Uncle Victor—a talented con artist with a penchant for bending the rules. Not exactly what one would call an ideal parent.

While other children were learning their ABCs and playing games, Gina was learning the tricks of the trade: the Fiddle Game, Three-card Monte, fortune telling, and most importantly, how to "communicate" with the dead.

"I suppose we could go out of town," he suggested, breaking into her thoughts.

"Great," she agreed eagerly. "San Antonio, maybe, or San Marcos. I wouldn't mind checking out the outlet mall. Or perhaps we could rent a cabin near Garner State Park."

"Or—we could go to Las Palomas."

"Where?" She'd never heard of it.

"Las Palomas. Down around McAllen, Texas. I'm sure I've mentioned the town to you before."

Perhaps he had; Gina couldn't recall. "What is there to do in Las Palomas?"

"You can talk to a ghost." He offered her a half-smile when she pinned him beneath her glare. "They want to hire you," he explained.

Gina fought to contain her frustration. "Correct me if I'm wrong, but isn't the whole point of taking a vacation to relax and not work?"

"They want you to contact the spirit of *La Llorona*," he continued, as if not hearing her objection.

"Wait. *La Llorona,* as in The Weeping Woman?" she asked, feeling a bit shocked.

"That's the one," Uncle Victor assured her.

"I thought she was just a legend."

"All legends have a basis in the truth," he said. "According to the good people of Las Palomas, *La Llorona* is real and haunting the *Rio Maldito,* which runs through their town. The town council would like to hire you to talk to *Llorona* and find out what's upsetting her."

"Please," Gina snorted, rolling her eyes. Everyone in Texas knew the legend of *La Llorona.* "I'll tell you what's bothering her. She drowned her own children and then regretted it."

Uncle Victor smiled indulgently. "Hence the reason this would make an ideal vacation. You already know the reason for the spirit's unrest. After you pretend to talk to the ghost, make up a story about this being the anniversary of her children's drowning. Then suggest the town's priest come bless the river and the souls of the lost children." He paused, giving his words time to sink in. "The town will put us up in the local B&B. We'll have to pay for our own meals, but the B&B serves free breakfast and dinners. Our costs will be minimal. And, when it's all over, we collect ten thousand dollars."

Ten thousand dollars! That was a lot of money.

"I don't know," she said hesitantly. "Maybe it would be better to just go to San Antonio, enjoy some good Mexican food, and maybe ride the riverboat."

"Gina. We need money." His tone was more serious than she remembered hearing it before.

"Since when?" She eyed him closely, afraid of his response.

His sigh was audible. "Since I got myself into a bit of a bad spot with a loan shark," he admitted reluctantly, suddenly sounding like a beaten man.

She probably should felt more shocked or surprised, but unfortunately, this wasn't the first time her uncle had gambled and lost. It was just the next time. "How *bad* a spot are we talking?" she asked, her heart dropping to her stomach.

"Bad. I owe Frankie Goldstein twenty thousand dollars."

Now she felt a tremor of alarm. Frankie Goldstein was one of Houston's scariest criminals; an evil man who'd killed more people than she wanted to think about.

"Why didn't you call Thomas?" Thomas Martin was not only her uncle's best friend, but he was her uncle's Gamblers Anonymous sponsor.

"Thomas died."

"What? When?" Why hadn't he told her?

"Last week. He had a massive heart attack."

"Oh, Uncle Victor." Sympathy for his pain washed through her. "Why didn't you tell me?"

He frowned. "I knew you would worry, and I didn't want to burden you."

"So what happened?"

"It was too painful for me to attend the GA meetings knowing Thomas wouldn't be there, so I stopped going. I thought I was past needing their help. It had been years since I last felt the urge to gamble. I thought I was cured." He sounded defeated. "Then after Thomas' funeral, I found myself sitting in the parking lot of the racetrack. I don't even remember deciding to go there. I sat there for a long time, trying to convince myself to leave." He grimaced. There was no need to point out that he hadn't. "One bet, I thought, and then I'd walk away. Just to prove I could do it. A tribute to Thomas, if you will. So I went inside and looked at the line-up. There he was. Thomas' Triumph. It was a sign from God."

"You bet on a horse based on its name?" She couldn't believe it.

"Not just because of his name," he assured her. "I looked at his stats. He had a solid record going into the race. None of the other horses had a chance against him. He was a sure thing." He gave a self-deprecating laugh. "In retrospect, I realize Thomas would have hated such a tribute, but at the time—" He shrugged. "I thought if I made a big enough bet, then we'd have enough money after paying back Frankie for you to stop working."

"What happened?" she asked, already knowing he'd lost but curious about the details.

He sighed heavily. "It was the damnedest thing. They were coming down the home stretch with Thomas' Triumph in the lead. And then... he stumbled." He shook his head as if he still couldn't believe it. "And lost the race." He raised his head to look at her. "I can't blame the horse. This is my fault, and you have every right to be mad."

Gina groaned. This wasn't the first time her uncle's gambling had gotten him—them—into trouble, but it had been so long since the last time she'd actually thought he'd learned his lesson. "Even if we take every penny in savings, we don't have that kind of money."

"I did try to explain that to Frankie."

"What did he say?"

"He was not sympathetic." Uncle Victor unbuttoned his shirt and pulled it apart, giving Gina a look at his bare chest. Dark purple fist-sized bruises covered his upper torso.

"Oh, my God." She stood to get a better look. "When did that happen?"

"Yesterday evening." She remembered he'd gone out to meet "friends" and she'd been asleep when he'd returned. "It looks worse than it is," he assured her.

She hurried around the desk and threw her arms around him, giving him a hug but afraid to squeeze too tightly. She felt sick to her stomach. "We should go to the cops."

"I don't think that's a good idea."

"Why?"

"Because Frankie would not appreciate it, a point he made clear to me this morning when he called me during your performance."

Gina returned to her chair, feeling overwhelmed as she sank down into it. "What are we going to do?"

"We go to Las Palomas. After we get paid, I'll send the money to Frankie; make sure we're good before we come back. You'll see. Everything will be okay."

It wasn't adding up. "Why would Frankie be okay taking ten thousand dollars when you owe him twenty?"

Uncle Victor's gaze dropped to his lap, and it took a moment before understanding hit her with a horrible punch that left her gasping for breath.

"Oh, no. Please tell me you didn't empty our bank account," she grit out between clenched teeth as she pulled out her phone. She opened her online banking app and scrolled through the account. Where there had been twelve thousand dollars before, now there was an even one thousand dollars—just enough to keep the account open without incurring monthly fees. How generous, she thought sarcastically as fury took over. "You son of a bitch! How are we going to pay our bills? Or eat?"

"I'm sorry," he said, his voice filled with genuine pain and regret. "I had to give him something to buy more time. He was going to kill me; and then he said he was coming after you."

"For a lousy twenty thousand dollars? Who murders people for that kind of money?"

"Frankie Goldstein does," he answered patiently. Then he rose from the desk and moved around it until he could crouch beside her chair. Taking both her hands, his smoky gray gaze held hers with warmth and love. "I will repay it—every penny. I promise."

Flashes of memory assaulted her: the way he held her at her mother's funeral, taught her to roller-blade and tended to her scraped knees when she'd fallen, his solitary standing ovation of her fourth grade school choir solo when she obviously couldn't carry a tune. The many nights he sat by her side until she fell asleep just to keep the bad dreams away. All of her life, when she'd needed him most, he'd been there for her. She couldn't walk away from him now and leave him to deal with his problem on his own. She knew he wouldn't blame her if she did, but he was family and you didn't abandon family, no matter how badly they screwed up.

"All right," she said, nodding slowly. "We'll go to Las Palomas, and I'll pretend to talk to *Llorona*. But after we get the money and pay back Frankie, I'm done. This is my last ghost whispering job. Okay?"

"Okay," he agreed, offering her a sad smile. "I understand."

"And Uncle Victor?" She gave him a stern look when he met her gaze. "If you ever gamble again, I'm done with you, too. Now, if you'll excuse me," she said, rising from her chair. "I need some time alone."

He stood when she did but didn't try to follow her out of the room when she left, seeking the solace of her bedroom. Thinking about the future was not something she could afford right now. She needed to pull off the scam of a lifetime. If she failed, well, Frankie would probably take care of her future for her.

Chapter Three

"You look very nice tonight, dear," Ruby Mae's delicate hands smoothed out the wrinkles in Dane's shirt as she complimented him. The frail appearance of the seventy-five-year-old woman made him want to reach out and steady her, but he knew she was tougher than she looked. Running the only Bed & Breakfast in town single-handedly required a great deal of strength and resilience.

"He does look nice, doesn't he?" Sylvia's stern look made Dane straighten up, his hands clasped behind his back as if standing at attention. "In his uniform. When he's not actually on duty." This last was said with a bit of a bite.

"Well, tonight's a special occasion." Dane was careful to keep all inflection from his voice. "You said you wanted to impress our guests."

Sylvia's disapproving gaze intensified. "Impress them—not intimidate them."

"I'm sure I don't know what you mean, Sylvia. I'm here on official town business and, as such, I'm required to dress accordingly."

He didn't need Sylvia aiming her narrow-eyed glare at him to know she was mad and he had every reason to believe this Gina Castillo was legitimate. After all, both Sylvia and the famous Mark Allen vouched for her. But the last thing he needed while he was acting police chief was trouble and as far as he was concerned, the most important step he could take in protecting his town was to send a strong message to all newcomers up front: *don't mess with my town.*

Frankly, he found the idea of talking to ghosts either creepy or laughable. He hadn't decided which, but, on the chance the ghost whisperer was legitimate, protecting the town also meant limiting the ghost whisperer's spiritual encounters to the genuine ghosts. To help with that effort, the town council had issued a moratorium on ghost impersonations. Still, knowing how teenagers—specifically the teenagers on the Events Team—could be, Dane decided he would escort the ghost whisperer around town, steering clear of areas where the teens might do their impersonations.

He'd never met a ghost whisperer before, so he wasn't sure what to expect. The Tangina Barrons character from *Poltergeist* sprang to mind.

This house is clean.

The soft shuffle of footsteps at the top of the stairs caught Dane's attention. He looked up—and nearly forgot to breathe. His eyes widened in surprise as he took in the woman descending the stairs.

Definitely not Tangina Barrons. More like Cassandra Nightingale from *The Good Witch*. Memories of his mother binge-watching the show flooded his mind, and he couldn't help but compare this woman to Catherine Bell's character.

She was tall and moved with the grace and ease of a dancer. Her skinny jeans hugged her curves, while a flowing peach silk blouse revealed just enough skin to pique one's interest. Straight black hair cascaded to her shoulders like a thick silk curtain, framing her delicate features. Her bangs swept to one side of her face, revealing almond-shaped eyes that hinted at a blend of European and Asian heritage.

As she drew nearer, Dane couldn't help but notice how young she appeared—maybe even younger than his own twenty-six years. A tentative smile played on her lips, causing Dane's pulse to race. Movie star good looks paired with a girl-next-door charm.

Shaking himself out of his trance, Dane turned to study the woman's companion. He was a distinguished-looking older man with hair silvering at the temples. He descended the stairs slowly, moving carefully, and Dane wondered if he was infirm? Or injured?

Dane reaffirmed his resolve to keep an eye on these two strangers as they made their way towards him. Something about them felt off, and he couldn't shake the feeling that trouble was soon to follow.

"Here you are." Ruby Mae's voice resonated with warmth and hospitality as she stepped forward to greet her guests. Dane could see that the newcomers had already won the old woman's affection.

"Ms. Castillo, it's a pleasure to meet you," Sylvia said, stepping forward to shake hands with the young woman. "I'm Sylvia Winters. I'm the one who emailed you."

"Mrs. Winters, it's an honor to be invited to Las Palomas," Gina Castillo replied with a velvet-edged tone that sent Dane's mind racing with thoughts of tangled sheets and naked bodies.

He clenched his jaw tightly and forced himself to maintain a neutral expression.

"We are delighted to have you here," Sylvia cooed with genuine excitement.

Gina turned slightly and motioned towards the man standing beside her. "Allow me to introduce my manager—and uncle—Victor Castillo."

The man took Sylvia's hand in his, covering it with his other hand. "It is always a pleasure to meet a beautiful woman," he said with a charming smile.

Dane knew instantly the man was a fraud. No honest man could deliver such a corny line and make it sound that sincere.

He was surprised to see Sylvia blush and nearly missed what she was saying.

"Allow me to present our escort tonight. This is acting police chief, Dane Wolfe."

An awkward silence fell over the group as all eyes turned to Dane and he realized Sylvia had just introduced him. "Dane Wolfe," he said, quickly reaching out to shake hands with each of the Castillos, noting that Gina Castillo's hand fit perfectly in his own. He may have held onto it for a moment longer than necessary, but no one seemed to notice. "If you all are ready, we can leave."

"You're giving us a police escort?" Gina asked, her tone polite but curious. "Are you expecting trouble?"

He gave her a cool smile. "I'm a cop. I always expect trouble."

There was a moment of silence before Sylvia's nervous laugh broke it. "Oh, don't mind Dane. He's here to give us a ride, although I'm perfectly capable of driving the Castillos myself."

"It's my pleasure," he said, moving to open the front door. "Shall we be on our way?"

At the police chief's gesture, Gina moved past him through the open door, hoping he wouldn't see how nervous she was. His presence affected her on a visceral level that left her senses humming with awareness.

He wore his dark blond hair cut short, but not so short one couldn't run their fingers through it. A heavy shadow of dark brown whiskers covered his strong jawline. On anyone else, it might have looked unkempt, but on Dane Wolfe, it was undeniably attractive in a rugged Texas cowboy kind of way. And who didn't love a cowboy?

She admired the way his blue shirt hugged his toned, sculpted chest and arms. The fabric stretched taut over his muscles, emphasizing the strength and power hidden beneath. She couldn't deny she found him extremely attractive. He was the type who made her dream of close encounters of the physical kind. She wondered if he was married or had a girlfriend and turned back to watch him descend the steps of the Bed and Breakfast, hoping to glimpse his left hand to see if he wore a wedding band. Then, noticing the police badge proudly pinned to his chest, glinting under the front porch light, she silently scoffed at herself. This man's job was to protect the town and its people from those who would harm them. People like her and Uncle Victor. If her performance as a ghost whisperer was unconvincing, the only close encounter she'd have with Dane Wolfe would be when he ran her and Uncle Victor out of town. Or worse, arrested them.

Tearing her gaze away from the man, she looked ahead to their ride and wasn't surprised to see a light tan dual cab pickup truck parked in the driveway. Sporty cars had never been her thing, so she couldn't help admiring the powerfully built Ford F250. Knowing Dane drove this machine made him that much more attractive to her—and that was unfortunate.

"You're taking us to the RV park?" She asked, understanding that was where *Llorona* normally appeared.

"Not until later. We thought we'd feed you first," Dane said.

"It's much too early for *Llorona* to make her appearance," Sylvia added. "She doesn't normally appear until sometime after midnight."

"I promised the town council that I'd have you at the VFW Hall by seven," Dane continued. "You're the closest thing we've had to a celebrity and everyone wants to meet you. The VFW is having a big barbecue dinner to raise money for the town's beautification effort. Your plates are complimentary, courtesy of the town council."

"Sounds like fun," Gina said, not actually meaning it. She was an introvert who found spending time with a group of people stressful. Make that a group of strangers and...

Shoot me now, she thought, glancing at Uncle Victor for reassurance. He gave her a warm smile. Unlike her, he enjoyed spending time with people; the more, the merrier. If she started feeling overwhelmed, he would gladly step in and divert attention away from her.

Gina headed around to the far side of the truck, knowing Uncle Victor would want to sit behind the driver. Before she could open the back passenger door, Sylvia was pulling it open.

"I don't mind sitting in the back," Gina offered. "Wouldn't you prefer the front?"

The older woman merely waved away her offer. "I'm perfectly happy sitting back here where I can keep your uncle company."

Gina thought she heard Dane snort, but when she glanced at him, his expression hadn't changed. The truck stood higher than most, thanks to a lift kit, and Gina worried that Sylvia, standing at five-foot nothing, might not be able to climb into it. She watched with some interest, therefore, as Sylvia positioned herself in the truck's open doorway with her back against the seat. Then, with seemingly practiced ease, Dane placed his hands at the older woman's waist and lifted her onto the seat.

"Thank you, my dear," Sylvia said gratefully once she was settled. "I still don't understand why you insist on driving this monster truck when a regular car would do just fine."

Dane chuckled indulgently as he helped her buckle her seat belt. "Now, now Sylvia, let's not start that argument again. I like my truck," he said with a hint of playfulness. "Besides, you know it comes in handy for pulling Harvey's old caddy out of ditches." He turned to Gina and explained with a wry smile. "Harvey has a bit of a drinking problem and every so often, when he's had too much, he drives his car off the road."

Sylvia waved a hand dismissively. "Oh please, Harvey doesn't drink. He just gets lonely and drives off the road on purpose so Dane will come rescue him."

Dane gave her seatbelt a last check before leaning in closer. "Maybe you should invite him over for some of your famous pecan pie," he suggested with a playful twinkle in his eye. "Who knows—you two might hit it off, if you catch my drift."

Sylvia gasped in shock. "Why, Dane Wolfe," she scolded, trying to sound offended. "I hope you're not implying that Harvey and I..." She trailed off, too flustered to finish her sentence. Then she huffed indignantly. "That man is at least twenty years older than me!"

"I'm only suggesting that the two of you could be friends," Dane clarified, turning to Gina with a charming smile and a wink.

Gina tried her best not to grin too widely in return. She couldn't help but enjoy the playful banter between the two of them. After Dane closed Sylvia's door, he moved to the front passenger door and stood by, ready to help her into the truck if needed. She climbed into the seat with ease, though a small part of her wondered what it would have felt like to have Dane's hands around her waist.

No, she scolded herself. She had a job to do, and flirting was definitely not part of it.

A few moments later, the truck roared to life with a deep rumble and Dane effortlessly backed out of the narrow driveway. As they drove down the winding road, Gina silently vowed to fight the attraction she felt for this man and keep her mind on her job.

Dane's attention was only half on the road as he drove. The other half was on Gina Castillo. She wasn't at all what he'd expected, and it threw him off. He'd been around beautiful women before. Why he felt like an awkward teenager around this one was a mystery.

But he liked mysteries.

"How does one become a ghost whisperer? Is it an ability you're born with or is it learned?" he asked.

"I've read cases where both are true," Gina replied. "Some people are born with the ability. Others develop the ability following a near-death experience. In my case, it's inherited." She hated lying. "My mother had the ability and passed it on to me."

"Her mother was Trina Star," Sylvia said, leaning forward to tap him on the shoulder, her tone of voice suggesting he should know the name.

He didn't. "Ah," he said, unsure what else to say.

Fortunately, Sylvia didn't press the issue. Instead, she began chatting with Victor Castillo. The sound of laughter in the back seat caused him to glance in the rearview mirror where he saw Sylvia and Victor leaning close together, their heads bent in private conversation. Dane thought they were getting along a little too well and wondered if he needed to be worried.

"My uncle's a horrible flirt," Gina said softly, pulling his attention back to her. "But I promise he won't take advantage of her."

Dane sighed. "Sylvia's not the one I'm worried about getting hurt."

She gave a chuckle. "I assure you. My uncle can look out for himself."

"I hope so. In the sport of flirting, Sylvia plays at a professional level." The minute the words left his mouth, he wished he could pull them back.

"In that case, I'd say she's met her match." Gina smiled, turning her gaze back to the road in front of them.

He slowed the truck to a stop at a traffic light, noticing the silence that had fallen between them.

"When you talked about your mother, it was in the past tense," he said. "Did she pass?"

"When I was five, they diagnosed my mother with cancer. I don't know if knowing she was dying made her death a year later easier or harder. Maybe a little of both?"

"I know what you mean. My father passed away when I was eleven. A brain aneurysm. He didn't suffer, but we weren't prepared to lose him." After he said it, he wasn't sure why he'd shared such a personal part of his life with a complete stranger, but it had felt right. "Not that anyone gets to control when they die, but it was hard on my mother, sister and me."

"I'm sorry," she said in a way that made him think she actually was. "Can I ask you a question, Chief Wolfe?"

"It's Dane, please."

"Do you like your job?"

"Sometimes," he said truthfully. "Las Palomas, mostly, is a quiet town and one's more likely to die of boredom than from violence. Although," he admitted, "a couple of months ago, we busted a drug operation. That was when our chief of police was shot."

"Oh, wow. I'm so sorry."

He shook his head. "It's okay. She's alive and currently out-of-town, recuperating. I'm only acting chief of police."

They reached the VFW hall and as Dane pulled into the parking lot, the aroma of smoked barbecue greeted them. Diego and Elise Juarez had donated the beef for tonight's fundraiser, and several ranch hands had spent the day smoking it. That, alone, would have drawn the entire town to the hall. The Double R Ranch was famous for its BBQ dinners.

At a glance, the parking lot looked full. Tourists and townies alike, had shown up for food and dancing. Dane took one of the parking spots in front reserved for the police and escorted his guests inside.

Sylvia, he noticed, looped her arm through Victor Castillo's as they strolled into the building. Staking her claim, he thought. While there were several single older women in town, there weren't that many single men over fifty, and none as well preserved or handsome as Victor.

Stopping briefly inside the door, Dane gave the room a quick scan.

At the far end, Boomer was mixing tunes. He ran the music for most of their events, which was how he got his nickname. Four man-sized speakers sat on either side of the temporary stage, emitting music at a low volume so people could carry on conversations while they visited and ate. It wouldn't be long, though, before Boomer would dim the overheads, start his light show and crank the volume on the music to a level more suited for dancing. While the area in front of the stage was left open for dancers, tables of various sizes were cleverly arranged throughout the rest of the space, ensuring diners had plenty of options. The tables holding the buffet stretched the length of the left wall. The booth where VFW volunteers were serving beer, soft drinks, and sweet tea was in the corner.

Dane made introductions as they moved to the reception desk where a woman was selling meal tickets. "Nita, I'd like you to meet Gina and Victor Castillo." Then, turning to Gina and Victor, he said, "Nita Garcia is in charge of the fundraiser. In fact, it's a well-known fact that if you want your fundraiser to be successful, you'll ask Nita to run it. The high school has new iPads this year, thanks to Nita."

He knew from the way she blushed that he'd embarrassed her, but she deserved all the praise he could lavish on her. "Nita is also, incidentally, the mayor's wife."

"Welcome to our town," Nita greeted them, smiling warmly as she shook their hands. "We're so glad you could come. There's plenty of food, but grab some now before they," she waved at the tables of seated diners, "go back for seconds. Dane, I trust you'll show our guests around?"

"Of course. This way," he gestured for Gina to precede him into the room, followed by Sylvia and Victor, still connected by interlocked arms.

As they went through the buffet, Dane made a point of introducing Gina and Victor Castillo.

"I'm not used to meeting this many people at one time," Gina confessed to him at one point. "I don't think I'll ever remember all their names."

He chuckled. "Don't worry about it. No one expects you to."

Reaching the end of the buffet, trays ladened with food, Dane guided them to a smaller table where the four of them could quietly sit and eat.

"I hope you don't mind," he said as they set down their trays. "If we sit with other people, you'll be kept so busy answering questions you'll never have time to eat."

He pulled out Gina's chair so she could sit, which earned him a surprised, but, he thought, pleased, look.

"Thanks." She smiled at him as he sat in the chair next to her and he wondered if she had any idea how her smile lit up a room.

Gina focused intently on cutting her brisket into bite-sized pieces. The scent of smoked meat and barbecue sauce filled her nostrils, but she found it difficult to focus on anything other than the handsome man sitting beside her.

Across the table, Sylvia giggled at something Uncle Victor said, her heavily lashed eyes batting flirtatiously. He responded by covering her hand with his and whispering something that made her other hand flutter to her chest.

Gina stole a glance at Dane and saw that he had been watching the older couple as well. Meeting her gaze, he winked, and they shared an inside joke once again.

"So, about this ghost whispering," he said, signaling a change in subject as he took a bite of his food and swallowed. "Is it like being a ghost psychologist?"

Gina chuckled and shifted comfortably into familiar territory. "In a lot of ways, yes," she agreed, lying as she claimed her mother's experiences as her own. "Most of the time, there is a reason a spirit refuses to cross over. I try to understand that reason and help them find peace if I can. Sometimes, they just have a message they want to give to a loved one who is still living. Once I can deliver their message, they can finally move on."

Dane nodded thoughtfully. "Have you dealt with many cases where the ghosts are intentionally terrorizing people?" he asked curiously.

Gina's heart skipped a beat, and she fought to keep her composure. "*Llorona* is terrorizing people? In what way?"

"Mostly screaming at them," he said matter-of-factly.

Her mind raced, trying to piece together the implications of this revelation. In all her years of ghost whispering, she had never encountered an actual ghost, much less one capable of making noises. Any noises generated during one of her ghost whispering sessions were made by Uncle Victor himself. Instantly suspicious, she couldn't shake the feeling that this *Llorona* haunting was being perpetrated by an unknown party on the unsuspecting residents of Las Palomas. Money might motivate her cons, but she liked to think she helped people. She wasn't trying to frighten anyone. She and Uncle Victor would have to act quickly to uncover any other players involved in this ghostly game. And if she could do so without jeopardizing herself, she would expose them for the frauds they were.

CHAPTER FOUR

FEELING DANE'S GAZE ON her, waiting for her response, pulled her from her thoughts. "I guess we'll see what we're up against tonight, won't we?" She tried to keep her tone light, but wasn't sure she succeeded.

At that moment, Uncle Victor pushed his chair back from the table and stood, reaching for Sylvia's hand.

"My dear, would you care to dance?"

Sylvia nodded, and Gina watched the two head toward the dance floor. A country-western tune was playing and Uncle Victor twirled Sylvia onto the dance floor where they melded seamlessly into the moving circle of dancers. Gina wondered why she was amazed to learn, after all these years, that her uncle could two-step. Seriously, was there anything he couldn't do?

She and Dane watched the older couple disappear from view and then exchanged another wordless smile. The silence stretched out between them as Gina racked her brain for something to say. Two women suddenly appeared at their table, saving her.

"Hey, Dane," the one standing closest to him said. She was a tall, stocky woman with an amiable smile and a sparkle in her eyes. Gina liked her immediately.

"Hello, ladies," Dane greeted them easily. "Are you having a good time?"

"Oh, yes," the other said breathlessly, not even glancing over at Gina. "Are you having a good time?"

While the words were innocent enough, the way she spoke them told Gina the woman had a major crush on Dane.

"Indeed, I am," he replied. "Ladies, may I introduce you to Gina Castillo? Gina's here to help us with—"

"Oh, hell, Dane," the first lady interrupted him with a laugh and a dismissive wave of her hand. "We know why Miss Castillo's here. It's why we came over. We wanted to meet our guest." She held out her hand to Gina. "Welcome to Las Palomas. I'm Kathy Danvers. I own Kathy's Café on Main Street."

Gina shook the woman's hand, finding her grip was warm and firm. Solid. Probably like the woman herself, Gina mused.

"And this is Emma Dorset," Kathy continued, gesturing to the mousy thin woman standing beside her. "She's a nurse over at the clinic."

Gina extended her hand in greeting, wondering if the woman would bother to acknowledge her. She did and, not surprisingly, Gina found the woman's hand cool to the touch and her handshake was the limp-fish kind that Gina despised. She was glad it ended quickly and hoped no one noticed her reaction.

"A ghost whisperer—wow!" Kathy exclaimed enthusiastically. "I bet you've seen some shit."

Gina couldn't help but laugh at the woman's bluntness. "I have, but you'd be surprised how often it's the living and not the deceased who are full of surprises," she replied, thinking of Lydia Calhoun Jones. "I think—"

"You look very nice this evening, Dane," Emma said, unaware that she'd interrupted the conversation.

"Um, thank you, Emma," Dane replied, clearly embarrassed. "You're looking very nice tonight as well."

He was being generous, Gina thought, mildly irritated now. Someone as thin as Emma shouldn't wear a formless maxi-dress in that shade of tan. It looked like she was wearing a burlap bag.

Kathy's gaze shot to Emma, and she seemed to make a quick decision.

"Well, we don't want to monopolize your time, do we, Emma? Come visit me at the diner when you get a minute. I'd love to show off some of the café's resident ghosts. Maybe I could even hire you to talk to a couple of them."

"Oh, sure. Sounds like fun." Gina hoped she sounded more sincere than she felt. Mentally, she was stuck on Kathy's announcement that the café had ghosts.

"Come on, Emma. I think I see Stuart over there. Why don't we see if he wants to dance?"

Emma resisted Kathy's pull on her arm and turned to Dane. "Dane, would you like to dance?"

Gina saw, rather than heard, Dane's sigh. He turned to Gina and gave her a look that she couldn't decipher. Then he grabbed her hand, pushed his chair back, and stood, leaving her with no choice but to stand as well.

"I'm sorry, Emma. I already promised the next couple of dances to Gina. It was nice seeing you both." He started for the dance floor, not waiting to hear Emma's reply. "Sorry about that," he said when they reached the edge of the dance floor, leaning close to be heard over the noise, his breath warm against her cheek. "I hope you won't think badly of me. Emma's nice, but I'm just not interested. I've tried every polite way I know to tell her that, but nothing seems to work."

Gina wasn't entirely unsympathetic to Emma's plight. With Dane standing so close, the woodsy scent of his aftershave aroused something primal within her. She struggled to ignore it and considered Dane's words.

"Well, I hate to tell you this and ruin your exit strategy, but I don't know how to dance."

"Then it'll be my pleasure to teach you." He smiled and gave her a wink.

Then, before she could think of a reply, he pulled her closer, took her right hand in his left, holding it slightly up and away from their bodies and positioned her left hand on his shoulder before fitting his right hand to the curve of her waist.

"All you need to know is one step back with your left foot, then two shorter steps back with your right, and repeat. Follow my lead and trust me to drive, okay?"

He waited for her nod, then studied the circling dancers until he found an opening. He gave her hand a gentle squeeze to warn her they were about to move, then he stepped forward, at the same time pushing her back slightly.

For the first several minutes, she focused only on moving her feet in sync with his. Eventually, though, she stopped counting steps. There was no need. Every time they were about to switch feet, Dane would signal her by applying subtle pressure at her waist.

Once she trusted his lead, she began to enjoy herself. Dane was a masterful dancer, steering them expertly past the other dancers. Gina couldn't help but admire the way he moved. He exuded a presence, and she wasn't the only one who felt it. It seemed everyone was aware of him, judging from the many glances he received as they danced past other couples. It wasn't just the women who watched him, either. The men did as well, but not out of jealousy, she thought. They respected him. To Gina, it spoke volumes about the man he was.

For a minute, she allowed herself the fantasy of believing they were together; that he was her date. She didn't allow herself to indulge in the fantasy too long. It would be dangerous to forget why she was in Las Palomas.

"You're a natural," he said, interrupting her thoughts as he pulled her a little closer so she could hear him. The feel of his hard body against hers sent a shiver of awareness racing through her.

"I think it's more a testament of your teaching than my abilities," she told him when she could speak.

"Even the best teacher can't teach grace and a sense of rhythm."

She gave a self-conscious laugh. "I can't tell if you're being honest or flirting with me."

"A little of both," he answered with a smile that had butterflies dancing in her stomach. "Even without Emma as an excuse, I wanted to dance with you, but I have to admit that it's worked out much better than I could have hoped. It helps that you're tall and your stride is more like my own, but you move around the floor like you've been dancing for years."

Not used to such compliments, Gina blushed and hoped he wouldn't notice in the dimly lit room.

When the song ended, he stopped. "Would you like to go back and sit down?"

"Not really," she replied, surprising herself because she meant it. She wanted to dance. More specifically, she wanted to dance with him. "But if you want to..."

"Are you kidding? I'm just getting warmed up."

As soon as the music started, he pulled her close, and they were soon circling the dance floor. Gina was just congratulating herself on mastering the dance when a passing couple executed a spin, with the woman stepping out and under the arm of her partner, only to end up back in his arms. All in time to the music!

"Want to try it?" Dane teased, his low voice tickling her ear.

She glanced up at him, wondering if she dared to say "yes." At the same time, she worried about tripping over her own feet during the execution of such a maneuver. He must have seen her desire to try because the next thing she knew, Dane used the hand at her waist to push her away from him, then guided her in a clockwise spin under his arm. Then he pulled her back into his arms and they continued around the dance floor. Except for a slight wobble on her part, they never missed a beat.

"Like I said. You're a natural."

"That was fun," she admitted.

When he pulled her into an even closer embrace, she didn't resist. He was the only thing keeping her grounded because her head was spinning from the flurry of emotions racing through her. She loved dancing and did plenty of it in the privacy of her bedroom, where no one could see. This took dancing to a whole new level. She loved the way the music pulsed through her.

It was more than the dancing and the music, though. It was the way she felt wrapped in Dane's arms. She shouldn't get used to it, but told herself it was okay to relax and enjoy the moment. There was no harm in that, right?

They didn't stop dancing when the song ended, but kept moving until the next one began. Again and again, until Gina lost track of the songs. When the tempo of the music slowed, so did they. Now, instead of circling the floor, they stayed in one place; swaying back and forth. No one else existed. It was only the two of them, their bodies pressed together. She rested her head against his chest and closed her eyes.

So wrapped up in her fantasy, Gina hardly noticed when the music finally stopped. Dane still held her close. She tipped her head back and found he was looking down at her. The smoldering heat of his gaze held her in place; confusing her, arousing her.

His head lowered and a voice in her head screamed that kissing him, especially in the VFW hall in front of the entire town, would be the biggest mistake of her life, but she wanted that kiss; wanted it more than she wanted her next breath.

His lips were so close now that every nerve, every fiber of her being, was focused on them. She could practically taste them.

Then someone slapped Dane on the back, jolting them both and shattering the moment.

Gina felt her face heat with embarrassment. What the hell had she almost done? Not only was he the chief of police, but she'd just met him.

Gina prayed for a hole to suddenly open in the floor beneath her and swallow her up. When that seemed unlikely to happen, she tried to think of an excuse to ditch Dane on the dance floor and walk away, preferably not stopping until she reached Houston.

As if sensing her emotions, Dane tightened his arms around her, giving her a reassuring hug before stepping back, putting some space between them so they could greet the newcomers.

Gina nearly groaned when she recognized the woman as Nita Garcia, the mayor's wife, which meant the man with her would be the mayor.

Wonderful. Nothing like being caught by the mayor nearly kissing the town's police chief. On her first night in town. She might as well write "slut" across her forehead.

She knew the best way to handle the situation was to act like nothing had happened.

Nothing had happened, she felt obliged to point out to herself.

"Gina, I'd like to introduce you to Mayor Sal Garcia and you remember his wife, Nita."

Gina held out her hand to the man. "It's very nice to meet you, Mayor Garcia."

"Please, call me Sal," the man said pleasantly. "We appreciate that you and your uncle could come on such short notice. We're used to dealing with ghosts, but *Llorona's* recent behavior has us baffled. Have you gone out to the RV park yet?"

"Sal, please," his wife scolded gently. "Ms. Castillo only arrived in town this afternoon. Please forgive him, Ms. Castillo," she said. "We're understandably anxious. Tourism is our primary source of revenue. We want people coming to see the ghosts and then staying a while to enjoy our shops and services; not running away in terror." While this last bit was said in a humorous tone, Gina knew the Garcias were concerned.

"I hope I'll be able to help," she said sincerely, though she wondered what kind of situation she was facing.

Nita Garcia patted her arm reassuringly. "I have a feeling you will. Now, Dane, have you introduced Ms. Castillo to Zelda and the others? No? Shame on you. Come with me, Ms. Castillo."

"Please, call me Gina."

"Then you must call me Nita."

She looped her arm through Gina's, leaving Gina no choice but to go with her to meet more of the town's residents while Dane stayed behind, talking to the mayor.

After an hour of meeting people, Gina used the excuse of needing to visit the restroom in order to get away. She took a little longer than necessary, enjoying the small respite from the crowded hall, then went in search of Uncle Victor.

She found him sitting alone at their table.

"I noticed you're having a good time tonight," he teased when she sat beside him.

She felt a blush heat her face. "Turns out I enjoy dancing," she said.

He laughed. "Dancing. Right. It had nothing to do with young Chief Wolfe."

"Well, maybe," she admitted. "I noticed you and Sylvia are getting along well."

He chuckled. "She and I are two of a kind; open to enjoying the moment and neither one of us interested in a long-term relationship."

"That's nice, I guess, but it sounds lonely."

He shrugged as much as to say to each his own. "In talking to Sylvia, I learned some interesting things about *Llorona*," he began, but she wasn't really paying attention. She was watching Dane across the room, talking to people, and at that moment, he looked up. Their gazes met and the rest of the room fell away until it was only the two of them.

They were lost in their own world for what seemed like forever. Then he smiled, and it was like someone had set off fireworks right there inside the room. Gina couldn't help but smile back.

When he looked away briefly to respond to something a person said, Gina realized it was already too late to keep her emotional distance from this man. She'd fallen for a total stranger. That never happened to her. Why now? Why this man?

"Hello?"

Gina turned, startled to realize Uncle Victor had been talking to her. "What?"

"Did you hear anything I said?"

"Sure. Sylvia was telling you about *Llorona*."

"Right, so what do you think? Maybe we should postpone going out there tonight."

Gina saw Dane heading toward them and suddenly felt short of breath.

"Gina?" Uncle Victor pressed.

"Yeah, yeah," she said, dismissively. "It'll be fine."

"Sorry about letting Nita drag you away like that," Dane said when he reached their table. "I hope it wasn't too awful."

"Of course not," Gina lied. She was trying to think of something else to say when Sylvia suddenly joined them, looking as excited as a kid on Christmas morning.

"Shall we drive out to Murphy's? It's nearly midnight."

All three turned to Gina, and she realized the decision to go was up to her.

"Do you feel up to going out tonight?" Uncle Victor asked, offering her an excuse to beg off. "You're not too tired?"

For a moment, she considered taking it, but with Frankie Goldstein after them, they didn't have the luxury of time. She forced herself to smile.

"By all means, let's do this."

CHAPTER FIVE

A FEW MINUTES LATER, once again sitting in the front passenger seat of the truck, Gina watched as they headed out of town. The last of the residential neighborhoods disappeared until only long empty stretches of road lay ahead of them. She noticed Dane sneaking glances at her and wondered what thoughts raced through his head. Was he regretting their shared moment on the dance floor? She wouldn't blame him if he was. It had been impetuous on both their parts. A fluke. It meant nothing; and certainly didn't mean she and Dane had a future together. She and Uncle Victor would be returning to Houston soon; maybe even tomorrow if her ghost whispering act was convincing enough.

Sensing Dane's gaze on her again, she turned to meet it.

"You're very quiet," he observed. "Everything okay?" He kept his voice low so only she could hear, not that she thought either Sylvia or Uncle Victor were listening. From the sound of it, the two were engaged in a lively discussion.

"Just taking a few moments to mentally prep myself. That's all." It wasn't a total lie.

"That's good. I was afraid that maybe..."

His voice trailed off as Uncle Victor's voice rose in volume. "Why do you want to be rid of *Llorona?* She's got to be one of your star attractions. It doesn't make sense."

"Oh, no," Sylvia corrected. "We don't want to get rid of her. Heavens, no. We want you to talk to her and find out why she's trying to scare off people."

"She doesn't normally attack the tourists," Dane admitted, joining the conversation. "She only started doing that recently. The last family was so frightened, they packed up their RV and left in the middle of the night. That's not good for business, so we want you to find out what's going on with her."

"I'll see what I can do," Gina promised, doing her best to sound like she had a clue how to go about doing that, while also wondering exactly what these families had experienced. Most of the ghostly noises she encountered were caused by old homes settling or wind hitting a house at the perfect angle to cause a whistling sound. There was nothing other-worldly about them."

"Murphy's RV park is up ahead," Dane said a few minutes later as they turned onto a long, winding road.

They continued on it until they reached a large, paved parking lot which, at this time of night, was empty.

A few minutes later, they climbed out of the truck and Gina thought she heard the babbling of running water.

The river must be close, she thought.

A single light pole stood in the middle of the parking lot, casting a dim glow by which to see. It was enough for Gina to make out the grassy area next to the parking lot.

"The river's over there," Sylvia said, confirming Gina's guess. "This way." The older woman didn't wait for a reply. Hooking her arm through Uncle Victor's, she headed off across the parking lot.

Dane moved closer to Gina and, glancing down at her shoes, offered her his arm. "May I? There's no walkway and the ground, in the dark, can make walking dangerous. Especially in heels."

She gave him a grateful smile while looping her arm through his. "That's very gallant of you."

"It is, isn't it?" He smiled and winked. "Or maybe it's an excuse to get close to you again."

"Why Chief Wolfe," she cooed in her best Southern drawl. "I do believe y'all are flirting with me."

"Guilty as charged." Then, in a more serious tone, "Is that a problem?"

Warmth spread through her. "No. No problem at all."

They fell silent as they followed the older couple who, by now, had disappeared into the night.

The further from the parking lot's overhead lamp they went, the darker it became. Gina didn't like feeling blind and was glad Dane was with her.

They finally moved past the trees and reached the open banks of the river and the night went from ominous to peaceful. There was something soothing about the gentle rippling sound of the water flowing downstream and the way the moon reflected off the water's surface. Standing arm-in-arm with Dane, Gina felt the moment couldn't be more perfect. She tried to commit every detail to memory so she could recall it days, weeks, even years, from now.

"Where do you want us to stand while you summon *Llorona?*" Sylvia asked, reminding Gina why they were there.

Reluctantly, she unhooked her arm from Dane's. "I think it would be best if all of you remained here by the trees."

She moved toward the river, stopping about a foot from the water's edge. According to legend, *Llorona* died on a riverbank. Gina had no idea if it was the *Rio Maldito* or some other river, but according to her mother, spirits were drawn to familiar places.

There was the added benefit that the noise of the river would mask the sound of her voice, easing the burden of "conversing" with the ghost. In fact, she was half tempted to stand there with her back to the group and nod her head as if she was listening to a ghost speaking.

She wouldn't do that, of course. The more realistic the performance, the better.

Glancing back at the group, she saw they were standing together at the tree line, watching her. It was too dark to see their expressions, but she could see Uncle Victor waving at her. She waved back, confused by the unusual gesture. It's not like she was leaving or anything.

She pushed it out of her mind. "I'm going to summon *Llorona* now, and it's important that you remain quiet." Without waiting for their response, she turned so she could look upstream.

Show time.

Closing her eyes, she let her head fall back slightly, arms relaxed and down by her sides. It was the pose her mother always assumed when summoning a ghost.

"*Llorona*, if you can hear me, please appear before me. I know you're troubled and I want to help." She paused, opening her senses to the night. A cool breeze, startling on such a warm night, wafted across the back of her neck, causing the tiny hairs to stand on end. Her heart lurched and adrenaline shot through her system, causing her to shiver.

Sometimes it felt like she really could summon ghosts.

Get a grip, she ordered herself.

"*Llorona*, if you can hear me, please show yourself." She spoke loud enough for the others to hear her and patiently waited for the right moment to cue the second act of her performance. It occurred when the slight breeze picked up, stirring the trees so the branches rubbed against each other, emitting an eerie groan, and the rustling of leaves became whispers in the night.

"She's here. *Llorona* is with us," she announced in a reverent tone, opening her eyes to stare at a spot three feet in front of her, not that her audience could see where she was looking.

"I don't see her," Dane commented, loud enough to be heard.

Gina felt slightly miffed that he had interrupted her session, but she decided not to make an issue of it because Sylvia was already shushing him.

"*Llorona*, I know you're troubled," Gina continued. "You left this life with unfinished business. Tell me what troubles you so I can help."

"No, Sylvia. I'm serious," Dane interrupted again. "Where's *Llorona*? I don't see her. Do you?"

"Well, no, I don't," came Sylvia's reluctant admission.

Gina momentarily paused. Had they really expected to see *Llorona's* ghost? She waited for Uncle Victor to quietly explain to them that only she could see spirits.

When he didn't, she started feeling uneasy. She spared a look over her shoulder. It was too dark to read their expressions, but their stance was no longer relaxed. She cast a quick glance at Uncle Victor, who ran his hand over the top of his head, signaling her to abort the performance.

Crap.

She didn't know what was wrong, but realized she should have paid more attention to whatever he'd been telling her earlier. Now she was going to have to think fast.

With an audible huff, she let her arms flap against her sides in a show of frustration. "She's gone." She started walking toward the group and, though it pained her to do it, glowered at Dane. "You frightened her away."

"I frightened away the ghost who's been terrorizing our town? Not likely," he scoffed, his once flirtatious tone turning suspicious. "Tell me something. Why is it that every other time *Llorona* appears, she's as plain to see as you or me? But tonight, for the first time in...FOREVER, she's invisible?"

Insufferable man! Hearing the challenge in his voice, she couldn't believe that less than an hour ago, she'd actually wanted to kiss him. Then his words sank in.

What did he mean by saying *Llorona* was visible? Gina had never in her life seen a ghost before. It was impossible. Wasn't it?

She needed time to think about this.

"Maybe you've only seen her when she wants you to see her. Had you considered that? I can see her when she does not wish to reveal herself to others."

Sylvia seemed to consider her explanation and nodded her understanding.

Dane didn't look convinced, but she saw doubt flicker across his face. "So you're saying that *Llorona* appeared only to you?"

Gina kept her expression neutral. "Exactly." Her next words were directed to the group. "I don't think *Llorona* will be back tonight. We'll have to try again tomorrow night."

"Of course, dear," Sylvia agreed, stepping forward to loop her arm through Gina's. They'd only taken a few steps when Dane called after them.

"Wait a minute. If *Llorona* confided in you, what did she say?"

The women stopped walking so Gina could look back and meet Dane's gaze. "I don't know; I don't speak Spanish."

Sylvia chattered the entire ride home, speculating on ways for Gina to translate *Llorona's* words the next time they spoke; everything from using Henri, her spirit guide, as interpreter to using a Ouija Board and letting *Llorona* move the pointer to spell out words while one of the Spanish-speaking residents translated them.

Gina paid little attention. Her focus was on the uncomfortable silence that had fallen between her and Dane. The moment they'd shared at the dance was like a distant memory; a suggestion of what might have been but never would be. Sometimes, reality sucked.

It was for the best, but she couldn't help feeling disappointed.

By the time they returned to the quaint Bed and Breakfast, Dane's demeanor towards Gina had noticeably changed. He was now cool and distant as he bid her goodnight, leaving her standing on the front porch as he hurried back to his truck. Sylvia, on the other hand, lingered on the front porch, taking her time saying farewell to Uncle Victor. Gina didn't stand around waiting, but went upstairs to her room. By the time her uncle finally made it upstairs, Gina was already snug in bed. Any discussion about their failed ghost whispering attempt would have to wait until tomorrow.

As she lay awake, unable to sleep, Gina made a promise to herself that she would not let this setback deter her from her goal. Tomorrow, she and Uncle Victor would devise a plan to stage a ghost encounter worth ten thousand dollars. With that money, they could pay off Frankie Goldstein and return to their home in Houston.

She determinedly pushed Dane Wolfe from her thoughts. She was done fantasizing about the man. But when she finally fell asleep, her dreams were filled with visions of a tall, handsome man with dark blond hair and warm golden-brown eyes holding her close as they danced under sparkling lights.

Chapter Six

THE NEXT MORNING, THE sun shone brightly in a clear blue sky. The temperature outside should have felt cool, but this November, it was unseasonably warm. Fortunately, the air conditioning was working in Kathy's Café where Gina and Uncle Victor sat for breakfast. They'd risen early, as was their habit, and had already made one quick tour of the town to get their bearings; not that it had taken long. Las Palomas was a tiny town.

At the center of the town, taking up a small city block, was Town Park. According to the plaque they read, there had once been a courthouse standing there, but it had burned down in 2004. Now, the only thing remaining of it was a single brick wall that separated the grassy side of the park from an area made up of concrete ramps in varying degrees of inclines and lengths. A skateboard park, Gina realized.

Sitting now in a booth at the front of Kathy's Café, Gina stared out the window, watching a man spray painting a mural on the side of the brick wall facing the grassy side of the park. There was an assortment of spray paint cans on the ground beside him. It was too soon to tell what the mural was supposed to be, but it was fascinating to watch. The wall was so large, Gina wondered how he could work on one small section without being able to see it in relation to the rest of the picture.

"Good morning," a cheerful voice greeted them, drawing Gina's attention away from the artist. Looking up, she recognized the woman.

"Good morning. It's Kathy, isn't it?"

The woman she'd met the night before smiled. "You remembered. I'm impressed."

Gina gestured to her uncle. "I'm not sure if you met my uncle last night. Uncle Victor, this is Kathy. She owns this café."

Uncle Victor held out his hand to shake Kathy's. "It's a pleasure to meet you."

"You, too," Kathy replied warmly. "Y'all are up early this morning."

"You know how it is," Gina replied. "Being out of town, sleeping in a different bed. Regardless of how comfortable it might be, sometimes it's hard to sleep in. So we got up and walked around town." She pointed across the street. "What's going on over there?"

"The painter? That's part of the town's beautification project. I'm not really sure what he's painting. No one knows except Peggy Olson, who's heading up the project, and hopefully the mayor. Every day, it's interesting to see a little more of the picture emerge."

Gina glanced back at the painter, who was in the process of spraying orange in a wide arc. She had no idea what it was supposed to be. Part of a rainbow, maybe?

"Can I start you folks off with something to drink?" Kathy asked, laying menus down on the table. "Coffee, maybe?"

"That would be great," Gina said. "With creamer and sweetener?"

"Sure thing." Kathy turned to Uncle Victor to get his order.

"Coffee please. Black."

As Kathy walked away to get their drinks, Gina and Uncle Victor turned their attention back to the painter. The man had switched to a can of bright blue paint, his movements precise and deliberate as he added more details to the mural. Gina found herself mesmerized by the swirls and shapes taking form on the wall, wondering what the finished piece would look like.

Suddenly, a loud crash startled them both. Gina whipped her head around to see that a waitress had dropped a tray of food on the floor. Instead of bending to pick up the mess, her attention was on two plates floating past her in mid-air. They continued gliding effortlessly across the room as if carried by invisible hands. Uncle Victor's eyes widened in disbelief, his mouth agape as he watched the surreal sight unfold before him.

Gina felt equally shocked and glanced up at Kathy, who had just returned with empty mugs and a carafe of coffee.

"It's just the ghostly wait staff at work," Kathy explained casually as she filled their empty mugs with coffee. "They like to keep things interesting around here. Don't worry, they won't drop your order."

Gina and Uncle Victor exchanged surprised looks before bursting into laughter. Gina shook her head, still half in disbelief at the illusion. "You had me going for a second there, Kathy. I thought my eyes were playing tricks on me. You can't even see the wires."

When Kathy's expression remained serious, Gina and Uncle Victor's laughter faded. "I'm afraid it's no trick. This café is haunted," she said, her voice low and solemn. "The ghostly wait staff are real. They've been here for as long as I can remember, making their presence known in subtle, and not-so-subtle, ways." She gestured to the plates, now gently landing on a table on the other side of the room. "I can't see them, but you can, right?"

Gina felt dumbstruck and it took her a moment to recover. "Um, yes. I can."

"Wow," Kathy exclaimed. "What I wouldn't give to be you. Some of them still think they work here and carry plates from the kitchen to the table and back again."

Gina felt a tingle of fear creeping up her spine, every nerve on high alert as she scanned the room for other signs of paranormal activity.

"Now, what can I get you folks to eat?" Kathy asked, setting the coffee carafe on the table. "Cook makes a mean omelet and the best damn French toast you'll ever eat. Plus, we have real maple syrup." She pulled packets of sweetener and creamer pods from the pocket of her apron and set them on the table by Gina.

They placed their orders and Kathy left.

"Do you think she was kidding?" Gina asked Uncle Victor, still uneasy at seeing plates floating across the room.

"Did you notice all the posters in shop windows and the notices on the bulletin board in the park? They all advertised ghost sightings. And last night, I overheard a couple talking about their trip here last year and how they saw not just one, but two ghosts."

"They probably mean they saw evidence of a ghost, like a floating light or something, don't you think?"

He shook his head, looking pensive. "You remember what happened at the river? Both Dane and Sylvia said they couldn't see *Llorona* after you said she was there, and they sounded surprised, like they expected to see her."

"Yeah." She dragged the word out as the memories from the ghost whispering session rushed back. "That didn't make sense to me. How can they see a ghost?"

"I don't know. Let's ask Kathy when she brings our food."

Gina nodded, and they didn't have to wait long before Kathy reappeared with a tray of food. Balancing the tray with one hand, she used her other hand to place their plates in front of them.

"This looks wonderful," Uncle Victor said, leaning forward to take an appreciative whiff of his food.

Gina had to agree. While her omelet didn't smell as good as Uncle Victor's French toast, it looked cooked to perfection and she could hardly wait to taste it.

"Kathy, I'm curious," Uncle Victor started before Kathy could turn to leave. "Have you ever actually seen a ghost?"

She gave him a funny look. "Sure, some of them. The ancient ghosts, like *El Muerto* and *Llorona*."

"That's interesting," he said. "Usually in our encounters, only Gina can see the ghost."

Kathy didn't seem to find this odd. "There's something about where Las Palomas is located that enables ghosts to appear. Our local coven leader, Katherine Hunter, says it's because Las Palomas sits at the juncture of two powerful ley lines." She shrugged. "I don't even know what that means."

"So, you've seen *Llorona*?" Uncle Victor asked, trying to keep them on topic.

She nodded. "Sure."

"Gina and I were at the river last night and while Gina felt her presence, I'm afraid she didn't manifest to me or the others with us. Perhaps you could humor me and tell me what she looks like?"

"I can do better than that. I can show you a picture of her."

Before either of them could react to this, Kathy headed for the back of the café, where a short hallway led to the restrooms. Mounted on the wall was a bulletin board. Kathy stopped in front of it and, after several minutes of searching, found the picture she was looking for and unpinned it from the board. When she returned, she handed it to Uncle Victor.

"Isn't that interesting," Uncle Victor said, stroking his beard like an old college professor might as he studied the picture for what felt like an eternity before finally passing it to Gina.

Her hands shook as she accepted it, her heart racing in anticipation and trepidation. She expected to see a blurry or faded figure, but what she saw was beyond her wildest expectations.

The woman in the photo stood by the river under the ethereal glow of the moon, her form radiant and otherworldly. Her flowing hair cascaded down her shoulders like a waterfall of mist, and her eyes glimmered with an ancient wisdom that seemed to hold secrets from beyond the veil.

The ghost's gown billowed in an unseen breeze, appearing both solid and insubstantial at the same time. She stood with one hand outstretched towards the water, as if beckoning to someone or something hidden in the shadows.

Gina felt a shiver run down her spine as she looked at the photograph. Unable to find words, she handed the picture back to Kathy, who quietly walked away to replace it on the bulletin board.

Alone at their table again, Gina met Uncle Victor's intense gaze.

"Houston, we have a problem," he said gravely.

Dane woke that morning thinking about Gina Castillo. He couldn't deny he was attracted to her, but that's all it was, physical attraction. That's all it could be, because he hadn't known her long enough for it to be anything more.

Yet he couldn't deny feeling drawn to her.

Driving into work, he was still trying to figure out what had come over him the night before to make him almost kiss her. He was an adult, for Christ's sake. Not some wet-behind-the-ears kid in the throes of his first crush, but damn if he hadn't acted like it. If Sal and his wife hadn't come along...

He didn't allow himself to finish that thought. What he needed, he decided, was a good cup of coffee to clear his brain. Something better than he could make on his office Keurig. Since Kathy made the best coffee in town, he would stop there first before going into the office. He placed a call to the police station to let them know he'd be a little late.

"Morning, chief," Chad answered the phone.

"How are things this morning?" Dane asked.

"Quiet, so far."

"Good. Did that background check come back yet on the Castillos?" He'd put in the request the day after Peggy's attempt to summon *Llorona* failed, the same day the mayor had asked Sylvia to contact Gina Castillo.

"Hang on, let me look."

Chad put him on hold and Dane listened to the sound of Muzak without really hearing it. A few seconds later, Chad clicked back on. "No, not yet."

"Okay, thanks for checking. I'm going to stop at Kathy's for coffee before I head in."

"You're planning to work today?" Chad sounded surprised.

"Yeah, why?"

"I figured you'd be spending the day with that really hot ghost whisperer. The two of you looked pretty, um, chummy last night, if you know what I mean."

"No, I don't know what you mean," Dane said, making his tone stern.

"From the way you were looking at her, I thought we were going to have to call the fire department. I mean—"

"I'm hanging up now," Dane interrupted and disconnected the call, refusing to be baited into admitting anything to Chad, even if Chad *was* his best friend.

It bothered him to think the entire town might know he had a thing for Gina Castillo, not that anyone could blame him. After all, she was stunningly attractive; slender but with curves in all the right places. Just thinking of her reminded him of the way her body had felt pressed up against his.

Damn it. He needed to focus on something else.

Reaching the café, he pulled into a parking place and climbed out of his truck, sending forth a small prayer that Kathy, having seen him drive up, had his coffee waiting for him in a to-go cup so he could be on his way without having to talk to anyone.

Fate, he quickly discovered, had other plans for him. Not only did Kathy not have his coffee ready, she wasn't even standing behind the counter. Instead, she was standing by one of the front booths, talking to none other than Gina and Victor Castillo. She looked over at the jingling of the small bell hanging from the door.

"Morning, Chief. Coffee's coming right up. Excuse me, folks."

Now that Gina and her uncle had seen him, Dane really had no choice but to walk over and say hello. After the near-kiss at the dance followed by what happened at the river, he hoped it wouldn't be awkward.

"Good morning, Chief," Victor Castillo greeted him warmly. "We were just enjoying some of Kathy's wonderful coffee." He gestured to the opposite side of the booth. "Please, won't you join us?"

"Well, I—"

Kathy walked over at that moment with an empty ceramic mug—not a to-go cup—and a full carafe of coffee. She set the empty mug down beside Gina's cup and, since Victor Castillo was clearly not sliding over to share his booth seat, Dane slid in beside Gina.

"Thank you," he said politely, very much aware of the woman sitting beside him. "I hope you both slept well."

"Yes. The accommodations are very comfortable," Gina assured him. "And Ruby Mae is a gracious hostess. She offered to make breakfast for us, but we wanted to get out and see the town."

"You're here at a good time of year," Dane told her, "when it's not as crowded. We had a rush in October. Halloween draws a lot of ghost hunters," he explained.

Gina and her uncle didn't seem to find it odd that people would come to Las Palomas to see a ghost. He had to remind himself that while Las Palomas was not a well-known tourist destination with the public, it was well known to those specifically in search of paranormal activity.

"I wonder, Chief Wolfe, if you could tell me where I might find Sylvia this morning?" Victor asked, drawing his attention.

"Sylvia's Saturday Séance Circle meets tonight, so she's probably at home setting up the table and polishing her crystal ball."

If either Gina or Victor noticed his sarcasm, they didn't comment on it.

"Then perhaps I'll call her. If the two of you will excuse me?"

Uncle Victor didn't give them a chance to say anything before sliding out of the booth and stepping away from the table. He disappeared from Gina's view, presumably to go someplace quiet to place his call, leaving her and Dane alone at the table.

Feeling self-conscious, Gina focused on taking a sip of her drink, even though she'd had enough coffee to float her back teeth.

Dane seemed equally focused on drinking his coffee.

The silence between them was on the verge of being extremely awkward when Uncle Victor suddenly reappeared at the table.

"Sylvia has invited me to go over and help her." He beamed at the two of them.

"Would you like a ride?" Dane offered.

"No, thanks." Uncle Victor waved his offer aside. "I understand her house isn't that far from here, so I'll walk. There is something you can do for me, though, if you have time."

"Sure. I'm happy to," Dane said, wondering what he was agreeing to.

"My niece is interested in seeing the town. Perhaps you wouldn't mind showing her around?"

"Oh, my God! Uncle Victor, you did not just ask this man to babysit me!" She sounded so mortified that Dane chuckled.

"It would be my pleasure," he said, suspecting, even as he agreed, it was probably a horrible idea.

"Are you sure?" she asked. "I don't want to take you away from anything."

"You're not," he responded, forgetting all about his plans to head to the office.

"Excellent. Then it's settled," Uncle Victor announced. "You two have fun, and I'll see you later." He walked off.

"When?" Gina called after him.

He stopped long enough to look back, smile, and shrug. "I'm not really sure."

This time, when he turned and walked off, Gina let him go. After he disappeared through the door, Dane became all too aware of the woman sitting beside him. She was too close and he was finding it hard to think. Pushing his coffee across the table, he slipped out of the booth and took the seat across from her.

That was better, he thought, picking up his mug to take a drink.

"Seriously," she said. "Please don't feel obligated to stay with me if you have better things to do."

"You don't want to spend time with me?" he asked, only partially teasing her.

"What?" She looked surprised, then grimaced and started over. "What I meant was, I understand if you have to work. I'm perfectly capable of walking around town by myself."

"Where's the fun in that?" He gave her a smile. "The main square here is the most interesting part of the town. When you're done with your coffee, why don't we walk around it? I'll point out the historical landmarks and give you some of the local color. Then we can take my truck and I'll show you some of the other interesting sites around town, including the sites of our more notable hauntings. How does that sound?"

She smiled. "That would be nice, thanks."

It sounded good to Dane as well. "How about we take this coffee to go?"

He signaled to Kathy to bring two to-go cups. When she came over with them, she set a bill on the table. He picked it up and handed it back to her.

"You can put their bill on my tab," he said, ignoring Gina's attempt to pay it.

He filled their cups from the carafe and waited until Gina had added sweetener and creamer to hers. "Ready to go?"

"Sure." Gina wondered if she sounded as breathless as she felt. She vowed to get her nerves under control as she followed Dane outside.

"That," he said, gesturing to the park across the street, "is where the old courthouse used to stand. After it burned down, the town rebuilt the courthouse a couple of blocks over and turned this space into a park."

She looked over at the park with admiration. The vibrant green grass and colorful flowers gave off an air of tranquility and calmness. "It's truly beautiful." Her gaze then shifted to the other side of the park, where the painter was hard at work.

Dane noticed her curiosity and explained, "That's part of our beautification project. The residents found the bare wall unsightly, so a graffiti artist was hired to transform it into a work of art."

"A graffiti artist?" She'd never heard of that before. She knew what graffiti was, of course, having seen it on the sides of train cars. "That's a real thing?"

"Yeah, apparently. One artist is pretty much the same as the next, as far as I'm concerned, but don't let Peggy hear you say that. She's very particular."

"Peggy?"

"Peggy Olson."

She rolled the name around in her head. "I don't think I met her last night."

"You'd remember if you had."

Gina waited for him to expound on that comment, but he didn't. Instead, he gestured to the wall.

"I don't get it, myself. We could have turned a bunch of five-year-olds loose with paint cans and it would look the same to me."

She smiled. "Not a fan of modern art?"

"I'm not sure this qualifies as art." At the sound of a car door shutting, he glanced over his shoulder. "Oh, crap. Speak of the devil. I don't think there's any way we can make a graceful escape or, believe me, we would."

Gina turned to see a dark-haired woman hurry across the street to join them. She wore a tailored slack suit that seemed a little too formal for such a small town and her hair was pulled back in a neat chignon. "I'm sure it won't be that bad," Gina assured him, trying not to sound too amused.

"Yeah? I'm willing to bet you've never met anyone like Peggy." He sighed heavily. "We might as well get this over with."

As the woman drew closer, Gina saw she was in her mid-fifties with fine age-lines around her eyes and mouth. Her makeup was not only perfectly applied, but, despite the heat, still appeared fresh. This was a woman who cared how she appeared in public.

"Dane, dear. I thought that was you," she greeted them. "And this, of course, must be Miss Castillo. I would have introduced myself to you last night, but you and Dane appeared to be... preoccupied." Her tone was filled with censure.

"Morning, Peggy," Dane greeted her, clearly choosing to ignore her comment. "Gina, I'd like to introduce you to Peggy Olson. She's in charge of the town beautification project." To Peggy, he said. "We were just admiring the artwork of the graphic artist you hired."

"Graffiti artist, dear, not graphic artist." She patted his arm. "It's all right. I don't expect you to know the difference. He's quite good, isn't he?" Her tone was that of a proud parent.

"That's right. Graffiti artist. I get the two confused." He winked at Gina and she fought to hide her smile. "What's his name again?"

"Miles Davis. He's from Denver." She looked at Gina. "I'm sure you've heard of him."

Gina silently repeated the name. "No, I'm sorry."

"Really?" Peggy sounded shocked. "Well, never mind. Modern art is not for everyone, but if you knew anything about it, you'd know that Miles is truly one of the more gifted artists of our time." The woman kept talking as if she hadn't just insulted Gina. "He started out as a runaway teen, defacing the sides of rail cars until an art critic discovered him. With the proper guidance, and underwriting, of course, his art took off. Now he's so famous, there's a long waiting list of people wanting him to create a piece for them. Shall

I introduce you? I mean, it's not every day you get to meet someone famous."

She started down the sidewalk toward the artist, leaving Dane and Gina no choice but to follow.

"If he's so busy, how did we get him so quickly?" Dane had to speak loudly for Peggy to hear.

"We almost didn't," she said, stopping so they could catch up to her. "At first, he was booked for the entire summer, but then later called me back and said he'd finished the job in San Antonio early and could fit us into his schedule. So," she shrugged. "Here he is." She beamed as if she, herself, had orchestrated the turn of events.

"Oh, Miles!" Peggy hollered as they reached the crosswalk that ran in front of the wall. "I want to introduce you to some people."

Gina thought the artist looked annoyed at the interruption, but he set his paint can down on his tarp and wiped his paint-stained hands on an already dirty cloth hanging from his waist.

"Miles, this is our acting police chief, Dane Wolfe, and Ms. Gina Castillo, a noted ghost whisperer."

Gina thought the artist looked nervous, shaking Dane's hand, barely even meeting Dane's gaze before looking away. Maybe it was a normal reaction to being around the police?

Interestingly enough, though, she discovered the artist had the same reaction when he shook hands with her, so maybe he was simply an extreme introvert. She offered him a smile, hoping to put him more at ease.

"Miles has won several awards for his work," Peggy went on. "But he's best known for his 3D representations. He did a marvelous rendering of the Alamo in San Antonio last month and before that, he was in Austin." She turned to him. "What was it you did there?"

"I did a scene of musicians playing with an overlay of a music staff with notes for the Austin City Limits Music Festival," he replied.

"Very nice," Peggy said, sounding indulgent. "We've commissioned him to do some work, but I can't tell you about it."

"It must be hard to be traveling all the time," Gina sympathized.

"Oh, Miles doesn't have to leave home," Mrs. Olson gushed. "He lives in an RV, traveling from one assignment to the next, with his wife and son."

"It's just me and my wife," the artist clarified. "We don't have a son."

Peggy gave a bark of laughter. "Of course you do. When I spoke to your wife last month, she said the three of you were traveling together. Josh. Yes, that's right. I'm sure she said his name is Josh."

"You're mistaken," he bit out. "I don't have any children. Now, if you'll excuse me, I'd like to get back to my work." He turned his back to them and bent down to retrieve another can of paint. "Stand back," he warned with a slight turn of his head before depressing the nozzle on the can. Paint sprayed forth, hitting the wall, and though it wasn't windy, the three automatically stepped back.

They waited a second, unclear of what to do, but when the artist showed no signs of stopping, the three turned and left.

"I'm positive his wife said they had a son," Peggy muttered when they finally crossed the street and reached the other side.

"Maybe you misunderstood what the wife said?" Dane's comment earned him a dark scowl.

"No, there's no mistake and when I find my notes, you'll see I'm right."

By unspoken agreement, they'd stopped in front of Peggy's white Lexus.

"I don't know, Peggy. You'd think the man would know whether he's got a son," Dane said in an overly patient tone of voice.

Peggy jabbed her car key in the air at him. "Don't take that tone with me, Dane Wolfe. I specifically recall talking to that woman. I told her about the park and she said—"

She continued to speak, but Gina, who felt like she was now intruding on the woman's meltdown, opted to stop listening.

An older couple in brightly colored tennis shoes walked past them at a surprisingly fast pace, no doubt taking advantage of the cooler part of the day to get in their exercise. At the far end of the park, a group of teens stood before a bulletin board, reading the notices posted there. Several younger children had appeared to play on the swing set while their mothers sat on nearby benches, chatting. She turned her attention back to the conversation between Peggy and Dane.

"—sick and tired of people not giving me the credit I'm due—"

"Peggy, no one feels that way—"

It didn't sound like the conversation was winding down, so Gina glanced into the nearest shop window and discovered it was a gift shop.

Perfect.

"If you'll excuse me," she interrupted them, shooting Dane an apologetic look. "It was nice meeting you, Peggy. I think I'll go inside to browse a bit while you finish your conversation. Excuse me."

Then, not giving either of them a chance to stop her, she pushed open the shop door and escaped inside.

Chapter Seven

THE INSIDE OF THE gift shop was full of display shelves filled with novelty items spanning the spectrum from kitchenware and cookbooks to toys and clothing, the majority with a ghostly theme. One could easily get lost in a store like this, which was exactly what Gina intended to do. Anything to avoid Peggy Olson, who seemed like the kind of person to suck the energy out of the people around her.

Gina browsed through the toys, remembering how excited she would get when her mother took her to the toy store. It wasn't often because they were always watching their money, so each trip had been a special treat. Her mother had seemed to enjoy the trips as much as Gina had.

Spotting a Slinky on the shelf, Gina picked it up and let it travel from one hand to the other, losing herself in a memory.

"What about that one?"

A man's softly spoken voice sounded from the other side of the rack.

"No," a second man whispered back, sounding impatient.

"Why? She's perfect. Look at those blond curls, blue eyes, and chubby cheeks. She looks just like a doll."

"I told you. We're not ready. I don't think you realize that once we do this, there's no going back. We can never undo it."

"You're scared," the first man replied sympathetically. "I understand. Really, I do."

"Thank you," the second man said.

The strange conversation sparked Gina's interest. What were they talking about? Setting the Slinky back on the shelf, she casually moved around the rack, making a pretense of examining the other toys.

As she came around, she spotted the two men. The tall one, with dark hair and linebacker build, was flipping through a book. Gina couldn't see what kind. The other man, also tall, was slimmer with neatly styled blonde hair. Both were nicely dressed in crisp dark-denim jeans and polo shirts.

As Gina studied them out of the corner of her eye, she noticed the blonde's attention on something across the room. Gina followed his gaze to a young girl, about four years old, standing beside her mother. She had curly blond hair, chubby cheeks, and looked like the doll she was holding.

Had the men been talking about that little girl? Gina replayed their conversation back through her head and an uneasy feeling came over her.

No, surely not.

Unable to shake the feeling, she moved to a display case closer to the men and picked up a book, pretending to browse its contents when, in fact, she was trying to eaves-drop.

"—understand that the first time will be scary, but think of how much fun it can be," the slender man encouraged. Gina recognized him as being the first speaker and dubbed him "Larry."

"I don't know," the linebacker replied noncommittally. Gina named him "Mo."

"Well, if you're not interested in a little girl, we could always take a boy."

"Are you upset?"

Gina jumped at the sound of Dane's voice. Her attention had been so focused on the two men that she hadn't noticed him coming into the shop. She turned to him now, uncertain whether she should say anything to him.

"If it's about what Peggy said about us at the dance, just ignore her," he continued. "Most people do. Being rude and unpleasant is just the way she is. After a while, you learn not to take her too seriously."

"Actually, I'd already forgotten about her," Gina admitted. "I don't let people like Peggy get to me."

He nodded. "Okay, but something is clearly bothering you."

His comment surprised her. "What makes you think I'm upset?"

He gestured to the book she held open before her.

"What? I was reading."

"Upside down?"

She looked down and this time focused on the pages before her. He was right. She blushed, hurriedly closing the book. "Yeah, okay," she said. "Maybe I was distracted."

It was on the verge of her tongue to tell him what she'd overheard, but at the last second, she changed her mind. She couldn't exactly accuse the men of being child predators based on a few snippets of conversation heard out of context. Besides, as a quick look around confirmed, the men had left the store and the little girl was still with her mother.

"I guess maybe Peggy's comments about us were more upsetting than I originally thought." It wasn't a complete lie.

"Don't let that witch make you regret our dance last night, okay? Because I don't regret it. Not a single moment of it."

"I wasn't regretting it, but wait... is she an actual witch?"

He laughed. "No way would the local coven allow her to join them."

Gina looked at him in surprise. "Are you telling me you really have actual witches here in Las Palomas?"

He shrugged, nonchalantly. "Of course." Then he cocked his head and gave her a teasing look. "Would you like to meet them?"

She smiled, feeling a ripple of excitement. "Yes, I would."

"Are you planning to buy that?" He gestured to the book she still held.

"No," she replied, placing the book back on the shelf.

"Then let's go. They aren't far from here. We can walk."

They left the store and started walking up the sidewalk parallel to Town Park. When they reached the end of the block, they turned left and kept walking until they reached the end of that block and crossed the street. Dane stopped then and gestured to the store in front of which they stood.

Gina studied the quaint-looking shop with the lacy-curtained front window and stenciled lettering that read *Katherine's Kozy Korner*.

"What is this place?" she asked.

"It's a bookstore and a coffee shop, owned and run by Katherine Hunter, mother of our chief of police. It's also headquarters for our local witch coven."

"The mother of your police chief is a witch?" She couldn't keep the skepticism from her tone.

He only shrugged. "What can I say? This is Las Palomas."

Dane opened the door for her, and they stepped inside. The store seemed empty, but they could hear voices coming from down a side hallway.

"Maybe we should come back some other time," Gina suggested hesitantly.

Dane shook his head. Sam had asked him to keep an eye on her mother and grandmother while she was out-of-town and, lately, he'd been remiss in that duty. For good reasons, of course, but even so, Sam's mother and grandmother could be real kooks at times.

He moved down the hallway, looking back only once to make sure Gina was following him. When he reached the first door on the left, he stepped into the open doorway and stared at the scene before him.

Sam's grandmother, Maggie Parrish—better known as "Nanna"—stood at the large table set in the middle of the room, her back to the door. Around the table sat four or five women, ranging in age from late fifties to mid-seventies. They were sprinkling what looked like dried grass over white crystals piled in the center of the table.

"That's right, ladies," Nanna was saying. "Be sure to cover the crystals entirely. If you don't, then the spell might not work."

At that moment, one lady on the opposite side of the table looked up and spotted them. Looking a bit like the cat that ate the canary, she froze and stared at them. It was enough to get Nanna's attention, and she turned to see what had distracted the woman.

As soon as she saw Dane, her face lit in a smile and she went to greet them. "Dane, it's so good to see you. What are you doing here?"

There was no point in lying. "Sam asked me to check in on you and Katherine while she's away," he said, looking around. "Speaking of, where *is* Katherine?"

"She and Zelda left this morning to head back to Florida to be with Sam."

"How's Sam doing?" he asked, his tone growing concerned.

Nanna smiled. "Physically, she's fine. Recovering nicely from her injuries. Mentally?" Nanna looked skeptical and shrugged. "It's hard to say. You know, she coded several times on the way to the hospital and once in surgery." He nodded, remembering how worried he'd been. Sam wasn't just his boss. She was also one of his closest friends, but every time he talked to her on the phone, she claimed to be fine, though her tone suggested otherwise. "She seems to do better when Zelda is there," Nanna continued. "She says she's ready to take the psych and physical evaluations and come back to work, but both doctors say she's not ready yet. Soon, though."

Dane would be glad when she returned. He'd thought he wanted the chief's job, but now he wasn't so sure.

"How are you doing?" he asked her. "It can't be easy running the shop all by yourself."

Nanna gave his arm a gentle pat. "Don't you worry about me. I have plenty of help," she said, nodding to the other women.

Then Nanna turned her attention to Gina. "Dane, dear. Aren't you going to introduce me to your friend?"

"Oh, I'm sorry." He felt like a school kid being chastised for bad manners. "Maggie Parrish, allow me to introduce you to Gina Castillo."

When Gina held out her hand in greeting, Nanna took it but didn't release it. Instead, she gently pulled Gina forward a step or two, bringing them closer together.

"You are the ghost whisperer," Nanna said, studying Gina closely. "It's a pleasure to meet you. I can tell the gift of second sight is strong within you." She closed her eyes, a focused expression coming to her face. "But you are not accessing your full potential," she finally said. "There's something blocking your ability. I can't see what it is. A past tragedy, maybe? Self-doubt?" She opened her eyes and gave Gina a tender smile. "You mustn't be afraid to be what you are." Then she gasped in excitement and released Gina's hand to clap hers together. "I have just the thing for you."

Without giving them an explanation, she hurried over to the table and sorted through the items before finding what she wanted. She held it out to Gina when she returned, and Dane saw it was some kind of delicate fabric pouch.

"What's in it?" Gina asked, holding the pouch up.

"A few herbs and dried flowers to enhance your senses and a small white crystal to promote healing and ward off evils spirits." Placing both hands around the pouch, she closed her eyes and muttered words under her breath that Dane couldn't make out. When she finished, she released the pouch and smiled. "That was just a small spell to help open your third eye, as we refer to it. Go ahead, put it on. You should wear it around your neck."

Gina looked dubious but smiled. "Thank you," she said. She held the pouch to her nose and inhaled. "It smells good." Then she slipped the pouch's long cord over her head. When she felt Dane's gaze on her, she shrugged. "It can't hurt to wear it, right?"

He had no idea but was saved from having to respond when his cell phone rang.

"Excuse me a moment," he apologized, seeing Chad's name on his caller ID and stepping into the hallway to answer the call.

"Dane, here. What's up?" he asked.

"There's been a break-in at Zelda's shop," Chad said. "The silent alarm was tripped. I'm here now and there's no one here. I called Zelda but got no response."

"Zelda's on her way to Florida," Dane replied. "Is there any damage? Or can you see if anything was stolen?"

"The only damage is to the back door. They had to break it to get in. I don't see any other damage, but there is a shelf in her shop that's empty. All the shelves around it have rocks on them. This one is labeled white crystals." He sighed. "Who breaks into a shop to steal a bunch of rocks?"

At that moment, the back door to the bookstore opened and a moment later, two women in their mid-sixties stepped into the hallway. One of them was holding a mesh bag filled with white rocks.

"Maggie," the other woman shouted. "We got the last of them—oh!" She abruptly broke off when she looked up and spotted Dane. "Hello, Dane."

"Hello, Mrs. Jones," he greeted her.

"I've told you a hundred times to call me Inez," she replied before the two women bustled past him to go into the break room where the other women sat. Dane didn't stop them.

"I think I know who broke in," he told Chad. "I'll take care of it. Can you do me a favor, though? Call someone over to fix Zelda's door for her."

"Will do," Chad replied, and then disconnected the call.

Dane put his phone away and went back to the open doorway.

"Are those crystals from Zelda's shop?" He asked of no one in particular.

His question was met with a moment of silence. "They are," Nanna admitted finally. "We always purchase our crystals from Zelda. She has the best quality stones. Unfortunately, we had an urgent need for crystals and she wasn't around, so we were forced to break into her shop. We plan to pay her for the ones we use and we'll return the ones we don't."

"And the damage to the door?" Dane pressed.

"Yes, yes. We'll pay for that as well."

Knowing Zelda wouldn't press charges, he reluctantly let the matter go, except...

"What do you need all those crystals for?"

"For the protection spells we place around the town, of course."

Dane rolled his eyes. "Of course."

Nanna narrowed her gaze at him. "Don't sass me, boy. We're doing this to keep you and everyone else safe."

"I have police officers patrolling the town who do that."

She waved her hand dismissively. "Nonsense. Evil will find a way past your officers. They're only human, after all. But they won't get past our spells. Now, if you don't mind," she said, practically pushing them down the hallway. "We have important work to do."

She herded them out the front door of the shop and then Dane heard the distinct sound of a lock being thrown. When he turned to glance back at the door, Nanna had flipped the "Yes, we're open" sign that hung there to "Sorry, we're closed."

He pulled out his phone and activated the screen long enough to check the time. "It's almost ten-thirty. Let's take my truck and I'll show you some of the haunted sites. We can even stop by the RV park again."

"Sounds good," Gina replied, at his mention of the RV park. Considering what she and Uncle Victor had discovered about the Las Palomas ghosts making themselves visible, last night's attempt to contact *Llorona* could only be considered a complete disaster. Though he'd not said anything this morning about it, she couldn't help but wonder if his plan was to test her abilities once they reached the RV park.

The two headed to his truck. After they climbed in, Dane slipped an ear bud into his ear before starting the truck. A few minutes later, they were on the road.

"I'm a little surprised this is your first visit to Las Palomas," Dane said. "Given your profession and how close you live."

Gina gave a half laugh. "I wouldn't exactly call five hours a short drive, you know. Besides, ghosts aren't exactly a novel experience for me." She watched him out of the corner of her eye as she spoke, looking for any reaction to her words. There was none. "Of course," she continued, "most of the ghosts I deal with aren't famous like a lot of yours are. I know about *Llorona*, but you have others?"

"There's *El Muerto*. The headless horseman. He shows up at the Double R Ranch, riding across the back pasture. And there's the old Winterson home. It's been empty for years, but folks say they've seen someone peering out the windows. I've investigated, thinking a vagrant might be camping out there, but never found anyone. After a while—"

His cell phone rang, interrupting him. He glanced at the screen and then gave Gina an apologetic look. "Sorry, I should take this."

He tapped his ear bud to accept the call. "Hi, Mom. Wh—"

Dane listened, and Gina could hear an excited female voice coming through the phone.

"Mom, slow down. I can't understand you." Dane sounded calm and patient, but Gina saw him glance in the rearview, and then the side-view, mirrors. "Who's in the house?" His tone grew sharp as he swerved into the right lane. "A snake? Are you sure? Of course, Mom. I realize you know what a snake looks like. Did it bite you?... Well, that's good. So what's the problem?" At the next intersection, he turned right. "Can't you just sweep it out the back door with a broom?... No, of course, I wasn't thinking." He rolled his eyes, then gave Gina an apologetic look. "I would never ask you to put your life in danger... Yes, I'm heading there now... A few minutes. I don't suppose you called Cody?... Because catching snakes is what he does... Well, considering all the time he spent at our house in high school, he's practically like a son to you. I think it's okay to impose." Dane shook his head. "No, Ma'am, I'm not trying to be cute or make light of this situation. Any idea what kind of snake it is?" He sighed. "Got it. No, I don't think it ate Winston. Where is it now? No, I'll find it. You stay where you are. I'll be there shortly... I have to hang up now so I can call Cody..." He sighed. "Okay, I'll call you right back."

He disconnected the call and glanced at Gina. "Sorry about this. Mom's not a big fan of snakes."

"I don't blame her. What kind of snake is it?"

He glanced at the screen of his phone and pressed a button. "'A big fucking snake.' I believe that's a direct quote."

Gina couldn't help but smile. Dane's mother sounded like a character.

Dane waited for his call to be answered. "Hey, Cody," he said after a moment. "I've got a situation and need your help. Can you meet me at Mom's house? And bring your snake catching gear... Don't know, but according to Mom, it's big enough to eat the cat. Thanks. See you in a few."

He disconnected the call as they pulled into a residential neighborhood. Gina studied the homes as they drove past. It was hard to guess the ages of the homes because Texas summers are hard on home exteriors, making them look older than they really are. Dane placed another call as he drove past the first two streets, then took the next left.

"Okay, Mom, I'm here," he said, pulling into the driveway of a modest one-story brick home. "Yes, I called Cody... No, stay in your room until I've checked out the situation. I'm hanging up now." He slipped the phone into his pocket, swearing under his breath. "I'm sorry our plans got interrupted."

"Oh, please. Don't worry about it. This is actually pretty exciting—so long as everything turns out okay."

"Thanks for understanding. Hopefully, this won't take long. It's probably best if you wait out here. Cody's a high school buddy of mine. He should be here shortly."

She nodded, then watched him get out of his truck and walk toward the house. He moved with an air of confidence, like he was used to dealing with crises. She found that appealing.

Once he reached the front porch, he paused to take a deep breath. Then, he slowly turned the door handle and pushed the door open, surveying the floor of the foyer before stepping inside. He wished his mother had been a little more forthcoming with information, so he'd have a better idea of what kind of snake he was looking for. According to his mother, she'd spotted the snake slithering across the mud room floor. Dane reasoned that because it was still blistering hot outside, the snake had been attracted to the coolness of the tile flooring. Unfortunately, the entire house was tiled, so there was no telling where it had ended up.

Until he knew where, and what kind of snake it was, he planned to exercise extreme caution.

The foyer opened into the formal dining room to the right and a small study that his mother used as her craft room to the left. He scanned the dining room floor, bending to see beneath the side buffet. No sign of a snake.

He turned his attention to the craft room. The walls were lined with bookcases and storage bins, neither of which offered a snake some place to hide. He checked the floor beneath the desk and craft table.

Nothing.

His gut told him the snake hadn't ventured too far from the mudroom, which meant it was in the kitchen or family room. He hoped like hell it had gone into the kitchen because he didn't like the idea of bending down close to the ground to check beneath the sofa and recliners.

He continued across the foyer, scanning the floors ahead of him before placing each foot. It was slow going, but soon enough, he reached the kitchen. Flipping on the overhead light, he scanned the floor as best he could, but the refrigerator blocked his view to the right.

He crept forward and was four steps into the room when a distinct rattling sound caused him to freeze.

Oh, shit!

One didn't grow up in this part of Texas without recognizing that sound.

Dane turned his head toward the noise. Curled on the floor on the other side of the refrigerator, in the shadowy corner where the cabinets met at right angles, was a snake. A very large and deadly rattlesnake. Coiled with its head raised, it was staring at him, its tongue vibrating rapidly as it tasted the air.

Shit! Shit!

Chapter Eight

For half a second, he considered shooting it, but the combination of paperwork he'd need to fill out for discharging his firearm and the grief his mother would give him for destroying her tiled floor had him considering other options.

"Dane?"

Cody. Thank God. "In the kitchen."

"And the snake?" Cody's voice drifted to him from the dining room.

"About four feet from my right foot. A big fucking rattlesnake. Go around the other side, so you can see him better."

He heard Cody's footsteps fade and then Cody appeared in his peripheral vision as he moved through the family room to enter the kitchen from the opposite side. He stopped at the far end of the kitchen island.

"Oh, yeah. That is one big motherfucker."

"Not helping," Dane said, not taking his eyes off the snake.

"Try to stay calm. They sense fear."

"Again, not helping."

Cody gave a soft chuckle as he moved a little closer. Now that Cody was in front of him, Dane could see that his friend was wearing tall snake boots, a thick long-sleeved shirt, and leather gloves. In one hand, he held a long net and a pair of snake tongs, while in the other, he carried a tall plastic bucket. He set the bucket down and laid the lid to one side. Then, with the net in one hand and the tongs in the other, both extended in front of him, he faced the snake.

"When I give the word, I want you to back up fast," he instructed.

"What about you?"

"Don't worry about me. You ready?"

"Ready," Dane said.

"Now!"

Dane took a gigantic step back and quickly moved to the other side of the island. At the same time, Cody stepped in front of the snake, blocking Dane from seeing what he was doing. A moment later, Cody lifted the net while holding the top of it closed with his tongs. The snake, writhing and twisting, hung in the netting. With deft moves, Cody transferred the snake, net and all, into the plastic bucket and secured the lid in place.

Only then did Dane release the breath he'd been holding. He turned to his friend, whose broad smile lit up his face.

"If I didn't know better, I'd say that little ol' snake scared you," Cody teased.

"Little my ass." Dane ran his fingers through his hair. "Thanks for coming out. I owe you."

"We'll call it even if you introduce me to the woman waiting out by your truck." Cody gave him a big smile.

He glared at his friend. "I don't know that I'm feeling *that* grateful."

Cody chuckled. "But you will anyway, won't you?"

"Sure," he said. "Why not? First, though, let me tell Mom it's safe to come out." He gestured to the bucket holding the snake. "I'd appreciate it if you'd take that outside."

With a grin, Cody walked out of the house with the bucket. Dane waited until he'd disappeared from view before walking down the hall to his mother's bedroom. Coming to the last door on the right, he knocked once, opened the door—and stared down the barrel of a shotgun.

"Don't shoot!" He jumped back into the hallway, off to one side. "Are you crazy? Mom, it's me."

"Don't be rude, Dane. And come help me down from here."

He waited for the sound of the shotgun snapping open before rounding the corner. His mother was standing in the center of her bed, the broken shotgun balanced in the crook of one arm.

"Really, Mom. I mean, what the hell?" He crossed to the bed and held out a hand.

She placed her free hand in his. "How was I supposed to know it was you? It could have been the snake."

"Snakes don't knock on doors and then turn the knob." He reached up and took the shotgun from her and held it while she climbed off the bed. When she held her hand out to take the gun from him, he hesitated, giving his mom a smile.

"Maybe I should hold on to this? I have someone with me, and I don't want her getting shot accidentally." Too late, he realized it was the wrong thing to say. Sure enough, as soon as the words registered, his mother's eyes lit up with interest.

"You brought a woman home to meet me?"

"No, Mom. I did not bring her home to meet you. She was in the truck with me when you called. I couldn't just leave her on the side of the road."

"Where is she?"

"Outside." With Cody doing his best to charm her, if he didn't miss his guess. He ground his teeth and forced himself to stop.

"Dane Wolfe, where are your manners? You left your date waiting outside for you? That's no way to impress a woman."

"She's not my date." But he was speaking to an empty room. His mother had given her hair a cursory pat as she hurried out of the room, leaving him holding the shotgun. For half a second, he considered hiding out in her room but knew if he didn't go outside and run interference, she'd have Gina looking through old family albums and planning their nuptials.

By the time Dane joined the others outside, Cody was introducing Gina to Dane's mother and damn if that didn't grate.

"I can't believe my son left you waiting outside," his mother said after shaking hands with Gina.

"It seemed like the right thing to do considering there was a big fucking rattlesnake in the kitchen," Dane muttered.

"Dane, watch your language," his mother chastised him. "You all come in and I'll get us something to drink." Cody was still holding the bucket with the snake in it and she gave it a pointed look. "Cody, you leave that thing outside, you hear? I don't want it back in my house."

"Thanks for the offer, Mrs. Wolfe, but I probably should get rid of it."

"Are you going to kill it?" Gina asked. There was no inflection in her tone, so Dane couldn't tell if the idea of killing the snake bothered her or not.

"Naw. We're strictly a catch and release operation, but I don't want to release him too close to town, so I'll take him for a drive first. Of course, the longer he's in this hot bucket, the more pissed he's going to be, so I best get on the road." He set the bucket in the bed of his truck before giving Dane's mother a kiss on the cheek. "Maybe next time." He turned to Gina. "Ma'am, it was real nice meeting you." Then he shook hands with Dane. "Take care, man."

"Thanks again for coming right out," Dane said. "Like I said earlier, I owe you one."

"No problem." Then, with a wave of his hand, Cody climbed into his truck.

As his mother and Gina walked into the house, Dane watched Cody drive away, half wishing his friend had stuck around so he wouldn't be left alone to deal with the "crazy" that was his mother. He loved his mother, but damn! Sometimes, it took a lot of energy to be around her. He gave half a thought to calling Jess, his sister, and ordering her to come home, but of course, that was impossible. She was away at college. Mom was his to deal with alone.

Feeling tired as the rush of adrenaline finally abated, Dane went back into the house where he discovered his mother pouring lemonade into glasses. Gina sat on the stool at the kitchen island.

"There he is," his mother exclaimed as he walked into the room to join them and took the seat next to Gina. "How about some lemonade?"

"Yes, thanks."

His mother placed a freshly poured glass in front of Gina.

"Thank you, Mrs. Wolfe."

"Sure thing, but please, call me Sarah," she said, setting another glass in front of Dane. "So what were the two of you up to this morning that I interrupted?" she asked before taking a sip of her drink.

Dane groaned at his mother's lack of subtlety, but Gina didn't seem offended. "Dane was about to show me some of the haunted places in Las Palomas."

"Have you been to the old courthouse and the hanging tree?"

"Is that the courthouse that used to be where the park is now?" Gina asked.

"No, she means the original courthouse, built back in the 1800s," Dane explained. "They used it until the mid-1950s when they built the one where the park is now. That one got hit by lightning and burned down in 2004. So they built the current one a couple of blocks from the park."

"The original courthouse used to serve as courthouse and jail," Sarah went on. "Back then, cattle rustling was a big problem. Suspected rustlers got a quick trial and an even quicker execution. Before the town got a marshal, the tree outside the old courthouse witnessed the hanging of many men. If you listen closely, you can hear rope rubbing against the tree limbs."

"It sounds... morbidly interesting," Gina said, a smile touching her lips.

"Oh, it is. You definitely need to take her there, Dane."

He sighed. "We were headed there when you called."

"Wonderful," his mother said with a smile that Dane recognized all too well. "Then don't let me stop you. But, since you're headed that way anyway, maybe you can stop by the VFW and drop off some cookies?"

"Yes, how convenient for you," Dane deadpanned. He shook his head, meeting Gina's gaze. "I walked right into that, didn't I?" Gina smiled as he turned back to his mother. "Why is it, again, that you can't take them?"

"Because I've had a very traumatic morning. It's not every day one finds a rattlesnake in one's home."

"Speaking of that," Gina interjected. "How do you think it got in?"

"I don't know." His mother said. "I know I didn't leave the back door open."

He'd been wondering the same thing. "It probably came in through the cat door." He cringed as soon as he realized he'd spoken out loud.

"Winston!" His mother gasped, her hand fluttering to the base of her throat.

"I'm sure he's fine," Dane said. Winston was his mother's Siamese cat who, in Dane's opinion, was too wily to be caught by a snake. At the look in his mother's eyes, though, he knew she wouldn't relax until the cat was found.

No sooner had the thought occurred to him, she set down her glass and headed down the front hallway, calling, "Here kitty, kitty."

Dane didn't think any self-respecting cat would answer to the moniker, but he set his glass down and followed her.

"I'll check the guest room," he told her.

A second later, he heard his mother's shout from her bedroom. "He's back here."

As Dane stepped from the guest bedroom, his mother appeared, holding the large cat in her arms.

"See, Mom? He's fine."

"We won't know for certain until we check him," she argued. "Grab a towel for me, please, and bring it to the kitchen," his mother requested as they passed the guest bathroom. "The lighting is better there."

Grabbing the towel, he carried it to the kitchen and spread it out on the island so his mother could set the cat on top of it.

"Okay, baby. Let's make sure that mean old snake didn't hurt you." His mother spoke calmly as she started running her fingers through the cat's fur.

"Mom, he's fine," Dane repeated, listening to the rumble of the cat's purring.

"We can't know that for sure until we've checked."

"Yeah, Mom. I think we can. If that snake had bitten Winston, he'd be dead."

Her hands stilled over the cat's fur as she stared up at Dane. He could see logic battling with emotion in her eyes. After a moment, logic prevailed, and she sighed.

"I guess you're right." Picking up the cat, she gave him a kiss and set him on the floor.

Good, he thought. Another crisis averted.

His mother grabbed the towel and carried it to the laundry room, pitching it to land on top of the washer. Dane picked up his lemonade from the side counter where it had been moved to make room for the cat. He downed the liquid and set the empty glass in the sink. Gina, he noticed, had also finished her drink. Time to go.

"Ready?" he asked her.

She met his gaze and then looked, uncertainly, at his mother.

"I guess so." She sounded hesitant. "If you're sure you're okay, Sarah?"

His mom looked pleased that Gina had asked and gifted her with a smile.

"Aren't you sweet for thinking of me?" She shot Dane a look that he ignored. "I'm fine, but don't let my son rush you. Would you like another glass of lemonade? Or something to eat?"

"No, Mom," Dane interjected, taking Gina's empty glass and setting it in the sink. "We're leaving."

"You promised to deliver cookies for me," she protested.

"I will. Where are they?" He looked around the clean, uncluttered kitchen and felt his blood pressure rising. "Please tell me you've made the cookies." He knew his mother too well.

"Of course they're made," she said indignantly. "They're just not baked—yet."

"Mom! What the hell?"

She put her hands on her hips. "Well, it's not like I could use the oven with a snake in the kitchen, now, could I?"

"Fine." Dane gave his mother a quick kiss on the cheek. Then he crossed over to Gina, took her by the hand and led her to the front door. "Call me when you're done. I'll come back for them."

"Wait! It'll only take thirty minutes to bake the entire batch. That's not really enough time to take Gina anywhere. Besides, what if another snake drops by?"

Dane turned to glare at his mother. Sometimes, she was the strongest woman he knew. At other times, he prayed he was adopted.

"What are we supposed to do while you're baking?" Dane was almost afraid to ask.

"Well, you could fix the toilet. And Gina, maybe you could help me?"

Dane felt like he was fifteen years old again. "Mom, Gina doesn't want to help you bake cookies, and I don't have time to fix the toilet."

"Actually, I don't mind," Gina said, not helping the situation. "Although, fair warning, I never really learned to cook." Seeing his mother's confused look, Gina explained. "My mother passed away when I was young, so our cookies were always store bought."

"That's a shame, but I could teach you. Would you like to learn?" his mother asked.

Gina's eyes lit at the offer. "Really?"

His mother laughed with obvious delight. "Of course. I always dreamed of teaching my daughter how to cook and while Jess, Dane's sister, learned what she needed to in order not to starve, she was always more drawn to sports and hunting, rather than baking."

Great, Dane thought. He'd seen that look on his mother's face before. He studied Gina with a critical eye, trying to gauge her reaction to his mother's suggestion, searching for the slightest hint that she might be uncomfortable.

"Do you mind if we stay?" Gina gave Dane a shy, almost embarrassed look.

How could he refuse? "No, not at all." Part of him resented the fact that he wasn't getting to spend time alone with her; another part was glad she was getting along with his mother. "If you ladies will excuse me, I'll let you bake while I go see what's wrong with the toilet."

If he'd expected either woman to acknowledge his statement, or the fact that he was walking out of the room, he was sorely disappointed. His mother had already walked over to a drawer and pulled out two aprons, one of which she handed to Gina.

"I don't want you to get those pretty clothes dirty," he heard his mother saying.

Gina took the apron and tied it about her waist. She was entranced by Sarah and excited about helping her.

"The first thing you need is a great recipe," Sarah said, pulling a well-worn card from a recipe box sitting on the kitchen counter. "This one used to be my grandmother's. I think you'll like it. Now, let's see what we need." She ran her fingers down the list of ingredients. "Would you mind getting the flour, brown and white sugars and baking soda from that pantry over there?"

Sarah must have seen Gina's confused look, because she smiled. "There's nothing better than cookies made from scratch."

Gina hadn't realized they'd be making cookies and wondered how Dane was going to react when he saw what they were doing. Then she decided that considering Sarah was his mother, he probably wouldn't be all that surprised.

She went to the pantry and found it well-stocked and neatly organized. "Do you do a lot of baking?" she asked, pulling the requested items off the shelf and carrying them over to the island.

"Not as much as I used to when the kids were younger," Sarah admitted, pressing buttons on the oven. "But yes, I like to bake, and I'm always looking for an excuse to do it."

She took the eggs and butter from the refrigerator just as they both heard a loud clatter from the back of the house, followed by Dane's cursing.

"Everything okay?" Sarah hollered.

"Yeah. Peachy," Dane yelled back, sounding none too happy. "Can you bring me a cup? One I can use to empty the tank."

"Just use the one by the sink." Sarah winked conspiratorially at Gina. "I know I'm biased, but he's grown into a fine man. I couldn't be prouder of him, but between you and me, he's better at chasing criminals and keeping the town safe than he is at fixing stuff around the house. I kept telling him I could call someone, but he wouldn't hear of it. Oh, there's a red mixing bowl in the cabinet there." She pointed. "If you'll get that, I'll get the measuring cups and spoons." She pulled these items from another drawer and carried them to the island. Last, she carried the stand mixer to the island and plugged it in.

"Shall we get started?"

Sarah called out an ingredient, and the amount needed, then watched as Gina measured out the right amount; along the way, offering her helpful tips, like the importance of pouring the ingredients into the measuring cup rather than using the measuring cup to scoop out the ingredients. "When you scoop," she said, "you get more of the ingredient than is called for in the recipe. That can give the cookies the wrong texture or taste."

Gina glanced up when Dane walked into the room fifteen minutes later, drying his hands with a towel. He stopped when he saw what they were doing.

"What the hell, Mom?" He sounded exasperated as he gestured to the ingredients and mixer sitting on the counter. "You said all you had to do was bake the cookies. This looks like you're starting from scratch."

"Dane Rylan Wolfe. Don't you take that tone with me," his mother reprimanded him. She opened the refrigerator door and pulled out two rolls of Nestlé chocolate chip cookie dough and set them down, a little forcefully, on the counter. "These are for the VFW. Gina and I will bake them while we mix up a batch of grandma's Choco-nutty Delights. Gina's momma never had a chance to teach her to bake and because neither you nor Jess ever showed much interest in learning, she and I are going to make a batch together."

"Choco-nutty Delights?" The look on Dane's face at his mother's reprimand wasn't nearly as funny as the look of longing that crept into his eyes at the mention of his grand-mother's cookies.

Gina had to work hard to suppress a giggle—and nearly succeeded.

"Laugh all you want," he told her with a grin. "But wait until you've tasted grandma's cookies and then tell me there isn't anything you wouldn't do for one. Best damn cookies ever!" He pulled out his phone and glanced at the screen. "It's nearly noon. I'm assuming this," he waved his phone around to encompass their baking, "will take some time?" He glanced at Gina. "Is there anywhere you need to be today?"

"Not until later this afternoon," she admitted, thinking that she and Uncle Victor needed to check out the RV park.

"Okay, that was your chance to get out of cooking," he said with a smile. "And you blew it, so I guess I'll head on over to the hardware store. Looks like the whole inside of the tank needs to be replaced. How about I pick up lunch on my way back?"

Both women agreed they liked that plan.

"Alright, then." He stepped closer to the mudroom and tossed his towel onto the washer. "Don't go all June Ward on me and throw that towel into the wash as soon as I leave," he told his mother, crossing the room to stand beside her. "I'm going to need it again and there's no point in getting another one dirty."

"Obviously," she said drolly. Then, changing her tone. "Let me get you some money."

"Keep it," he told her, kissing her cheek. "I got this. Love you."

"Love you, too," his mother replied with a smile, patting his cheek.

To Gina, he asked, "Walk me to the door?"

She nodded and followed him.

"You don't have to stay, you know," he told her as soon as they both stood on the front porch. "I can take you back to the B&B right now. Mom will get over it. Then I can come get you as soon as I finish here and we can resume our tour of haunted Las Palomas."

She smiled, touched by his concern. "No, really, I'm actually having fun. I like your mother."

He hung his head and shook it. "You poor, demented woman. You are in so much trouble. Making cookies is a gateway activity. Before you know it, she'll have you over here crocheting doilies or giving you sewing lessons."

"I think I might like that," Gina admitted.

He smiled. "Really? Okay, then. Just remember, I warned you. Oh, and be sure to keep that apron on. Mom really gets into her baking and by that, I mean, there'll be flour everywhere, including your clothes."

"Thanks for the warning," she said with a grin.

"I guess I'm out of here." He started across the lawn to where his truck was parked but stopped after taking only a couple of steps to turn back to her. "Thanks."

She wasn't sure why he was thanking her and was sure her face reflected her confusion, but he didn't bother to explain. He just climbed into his truck and drove away.

What he didn't understand was what an opportunity like this meant to her. Her mother's death meant she'd never baked cookies with her and while Sarah wasn't her mother, Gina was still enjoying the experience.

With an inward smile, she hurried back inside.

CHAPTER NINE

FINDING WHAT HE NEEDED at the hardware store didn't take nearly as long as checking out with his items. Not that the lines were long, or the store was busy. It was because everyone Dane ran into at the store wanted his opinion of the lady ghost whisperer. He suspected their interest was less about whether he thought she could resolve their *Llorona* problem and more about his personal involvement with her. Apparently, the private moment he'd shared with Gina on the dance floor had been witnessed by—well, just about everyone in town.

He dealt with the inquiries as politely and professionally as he could without engaging in any lengthy conversations. He wanted to get back home as soon as possible to make sure his mother and Gina were still getting along.

The last girlfriend he'd brought home had spent one afternoon with his mother and laid down an ultimatum: he could have one woman in his life—his mother or her. Dane didn't do ultimatums, and the relationship ended badly.

Fortunately, the ex-girlfriend had moved away from Las Palomas shortly after that, but just the memory of it made Dane hurry a little faster across the parking lot. He was back in his truck and heading for The Waterin' Hole to place a to-go order when his phone rang.

"Dane, it's Jan Stuart," the caller said when he answered.

"Hi, Jan. Is everything all right? You sound upset." Jan, who was a year older than Dane, was normally a cheerful, positive person. He'd only known her to have a bad day once in all the time he'd known her and that was back in high school when she'd caught Roger, then boyfriend and now husband, flirting with Sunny Martin. Dane sure hoped Roger had done nothing that stupid again.

"It's Maizy." Their three-year-old daughter. "Someone tried to take her."

"Take? As in—?"

"Kidnap. Abduct!" Clearly upset, her voice was rising in pitch and she was speaking faster. "My baby. Some man tried to take my baby. From right out in front of our house."

"Where's Maizy now?"

"With me. Still at the house. We're inside."

"Are your doors locked?" Dane infused his tone with calm even as he flipped on his siren and took the next corner with squealing tires.

"Yes."

"Where's the man now?"

"I don't know. Rufus chased him off while I ran inside with Maizy and locked the doors."

"Okay. Keep Maizy with you in the house. Don't go any-where near the windows and don't open the doors to anyone but me or Chad. I'm on my way. Is Roger in town?" Her husband drove an eighteen-wheeler and was often gone for days at a time.

"No. I expect him back tomorrow."

Not good, Dane thought. "I'm going to stay on the phone with you, but I need to radio Chad." He reached out to grab the radio handset.

Dane squeezed the talk button on the side. "Wolfe to base. Come in, base."

"Where the hell you been? I thought you were coming in?" Chad asked, by way of answer.

"Change of plans. I need you to get over to Rog and Jan's house. Someone just tried to kidnap Maizy."

"She okay?" Chad asked, suddenly serious.

"For now. I'm on my way. Bring Steve with you."

"Do we have a description of the perp?" Chad asked.

"Not yet." The thought of a kidnapper lurking around the house, waiting for a chance to break inside, had him pressing down a little harder on the gas pedal. "I'm almost there. Signing off."

He turned down the next street and replaced the radio handset. "I'm here," he said to Jan a few minutes later, pulling in front of her house. "I'm going to hang up while I check the property."

"Okay."

Disconnecting the call, he climbed from his truck and un-snapped the safety strap on his gun. With one hand resting on his weapon, ready to pull it at the first sign of trouble, he started around the side of the house. Finding no one, he continued around to the back. Rufus, the Stuart's black lab, was sitting by the back door. Upon seeing Dane, he trotted forward, happily wagging his tail.

"Hey, boy," Dane greeted the animal, giving his head a quick pat while scanning the backyard. If the kidnapper was still on the premises, the dog wouldn't be so relaxed. He and Roger took Rufus duck and hog hunting with them so the animal was a well-trained tracker. He wouldn't stop tracking a scent unless there was nothing left to track—suggesting the perp had driven off in a vehicle he'd parked nearby.

Still, Dane believed in being cautious. "Come on, boy. Let's see what's in the garage." The dog obediently followed along and once they reached the detached garage, he trotted through the side door beside Dane, tail still wagging. Convinced no one was hiding behind the large mesh bags of duck decoys or yard equipment, Dane went back outside.

The sound of sirens coming from the direction of the street told him that his officers had arrived. A minute later, Chad and Steve joined him in the driveway.

"Anything?" Chad asked.

"Looks like he bolted. Maybe a neighbor saw something. Go have a chat with them while I go talk to Jan."

The men nodded and left. Dane pulled out his phone to call Jan and let her know he was coming inside. She met him at the front door, holding Maizy.

"He's gone," Dane assured her once she let him in. Rufus had slipped inside while the door was open and upon seeing him, Maizy began squirming in her mother's arms.

"Ow, Mommy. My wants down."

Dane could see Jan's reluctance to release her daughter, but the child gave her little choice. "Stay in the front room where I can see you—and do *not* go outside," Jan hollered as Maizy ran off to play.

"Are you okay?" Dane asked her, watching her rub the spot above her right eye hard enough to turn the skin red. She looked up at him, her gaze desperate and pleading. He knew that at this moment, she didn't need him there in his capacity as a police officer. She needed the comfort of her husband and, in his absence, the comfort of an old friend was the next best thing. He started toward her and opened his arms. She accepted the invitation and wept silently against his chest.

He simply held her, murmuring words of comfort. As expected, her moment of weakness didn't last long. After only a couple of minutes, she gave his back a couple of pats and stepped away.

"Sorry about that," she said, turning to discreetly wipe her eyes.

He gave her a sympathetic smile when she turned back to him. "Don't be. You have every right to be upset. Can we talk about what happened? It's better if we go over it now, while it's all still fresh in your head."

"Yeah, I'm good. And I want that—" she glanced over to see if Maizy was within hearing distance and then lowered her voice, "bastard caught."

She took another deep breath. "We'd just finished lunch. I was finishing up the laundry while Maizy was playing in here. I don't know whether she got the front door open herself or if that man actually had the nerve to come into my house, but one minute everything was fine and the next, Rufus is having a fit at the front window and I can hear Maizy yelling outside. I ran to the front room to see what was going on." She paused. "The only thing that scared me more than finding Maizy gone and the front door cracked open was seeing that man in the front yard, bent over Maizy, trying to pick her up. He was having a hard time because Maizy was kicking and squirming on the ground." Here she stopped and a small smile touched her lips. "When she doesn't want to be held, it's almost impossible to pick her up. Anyway, Rufus shot past me, teeth bared and growling. I think he would have torn out the man's throat if he'd gotten a hold of him. The man knew it, too, because he turned and ran. I didn't even try to call Rufus off. I just grabbed Maizy and ran inside."

"You did exactly right, Jan. What can you tell me about the man? Did you get a look at his face?"

"No. He was wearing a baseball cap. It was dark navy maybe, but I don't remember if there was any writing on it. He had it pulled low so his face was in shadow." Her voice was filled with disgust. "He was about my height, I would guess."

That would make the perp about five foot six or seven. "What about his build?"

She shook her head. "I don't know. Average? He was wearing an over-sized plaid shirt, navy and gray, I think, and jeans. I don't know. The only thing on my mind was getting to Maizy. I guess I should have paid more attention."

He gave her shoulder a sympathetic pat. "It's okay. Did you notice if he got into a car or truck?"

"No, but like I said, I didn't stand around outside."

"Have you gone anywhere new lately?"

She shook her head, then stopped. "I took Maizy to Town Park the other day to play, but that's not necessarily new. We go there once a week."

"Seen any strange vehicles in the neighborhood?" Again, she shook her head. "That's okay." Dane didn't want to alarm her, but she'd given him very little to go on. He glanced over to where Maizy was quietly playing with a stuffed horse, Rufus laying close by.

There had been no child abductions in Las Palomas as far back as he could remember and he had to wonder why now? Why Maizy? Anyone who looked at their house could see they were not affluent, so kidnapping Maizy for money made little sense. So, if not for money, was it personal? Or had a human trafficking ring come to town?

"Is there any reason to think that this attack might have been aimed at you or Roger?"

"What? I don't understand."

"Do you have any enemies?"

Jan looked like the question was absurd, but she gave it a moment's thought before finally shaking her head. "No. I can't think of anyone who would hate us enough to take our child."

Dane hadn't thought so either, but he'd had to ask.

"Would you mind if I asked Maizy a few questions?"

Jan bit her lip, clearly torn. Dane understood. The last thing he wanted to do was upset the child. "She got closest to the man. There might be something she could tell us that will help."

"All right," Jan agreed, sounding reluctant. Maizy looked up as they walked over to her and held her stuffed horse up to Dane, her eyes alight with interest.

"Play with me?"

He smiled, joining her on the floor and accepting the stuffed toy. "What's your horse's name?"

"Her name is Buck," she said matter-of-factly. "Her's a boy." She held up a second horse. Unlike the first buckskin colored one, this one's coat was a dark chestnut. "This is Princess. Her's a girl."

Dane pretended to trot the stuffed animals around on the floor. "Buck is fast."

Maizy nodded sagely. "Her likes to run fast."

Dane was trying to figure out the best way to broach the subject of the attempted abduction without alarming the child.

"Did you play with your horses this morning?"

She frowned. "Horses like to run outside, not inside."

"Did you take them outside this morning for a run?"

She stopped trotting her horse around and glanced up at her mother.

"It's okay, Maizy. You can tell Uncle Dane the truth. You're not in trouble."

Maizy turned back to Dane and nodded.

"How did you get outside?" he asked her, trying to understand how a three-year-old could reach the doorknob. "Can you show me?"

She jumped to her feet and ran to the entryway, stopping beside an empty plastic milk crate Dane hadn't noticed before. It was already sitting upside down. The toys that had presumably been stored inside lay scattered behind a chair.

As he watched, she pushed the crate closer to the wall beside the front door and, after a few false starts, climbed on top. Once she was standing on the crate, the front doorknob was easily within her reach. She was surprisingly strong for a three-year-old, or at least Dane thought so, because she had no trouble turning the knob. The weight of the door caused it to open a crack. Maizy then laid belly down on the crate so she could slip off. She moved it out of the way and slipped her fingers into the crack. Then she pulled the door open far enough to slip outside.

The little girl turned back to him, a huge smile on her face; clearly proud of her accomplishment.

Dane, who'd stood up to watch the demonstration, glanced over at Jan, whose eyes had gone wide with surprise. As Maizy returned to her horses on the floor, Dane pushed the door closed. Then he went back to sit on the floor with Maizy.

"So you took your horses outside to run earlier," he said. "What happened then?" Dane waited for Maizy to reply, but she remained silent, a troubled frown now replacing the smile she'd worn seconds before. Dane gave her a few seconds before prompting her. "Did someone stop to talk to you?"

She nodded but kept trotting her horse around on the floor.

"Did he say anything?"

"Her lost her's puppy." Maizy looked sad.

"Did he ask you to help him look for it?"

Maizy nodded. "But my not see it."

"And you told him that?"

She nodded. "Her wants me to take her hand but I not want to. Rufus started barking, but her can't get out."

"What happened after that?"

Maizy looked from him to the horse she held. Then she grabbed the horse and held it up in both hands.

"He grabbed you?" Dane asked.

She nodded again. "Mommy says, run fast from strangers." She glanced over at her mother. "I tried to run, Mommy, like you said, but her hold me." She glanced up at her mother, her little lips trembling, making Dane feel like the worst kind of person for putting the child through the ordeal again.

"It's okay, honey," Jan soothed, moving to sit beside her daughter on the floor so she could pull the child into her lap.

"How'd you get away?" Dane asked, curious. "If he was holding you?"

Maizy wrinkled her nose. "I got soc-o-lez."

Dane furrowed his brows, trying to understand. Finally, he looked at Jan for an explanation. Her lips twitched into a smile.

"Maizy, why don't you show Uncle Dane what that means."

Maizy hopped out of her mother's lap and gestured for him to stand. Once he complied, she held her arms up to him so he could pick her up. He worried slightly that being held by another man so soon after her ordeal might traumatize the girl, but she knew him and obviously trusted him.

"Pick her up," Jan instructed.

Dane placed his hands under her arms and lifted her. Suddenly, Maizy started kicking both feet and arching her back, throwing him off balance. Caught so unexpectedly, there was no way he could have held onto her and he barely controlled her fall to the floor. Worried she might have gotten hurt, he was relieved when she looked up at him and giggled.

"When Maizy doesn't want to be held, she goes all soccer-legs on us," Jan explained. "I'm not surprised that—cover your ears, Maizy—" the little girl quickly slapped both hands over her ears, "—asshole couldn't hold on to her."

Maizy, who clearly could still hear every word, took her hands away from her ears without needing to be told and seemed unfazed by her mother's profanity. He suspected the girl had heard much worse from her father.

Dane chuckled.

"You did good, Maizy. Did you see the man's face?"

She nodded, leaving Dane to wonder whether it would be worth bringing in a sketch artist to talk to her. The town didn't have a sketch artist, but maybe the graffiti artist working on the mural could do portraits? He made a mental note to ask him. In the meantime, "Could you tell me what he looked like?"

"Her smell bad." Maizy screwed up her nose and mouth in disgust. "Her need a bath. And her have a spot, right here." She pressed a finger to the side of her nose.

"What kind of spot?" Dane asked.

"Black."

"Does she know her colors?" Dane asked Jan, wondering if Maizy was old enough that he could depend on any of these descriptions.

"Yeah, of course."

Okay, so the perp had a black spot on his face. A mole, maybe?

Just then, a knock sounded on the door seconds before Chad and Steve strode inside.

"We finished checking with the neighbors," Chad announced. "Everyone's fine and Mrs. Walinsky remembers seeing a dark truck this morning parked several houses up from here. She doesn't remember the make, model or license number, or if the plates were in-state or out."

"That's not much to go on," Dane acknowledged. "Let's increase patrols around the schools, the park and through the neighborhoods. Anyone sees something suspicious, call it in." He turned to Jan. "I'll have one of my men stay here with you."

"Thanks, but we're not staying here. I'm going to pack an overnight bag and then Maizy, Rufus and I are going to my parents' house to stay. At least until Roger is home."

"Steve will stay with you while you pack and then follow you over to your parents," Dane said, glancing at Steve long enough to see the man nod that he understood his instructions.

"Thanks, Dane." Despite her earlier assurance, Jan sounded relieved to know she'd have someone watching over them. She gave him one last hug before he stepped outside with Chad and Steve to give her time to pack their bags.

"If Jan and Maizy are the specific targets, then I don't need to tell you that the perp might already be at her parents' house. So call ahead and then be sure you secure the place before you leave, but don't go far. I want you to check in at regular intervals until we're sure this was a random occurrence."

"Will do," Steve said.

Dane turned to Chad. "I need to pick up Gina—I left her at my mom's—and take her back to the B&B. Her uncle was supposedly with Sylvia, but I want to get a look at what they drive."

Chad looked shocked. "You don't honestly believe it could be the uncle, do you?"

Dane sure as hell hoped not, but he couldn't afford to let his personal feelings for Gina make him careless. "No stone unturned, my friend. No stone unturned."

Chad nodded thoughtfully.

"Go back to the office and hand out patrol assignments. Then call around to the nearest towns to see if they've had any abductions or attempted abductions."

CHAPTER TEN

"Oh, wow! At the risk of sounding boastful, this is the best cookie I've ever eaten," Gina said around a full mouth, savoring the chewy flavors of the cookie. "I can't believe I made it. You are a great teacher."

Sarah's eyes gleamed as she chuckled at Gina's reaction. "I don't think I deserve that much credit. You're a natural cook. All I did was provide the recipe. You did the rest."

They had baked the Nestle Toll House cookies while mixing the ingredients for Grandma's cookie recipe. After the Nestle Toll House cookies were baked and bagged for the VFW, it had become obvious that Dane had been delayed, so they'd hopped into Sarah's car and delivered the cookies themselves. Sarah could have dropped Gina at the Bed and Breakfast but Gina had wanted to go back with Sarah and finish the batch of Grandma's cookies that she'd started.

"I want you to know how much I appreciate the baking lesson and, well, just the time you've taken today to spend with me. It's been nice." They'd spent the last two hours baking cookies, drinking coffee and talking; not about anything too personal, but the conversation had never grown awkward. It turned out that the women shared many common interests.

Sarah was an accomplished seamstress, and Gina had always wanted to learn how to sew. Both crocheted. Gina was an avid photographer and shared her knowledge of photo journaling with Sarah, who was looking for a better way of saving family photos and wasn't into the more traditional scrapbooking.

Impulsively, she gave Sarah a hug because there were no words to explain how much this afternoon meant to her. Judging from the way Sarah hugged her back, she thought maybe Sarah understood without needing further explanation.

Sarah's cell phone rang, interrupting the shared moment. She sniffled and gave Gina's back a couple of quick pats before pulling away. Her voice, when she answered the phone, echoed her emotion.

"Hello, dear," she answered the phone. "Is everything all right? What? No, no, we're fine... Yes, Gina is here with me... Don't be ridiculous. We've had a marvelous afternoon... Yes, we ate without you. No, that's all right, dear. We'll see you shortly."

"We were right," she said, disconnecting the call. "Some police business came up he had to deal with, but he's on his way back."

"Thank you so much for letting me stay," Gina said. "I really had a good time."

"Me, too," Sarah admitted with a smile.

Gina stood and headed over to the kitchen sink. "The least I can do is clean up the mess I made."

Sarah seemed about to refuse her help, but then thought better of it.

"Thank you." Gina couldn't mistake the heartfelt gratitude in the woman's tone. "Dane's never brought home a girl before who offered to help me with dishes."

She joined Gina by the sink and after Gina rinsed off the bowls and utensils they'd dirtied, Sarah loaded them into the dishwasher. With both of them working, they finished quickly.

Moments later, Gina heard a truck pulling into the driveway. Then, the front door opened.

"I'm back," Dane shouted from the foyer.

"We're in the kitchen," his mother called out as they turned to greet him.

When he came around the corner, Gina thought his smile looked strained.

"Everything all right?" his mother asked.

"Yeah, everything's fine." His tone suggested otherwise, but it wasn't Gina's place to ask and Sarah didn't press him for more information. Gina wasn't sure whether his silence was to keep his mother from worrying or because she, a relative stranger in town, was standing there.

"I need to go into the office for a while," he said apologetically. "I'll come over tomorrow and finish the toilet. In the meantime, can you just use the one in the master bath?"

"That's fine, honey. Don't worry about it."

"Thanks." He nodded, solemnly. "You have those cookies ready? I'll drop them off when I take Gina back to Ruby Mae's."

"No need. We already took them."

He shook his head. "I'm sorry again for the delay."

"Don't worry about it. Gina and I have spent a lovely afternoon together, just talking."

"About what?" He sounded worried.

"Not about you," Gina assured him with a smile. "But only because we ran out of time. Your mom was just about to break out your high school yearbook."

"Then it sounds like my timing was perfect." He walked into the kitchen to where the cookies were sitting on a cooling rack and ate one. "These are fantastic." He reached for another, but his mother smacked his hand.

"Don't eat them all. I'm sending some back with Gina. After all, she baked them."

"No, really," Gina said. "I couldn't." Actually, the problem was that she wasn't sure she could resist eating them if they were in her room and she sure didn't need the calories.

Sarah, who'd already started putting cookies into a baggie, stopped and there was a look of disappointment in her expression. "You don't want any? Not even to share with your uncle?"

How could she refuse? "Well, they *are* very good," she admitted with a smile. "Okay, maybe a few. And thank you. Uncle Victor has a real sweet tooth and will enjoy them."

A few minutes later, it was time to go. Standing at the front door, holding the bag of cookies, Gina exchanged another hug with Sarah. "Thank you again for everything. I had a good time."

Sarah smiled. "Me, too. I hope you'll visit me again while you're in town."

"I would like that," Gina admitted, wondering if she'd be in town long enough.

After Dane hugged his mother goodbye, he and Gina climbed into the truck. They drove for the first couple of minutes in silence, each lost in his or her thoughts. Then, out of the blue, Dane spoke.

"Thank you."

"For what?"

"For being, I don't know, cool? About spending the afternoon with my mother after I bailed on you. I'm sorry I put you through that."

"Dane, if I hadn't wanted to stay, I could have had your mother drop me off when we ran the cookies to the VFW. I wanted to spend more time with her. She's terrific."

He looked surprised. "Really?" He gave his head a slight shake. "Wow. I didn't see that coming."

That made her curious. "What do you mean?"

"I've brought home about a half-dozen girlfriends in the past ten years and not a single one enjoyed spending that much time with my mom."

Gina wasn't sure how to respond to that. Should she point out the obvious? That she wasn't his girlfriend?

She went a different route.

"Maybe it's because I miss having my mom around." She shrugged dismissively, hoping he wouldn't hear in her tone just how much the time spent with his mother had meant to her.

"No, I get it," he said quietly. "When my father died, he left us with a large amount of debt." He smiled. "Hank Wells, who's the president of the local bank, let me pay it off over time by working odd jobs for him. I ended up spending a lot of time over at Hank and Mindy's place, helping them renovate their home. They became like a second family to me. And Hank became like a surrogate father. When other boys might have turned to drugs or crime, or even run away from home, Hank was there for me."

"Sometimes the best father you have isn't your biological one," Gina admitted. "I never knew who my father was. Just a one-night stand my mother had, I guess, but I never felt like I was missing a father because I've always had Uncle Victor. My mother's death hit us both hard, but at least we had each other."

The atmosphere between them grew heavy with shared emotions and for a full minute, neither spoke.

"Someone tried to abduct the daughter of a friend of mine," Dane finally said, breaking the silence.

Gina gasped. "Oh, my God. Is she okay?"

"She's fine, but it scared her and her mother."

"I'm so sorry," Gina said, hearing in his tone how upset the whole thing had made him.

"Yeah. The guy came right up into her front yard and if Maizy hadn't started kicking so he couldn't hold on to her, it might have been a lot worse."

"Did you catch the guy?"

Larry and Mo came to Gina's mind.

"No, and we weren't able to get much of a description, either," he said, pulling into Ruby Mae's driveway. "A man wearing a dark baseball cap, possibly with a mole on his face. The neighbor reported seeing a truck parked up the street, but fifty-percent of the motor vehicles in town are trucks, so that's not much help."

"Does Maizy have blonde hair?"

Dane gave her a funny look. "That's kind of an odd question. No, she's brunette, why?"

She sighed. "When I was in the gift shop earlier, I overhead a couple of men talking about taking a blonde girl. There was a blonde girl in the store with her mother at the time. The conversation just struck me as odd, that's all."

"Tell me what you heard."

So she did, word-for-word. Then she described the men. "I only overhead a little bit," she conceded.

"Taken out of context, it sounds bad," he admitted. "I'll keep an eye out for them. Thanks."

"I hope you catch whoever it is," she finally said. It sounded lame, even to her, but she didn't know what else to say. She reached for her door handle. "Thank you for this afternoon. I had a good time."

"I'd still like to take you to see the sights, if you're interested."

She smiled, her heart speeding up with anticipation. "I'd like that."

"Maybe tomorrow?"

"Sure. Provided we're still here."

"You will be," he assured her. "Llorona usually only shows up during a full moon, which is in a day or two. Bill, who owns the RV park, will call me or Sylvia if Llorona shows up before then. In the meantime, we might as well check out the other sights in town."

"Sounds good," she said. "Why don't I give you my cell phone number and you can call me once you have a better idea of what your day's going to look like?"

He seemed relieved at the suggestion. "That works."

It didn't take them long to exchange numbers and then, with no more excuses to keep her there, Gina opened her door.

"Is your uncle here?" Dane asked just as she stepped out of the truck. She stood in the doorway and glanced at the four vehicles parked in the driveway a short distance in front of them.

"Doesn't look like it. Why?"

"No reason."

He held her gaze for a full second, nothing of his thoughts showing in his expression. She might almost have dismissed the comment as completely random, but then it occurred to her why he'd asked. Anger shot through her.

"Are you seriously accusing my uncle of being your child abductor?" He held up his hand to interrupt her, but she ignored him. "Not only is that ludicrous, but it's highly insulting. For your information, my uncle and I drove down in my car; a sandstone-colored GMC Acadia. We are *not* driving a truck." She got out of his truck and might have slammed the door shut a little harder than necessary.

With righteous indignation, she walked around the front of his truck to the edge of the walkway leading to the front porch of the Bed and Breakfast. There she stopped and glared at him through his now open window.

"Gina—"

"Just in case I might be lying, maybe you should come inside and ask Ruby Mae? She took our make, model and license plate number when we checked in."

He remained silent and the look on his face reminded her of Uncle Victor's expression the day he'd taken his eighteen-year-old beagle, blind and suffering with severe arthritis and kidney failure, to the vet for the last time. It was the expression one wore when doing the right thing was the last thing one wanted to do.

She looked away, giving herself a second to calm down, only half conscious of the cloudless blue sky or the distant sound of children playing down the street.

"Gina, I'm sorry," Dane finally said. "For what it's worth, I don't think your uncle is our guy, but right now, I have a whole town filled with out-of-towners. Since I don't have any good leads to follow, I have to do this by process of elimination. The more people I can eliminate, the better."

Hearing his apology, she turned her gaze back to him. "I get that you have a job to do and you don't know us. If it will make things easier, Uncle Victor and I will leave tomorrow. That will be two less out-of-towners you have to deal with."

Dane was shaking his head before she'd finished speaking. "No, please don't leave town." For a moment, she thought he was telling her that because he wanted to spend more time with her. His next words shattered that illusion. "You haven't talked to *Llorona* yet."

"Right." What had she been thinking? The closeness she'd felt toward him and the moment they'd shared on the dance floor. It all vanished in the face of a harsh reality. He didn't know her. Hell, they weren't even friends.

Shaking her head at her own naiveté, she turned and started up the front walkway. She half hoped he'd stop her and tell her... what?

She realized there was nothing he could say and wasn't surprised when she heard the truck shift gears before backing out of the driveway. It took everything in her not to look back as he drove off.

Once inside the Bed and Breakfast, she hurried up the stairs, grateful when she reached the sanctuary of her room without running into anyone. She tried calling Uncle Victor, but he didn't answer. It was too early to go downstairs to dinner, and she didn't really feel like talking to anyone at the moment, so instead, she grabbed her Kindle and settled into the bedside chair to read.

It was almost dinnertime when Uncle Victor finally texted her to tell her he was staying with Sylvia. She texted him back, reminding him they had a job to do but his response was to tell her the police had asked everyone to stay inside that evening. Then, echoing Dane earlier, he told her that if Llorona appeared at the RV park later that night, the RV park owner would call Sylvia, at which point, he and Sylvia would come get her.

Unable to do anything else, Gina joined Ruby Mae and a few of her other guests for dinner. She remained downstairs, making polite conversation long enough to not appear rude and then about 8:00 p.m., claimed she was tired and went back to her room.

Settling onto her bed, she used the Wi-Fi access code Ruby Mae had given her earlier to surf the Internet for everything she could find on *Llorona*. When it came to ghost whispering, it never hurt to learn as much about the ghost as possible.

Hours later, no longer able to keep her eyes open, she fell asleep and dreamed of a weeping woman in white.

Chapter Eleven

The next morning, after showering and dressing, Gina called Uncle Victor.

"What?" His groggy voice answered after four rings.

"Good morning to you, too. Were you still asleep?"

"I was," he grumbled. "Not anymore, thanks to you. What time is it anyway?"

Gina pulled the phone away from her ear briefly to glance at the time. "Seven-thirty."

"Crap," he cursed in response. "I need more than two hours of sleep."

"You only went to bed two hours ago? What have you been doing all night? Wait, don't answer that." A mental image of her uncle and Sylvia together in bed formed before she could shut it down. "We really need to talk. When are you coming back?"

"Noon."

"No. How about I meet you at the café in an hour?"

"What's so urgent that it can't wait?"

"You mean other than the fact that I'm supposed to talk to a rogue ghost and the town's acting police chief practically accused you of being a child predator? You're right. There's nothing important going on."

A heavy sigh came through the line. "Fine. I'll meet you at Kathy's Café in an hour. But I'm not discussing anything serious without coffee."

"But—"

She realized he had already hung up on her and knew that if she called him back, he wouldn't answer.

Damn it. Nothing about this trip was going as expected.

"Here you go, Hon," Kathy said, setting a mug of coffee on the table. "You look like you could use a cup."

Gina had tried to hurry but it had still taken almost an hour to dress and walk to the café. She ruefully touched a hand to her hair. "That bad, huh?" Then, remembering her manners, added, "Thanks for the coffee."

"You look better than most of the tired faces I see this time of morning," Kathy said with a smile, pulling out packets of sweetener and creamer pods from her apron pocket and setting them on the table next to the coffee.

Gina picked up a creamer pod, tore off the foil seal and dumped the contents into her coffee. "Do you get a lot of late-night partiers?" she asked, trying to make conversation.

Kathy chuckled. "Nope, late night ghost hunters."

Gina rolled her eyes at herself. Of course, that made sense. "Any good sightings?"

Kathy shook her head. "Not yet, but I expect there will be some soon. It's almost a full moon. The older ghosts like to come out then." Gina took a sip of coffee and willed the caffeine to give her a jolt of energy.

"Are you by yourself this morning?" Kathy asked.

Gina hoped not. "Uncle Victor should be here shortly."

"I'll come back and check on you in a few minutes, then."

"Thanks," Gina replied gratefully.

As Kathy walked away, Gina turned to gaze out the window at the bustling street. Despite the early hour, there were already many people going about their daily lives. She found comfort in watching them, a sense of normalcy amidst the chaos of her current situation.

Kathy gracefully glided over fifteen minutes later, her footsteps making barely a sound as she refilled Gina's coffee. The steam from the cup rose in a warm, comforting swirl, filling the air with its rich aroma.

"No sign of him yet?" she asked, her voice laced with concern.

Gina let out an exasperated sigh. "No, not yet." She couldn't hide her irritation this time. "Could I have a few more minutes?"

"Of course, dear. Take your time," Kathy replied with a gentle smile before walking off.

Gina returned to gazing out the window, trying not to think too hard, when a familiar tan truck caught her attention. Her heart skipped a beat as she watched it park across the street and Dane stepped out. A wave of emotion washed over her at the sight of him and she couldn't tear her gaze away even if she tried.

As soon as he entered the café, Gina felt his presence like a magnet pulling her towards him. She watched as he scanned the room and her heart raced when their gazes met. She debated on how to react—should she smile, frown, or turn away? Before she could decide, he was walking towards her.

"Do you mind if I join you?" he asked, his voice low and hesitant.

Gina momentarily felt taken aback, but nodded and gestured to the seat across from her. "Please."

Kathy had also noticed Dane's arrival and brought over an empty mug and filled it with steaming coffee. Its rich scent wafted towards them as she left the table.

"I ran by Ruby Mae's this morning, looking for you."

"You did?" she asked. "Why?"

"I thought if I showed up in person, you wouldn't be able to hang up on me."

Gina's heart softened towards him. If he had purposefully come looking for her to apologize, the least she could do was tamp down on her irritation and be gracious.

"About yesterday—"

"I understand you were just doing your job," she said, trying to gracious. "No need to apologize."

"I wasn't going to," he replied confidently.

Gina immediately felt annoyed, but before she could say anything, he spoke again.

"Gina, I wouldn't be doing my job if I ruled out your uncle as a suspect solely because I like his niece." A gleam of emotion—dark and hungry—lit his eyes.

"Oh," was all she could manage, feeling both flattered and uneasy at the same time. "You like me?" Her words slipped out before she could stop them.

His gaze locked with hers, his voice sincere as he admitted, "I do. And I hope you'll give me a second chance by letting me take you around town this afternoon to show you some of those haunted sights I intended to show you yesterday."

Gina couldn't deny that his offer intrigued her. It made her feel like a schoolgirl being asked out on a first date. Dane's next words, however, reminded her it wasn't a date.

"Your uncle is welcome to join us, of course."

"Thanks. I'll ask him when he finally gets here." She glanced at her phone and pressed the button to activate the screen. "He's late, as usual."

"Damn, I should have offered him a ride while I was at Ruby Mae's. It didn't occur to me he wasn't with you." Dane's regretful tone made Gina soften towards him once again.

She dismissed the comment with a graceful wave of her hand. "No need to feel bad. He's not at Ruby Mae's." Dane's eyebrows raised in question. "I'm embarrassed to say that he spent the night with Sylvia."

Dane let out a low whistle. "Wow. They didn't waste any time, did they?"

Gina shook her head incredulously. "You're not shocked by this?"

A deep chuckle rumbled through Dane's chest as he shook his head, amusement dancing in his eyes. "Sylvia may look like a Sunday school teacher, but she's far from it. That woman sees more action than Rambo."

Gina couldn't help but shake her head in disbelief. "Uncle Victor's the same way. I would have thought once you hit fifty, your social life slows down. His seems to have picked up instead."

A comfortable silence fell between them as they each sipped their coffee. Suddenly, Gina heard a loud rumbling noise break through the quiet chatter around them.

"Sorry," Dane apologized with a sheepish grin, covering his stomach with his hand in embarrassment. "I left this morning before eating."

Gina gave a soft laugh in response, touched by his gesture. "I appreciate you sacrificing breakfast in order to come talk to me." She glanced around expectantly, hoping to see Uncle Victor arrive soon, but there was still no sign of him. "I was going to wait for Uncle Victor, but it doesn't seem like he's coming anytime soon, and I'm absolutely starving. If you haven't already made other plans, would you like to join me?" Even as she asked, she couldn't help questioning the wisdom of it all. The more time she spent with Dane, the more she liked him, and it was going to make leaving town in a day or two that much harder.

Dane's face lit up with a warm smile, his eyes crinkling at the corners as he spoke. "Thanks, I'd like that." He scanned the bustling restaurant and caught Kathy's eye, signaling for her attention. A moment later, she appeared at their table with menus in hand, though neither of them really needed them. After perusing the options, Dane confidently ordered the three-egg southwest omelet with a side of fluffy butter-milk pancakes while Gina opted for scrambled egg whites and a platter of fresh fruit.

"If I ate what you ate, I'd be starving an hour later," Dane commented after Kathy left to put in their order.

Gina chuckled and sipped her coffee. "And if I ate what you ate, I'd be as big as a house. Either you have a very high metabolism or you work out regularly."

He gave a knowing smile that made her cringe inwardly. Oh, God. She was acting like a giddy schoolgirl all over again. *Oooh, what big muscles you have. You must work out.*

Could she be any more obvious?

Maybe she was trying too hard to be casual. Or maybe she was being too sensitive. Or...

She took another sip of her coffee, hoping to quiet the internal tirade.

"I went back to Mom's last night to fix her toilet," Dane said after a few minutes had passed. "She couldn't stop talking about you." He imitated his mother's voice, complete with exaggerated hand gestures. "Did you know Gina is practically a professional photographer? She creates beautiful books with her photos instead of just scrapbooking them like us old-timers do. Isn't that fascinating? She showed me one of her books online. And don't even get me started on her cooking skills. She has natural talent. Whoever marries that girl will have to watch his weight." He glanced across the table at Gina and grinned. "She really likes you."

Gina smiled back, feeling a warm glow in her chest. "I like her, too."

"She won't forget you offered to show her how to do that picture book," Dane warned her. "When she sets her mind to something, she can be like a dog with a bone."

"It's not a problem. I'm actually looking forward to showing her," Gina replied, her voice filled with genuine eagerness.

Just then, Kathy arrived with their orders, and they ate in comfortable silence for a few minutes. Gina realized she was hungrier than she thought and had to resist the urge to devour her food. She looked up to find Dane studying her.

"What? Do I have a piece of pineapple stuck in my teeth or something?" She ran her tongue over her teeth to check.

"No, it's not that."

"Then what?"

"You genuinely sound sincere about teaching my mother how to save her photos before you leave."

Confusion crept into Gina's expression. "It's just digital scrapbooking and, of course, I mean it. Why wouldn't I?"

He shrugged. "I didn't expect you would stay in town that long."

"Even if I don't get around to it before I leave, there's this amazing thing called the Internet—you might even have it here in Las Palomas. We can still connect through phone or video chat after I leave." She flashed him a teasing smile.

"I guess I just assumed once you finished your assignment with *Llorona*, you'd move on to your next big project and be too busy to bother with—"

His words trailed off, leaving an unspoken question lingering between them.

Gina delicately placed her fork on her plate, her stare intensifying as she locked eyes with him. "What? That I'd bail on your mom?" She shook her head in disbelief. "People are not always who they appear to be." Her gaze softened, and she took a deep breath before opening up to him in a way she rarely did. "I don't have many genuine friends, so I value and treasure each one."

Dane reached across the table and took her hands in his, his touch warm and comforting. "Gina, I apologize. I didn't mean anything by it. I honestly thought that with your job, you must meet so many people that—"

"That I'd forget about your mom as soon as I left town?"

"Something like that," he admitted sheepishly. "But if I'm being completely honest, my thoughts were more selfish. I wasn't just thinking about my mom."

It took a moment for his words to sink in. When they did, Gina was taken aback.

"I could never forget you," she blurted out before realizing what she had said. A flush crept up her neck and spread across her cheeks, but she couldn't look away from Dane's intense gaze. She wanted to see how he would react to her confession.

"I'm glad to hear that," he responded in a low drawl that sent shivers down her spine. "Because I feel the same way." He gave her hands a gentle squeeze.

His words warmed her from within, like a ray of sunshine after a long winter. Feeling suddenly self-conscious under his intense scrutiny, she quickly scanned the room for something—anything—else to talk about. Her gaze landed on a booth across the room where two men were eating breakfast. They looked familiar, and it took her a minute to recognize them.

Larry and Mo!

"Gina, are you okay?" Dane's voice broke through her thoughts. "You look troubled. Was it something I said?"

"What?" She turned to him in confusion. "No. Nothing you said. It's them. Larry and Mo." When he gave her a confused look, she added, "The two men from the gift shop. They're sitting in that booth over there" She cocked her head in the direction of the booth.

Without another word, Dane got up from the table and made his way over to the counter, where Kathy was ringing up a bill for a guest. While waiting for her to finish, he discreetly glanced around the room, letting his gaze linger on the two men in the booth. Gina watched him closely, noticing how he exchanged words with Kathy before her eyes flickered towards the suspects and then back to Dane. When they finished their conversation, Dane rejoined Gina at their table.

Gina watched him expectantly as he sat back down. "Well?" she finally asked, her voice teetering between anticipation and dread.

"I don't know," he responded, voice low. "It's not like they're wearing signs that say 'child predator.'"

"But we can't just do nothing," she protested.

"Gina, I don't have cause to arrest them," he replied, running a hand through his blond hair in obvious frustration.

She sighed heavily; the sound filling the small space between them. It seemed there was no simple solution to this problem.

"What I will do, though," he continued, breaking the silence, "is assign one of my guys to follow them."

Relief washed over Gina. "Good." The men might not be guilty, but it made sense for someone to keep an eye on them.

"Now, as much as I hate to say this," he said apologetically, "I've got to head into the office for a bit. Can I drop you someplace?"

"Um... no, thanks," she said hesitantly, glancing around the diner. Uncle Victor was nowhere in sight. "I'd better wait for my uncle. If he doesn't show up in the next thirty minutes, I'll leave."

Dane nodded understandingly and slid out of the booth. "Okay, then," he said, standing. "I already paid our tab, but Kathy won't kick you out and coffee refills are free."

"Thank you so much," Gina replied gratefully. "You didn't have to do that."

He smiled kindly at her. "I wanted to."

Gina's heart swelled with a mixture of emotions: gratitude, regret, and something else she couldn't quite name.

"Well, thank you—again," she said, her voice barely above a whisper. "Maybe you'll let me get the next one?"

"I don't think so," he responded gently, pulling his phone from his pocket and checking the screen.

"Oh." The word came out as more of a breathy sigh than an actual response. A lump formed in Gina's throat as she realized perhaps, she had misread their recent interactions. "I understand," she said, before turning away to hide her disappointment.

"Wait? What?" He had turned back towards her, confusion etched on his face. Then realization dawned and his eyes widened. "No, no! That came out wrong. What I mean is, next time we go out—and I hope there will be a next time—it will also be my treat. I'm old-fashioned like that."

Feeling relieved, a teasing smile spread across her face as she replied, "Well, if you insist…"

His smile mirrored hers. "I do. Now, with that settled, I really must go." He glanced at his watch before continuing. "I'll call you after lunch to see what time works for you to go look at those other sites."

Gina nodded, her excitement building at the thought of spending more time with him. "That sounds good."

"Great." With one last smile, he left the café, Gina's gaze following him hungrily. Damn, the man looked good coming or going. She couldn't wait for their next encounter.

Chapter Twelve

Uncle Victor walked into the café ten minutes after Dane left, looking contrite.

"I'm sorry," he said before she could say a word. "I had every intention of returning to the B&B last night. After the séance ended, I helped Sylvia clean up, and she invited me to stay for a drink and, well, one thing led to another..."

Gina could practically hear the words *bada-bing, bada-boom* hanging in the air between them. "Must have been good," she said, dryly, "considering you couldn't even get here on time for breakfast."

He had the decency to look embarrassed. "She's a very, um, enthusiastic, lover."

Fortunately, before he could continue, Kathy appeared at their table with a mug of coffee.

"Thank you, my dear," Uncle Victor greeted her, accepting the mug. He took a swallow and sighed. "You make the *best* coffee."

Kathy chuckled at the compliment. "Would you like to see a menu?"

He shook his head. "No, I know what I want, but ladies first. Gina, what would you like for breakfast?"

"I've already eaten, thanks. I got tired of waiting."

He seemed surprised, but recovered quickly. "Ah, yes, of course. In that case, Kathy my dear, would you be so kind as to bring me two eggs, over hard, bacon, hash-browns and wheat toast?"

"I'll be back shortly with your food," she told him before walking off to deliver his order to the kitchen.

"I'm sorry you had to eat alone," he apologized.

"I didn't." She was mad at him and didn't feel like elaborating, but he was staring at her, eyebrows raised expectantly. "Dane joined me."

"Ahhh. Wasn't that nice of him?" There was a twinkle in his eyes.

She knew he was baiting her, but she refused to get sucked into a conversation about her and Dane. Even though her uncle had apologized, twice, the apologies had been platitudes, offered hoping to avoid a fight. She wasn't about to let him off that easily. Despite what he might think, this discussion wasn't over.

So, while he sipped his coffee, she waited patiently in silence, knowing he couldn't ignore her forever. After his fourth swallow, he sighed and set the mug back on the table, where he cradled it between his hands. Reluctantly, she knew, he met her gaze.

"You're upset. I understand."

"No, I don't think you do." She glanced around to see who might overhear them and lowered her voice. "Given the circumstances under which we left Houston, I was worried sick about you, imagining all sorts of horrible things. And all the while, you're out bumping uglies with Sylvia Winters!" Giving vent to her anger only made her angrier. "And did you know that someone tried to kidnap a little girl yesterday and Dane wonders if that someone is you!"

"That's ridiculous," he said.

"Of course it is, but we don't need him or his men following you around town. Not when we still need to go to the river and—"

She snapped her mouth shut as Kathy arrived with her uncle's breakfast.

"This looks wonderful," he told her, picking up his fork. He took a bite of the eggs and closed his eyes. "Every bit as good as it looks."

Kathy pulled his bill from her apron and laid it on the table. "Let me know if you want anything else."

Gina forced a smile onto her face and thanked Kathy, because she was not the source of her irritation. After Kathy left, Gina decided she needed to do something about the six cups of coffee coursing through her system.

"I need to pay a quick visit to the ladies' room," she told Uncle Victor. "Then you and I are going to talk."

His mouth was full, so he nodded and waved her away.

Returning several minutes later, she found Uncle Victor was gone and a teenage boy wearing an apron was bussing their table.

WTF? she thought, looking around the café.

"He left," Kathy called out from behind the counter.

Gina walked over to her. "Seriously? I didn't think I was in there that long."

"Sorry, Hon. He got up as soon as you disappeared into the ladies' room, paid his tab and walked out. It wasn't that long ago. If you hurry, you might still catch him."

Gina thanked her and rushed outside. She scanned the streets in both directions, hoping to see him sauntering along but knowing she wouldn't. He'd had the car. Why he'd ditched her, she didn't know, but after last night's stunt, it was adding insult to injury and if he thought giving her more time would help her calm down, he had another think coming.

At that moment, her cell phone vibrated. Pulling it from her pocket, she glanced at the screen to see a text from Uncle Victor.

> *Need a nap. Talk later.*

She sighed, frustrated. There would be no talking him out of his nap. So with Dane working and Uncle Victor napping, she was on her own.

With nothing pressing to do, Gina pondered how to spend her free time. She considered heading to the RV park to plan her next conversation with the ghost of the wailing woman, but it was too far to walk and would be pointless without Uncle Victor to help. So she resigned herself to waiting until after his nap.

The reminder of how he had left her alone sparked new irritation at her uncle, so she decided a stroll around the park might help improve her mood. The temperature outside was warm, but not uncomfortably so. As she crossed the street, she paused to consider which direction to take. Turning left would take her past the colorful wall mural where she had met the surly graffiti artist. Deciding she didn't want a repeat encounter with the man, she headed in the opposite direction.

At the far end of the park, the large bulletin board caught her attention. Gazing out the café window earlier, she had noticed multiple people stopping to read it and was now curious to see what it contained.

The first thing that caught her eye when she reached it was a detailed map of the town mounted behind a sheet of Plexiglas. A bright red "You Are Here" sticker marked the corner of the park where she currently stood. Below the map, arranged by category, was a list of the stores surrounding the park and their map coordinates.

Attached to the edge of the map, a set of park rules were displayed in bold lettering: all trash must be disposed of in the marked bins, minors under the age of fifteen must be accompanied by an adult, pets must be kept on leashes, and discharging fireworks was strictly prohibited due to a current fire ban.

The other side of the board was made of cork, its surface covered with a variety of ads, some faded and weathered with time, while others crisp and new. Items for sale, requests for help with household or yard work, and notices for upcoming town events were just some of the postings that adorned the board.

Then she caught movement out of the corner of her eye. Turning, she saw two men exiting the café.

Larry and Mo.

Gina looked around discreetly, hoping to spot the police officer Dane had tasked with monitoring the pair. But either he or she was very skilled at staying hidden, or they hadn't arrived yet.

It didn't matter to Gina, though; she had nothing better to do so she would keep an eye on them. She wondered how long it would take for her to uncover their true intentions.

⸺◆O◆⸺

Sitting at his desk at the police station, Dane glanced at his watch. Eleven o'clock.

He'd call Gina soon. If she hadn't eaten lunch yet, he'd see if she was interested in grabbing a bite with him. He tried not to think about how much he was looking forward to seeing her again; like they'd been apart for days, instead of hours.

It wasn't just his physical attraction to her, though. He felt drawn to her in other ways. She was witty yet naïve; strong, yet vulnerable. He found himself intrigued, entranced, and oddly protective of her.

The incident at the river flashed through his head. He hadn't forgotten about it, or the way Gina had told them *Llorona* was there when she plainly wasn't. It was more like he'd chosen to place the memory on a shelf, for now. When the time was right, he'd take it down and examine it again.

His fear, of course, was that she was a fraud; a con artist. Out to take the town for its money. If that were the case, though, he'd be a hypocrite to condemn her when the town was guilty of its own deceptions. And if Gina Castillo was a legitimate ghost whisperer, then it was important that he keep her from discovering the truth about the town. He didn't want to think about how mad she'd be at him if she discovered the truth because, God help him, he liked her. And that was a problem.

The lines of right and wrong were blurry enough without complicating them with emotions.

The sound of his phone ringing broke into his thoughts. He looked down to see Steve's name on the caller ID.

"Dane here," he answered.

"Just checking in," Steve said. "I relieved Chad around eight this morning at Jan's folk's place. He went home to sleep. Roger got here about forty-five minutes ago."

"How are they doing?"

"Still shaken, like you'd expect, but they're holding it together. Roger says he's got some time off coming, so he's thinking of taking Jan and Maizy to San Antonio for a couple of days, at least until things calm down."

"That's probably not a bad idea," Dane admitted. "I'd like to make sure you or Chad are with them until they're gone—maybe even follow them until they are safely out of town."

"You got it, Boss."

The men talked for another minute before hanging up. Dane felt better that Roger and his family would be safe, but he didn't think for one minute the child predator had left town after one failed attempt. His thoughts turned to the two men Gina had pointed out at the café. What were the chances they were the perps? With a sigh, he looked at the day's roster to see who was working. Then he picked up his phone to make the arrangements.

It was noon and Gina stood outside a store, pretending to window shop. Glancing around, she realized Larry and Mo had wandered off and she didn't know where they'd gone. It was a good thing she wasn't a cop because she sucked at surveillance. Maybe if the men had been a little more interesting, she would have been more attentive. If those men were criminals, they were either brilliant or the most boring criminals in the world.

She'd followed them from one store to the next while they'd shopped, catching bits and pieces of conversation, but nothing that sounded like plans to kidnap a child. For Gina, who had to be one of the few women in the world who actually hated to shop, it was a grueling morning and she was more than ready for it to end.

So she was immensely relieved when her phone rang.

"Hi," Dane greeted her. "I'm done with work. Can I interest you in lunch, followed by a trip to the old courthouse?"

"I'd like that," she replied.

"Great! Are you still in front of The Magic Shop?"

"I am," she replied, wondering how he'd known.

"See you in five." He hung up and Gina looked around. Maybe he had someone watching Larry and Mo after all.

CHAPTER THIRTEEN

LUNCH CONSISTED OF BURGERS and fries at one of the local bars. Gina thoroughly enjoyed every bite. They kept the conversation light, with Dane sharing more of the town's history and a few anecdotal stories of tourists whose ghost hunting enthusiasm had resulted in unforeseen, albeit comical, consequences. Gina particularly enjoyed the story of the man who hoped to get a selfie with *El Muerto*, the headless horseman who rode across the pastures of the Double R Ranch. Unfortunately, the man succeeded only in garnering the attention of the ranch's prize bull, unoriginally but aptly named *El Diablo*. In a chase worthy of Pamplona's *Running of the Bulls*, *El Diablo* pursued the ghost hunter for three hundred yards before the man could scramble through the barbed wire fence to the safety of the other side.

"He threatened to file charges against Roy Richardson for having dangerous animals on his ranch," Dane told her. "Can you believe it? Sam Hunter, our police chief, may have suggested to him that because he had worn a red shirt, that he had intentionally provoked the animal and that Roy would be within his rights to file a countersuit." He shrugged. "I don't know if that's right, but she can be pretty convincing when she needs to be. Anyway, the guest left and I'm pretty sure he's not been back to town since."

Lunch ended shortly thereafter but fortunately, Gina thought, not their time together. Soon they were in Dane's truck driving toward the old courthouse, which was located a couple of blocks south of Town Park.

When it came into view, Gina thought it looked like a hundred other small-town courthouses, built in an era when appearance, not energy efficiency, governed architectural design—which meant she loved it. It was a mammoth square stone structure standing two stories tall. Wide brick steps led up to a wide portico where four giant two-story high columns stood sentry. Gina saw that the windows on the lower level were boarded, and the wooden double-front doors were chained and locked.

"Wow. This is really something," she admired as Dane pulled into one of the parking spots along the curb. "How long has the building stood empty?"

"Since the shooting in 1954." He put the truck in park but didn't turn off the engine.

"Shooting?"

"Yeah. It happened in March of that year. Back then, the police department and jail cells were in the back of the courthouse. Donny Rangel was being held prisoner for stealing the Stanford Diamond. He was scheduled for transport to Houston and a couple of Texas Rangers were on their way to pick him up. No one knows for sure how it happened, but that morning, before the Rangers arrived, Rangel had an altercation with one of his guards in the process of being moved to a new holding cell. Rangel got the guard's gun and everything went south after that. In his attempt to escape, Rangel shot five people before an officer put him down—permanently."

"That's horrible." Gina exclaimed, trying to imagine what it must have been like.

"Yeah, things like that didn't happen much back in those days, so it really affected the town. Not that it would be any less horrible if it happened today," he quickly amended. "Anyway, it left the town shaken, and no one wanted to go back into the building to work. Bad juju and all that. So they built a new courthouse where the park is now and a new police station across the street. This building remained empty, and the town was trying to decide whether to tear it down when rumors started about it being haunted. People saw lights on inside at night, even though the electricity was off, and there were reports of strange noises. We still get reports of lights and noises. Once, Nita swears she had a *Sixth Sense* moment when she was inside the building. The air got suddenly cold, and she caught a flash of pink disappearing through a doorway."

"What was it?" Gina asked, caught up in the story.

"Yolanda Glossup. She was the department's secretary and one casualty in the gunfight that day. The locals call her The Pink Lady because her ghost is still wearing the pink sweater and cardigan set she had on the day she died. Now and then, she shows herself."

"I can understand how this would be a popular stop on the ghost tour."

"Ghost tour?" He sounded confused.

"Yeah, you have one, right? Like the 'Haunted New Orleans' tours," she made air quotes with her fingers, "where they walk or bus you through town, stopping at places like Madame Delphine LaLaurie's haunted mansion."

"We don't, but it's a great idea. I'll bring it up at the next town council meeting." He smiled as he put the truck in gear and began backing up.

"We're not going inside?" She'd hoped that "showing her the courthouse" had meant more than viewing it from the street.

"Patience," he said with a smile. "We'll go inside in a minute, but first, I want you to experience the Hanging Tree around back."

Gina's hand rose to the base of her throat. "Thanks, but I'll pass."

He looked momentarily confused, then chuckled. "Funny."

Dane drove along the driveway that led to an empty lot behind the courthouse, the tires of the truck crunching against the dirt and gravel surface.

"Back when the town was first established, that," he pointed to a massive tree standing at the far end, "was the town's hanging tree."

The tree loomed larger and larger as Dane drove towards it. Its trunk was thick and gnarled, with deep grooves and knots stretching along its surface. Gina couldn't help but shiver as they got closer.

"Oh my God," she gasped.

"I know, right?" Dane agreed with a smirk. "The tree is massive."

Gina leaned forward in her seat, trying to get a better look out the front windshield. About twenty feet up, a massive branch extended from the main trunk like a giant arm reaching out from the tree. It was strong and sturdy, as thick as Gina's waist. Hanging from it were frayed ropes, their ends dangling towards the ground like eerie tentacles.

As they slowly drove forward, Gina noticed the branches and leaves of the tree begin to rattle and shake as if caught in a strong wind. She instinctively braced herself against the door and looked at Dane with alarm.

"Cool, right?" he said nonchalantly. "Legend says that this disturbance is caused when the ghosts of the hanged men start swinging at the end of their ropes. I was hoping you could tell me if that's really what it is, since you can see ghosts."

Was this another test to gauge her abilities?

She leaned forward, gazing up through the windshield as her mind raced with uncertainty. What should she do?

Should she pretend to see something she didn't or reveal the truth? Either choice held risks.

Lowering her head, she pressed her lips together and feigned a shudder. "Consider yourself lucky you can't see it," she muttered. "The criminals may have moved on, but it's the ghosts of the innocent—those wrongly hanged—that remain here; seeking justice."

He stared at her for a long moment, and she feared she'd been caught in her lie, but then his expression changed and he looked distressed. "I'm sorry. I wasn't thinking." He sounded genuinely contrite as he shifted the truck into gear and drove back towards the front of the courthouse. "I never considered how disturbing a sight it might be for someone who can see ghosts. Maybe we should go."

She placed a comforting hand on his arm, wanting to ease his guilt. "I'm fine, really. And I would still love to explore the inside of that old building."

He glanced skeptically at her as he stopped the truck in front of the courthouse. "Are you sure?"

She nodded, and he pulled into one of the front parking spots. "Okay, but only if you promise to let me know if you see anything too disturbing."

"I will."

She didn't wait for him to open her door, but got out and met him on the front sidewalk. After climbing the steps leading up to the courthouse doors, Gina stood on the portico, looking around while Dane sorted through his keys. Finding the one he wanted, he unlocked the padlock and removed the chain.

"Shall we go in?" He pulled open the door and held it, letting her go ahead of him.

Darkness loomed before her. Taking a breath, she stepped over the threshold.

Inside, she was relieved to discover that it wasn't nearly as dark inside as she'd expected, thanks to the sunlight filtering in through the upper-story windows.

She looked around the inside, feeling her breath catch in her throat. "What a magnificent building."

The lobby was a large open area with marble flooring and walls and a two-story high ornate ceiling. She'd expected the air to smell musty, but it didn't. There were no cobwebs hanging in the corners nor was there a thick layer of dust covering the few remaining pieces of furniture.

"Someone's taking care of this place," she observed. "Considering how long it's been empty, I expected broken furniture, litter on the floor, graffiti on the walls, dust everywhere—and spiders."

"Rumors of it being haunted keep the vandals away. As for the dust and spiders," he continued with a smile, "there are still some members of the town council who don't mind coming into the building. They take turns coming out once a month to clean." He gestured around them. "This, as you can see, is the lobby."

She studied the building; appreciating the richness of the wide marble staircase on the left. The balusters and newels were constructed of a dark wood that Gina thought might be cherry or rosewood. Its railing ran the length of the staircase and then continued around the perimeter of the second-floor balcony.

"Up there," he pointed to the second floor, "are the two courtrooms, each having its own judge's chambers."

Through the wood banister, Gina saw the two sets of double doors leading to the separate courtrooms.

He gestured off to the right. "Over there is where people checked in for cases or paid fines."

A long counter with four bank teller-like windows ran along the right wall. Past it, at the far end of the room, a hallway led further into the building.

"Where does that go?" She pointed to it.

"The old police department and holding cells. The shooting took place back there."

"Can we go back—?"

Dane's cell phone rang, interrupting her. "Sorry," he sighed, pulling it from his pocket to check the caller ID. "I need to take this." He answered the phone and told whoever was on the other end to "hold on a second." Then to her, he said, "cell phone reception in this building is for crap, so I'm going to step outside. Are you okay in here by yourself?"

She smiled at him and quipped, "I ain't afraid of no ghosts."

He chuckled. "Okay. This shouldn't take long."

She watched him until he'd disappeared through the front doors before continuing her trek across the lobby. She loved exploring old buildings. They were full of history and she enjoyed seeing what she could find. She had almost reached the hallway entrance when a noise stopped her.

Unsure of what she'd heard, she strained to listen, hoping to hear it again.

Just as she was about to brush it off as her imagination, the distinct sound of a drawer closing and the faint tap-tap-tapping of footsteps filled the air.

Her heart racing, she debated whether to go get Dane or investigate on her own. She knew he would be back soon enough and reassured herself that it was unlikely to be vandals, so it must be one of the town council members cleaning. However, she couldn't ignore the fact that the front entrance had been chained and locked when they'd arrived, with no vehicles parked outside.

Could there be another entrance? Or perhaps... it was a ghost?

No, she reasoned. *There is no such thing as ghosts. The Pink Lady is nothing more than the product of over-active imaginations.*

The problem was, she was having a hard time convincing herself. Despite her fear, Gina's curiosity got the best of her and she followed the sounds down the hallway. As she neared the end, she felt a chill creep over her skin and the hair on her neck stood up. Looking back towards the lobby, everything seemed darker somehow, making her doubt what she saw.

Just as she started back to the lobby, she glanced back and caught a blur of pink movement disappearing through an open doorway. A chill ran up her arms and along her neck. She tried to shake off the *Sixth Sense* moment as the chorus from the *Ghostbuster* song played in her head, mocking her.

I ain't afraid of no ghosts.

Gathering all her courage, she continued walking, finally reaching the last doorway at the end of the hall. Peering inside, she saw a woman, wearing a fitted pencil skirt with matching delicate pink cardigan and top, standing before a large filing cabinet. She seemed unaware of Gina's presence.

Gina stepped into the room, stopping just inside the doorway so as not to alarm the woman. "Hello. I hope you don't mind. I saw you come in here and followed you."

Ignoring her, the woman crossed the room to the desk and sat down.

"I'm here with Dane," Gina offered, wanting the woman to know she wasn't some random stranger coming in off the street.

Still, the woman ignored her. For a couple of heartbeats, Gina grew irritated at the woman's rudeness, but the irritation vanished an instant later as confusion set in. Everything about the woman screamed otherworldly, from her perfect bouffant hairdo, straight out of a vintage magazine, to her outdated attire.

Shivers running down her spine, Gina couldn't tear her gaze away from the woman. Her mind was reeling with questions and disbelief. Then she heard heavy footsteps echoing down the hallway. Across from her, the woman at the desk looked up. Then, in the blink of an eye, she vanished.

"Are you okay?" Dane asked, stepping into the doorway, his concerned tone breaking through her trance-like state, bringing her back to reality.

Trembling slightly, she finally found her voice. "I... I think I saw a ghost. A woman in a pink sweater set and skirt."

Dane nodded, seemingly unsurprised. "The Pink Lady."

He strode further into the room, navigating past the various desks until he reached the far wall. Once there, he stopped in front of a framed picture and pointed at it with his finger. "Was this her?"

Gina followed him over, her curiosity piqued by the picture. It was a department photo taken in front of the courthouse, and she immediately recognized the woman Dane was indicating.

"Yes," she replied simply, finding it hard to talk. Her mind still spun from the fact that she had just encountered an actual ghost.

"That's Yolanda Glossop. The one I told you about," he said solemnly, his eyes lingering on the photograph. "Listen, I hate to cut the afternoon short, but that call I took was the station. I'm needed back there." He gestured toward the door, indicating they should leave. "Shall I drop you off at Ruby Mae's? Or is there someplace else you want to go?"

"Ruby Mae's would be great, thanks." *And with luck, Uncle Victor is awake and planning out our next steps.*

The drive to Ruby Mae's was quiet. Gina couldn't shake the image of the Pink Lady from her mind, or the fact that she'd seen a real ghost.

A few minutes later, Dane pulled into the driveway of the Bed and Breakfast.

"Thank you so much for lunch and the tour of the courthouse," she said when he'd pulled to a stop. "I had a really great time."

"Good, then maybe you'd consider going out with me again?"

Her cheeks flushed with excitement as she replied, "I think I could be persuaded." She knew that spending more time with Dane meant risking him discovering her secret, but she pushed the thought aside, ignoring the warning bells in her head.

Unaware of her inner turmoil, Dane parked the truck and, walking around to the passenger side, opened her door. She accepted his help getting out, enjoying even more the way he held her hand longer than necessary.

They walked in silence along the front walkway and up porch steps.

"Can I call you later?" he asked, his voice low and husky.

Her heart skipped a beat. "Yes, I'd like that," she replied, her smile widening.

With a soft touch, he took her hand in his and stepped closer. The proximity made her pulse race with anticipation.

"There's something I've been wanting to do since the dance." He stepped closer, his breath warm against her cheek. "May I kiss you?"

Her heart fluttered in anticipation as she gave him a breathless nod. This was everything she had fantasized about.

He closed the distance between them until she could feel his warm breath on her lips.

Just as their lips were about to touch, he suddenly stepped away from her. Confused and frozen in place, Gina watched as Dane turned towards the sound of the front door opening.

"Hello, Chief," a cool voice greeted them. Uncle Victor stood in the doorway, a hint of amusement in his tone. "So nice to see you again." He turned to her, not bothering to hide his smirk. "Ah, Gina, you're back. How nice. We must make plans to confront *Llorona*."

"If you want, I can take you out to the RV park tonight," Dane offered.

Before Gina could thank him for the offer, Uncle Victor was waving it aside. "That won't be necessary," he said. "I know you must be busy with a potential kidnapper in the area. Besides, it seems the ghost finds the presence of a lot of people disturbing, so perhaps this one night, Gina and I could try to contact her alone?"

"Okay. I suppose we could give that a try," he said somewhat reluctantly. Then he turned back to Gina. "I'll call you later?" His voice was low and smooth, like silk sliding over bare skin.

"I'd like that," she told him.

He leaned down and placed a gentle kiss on her cheek, sending shivers down her spine. "To be continued later," he whispered with a wink before walking away.

Gina felt her cheeks heat at his words.

"Do I need to remind you it's not wise to become romantically involved with the locals?"

She turned to Uncle Victor, surprised by his stern tone. "Says the man who has never followed his own advice." Brushing past him, she headed for the staircase, needing some space to gather her thoughts. Partway up, she stopped and looked back at him. He was still standing in the open doorway, his expression unreadable. "Are you coming up? We need to talk." He closed the front door, then turned to her. She noticed the worry etched on his features. "Look, if you're worried about me getting my heart broken, then don't. I'm going to be careful."

"I know you will." There was something heavy weighing on his mind. She could tell by the way he avoided eye contact and gave her a forced smile.

"Are you okay?" she asked, growing concerned.

"Of course," he replied, trying to infuse sincerity into his tone but falling short. Gesturing for her to continue up the stairs, he followed her.

Once inside her room, Uncle Victor took a seat in the corner armchair while Gina sat on the edge of her bed.

"So, what is it you wanted to talk about?"

CHAPTER FOURTEEN

IT WAS HOURS LATER and Gina was fast asleep when knocking at her door jolted her awake. She sat up in bed, her mind still foggy. "Yeah, I'm up," she answered in a hushed voice, not wanting to disturb the other guests.

The knocking ceased, and she heard footsteps retreating down the stairs. For a moment, she considered going back to sleep, but with a groan, she threw off the covers and rose from the bed, already fully dressed. She quickly slipped on her shoes and checked her reflection in the mirror, making sure her makeup hadn't smudged during her nap. Quickly running a brush through her hair, she was ready to go.

Quietly making her way down the stairs, she opened the front door and stepped outside. The guest parking lot was surprisingly empty as she made her way towards their car where Uncle Victor was waiting for her.

They had agreed earlier to wait until nearly midnight before driving out to the RV park. They needed to explore the area where *Llorona* usually appeared and make a plan to convince the town that *Llorona* had been dealt with.

She hadn't told Uncle Victor about her encounter with The Pink Lady at the courthouse—how she had come face-to-face with the ghostly apparition while Dane conveniently stepped away for a phone call. She was still trying to understand what had happened, considering all logical explanations before jumping to paranormal conclusions. Maybe the woman was simply a distant relative of the original victim, hence their resemblance. And perhaps Dane had orchestrated this entire incident as part of an elaborate prank. In which case, ha. Ha. The joke was on her.

This time.

What Dane didn't know was she and Uncle Victor were masters at deception. They'd better be. Their lives now literally depended on it.

As Gina slid into the passenger seat, she caught the tantalizing aroma of freshly brewed coffee. Her gaze flicked from the Styrofoam cup in Uncle Victor's hand to the second cup nestled in the cup holder.

"Is that for me?" she asked hopefully.

"It is," he confirmed with a smile. "Ruby Mae had a pot going. We're not her only guests venturing out this late at night in search of ghosts. Unfortunately, we seem to be the last ones awake. Everyone else has already left."

Gina nodded, now understanding the reason for the empty parking lot.

"Thank you," she said gratefully, raising the cup in a half-toast before taking a much-needed sip. The warm liquid flowed down her throat, and she knew the caffeine would soon work its magic on her tired mind.

"What do we do if there are others already at the site waiting for *Llorona?*" she asked, voicing her concern.

"Hopefully, they won't be at the RV park," he replied easily. "I heard most of the action tonight is at the Double R Ranch, where *El Muerto* is expected to ride."

Gina felt a twinge of disappointment at missing out on seeing the headless horseman, but duty called.

"Do you think *Llorona* is real?" she couldn't help asking, finally giving voice to her fears.

Uncle Victor shook his head. "I don't know. We both saw the photo. You should be ready to handle surprises."

Not exactly the comforting words she'd hoped for. She took another long sip of her coffee, the warm liquid soothing her nerves as she sat in silence with Uncle Victor on the drive to the RV park.

"Looks like not everyone went to the ranch," she observed a few minutes later when they pulled up to the entrance of the RV park. The lot where Dane had parked the other night was now over half full.

"Indeed," Uncle Victor replied, his tone sounding almost disappointed. Instead of turning, he continued driving.

"Did you change your mind?" Gina asked hopefully, her heart fluttering at the thought of getting to spend another day with Dane.

"No," Uncle Victor replied, crushing her fantasy. "But I think we'll have better luck further up."

As they drove up the road, she couldn't see how this was better. There were no streetlights in this area and the resulting darkness was so thick, she could barely see her hand in front of her face.

After driving for about three hundred yards, Uncle Victor suddenly executed a three-point turn and pulled off onto the side of the road, now facing the direction from which they'd just driven. When he turned off the engine, Gina looked out the window and saw nothing but the impenetrable darkness of night.

"Yes, I can see how this would be better," she said sarcastically, feeling on edge.

"Don't tell me you're afraid," Uncle Victor challenged, his mocking tone only adding to the uneasy feeling in her gut.

"I can't see anything," she retorted, trying to see where the side of the road ended, and the woods began.

"Don't worry. I'll protect you from the boogeyman," he said nonchalantly.

"Ha. Ha." She forced a laugh. "The boogeyman isn't real." Nevertheless, the thought of something lurking in the dark made her skin crawl.

"Like ghosts aren't real?" Her uncle's joke hit a little too close to home.

Then he opened his car door, flooding the interior with light, and she had to squint against the sudden brightness.

"Warn a girl next time, would you?" she snapped, annoyed but also grateful for any source of light.

Taking a last sip of coffee and placing the cup back in the cup holder, Gina opened her door and climbed out. When they both closed their doors, they were once again plunged into darkness and her mind raced with thoughts of what horrors lurked in the shadows.

Suddenly, she heard a rustling in the trees, and her heart leaped into her throat.

"What was that?" she asked, sounding breathless.

"Boogeyman," he replied and this time, he chuckled darkly.

She knew he was joking, but had the noise really been just an animal? She hoped that, when she spoke next, her voice sounded steadier than she felt. "What's the plan?"

"This section of land is part of a game preserve. The river separates it from the RV park. As I recall, Llorona first appeared on this side of the river, so we'll examine this side first," her uncle replied calmly.

"How are we supposed to do that? I can't see a thing."

She heard a muted click and a narrow beam of light suddenly appeared, cutting across the night. The beam originated from her uncle's hand and when he saw her looking, he raised his hand so she could see the small flashlight.

"I borrowed this from Ruby Mae," he explained. "There's a path through the woods that will lead us to where *Llorona* appeared."

"How do you know?" Gina asked, surprised.

"Because while you were distracting the police chief, I was out here scouting," he said with a sly smile. "The path is that way."

She stared into the pitch-black of the forest and let out a resigned sigh. If there was a path, she couldn't see it. "No, please. After you."

He started past her, the bright beam of the flashlight cutting through the darkness, revealing a footpath through the trees.

Gina's nerves were on edge as she listened to the sound of their footsteps echoing through the quiet woods. She could hear something else too—the sound of rushing water getting louder with each step they took.

Lost in her thoughts, she was surprised when Uncle Victor turned off the flashlight, plunging them both into a thick blackness that seemed to swallow her whole. Before she could react, she collided with him.

"What th—" she said before he quickly turned around and silenced her with a finger pressed against her lips.

Why had he stopped?

Understanding she couldn't risk making noise to ask, she strained to see past him, through the trees to the river. The lights of the RV park were barely visible and allowed her to just make out the shapes of tourists gathered on the other side.

Did he think the tourists would hear them creeping through the woods? Over the sound of the river?

Not likely.

Then a collective "ooohhhh" reached her ears just as a glowing figure moved into her field of vision. Gina tracked the figure's movement, wishing she was closer because she kept losing sight of it when a tree blocked her view. From what she could see, though, the figure—made entirely of soft, glowing light—was a woman with long hair and a long, flowing gown.

Llorona!

Gina's breath caught in her throat as she watched the spirit glide gracefully along the water's edge. Her movements were accompanied by a haunting wail that grew louder and more tortured with each passing moment. *Llorona* raised her arms and sent tendrils of mist swirling around her in a mesmerizing dance.

Just then, a darker shadow, lurking at the edge of her vision, broke Gina's trance. She couldn't make out what it was before it disappeared again, but she knew it wasn't just her imagination.

"Did you see that?" she whispered to Uncle Victor, barely able to form the words.

"By the trees?" he replied quietly, confirming that he had also seen something.

A flicker of light had Gina's gaze returning to *Llorona*, who was now moving away from the river—and heading directly for them!

Breath caught in her throat and, heart racing, she watched the ghostly apparition's approach.

Closer.

Closer.

Suddenly, there was a brilliant flash of light and a deafening *bang*!

Momentarily blinded, Gina didn't see the shadowy figure until it slammed into her with intense force, knocking her to the ground.

"Shit!"

For a nanosecond, Gina thought she'd muttered the curse out loud, then realized it hadn't been her. The voice had been male—but not Uncle Victor's. A teenage boy's voice.

In that moment, everything seemed to happen at once. Uncle Victor snapped on his flashlight just as *Llorona* bent over the fallen figure. The beam of light caught her face, revealing her to be a very much alive teenage girl. Then, another boy appeared out of nowhere to join *Llorona* and the first boy. Gina's mind raced as she confronted the three of them.

With a sudden burst of energy, the teenagers took off into the woods.

"Stop them!" Gina yelled, scrambling to her feet with Uncle Victor's help, but they were already too far behind and stumbling through unfamiliar terrain.

Minutes later, Gina heard an engine roaring to life. She knew it was the teenagers making their escape. In a burst of determination, she sprinted towards the source of the noise, a clearing up ahead. But it was too late. The truck was already disappearing down a dirt road, its taillights mocking her failed attempt to catch the mysterious trio.

Gina's rage simmered underneath the surface as she and Uncle Victor made their way back to the Bed and Breakfast several minutes later.

"Can you believe it?" she seethed. "Those kids pretending to be *Llorona*."

"The nerve," he responded with a smirk. "It's hard to trust anyone these days, I guess."

She smiled, aware of the irony. "At least now we know the town's problem isn't a real ghost," she said.

"Do you think you can describe them well enough to Dane?"

Gina thought back to her encounter in the woods with the teens and her face broke out in a smile. "Oh, yeah. I can."

If she was truthful, she was enormously relieved. She'd actually worried that she'd have to confront a ghost; the living spirit of the dead. Instead, *Llorona* was nothing more than a teen prank.

The town's problem could be easily solved once the teens were caught and it would be the easiest money she'd ever made.

Uncle Victor could pay off Frankie Goldstein when they returned to Houston. They would be safe, once more.

Then she realized, that when they left, she may never see Dane again and that cast a damper on her good mood.

CHAPTER FIFTEEN

GINA NERVOUSLY FOUND DANE'S name on her phone and hit the call button. She took a deep breath and waited, feeling her heart race with anticipation. Finally, a voice answered on the other end.

"Gina, good morning. What's up?" Dane's voice was warm and familiar, causing an unexpected rush of emotions in Gina.

"I know it's early," she began hesitantly. "I hope I'm not bothering you."

"Not at all," he assured her. "Just catching up on some paperwork." She could hear papers shuffling in the background.

Gina struggled with how to tell him about their encounter the night before. "Uncle Victor and I went to the RV park last night as planned."

"How'd it go? Did you see *Llorona?*"

"Sort of," she said evasively.

There was a moment of silence before Dane asked cautiously, "What does that mean?"

Gina stood up from the edge of her bed and began pacing back and forth across her room. Just say it, she told herself sternly. "The *Llorona* we saw last night was not a spirit or ghost. It was a teenage girl dressed up in a costume and covered in some kind of glow-in-the-dark paint."

She fell silent, waiting for his reaction. To her surprise, he didn't sound shocked or disbelieving. "Are you sure?" he asked calmly.

Gina was taken aback by his response. "Yes, I'm positive," she said firmly. "I got close enough to see her clearly. In fact, we practically ran into each other. One of the boys with her *did* knock me down. Trust me, they were very much alive."

Dane's response was a heavy sigh. Gina felt guilty for having to share bad news with him. "Tell me everything."

So she did, from the trek through the game preserve, to seeing the ghostly *Llorona*, to the bright light and loud bang, ending with the teens driving off into the night. "I don't know why these kids are dressing up and scaring tourists," she continued. "But I thought you should know so you can stop them. It's sad that they have nothing better to do with their time."

"I don't suppose you got a look at their license plate?"

"No, sorry. All I saw was a dark pickup."

"Well, I appreciate you telling me about it."

Now for the hard part, she thought. "At least your *Llorona* problem is solved," she said, trying to lighten the mood.

"What?" He sounded confused.

"I was hired to confront Llorona and stop her from terrorizing the town. Well, I confronted her last night and after getting caught, I doubt those kids will try anything like that again." She shrugged, even though he couldn't see her. "It's really a shame, too. I've enjoyed my time here in Las Palomas, but now that the job is done, I need to get back to Houston. As soon as I collect my fee, that is."

"You can't leave," Dane protested.

She couldn't help but smile. "I know. I feel the same way but maybe I can come back for a visit."

"No, that's not what I meant. You haven't completed the task we hired you for."

Wait... what? "Excuse me?"

"The thing is, *Llorona* is an actual ghost. I've seen her myself. The kids playing near the river last night may have created a distraction, but that doesn't change the fact that the actual ghost is scaring away tourists."

She wanted to tell him that ghosts weren't real but that wouldn't sound good coming from a supposed ghost whisperer. "I know it's hard to accept that it was a teen prank all along," she said, not unkindly.

"We're paying you to solve the issue with *Llorona*—the actual ghost. If you need to leave, I understand, but you'll end up leaving without getting paid."

Gina felt her patience wearing thin. She didn't want to go over his head, but she would. "Dane, I called you as a courtesy, but I think it's time I called Mayor Garcia."

"You're welcome to call him, but his answer is going to be the same as mine. I'm sorry if that disappoints you. We still have a problem, and if you can't stick around to help us with it, then we'll find someone who can."

The man was being obstinate. Any feelings of affection she'd developed for him were quickly evaporating. They were at an impasse. Any other time, she'd cut her losses and leave town, but it would be suicide, literally, for her and Uncle Victor to return to Houston without Frankie's money.

"Fine," Gina responded curtly. "I'll call him."

"Fine." She heard him sigh. "I don't want to fight with you. Can I take you out for breakfast?" he asked.

She looked at her phone incredulously. Was he serious? "Thanks, but I've already eaten," she lied.

Dane couldn't possibly miss the frost in her tone, or what it meant.

"Some other time, then," he replied politely, but with a hint of chilliness.

"Sure," Gina matched his tone with equal politeness. "Goodbye."

As soon as she hung up, Gina felt like crying. Whether from anger or heartache, she wasn't sure. Maybe both. She decided to get dressed and consult with her uncle before calling the mayor. Maybe he had advice on how to handle this situation, because right now, it seemed hopeless, like she was stuck in quicksand and sinking fast.

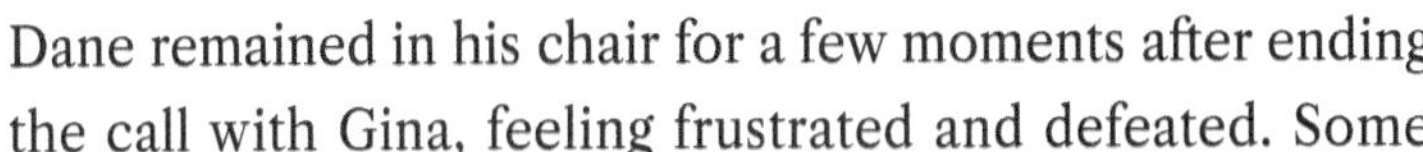

Dane remained in his chair for a few moments after ending the call with Gina, feeling frustrated and defeated. Some days, he couldn't stand this job, and today was quickly becoming one of those days. He never intended to develop feelings for Gina Castillo, but fate seemed to have different plans for him. And now, any chance he had with her had been blown to pieces.

Letting out a heavy sigh, he retrieved the mayor's number and dialed it.

"Sal, we have a problem," he said once the mayor answered. He explained his conversation with Gina and waited for Sal's response.

"You need to fix this, Dane."

Typical. "Why is this my responsibility?"

"Everyone in town saw the two of you on the dance floor. You have chemistry together. Use it to convince her she's wrong about the teens being the source of our problem."

"I'll do my best, but she's not going to be easy to convince."

"Sometimes pillow talk can be effective." This comment made Dane's temper flare.

"Mayor Garcia," he interjected sternly. "You are very much mistaken if you think I will sleep with Gina Castillo just to protect the town."

The mayor quickly apologized, his tone contrite. "It was a mistake, Dane, to say that. I saw you two at the dance and made an assumption. I don't even know what I was thinking. It was inappropriate of me, and I apologize."

Dane hesitated before accepting the apology. He wanted to hold on to his anger, but he had enough on his plate without getting into a conflict with the mayor.

"I hate to cut our conversation short, but I have to take this call," Sal interjected. "My secretary just informed me that

Miss Castillo is waiting for me on hold. Thank you again for giving me a heads up."

Dane slammed his phone down on the desk, cursing under his breath as he ran a hand through his hair. What a shit day this was turning out to be.

A familiar voice interrupted his seething thoughts. "Problems, Bro? I can come back later."

Dane looked up to see Diego Juarez standing in the office doorway, looking every bit the cowboy he was in his faded jeans and beige chambray shirt. The two burgundy "Rs" embroidered over the left pocket were a trademark of the Double R Ranch uniform.

"Just another day in paradise," Dane sighed, forcing a smile for his longtime friend. "Come on in. I could use a cup of coffee. You want one?"

"Sure," Diego replied, taking a seat in one of the guest chairs while Dane went to the side wall lined with file cabinets. He opened the Keurig sitting on top, dropped a coffee pod inside, and started brewing a cup.

"How are Jan and Maizy doing?" Diego asked, concern evident in his tone. "I heard about the kidnapping attempt."

Dane wasn't surprised—news traveled fast in their small town. "They're holding up as best they can," he said, before handing Diego a cup of freshly brewed coffee. He knew his friend took it black.

"Any leads on the kidnapper?"

Dane let out a frustrated sigh as he loaded another K-cup and pressed the brew button. "No," he admitted, turning to face Diego with his back against the file cabinets. "And it's damn frustrating."

Diego raised an eyebrow in understanding as he took a sip of his coffee.

"Is Sal giving you a hard time about it?" When Dane looked surprised, Diego explained. "He was speaking loud enough for me to hear him across the room."

It made sense. Sal only had two volumes: loud and louder.

"Actually, no. He didn't even bring it up. He's more upset about Gina Castillo running into *Llorona* last night."

The Keurig gurgled and gave its final cough, signaling that Dane's coffee was ready. He spooned sugar into his cup before returning to his desk.

"Problem solved then, right? No scary *Llorona*," Diego joked.

Dane shook his head. "Not exactly. Damn kids. We made it clear that the river is off-limits until further notice."

Diego paused with his cup halfway to his lips. "Oh, shit. What happened?"

"Gina happened," Dane grumbled. "She got too close and saw their faces. Well, one of their faces, at least. Now she thinks it's just a group of kids causing all this trouble. She thinks she's scared them enough that they won't try anything again. Now she wants her fee so she can leave town as soon as possible."

Diego studied him for a moment. "What's really bothering you? The incident with the kids or Gina potentially leaving town?"

Dane gave him a wary look. "What are you talking about?"

"Don't play dumb. I saw you with her the other night. You haven't looked at someone like that since junior high when

Susan Wells gave you your first kiss behind the gym. You have feelings for her."

Dane took a sip of his coffee, noticing its overpowering sweetness. He had added the sugar in hopes of a quick burst of energy. Hopefully, by the time the sugar crash hit, the caffeine would kick in and offset it.

"Even if I do like her, it doesn't matter now. She probably hates me." He didn't want to discuss his personal problems anymore and studied his friend's face. Diego looked just as exhausted as Dane felt. "Why are you here so early?"

Diego set down his empty cup and leaned back in his chair, regarding Dane with a mix of curiosity and concern. "It's a social call, kind of. Elise wanted me to ask you and Gina to the ranch for dinner this weekend."

Dane felt a knot form in his stomach at the thought of facing Gina after their awkward encounter. "I'm not sure that's a good idea," he said slowly, weighing his words carefully.

Diego gave him a sympathetic smile. "Don't worry about it, man. I can always tell Elise that you're busy with work or something." He nodded understandingly before changing the subject slightly. "Is there anything I can do to help? Maybe track down those teens responsible for this mess and give them a talking to?"

Dane shook his head. "I appreciate the offer, but I think it's best if I handle this one myself." Dane stood up from his desk, feeling the weight of the upcoming tasks pressing down on his shoulders.

Diego also stood. "Alright, man. Just let me know if you change your mind. And take care of yourself, alright? Don't let this whole *Llorona* mess get to you."

Dane managed a small smile. "I won't, don't worry." He walked his friend to the door, grateful for the support despite everything else going on.

After Diego left the office, Dane closed the door behind him and took a deep breath. He needed to focus, to come up with a plan to deal with the situation at hand. He couldn't afford to be distracted by thoughts of Gina or anything else.

Returning to his desk, he reached for his phone, his fingers tapping out a familiar number. The dial tone filled the room as he waited for someone to pick up on the other end.

"Hey, it's me," he spoke into the phone, his voice steady despite the whirlwind of emotions inside him. "We need to talk about last night. Someone ignored those orders. Not only did they put on a show, they got caught by the ghost whisperer."

"Oh, shit."

Dane liked Dylan and had hoped he'd had no part in last night's haunting. The shock in the young man's voice was proof enough for Dane of his innocence. "Any idea who it might have been? One female; two males."

"Yeah." Dylan sounded disgusted. "I think I might know."

"Good. Call them and tell them I want to talk to them in person, at Spook Central, in an hour. Got it?"

"Yes, sir."

He disconnected the call and pushed away from his desk. "Damn, kids," he muttered to himself. They were probably just out having fun.

Well, let's see how much fun they have when I kick their collective butts and threaten to throw them in jail.

CHAPTER SIXTEEN

IN KATHY'S CAFÉ ON the other side of Town Park, Gina let out a sigh and met her uncle's concerned gaze across the booth. The buzzing chatter and clinking of silverware filled the air, but she could hardly hear it over the rush of emotions pulsing through her. The breakfast she'd just eaten felt like a leaden weight in her stomach, making her ill.

She leaned across the table, her voice dropping to a conspiratorial whisper. "Is there a chance Dane and Mayor Garcia are both right? That those teenagers aren't the problem and *Llorona* is an actual ghost?" She glanced toward the board where the picture of Llorona was pinned, remembering that while the figure in that photo had been semi-transparent, it hadn't looked photoshopped.

The seed of doubt had been planted and she let out a sigh. "There's something I haven't told you. Dane took me to the court house and when he went outside to take a call, I saw a lady. I followed her into one of the offices and I tried to talk to her, but she ignored me. When Dane finished his call and came back to join me, she vanished."

"You mean, she left the room?" he asked.

She vigorously shook her head. "No, I mean she disappeared into thin air. I told Dane about it and he said it was The Pink Lady; the spirit of a woman who was shot back in the nineteen-fifties." She paused, letting her words sink in. "What if ghosts are real?"

He shook his head. "You were there last night. You saw the costume and heard all the wailing and noise those kids were making. No. Even if ghosts are real, that's not what we're dealing with here." He reached over to pat her hand lying on the table just as his phone rang, breaking the tense atmosphere. Gina assumed it was Sylvia calling until she saw his anxious expression after glancing at the caller ID. There was only one person who could make her uncle react that way.

Frankie Goldstein.

She met his equally troubled gaze over the table.

"I'd better take this," he said with a sigh.

She nodded and watched him slide out of the booth to head outside, wondering why Frankie was calling. Was it to tell them their time was up? Even so, they couldn't return to Houston without his money.

She couldn't bear to think about it.

Instead of focusing on the problem, she admonished herself, she needed to think of a solution.

Perhaps there was another way to come up with the money. She could apply for a personal loan from her bank or take out a second mortgage on her house.

Neither solution was the quick fix they needed.

Just then, Uncle Victor walked back into the café.

She could tell from his expression and the short duration of his call that it wasn't good news. The tension in the air only grew thicker.

Gina leaned in eagerly as Uncle Victor settled back into his seat, her eyes searching for any sign of hope. "What did he say?" she asked anxiously.

"He wanted to know why we left town. I told him we're trying to get the money we owe him, but these things take time." He took a sip of his coffee. "However, I'm afraid Frankie is not a patient or understanding man," he sighed. "He made it clear that he wants his money soon—or else."

Gina's heart felt like it dropped to the pit of her stomach. "Or else what?" she pressed, feeling a sense of dread wash over her.

The silence that followed from her uncle was far from reassuring. Gina knew this was not good.

"Okay, here's the plan," she began quickly, trying to think on her feet. "Plan A—I will try my best to convince Dane that the teenagers are the ones scaring off the tourists, so we can get paid. And if Plan A doesn't work, then we'll have to resort to Plan B, which means going back out to the river and putting on the performance of a lifetime." She reached out and gently squeezed Uncle Victor's hand, unable to hide the worry in her own voice. "But either way, I am getting that money."

His smile did little to ease her concerns as she looked into his worried eyes.

"Have I told you how much I love you?" he asked sincerely. "You're like a daughter to me."

Tears threatened to spill from her eyes as she fought to hold them back. "I love you, too, Uncle Victor," she said softly. "Which is why I don't want anything bad to happen to you." Taking a deep breath, she released his hand and tried to regain her composure. Glancing at their empty plates, she suggested with determination, "Since we're done with breakfast, why don't we head out to the river right now? We need to figure out how to convince the town council that I'm speaking to *Llorona.* Maybe we can rig lights or a speaker into the trees, or something."

"During the day?"

Gina huffed. "Why not? It's starting to seem like during the day is the only time no one's actually out there."

Uncle Victor's eyes flicked to his phone. "I can't go right now," he said, his tone apologetic. "I promised Sylvia I'd meet her at eight-thirty."

Gina's frustration boiled over. "Seriously? Isn't this more important than whatever you have planned with Sylvia?"

A mischievous glint sparked in his eyes as one of his eyebrows shot up. "As far as you're concerned, what I'm doing with the delightful Ms. Winters is simply conducting research," he teased. "Plus, we can always go out to the river later."

She huffed in frustration, crossing her arms over her chest. "What am I supposed to do in the meantime?"

"I'm sure you'll figure something out. I've got this," he assured her, reaching for the bill and smoothly sliding out of the booth. With a confident stride, he made his way to the register. She watched as he paid and then disappeared through the front door, leaving her alone with her thoughts. The clink of plates and chatter of other diners seemed far away as she mulled over her options for how to spend the next few hours until Uncle Victor was ready to work.

Asking Dane to show her the sights was out of the question now, so she decided to explore the town on her own. Going outside, she crossed over to Town Park and strolled along the sidewalk, gazing around. She'd almost reached the end of the block when a group of teenagers walking along the sidewalk across the street caught her attention. The girl, in particular, looked familiar.

She tried not to stare as she studied the girl's features. Then it hit her—this was the girl who'd played *Llorona* last night. The two boys with her were probably her accomplices.

Feeling a rush of excitement and determination, she decided to follow them, hoping to get the evidence she needed to prove they were behind the town's *Llorona* problem. Maybe then Dane and Mayor Garcia would believe her, and she and Uncle Victor could collect their payment and return to Houston.

With determination fueling her steps, Gina crossed the street and trailed behind, keeping a safe distance so as not to draw attention to herself. Fortunately, the teens too absorbed in their conversation to notice her.

For four blocks, Gina followed them, until they reached the local high school. Rather than make their way towards the main entrance, they walked down the length of the school and then around the corner, heading to the back of the school. When Gina reached the corner, she pressed herself against the rough bricks and cautiously peered around it. The teens were crossing the vast parking lot, heading towards the field house. Instead of entering, they passed it and went into a temporary building a short distance away.

Then the sound of an approaching vehicle caught her attention, and she looked away from the temporary building in time to see a familiar tan truck pulling into the parking lot. Quickly, she ducked her head back around the corner so she wouldn't be seen.

Dane was the last person she expected to see here.

A part of her wanted to go to him and point out the building into which the teenagers had disappeared.

Something held her back; a gut feeling that told her to wait. She listened intently as Dane's truck came to a stop and his engine shut off. A moment later, she heard the sound of his door opening and closing, followed by heavy footsteps growing fainter as he walked away. Taking a chance, she cautiously peeked around the corner once more.

To her surprise and confusion, Dane was heading straight for the temporary building and something about his determined stride made her uneasy. She couldn't shake the feeling that there was more going on here than met the eye.

CHAPTER SEVENTEEN

Dane walked across the high school parking lot, headed for Spook Central. The town elders had entrusted the duty of haunting the town to teenagers for a reason. It wasn't just because the teenagers enjoyed impersonating ghosts, although they did. It was because teenagers were less likely to fall asleep during those late-night hours.

However, entrusting such a responsibility to teenagers came with its challenges—sometimes their excitement impeded following rules.

He thought back over the conversation with Gina and couldn't help but worry about last night's incident. He could only hope that their mistake wouldn't cost the town its future.

As Dane swung open the door to the building, he saw the three teenagers slumped in a despondent silence. Their eyes darted up to meet his, and he sensed the fear and apprehension radiating from them.

Good. Maybe they weren't just brainless troublemakers after all.

Stepping forward, he planted himself firmly in front of the door, blocking any chance of escape. He rested his hands on his belt and gave them his sternest look—the one he reserved for interrogating suspects.

"Someone care to explain what happened last night?" he demanded.

The teens exchanged nervous glances, silently deliberating over who should speak up first.

Finally, one boy nodded and cleared his throat. "Well, you see, the new *Llorona* costume arrived a few days ago," he began.

Dane remembered the town voting on whether to spend money replacing the old gown, so he simply nodded and let the boy continue.

"According to protocol, all new costumes have to go through a test performance before being used in public," the boy explained. Again, Dane nodded in agreement; he was well aware of the rules. "Well, Murphy's is practically empty because *Llorona* scared everyone away, and we figured most people would be at the Double R Ranch to see *El Muerto*. So, we thought it would be the perfect time to do a test run. We came in through the game preserve, so we didn't notice the cars in Murphy's parking lot. It wasn't until it was too late that we realized people were there."

He shrugged helplessly. "At that point, we figured we might as well finish the performance. So that's what we did."

The other boy chimed in eagerly, gesturing to the girl. "And let me tell you, that new costume is amazing. Dee looked absolutely awesome in it."

Dane nodded slowly, remaining silent for a moment and allowing the tension in the room to build. Finally, he spoke again. "Now, what about this flashbang I heard about?" A flicker of recognition sparked in Dane's mind as he remembered where he had seen the boy before. "Kent, isn't it?"

Kent's face flushed with embarrassment. "Uh, yes sir. See, I may have found one that you and Chad—um, Officer Lucero—left behind."

Dane recalled the night of July Fourth, when he and Chad had confiscated several dangerous incendiary devices. "Go on." His tone was a mixture of curiosity and accusation.

"I didn't think it would hurt," Kent shrugged. "You never gave me a chance to see what it could do. I was just curious." His gaze narrowed slightly. "Didn't you blow up the ones you confiscated?"

Busted. He, Chad and Steve had been just as curious about the flashbangs as the teenagers, so they'd snuck out to Howard Burn's farm to set them off.

"How do you know about that?" Dane asked, legitimately curious.

"Howard Burns is my grandma's sister-in-law's cousin," Kent said matter-of-factly. "I overheard him telling my grandma how much fun you guys had setting them off."

Dane let out a sigh. "So, you used one as part of your performance?"

Kent nodded eagerly. "We hadn't planned on it. I kind of forgot I had it in my pocket. When we saw some people sneaking through the woods behind us, I remembered the flashbang. You know they're not really that dangerous, just loud and bright. I thought it would temporarily blind the people sneaking up behind us so we could make our escape. Only, I never set one off before and it went off sooner than expected. We ended up blinded and ran in the wrong direction."

Dee chimed in beside him. "We didn't expect to run into the ghost whisperer—literally." Her expression turned apologetic. "I'm so sorry, Chief Wolfe. I'm pretty sure she saw me."

Dane nodded solemnly. "She did, but because you were covered in paint, she's not sure if she can make a positive ID."

The first boy spoke up nervously. "Are we in trouble?"

"I should arrest you." Dane paused, and watched their faces closely, taking satisfaction in the way they paled and shifted nervously under his intense gaze. "But I'm not going to," he continued, his tone firm and authoritative. "Just so we're clear—no more *Llorona* impersonations. Next person to do it before we get the all-clear from The Town Council gets thrown in jail. Understood?" The teenage group nodded quickly. "Okay, get out of here," he commanded, dismissing them with a wave of his hand. "I'll lock up."

With a heavy sigh, Dane watched as they scurried away, eager to escape his authority. As he locked up Spook Central, he felt mentally drained. The fear of a child predator roaming their small town had compelled him to do everything possible. He had even reached out to neighboring law enforcement offices, hoping for leads or information on similar incidents. He and his officers were working extra shifts, tirelessly keeping watch over the town and its residents. And now this stunt.

The only thing that had kept him going was the prospect of spending time with Gina later on, but now even that was gone.

He pulled out his phone after he locked up and made his way towards his truck. Sometimes even a grown man needed to hear his mother's voice.

"Dane? Is everything okay?"

He could hear the concern in her voice and reassured her quickly.

"Yeah, why would you ask?"

"You don't normally call this early."

He glanced at his phone's clock and furrowed his brow. "It's almost ten," he answered as he walked to his truck and climbed in.

"So, everything is okay?"

"Yes, everything is fine," he confirmed with a sigh. Sometimes talking to his mother was a challenge. "I thought about coming over for a bit."

"Don't you have work?" his mother asked, a hint of worry still present in her voice.

Dane let out another sigh, his eyes tired and his body exhausted. "I've been working all night," he explained. "I need a break." He leaned back in his seat, rubbing his temples to ease the tension building there. The thought of another long day at the office was daunting.

"Why don't you use this time to show Gina around?" his mother suggested. "You can't have shown her everything our town has to offer already."

He started up his truck, welcoming the cool blast of air from the A/C. This call was taking longer than expected and he regretted not just driving over to her house instead.

"She might not be speaking to me," he replied wearily.

His mother's disapproval was obvious in her tone. "And why might that be?"

Taking a deep breath, he relayed the conversation he had with Gina that morning. It didn't end well, and he knew his mother would be disappointed when she learned Gina might be leaving town today.

"We didn't exactly part on friendly terms," he finished with a defeated shrug. "So even if she stays, I doubt she'd want to spend time with me."

"You're giving up? That's not like you," his mother chided.

He felt a lecture coming on, and he wasn't in the mood for it. "I'm heading over now," he changed the subject abruptly, hoping to avoid any more comments about his love life.

The line went quiet for a moment before his mother spoke again. "Did you say it's almost ten?"

"Yes," he confirmed.

"Oh... well, now's not a good time. I have a... a thing."

Dane resisted the urge to roll his eyes. His mother always seemed to have some excuse for not wanting him to come over. "That's fine," he replied with forced politeness. "I can let myself in."

His mother's response was sharp and strained. "No, please don't," she said, her tone carrying a hint of frustration. "I'm in the middle of a project and I have stuff spread out everywhere."

Dane rolled his eyes. "Mom, I've seen the house messy before," he reassured her. "I won't judge."

She snorted. "Like I care what you think of my housekeeping skills," she scoffed. "I've been working on Christmas gifts for you and your sister, and I'd appreciate it if you didn't come by and spoil my surprise."

"Oh, okay." His mother was always making things for him and his sister.

"Come over for dinner, instead. It'll give us more time to catch up and visit."

He knew that with his sister away at college, his mother got lonely living all alone in their childhood home. "Okay, yeah, that sounds great. What time?"

"Come by at six."

"Okay, Mom. See you then."

He disconnected the call, and with no good excuse not to, headed back to the station.

Chapter Eighteen

GINA WAS STILL STANDING at the corner of the high school trying to decide what to do when the three teens left the temporary building and headed across the football field, back toward town. Dane emerged from the building a couple of minutes later, his posture tense as he made his way back to his truck. He sat there for several minutes, talking to someone on his cell phone, before driving away.

Finally alone, Gina headed toward the temporary building, driven by curiosity. When she tried the door, she found it locked.

Not a very sophisticated lock, she thought, studying it. In fact, it was a simple doorknob lock. Someone who knew what they were doing with a credit card could probably get the door open pretty easily.

Of course, that was technically breaking and entering—and she doubted Dane would be very understanding if he caught her.

So don't get caught. Uncle Victor's voice echoed in her mind.

Who would have thought that the skills Uncle Victor had taught her would come in handy one day? She reached into her pocket and pulled out her phone. Then she slid open the slot on the back of the case to reveal her driver's license. Memories of her childhood lessons flooded back as she carefully inserted the card into the crack between the door and frame, making sure not to lose her grip. The last thing she needed was for it to slip through and land on the other side of the locked door.

It took longer than she expected, but eventually she felt a satisfying click as the card slipped under the angled end of the slant-latch, forcing it back and allowing her to open the door. With a triumphant smile, Gina stepped inside the building- grateful for Uncle Victor's unconventional teachings once again.

She closed the door behind her and took a moment to survey the room. Sunlight filtered through the windows, casting a warm glow over the space and making it unnecessary to turn on the overhead lights. To her left stood a sturdy plastic folding table, large enough to comfortably seat eight people, with matching folding chairs scattered around it. Against the wall behind the table was a small but functional kitchenette, complete with sink, cabinets, a Keurig coffeemaker, and a microwave. A refrigerator hummed quietly next to the counter and when Gina opened it, she found it stocked with cases of bottled water and cans of soda.

Next to the refrigerator, sitting on the floor, were several small-sized packing boxes. The flaps of the top one were closed but not sealed. Gina pulled them open and discovered a supply of spray paints. Her first thought was that these were supplies for the graffiti artist, but she quickly changed her mind after pulling out several of the cans and discovering they were all the same: Rust-Oleum Specialty Glow-in-the-Dark Green.

Curious.

She put the cans back in the box and folded the flaps the way she'd found them.

On the opposite side of the room was a cozy sitting area, complete with an inviting area rug, television, end table with lamp, and an assortment of colorful bean bag chairs. The remote control for the TV sat on the floor beside one of the chairs, clearly showing this was a popular hangout spot for teens looking to pass time between classes (or, more likely, while skipping them altogether).

Beyond the kitchenette, along the left wall, stood a set of sturdy bunk beds. On each bed was a clear plastic zip-bag containing sheets and a folded comforter across its foot.

Nice, she thought facetiously. Just what every student needs—a place to lounge and sleep instead of attending class. She shook her head. What was the educational system coming to?

Opposite the bunk beds stood a clothes rack on wheels, stretching at least five feet long. From it hung an intriguing assortment of costumes, all of them in the same shade of pale-green.

She wondered if the drama class used this building. If so, it seemed like an odd location. Wouldn't they locate the building closer to the school auditorium?

Absently, she began browsing through the costumes until one caught her eye. She pulled it out and hung it sideways on the bar to get a better look. The gown was uniquely old-fashioned, yet not actually old. As she ran her fingers over it, she noticed a thin layer of paint covering its surface.

Curious, she went back to the box of spray paint and withdrew one of the cans. Carrying it over, she held the lid next to the costume. Not just any paint, she realized. It was the same glow-in-the-dark paint. At night, under a full moon, this gown would give off an eerie aura. Without hesitation, she returned the paint can to the box and snapped a photo of the costume on her phone before hanging it back up where she found it.

Her curiosity led her further into the building, her footsteps echoing on the worn linoleum floor. She opened a door at the back of the room and found herself in a bathroom with yellowed tiles and a chipped vanity.

She bent down to look under the sink and noticed a small toolbox sitting there. Opening it up, she was surprised to find it filled with Halloween make-up and glow-in-the-dark paint. She was starting to think the drama department had little to do with this building.

As she moved back to the center of the building, her eyes scanned the room, connecting dots and unraveling mysteries. She snapped more pictures of the various objects scattered around the space, capturing photographic evidence, before carefully tucking her phone back into her pocket.

It was the calendar hanging on the wall that caught her attention next. Going over to study it, she saw the names "*Llorona*" and "*El Muerto*" written on several dates. Beneath those names were two or three other names like "Dee," "Ryan," and "Kyle." Student names? she wondered.

The entries for this week—the week she was in town—were crossed out with a large red "X." Coincidence?

She was thinking not.

Pulling the calendar from the wall, she flipped through the pages for prior months. Every month, she found similar entries. On each date when an entry was made, a small black circle icon also appeared, indicating those were days when the moon was full.

She withdrew her phone again and captured images of several pages before carefully hanging the calendar back on the wall. As she stood there, her hands trembled with a mix of emotions. Was it anger or disappointment? She couldn't quite tell. One thing was certain though—there was a group of people in Las Palomas who were pretending to be ghosts. But why?

She could see teenagers orchestrating such a prank on the town and its tourists, but the trailer was school property, as, presumably, were the supplies and costumes within. All of it was too expensive for a handful of kids to afford, so they had the support of the school and whomever was footing the bill. Plus, Dane was somehow involved. How else would he have known to find the teenagers here?

She didn't like the conclusion she was forming; that there was more to these hauntings than simple teen pranks.

Feeling unsettled and unsure of what to do next, Gina locked the door behind her and began making her way back to town. Thoughts swirled in her head as she navigated the streets, wondering how she should handle this new discovery.

Chapter Nineteen

An hour later, Gina sat on a wooden bench in Town Park, her gaze fixed on the bustling playground before her. The sounds of children's laughter and shrieks of delight filled the air, a stark contrast to the turmoil brewing within her mind. Every so often, she would glance over at the graffiti artist working intently on his mural. His skilled hands moved with purpose, adding vibrant colors and intricate designs to the once plain brick wall. Normally, his artwork would have fascinated her, but at the moment, she couldn't muster up any interest in it. What she had learned that morning consumed her thoughts.

Why the charade?

The answer was simple: money. Ghost hunting enthusiasts from all over the country flocked to this small town for a chance to see a ghost. And while they were here, they spent money on food, lodging, and souvenirs. It was all about keeping customers satisfied and coming back for more. But lately, things had taken a dark turn. Did the teens think it was fun to terrorize the tourists?

Or could there be another explanation?

Dane's words from earlier rang in Gina's head. He had claimed that the real *Llorona* was behind these attacks. Could he be telling the truth? Then again, how could she trust someone who had lied about knowing of the teenagers' involvement?

Gina's thoughts came to a halt as she reached a mental stalemate. The weight of her own deceit hung heavy on her conscience as she struggled with what to believe.

To make matters worse, she was still short ten thousand dollars and they were running out of time. She couldn't help but wonder what Frankie would do if Uncle Victor didn't call him soon to say they had the money.

Images of Uncle Victor's bruised torso flashed before her eyes. She couldn't bear the thought of him enduring another brutal attack.

A sense of despair overwhelmed her as she stared off into the distance, her eyes settling on a car slowly making its way down the main street. The driver and passenger caught her attention immediately. They were not your typical ghost-hunting tourists. Their sharp features and hardened expressions made them appear dangerous, and she didn't like how they surveyed their surroundings, like they were searching for something. Or someone.

A cold sense of dread settled in her stomach as she stared at the car until it disappeared down the street.

Her hands trembled slightly as she reached for her phone and dialed Uncle Victor's number.

"I just spotted two men in town who looked like they make their living beating people up," she said anxiously as soon as he answered. "What if Frankie sent them here to find you?"

"Slow down." Uncle Victor's tone remained steady. "Just because you saw two tough-looking guys doesn't mean they're working for Frankie. It could be anyone. I mean, this town is no Disneyland. Let's be rational about this."

She thought back to what she had seen and begrudgingly admitted that maybe she had jumped to conclusions too quickly. After all, hadn't she been thinking about Frankie and his brutal ways just before spotting the two men? With a heavy sigh, she conceded, "Yeah, okay. Maybe you're right."

"I know I am," Uncle Victor replied, his voice smooth and calm like a gentle stream. "Frankie deals in big money. Ten thousand is small change to him. Don't get me wrong; he wants his money back, but I doubt he'd send anyone all the way down here to collect it."

She couldn't shake off the unease settling in her stomach, but what her uncle said made sense. Still, she wanted to be cautious. "Just keep your eyes open, okay?" She waited until he grunted his agreement before changing the subject. "Listen, I found out something important this morning. I need to tell you about it."

"Okay, I'm listening."

"Not over the phone." She didn't know if he was back at the Bed and Breakfast or still with Sylvia. Either way, she didn't want anyone overhearing their conversation. There was no telling who in the town was involved in the deceit. "Let's meet for lunch."

"Can't. I promised Sylvia I'd have lunch with her. Can it wait?"

"I suppose it will have to." Disappointment laced her tone, but Uncle Victor didn't offer to change his plans and they exchanged goodbyes.

Feeling like she was riding on a runaway train headed towards a brick wall, Gina placed a call to her bank manager in Houston.

"Hi Michael, it's Gina. How are you doing?"

"I'm well, Gina. Thank you for asking. How can I help you?" His professional tone was reassuring.

Michael had been the bank representative assigned to Gina when she had needed a loan to purchase the house she shared with Uncle Victor. He had also been a valuable resource over the years, providing guidance on how to manage her money wisely and potentially invest it for the future.

Gina took a deep breath before speaking, hoping she wouldn't have to disclose too much personal information. "Can I take out a loan, using my house as collateral?"

There was a moment of silence before Michael responded, his tone turning serious. "You make a decent income, but as you know from our previous discussions, your profession doesn't offer a steady stream of income. That makes you a high-risk borrower. If you want to come in, we can take a look at the numbers."

"Yeah, that'd be great. I'll let you know when I'm back in town." A heavy sigh escaped Gina's lips. She'd been hoping for an easy answer and while the news was not entirely unexpected, the weight of disappointment was bearing down on her. "Thanks, Michael."

She ended the call, sinking deeper into her thoughts as she wondered what other options she had if the town refused to compensate her for solving their supernatural dilemma.

She placed another quick call, this time to her good friend, Carla.

"Hey, girl," Carla answered. "How's the assignment going? What's Las Palomas like?"

"It's small," she replied.

"What's up? You sound stressed."

"I am, a little," Gina admitted. "I'll tell you about it later but right now, tell me, how's the real-estate market for sellers?"

There was a pregnant pause on the other end of the call.

"Are you selling your home?" Carla finally asked.

"Maybe," Gina admitted. "Uncle Victor—"

"Shit," Carla interrupted. "Not again." She knew all about the problems Uncle Victor's gambling had caused over the years.

"Afraid so."

Carla sighed. "Well, actually, now is a good time to sell. I have several clients who'd be interested in your house if you're serious about selling. Just give me the word."

The pressure around Gina's chest loosened ever so slightly. "Thanks, Carla. I'll be in touch."

They said their goodbyes and disconnected the call.

"Gina?"

The familiar voice broke through her thoughts and Gina turned to see Sarah Wolfe walking towards her with a warm smile on her face. Nervously, Gina returned the smile, wondering if Sarah had spoken to Dane this morning. Would she still be this friendly if she had?

"Hi." Gina tried not to let her unease show as she greeted the woman. "How are you doing today?"

"Good. I'm just running some errands. Mind if I join you?" Sarah gestured towards the empty bench seat next to her.

"No, not at all." She moved over to give Sarah room.

"What have you been up to this morning?" Sarah asked.

"Just had breakfast with my uncle at the café and then took a walk around town, enjoying the sights." Gina couldn't bring herself to tell her the truth, so she told a small lie instead, feeling like she was starting down a slippery slope. How many more lies would she have to tell before everything came crashing down? "Anyway, here I am, killing time in a park." She let out a forced laugh. "The thrilling life of a ghost whisperer, right?"

"My morning has been a wild ride," Sarah exclaimed with a laugh. "First, I whipped up enough chicken salad to feed an entire army, then I tackled the never-ending task of tidying up the house." The two women shared a knowing smile, both familiar with the endless cycle of household chores.

"I also attempted to start a Shutterfly album on the computer, but I'm afraid I might be in over my head," Sarah admitted sheepishly, rubbing her temples in frustration.

"What seemed to be the problem?" Gina asked, genuinely curious about Sarah's struggles.

"Well, I picked a theme for the album, but I couldn't figure out how to actually add the pictures. It's probably something simple that everyone else knows, but I'm not very tech-savvy," Sarah explained with a shrug. "I've only ever used computers for work and they had their own specific program."

Without thinking, Gina blurted out, "I'd be happy to help you."

Sarah's face lit up with gratitude. "That would be amazing—if you have the time? I don't want to inconvenience you."

Gina couldn't help but smile at Sarah's enthusiasm. "Actually, I don't have any plans this afternoon," she admitted.

Sarah clapped her hands excitedly. "Perfect! Have you eaten? If not, I have chicken salad for sandwiches."

Gina hesitated a moment, worried that Sarah was meeting Dane and had invited her to join them. "I don't want to intrude on any previous lunch plans you may have made," she said cautiously.

Sarah shook her head, reassuring her. "No, I dropped off chicken sandwiches at the police station for Dane and his colleagues. I was on my way back home when I saw you sitting here."

Gina's worries dissipated and she couldn't help but feel touched by Sarah's kindness. "In that case, I would love to have lunch with you," she replied with a genuine smile.

CHAPTER TWENTY

AFTER A FANTASTIC LUNCH, Gina helped Sarah sort through dozens of family pictures. Some were already in digital format but there were a few printed copies that they scanned using Sarah's all-in-one printer. Then Gina showed Sarah how to load the pictures into her album.

Gina showed Sarah how to add, delete and move pages around, how to add new backgrounds and embellishments to her project and how to resize and crop pictures, all while having more fun than she'd expected. Sarah was fun to be around and getting to see pictures of Dane growing up was priceless. She'd noticed how the ever-present smile on the young boy's face disappeared after his father died, replaced by a more serious expression. Not that he never smiled, but the smiles were less prevalent.

The pictures she'd seen of Dane's sister, Jess, showed a beautiful, spirited woman kayaking through rapids, skydiving, snowboarding and motocross racing. From the number of such pictures, Gina wondered when the girl had time to attend college.

"You have a real knack for this," Sarah observed as Gina helped her put the finishing touches on a Shutterfly page layout.

"So do you. That photo blossom you created two pages back turned out really well. I might have to steal that idea for my next album."

Sarah glanced at the time on the computer. "Oh my gosh, look at the time. Is that right? Is it almost five?"

Gina pulled out her phone to check the time. She hadn't realized it was so late. "I should probably go." Uncle Victor would expect her back at the Bed and Breakfast. "This was really fun." It surprised her now to realize how much she meant it.

"It was fun for me, too," Sarah replied. "I hate to see the day end. Why don't you stay for dinner? The roast is nearly done. I can take you back to the B&B after we eat."

"I wish I could stay. That roast smells wonderful." They had taken a break mid-afternoon so Sarah could put a roast in the oven and for the past hour, it had filled the kitchen with an aroma that made Gina's mouth water. What she wouldn't give for a home cooked meal by someone who knew what they were doing. "Uncle Victor is expecting me for dinner." After making such a big deal about talking to him in person, she didn't dare cancel on him. "In fact, I should call him to come pick me up."

Sarah sighed. "If you're sure." Then her face brightened. "You know, I have enough food for both of you, and I wouldn't mind getting to know your uncle."

Gina smiled at Sarah's persistence. "I'll ask."

"Good. I'll just go check on the roast while you make your call."

Sarah left the front room that also served as her craft room while Gina pulled out her cell phone to make the call. An unread text appeared on the screen. It was from Uncle Victor and she wondered why she hadn't heard it come in but then remembered that she'd put her phone on vibrate earlier that morning, while she was at the school, and must have forgotten to take it off.

Already expecting what was coming, she opened the message.

> *Something important came up. Can't make dinner. Talk to you tonight.*

Damn it. He knew she needed to talk to him. If he'd blown her off so he could spend more time with Sylvia, Frankie Goldstein's wrath would seem trivial compared to hers.

"Everything okay?"

Gina hadn't heard Sarah come back into the room and realized she must have been frowning.

"Yeah, everything's fine. Looks like I can stay for dinner after all."

"Wonderful. Will your uncle be joining us?"

"No. It'll just be me."

"Okay, then. I need to finish making dinner. You're welcome to watch TV in the other room."

"Is there something I can do to help you in the kitchen?"

Sarah smiled. "I was hoping you'd ask. I'll put you to work making the rolls while I peel potatoes and start the salad."

"That sounds like a lot of food. I hope you're not going to all that trouble just for me."

Sarah waved her concern aside as she turned to lead them to the kitchen. "No. I love to cook almost as much as I love to eat, and leftovers never go to waste around here."

The women set to work in the kitchen, with Gina following Sarah's directions. Soon, the smell of rolls baking in the oven mingled with the savory scent of the roast beef. Gina's mouth watered.

"Is there something else I can do?" Gina asked.

Sarah, who had just started the salad, spared a quick glance at the kitchen clock. "Would you mind setting the table while I clean up some of these pots and pans?"

"Sure. Just tell me where you keep the plates."

"Here, I'll get them." Sarah walked over to a cabinet and pulled out the plates. "This should do it," she said, handing them to Gina. "We'll eat in the formal dining room."

"Okay."

Gina headed into the front room, her thoughts turning to Uncle Victor. What had come up that was so important for him to cancel?

Probably sex with Sylvia, she thought derisively. That thought was disturbing.

When she realized Sarah had given her three plates, she carried the third one back into the kitchen.

"I think you gave me one too many," she told Sarah.

"No, three is correct." She took the plate and, carrying it back into the dining room, set it on the table, leaving Gina feeling confused.

Then, from outside came the rumble of a truck's engine.

Please be the neighbor's truck.

The engine shut off and moments later, she heard a truck door slam closed. The clatter of pots and pans from the kitchen faded as every one of Gina's senses focused on the noises coming from outside.

When she heard the thumping of boot steps on the front porch, she only had time enough to wish the ground would swallow her whole before the front door opened and Dane stepped into the foyer.

Despite her anger, her heart gave a brief flutter at the sight of his tall, muscled frame. When he saw her, he stopped short, his eyes going wide. He was obviously just as surprised to see her as she was to see him.

Sarah stepped into the room before either of them recovered from their shock.

"Dane, honey. Right on time. Dinner is ready."

Twenty minutes later, sitting across from Dane at the dining table, Gina was sure this would be the longest, most excruciating meal she'd ever suffered through. She and Dane had exchanged only a few painfully polite words when he'd come back from washing his hands, but then Sarah had walked in with their salads, and they'd taken their seats. If Sarah noticed they weren't speaking to one another, she didn't comment on it. Instead, she carried the burden of conversation with finesse, asking Dane about his day and then telling him about the afternoon she'd spent with Gina.

"You two sit here while I bring out dinner," Sarah said when they'd finished their salads. "I hope you'll forgive me, but I waited to mash the potatoes. I hate cold mashed potatoes, don't you? This will only take a couple of minutes."

Pushing away from the table, she gathered up their salad plates.

"Would you like some help?" Gina asked, praying Sarah would accept her offer and not leave her alone with Dane. Throughout the salad, Gina's thoughts had dwelled on the memory of seeing him at the school, which only renewed her anger.

Sarah waved her offer aside. "No. I'm sure you and Dane can find something to talk about while I'm gone."

Well, hell.

Gina watched her disappear and then felt Dane's gaze on her. When she turned to meet it, he gave her a polite smile. "It sounds like you and Mom had a pleasant afternoon together."

"We did," she said. "I enjoy your mother's company." She paused, considering the wisdom of asking what was uppermost in her mind. She opted for a round-about approach. "How was your day?"

"Pretty routine," he said slowly.

They fell silent as they listened to the whirring of the mixer at work in the kitchen.

"Any update on those teens from last night?" She kept her tone deceptively light; she could have been asking him about the weather. "I still wonder what they were doing at the river dressed that way."

Dane picked up his glass of iced tea and took a long drink.

Buying time to think about how to answer, she surmised.

"I'm sure it was just a prank." His tone was clipped; a clear signal he didn't want to talk about it.

"All right, that should do it." Sarah's voice floated to them from the kitchen, signaling she had finished the potatoes.

Screw the round-about approach.

"Is that what they told you when you talked to them this morning at the school?" Gina asked him in a hushed voice. "That it was just a prank?"

His surprised expression was both priceless and satisfying. He didn't have time to respond because Sarah walked in at that moment carrying a platter of sliced roast beef in one hand and a bowl of freshly mashed potatoes in the other.

Gina suspected he wouldn't want to continue this conversation in front of his mother, so she wasn't surprised when he glowered at her but remained silent.

They started passing the food around and when Gina handed the bowl of mashed potatoes to Dane, their gazes locked momentarily; his was hard to interpret, but she knew her own was accusatory.

The food smelled exquisite, but Gina could have been chewing cardboard for all she noticed. Her full attention was on Dane, though she refused to look directly at him or meet his gaze.

"Oh, dear," Sarah muttered several minutes later, her gaze moving over the table. "I forgot the rolls. Excuse me for one second."

Dane and Gina watched her disappear into the kitchen before turning to face one another.

Dane picked up the conversation where they left off. "How do you know I was at the school this morning?" His whisper sounded more like a growl. "Were you following me?"

"Don't flatter yourself." He cocked an eyebrow at that. "I was following them."

Sarah reappeared with the rolls, and the two fell silent again. Refusing to meet Dane's gaze, Gina turned her attention back to Sarah, who was soon regaling her with stories about her bunco group, not that Gina was paying close attention. Why couldn't Dane be honest with her?

A small, more rational, voice in her head reminded her she was guilty of her own deception.

That's just different.

So absorbed in her thoughts, she was slow to notice when Sarah suddenly stopped talking. Curious about what had drawn the woman's attention, Gina followed her gaze and saw Dane shoving half a roll into his already full mouth.

"Dane, honey, please," Sarah admonished him. "What's got into you? Slow down and chew your food before you swallow it."

"Did you make more rolls?" He mumbled around a mouthful of bread.

Gina glanced at the basket in some surprise. A second ago, when she'd reached into the basket to grab a roll, her first, there had still been three or four left. Now, the basket was empty.

"Lucky for me and Gina, I put a fresh batch in to cook before I brought the food in. They should be about done. I'll go check on them."

She folded her napkin, laying it on the table beside her plate, and rose. Picking up the empty basket, she gave Dane a curious look before leaving the room.

Dane watched her go and, as soon as she disappeared through the doorway, turned to Gina. She saw him forcefully swallow the food in his mouth so he could speak.

"What do you mean, you were following them?" He hissed at her.

"Three more minutes," Sarah hollered from the kitchen.

Gina kept her voice to a loud whisper. "I spotted them when I was at Town Park this morning, so I followed them. Turns out they went to the high school. As soon as they went into that building by the field house, I was going to call you and let you know I'd found them. Imagine my surprise when you pulled into the parking lot before I could place my call. And then, you went into the same building after them. It's almost like you'd planned to meet them there."

"I can explain that," he blurted.

"Oh, I'm sure you can, but I'm more interested in hearing you explain the contents of that building the four of you disappeared into."

She could tell that surprised him. "What do you mean?"

"You know, the costumes and the glow-in-the-dark paint. I found the calendar to be especially interesting, what with the names and all."

"How'd you get in? I locked the door."

"Are you sure?" She gave him her best innocent look.

His expression was impossible to read. Any reply he might have made was cut off when Sarah walked back into the dining room carrying the basket of fresh rolls. She purposely set them on the table between her and Gina.

"As I was saying," Sarah continued, as if she'd never left the table. "When Nita won the money, you should have seen Peg's face. I thought—"

"Mom, do you have more tea made up?" Dane held up his glass to show it was empty.

If Sarah was perturbed, she didn't show it, but her tone sounded strained when she spoke. "No, but I can make some more."

Dane set his empty glass on the table as she left the room and then pinned Gina beneath his steely gaze. "Breaking and entering is a crime. I could arrest you."

She shrugged again. "You could try. Without proof, I doubt the charges would stick. But arresting me shouldn't be your biggest concern. I figured out what you're doing and I've a good mind to go to the press with it. I can see the headlines now." She used her fingers to make air quotes. "Small town fakes ghost hauntings," she quipped, letting her hands fall back to the table. "This is exactly the kind of scam reporters like to expose."

"It would ruin the town if that got out, but I don't think you'll tell anyone."

"And why is that? You think you can stop me? Maybe make me disappear? My uncle knows I'm here. Are you going to make him disappear, too?"

That seemed to surprise him and some of the fight went out of him. "Jesus, Gina, is that what you think? Really? That I'd be capable of something like that? I would never hurt you. I thought there was something special between us. I'd hoped you thought so, too."

A horrifying thought hit her. "Is that why you danced with me the other night? And spent all that time with me? Having lunch. Seeing the sites. Introducing me to your mother?" She had to swallow the sudden lump in her throat. "You wanted me to fall for you, so even if I learned the secret, I wouldn't tell anyone?"

"What? No, of course not. It's not like that."

She wasn't listening. Once she'd voiced the suspicion, she couldn't let it go. As the possibility morphed into probability, Gina felt a sharp, stabbing pain that made it hard to breathe. "Almost kissing me was a nice touch," she commented with derision. "Very believable. I completely fell for it." She looked away, no longer able to meet his gaze. "Aren't I the pathetic one?" This last was said more to herself than to Dane.

The tapping of Sarah's heels told her the woman was returning and suddenly Gina couldn't face her; couldn't face him.

Quickly laying her napkin down, she pushed away from the table and rushed to the front door, nearly blinded by sudden tears. She didn't know whether those tears were from anger or hurt. At the moment, she didn't care. She only knew that she needed to get away.

She was out the door and halfway across the front yard when an iron grip on her upper arm pulled her to a stop.

"Gina, damn it. Wait. Please." She wrenched her arm from Dane's grasp and whirled around to face him, ready for a fight. He put up both hands, palms out, in a gesture of surrender. "I only want to talk."

"I don't feel like talking," she spat, angrily wiping a tear from her eye.

"Good, because I think you've said enough. It's my turn to talk, and I'd appreciate it if you'd listen. What's going on with those teens and what you found in that building—that's not my secret alone to share—and it has nothing to do with why we hired you."

"But—"

He held a hand up to stop her. "Still my turn to talk. Now that you know, I'll explain everything to you, but please, not out here. Let's go back inside and finish our meal. Mom's probably freaking out, wondering what I did to upset you."

Gina felt bad about having walked out on Sarah, but wasn't sure she was ready to go back inside. Dane must have sensed her reluctance.

"It's okay. Once we explain it to Mom, she'll understand."

He waited for her to nod her agreement.

"Okay, good. But first, I want to set the record straight. With a town full of tourists and an attempted child snatching case to deal with, as the town's acting police chief, the last thing I have time for is babysitting out-of-town guests. Besides, Sylvia is your official town liaison, not me. Her job is also not to keep an eye on you. It's seeing to it that you're comfortable at Ruby Mae's, answering questions you may have about *Llorona* or the assignment and ensuring you have what you need to complete the assignment. It's also her job to notify us when *Llorona* shows up."

He shook his head when she opened her mouth to ask a question. "Later. I promise to answer your questions, but first," he stepped closer and, using the side of his forefinger, gently lifted her chin until he could look into her eyes. "The reason I danced with you and spent so much time with you is because I wanted to. From the moment I met you, I felt this instant connection to you. I don't know. Maybe that's crazy sounding, but it's the truth. I knew you wouldn't be here long, and I wanted to see where this thing between us might lead." He sighed and let his hand fall back to his side. "I was hoping you felt the same way." He looked away then and gestured toward the house. "Shall we go back?"

She had a decision to make and no time to think about it. Trust Dane. Believe what he'd told her—all of it. Or walk away and protect herself from the hurt of learning this was all part of a bigger lie.

She wasn't aware of weighing the pros and cons; wasn't aware that she'd made a conscious decision. Instead, Gina drew in a deep breath and let it out slowly, then nodded. "Okay."

He gave her a tentative smile of appreciation. They started back toward the house, walking together. When they reached the front door, Dane stopped before opening the door.

"There is one more thing."

She turned to him, curious.

"When I started to kiss you the other night? That was because I *wanted* to kiss you; more than anything." He paused, holding her gaze. "I still want to."

Before she had a chance to respond, he opened the front door.

Chapter Twenty-One

Like two guilty kids, they stopped just inside the foyer, while Sarah scrutinized them from her seat at the head of the table, a mug of coffee in her hands.

The silence seemed interminable to Gina.

"I trust the two of you have worked things out?" Sarah finally asked. "I realize it's none of my business but since you've had me hopping up and down like a deranged rabbit for the past hour, I feel I'm entitled to some explanation." Her tone was serious, but she didn't sound angry with them.

Gina was at a loss for words. She felt horrible. "I'm so sorry, Sarah," she began. "I..."

What could she say?

Unlike her, Dane seemed unfazed.

"I told you what happened to Gina and her uncle last night."

Wait—Sarah knew? That news surprised Gina, but she remained silent and let him continue.

"This morning, Gina spotted the teens at the café and followed them so she could tell me where to find them." Here he grimaced. "Unfortunately, they were headed to the Events building to meet with me. I'd called Dylan earlier and asked him to find out who they were and tell them to meet me there. After we left the school, Gina went inside the building and looked around." He frowned down at her. "I'd still like to know how you got in, because I know I locked that door."

She didn't think it mattered now, so told him the truth. "I used a credit card to jimmy the lock."

A surprised laugh burst from him and a gleam shone in his eyes. "I'm going to have to keep my eye on you."

"The Town Council will need to be told," Sarah said, reminding them of the seriousness of what had happened. "But I suppose it can wait until tomorrow, don't you, Dane?"

"Yes, it can definitely wait. First, Gina and I have things to discuss."

"I'm sure the two of you will work things out," Sarah replied confidently. "But you can talk later. Right now, it's time for dessert. I spent hours this morning making this pie. It would be a shame to waste it."

"Sarah, I can't remember the last time I had pecan pie that good," Gina said later, checking her plate to see if she'd left any crumbs. "I can't believe it's homemade."

"Thank you, but really, it was nothing," Sarah said. Her tone, on the other hand, said she'd appreciated the compliment.

Seeing that everyone was finished, Gina stood and gathered the empty plates.

"Here, let me take those," Sarah said, also getting up from the table and reaching for the plates. "Why don't you two go sit in the family room? I'll clean up."

"Oh, no, you don't," Gina replied, holding the plates out of Sarah's reach. "You cooked dinner, so let us clean up."

"Nonsense," Sarah waved her suggestion aside. "You're our guest. We don't let guests do the dishes."

"I'd like to think I was more in the friend of the family category," Gina objected.

Sarah looked momentarily horror-struck. "Yes, of course you are."

Gina smiled. "Then, as your friend, I insist on helping because that's what friends do."

Dane stood and laid a hand on his mother's shoulder. "Go into the other room, Mom, and relax. We've got this."

Sarah looked from Dane to Gina and then, perhaps realizing she'd lost the fight, smiled her thanks. "I appreciate it. You can just rinse the dishes and put them in the sink. I'll load the dishwasher later."

"Yeah, fell for that one before," Dane scoffed and then, in a falsetto voice, said, "Really, Dane. How hard is it to place the dishes in the dishwasher after you've rinsed them off?" His voice went back to normal. "Go! Sit down. This won't take long."

As Sarah capitulated and headed into the living room, Dane and Gina carried the dinner dishes into the kitchen and set them on the counter by the sink. Sarah must have washed pots and pans as she'd used them because none were sitting on the stove and only one was soaking in the sink.

Dane opened the dishwasher and Gina saw it was full.

"Are they clean?" she asked.

Dane pulled out the lower rack and, after plucking out a pot, studied it. "They look clean, but that doesn't mean anything. Mom washes the dishes before putting them into the dishwasher. I'd better ask."

Gina started scraping the small amounts of food left on the plates into the trash while Dane went to find his mother. He was back a minute later.

"Clean," he announced.

"Why don't you put away the clean dishes while I rinse off the dirty ones?"

"Sounds like a plan." He looked at the pot in his hand, then raised his voice and called out. "Hey, Mom. Where do you keep your pots and pans?"

"No, Sarah. Sit back down," Gina shouted, not knowing whether to laugh or be irritated. "We've got this." She turned to Dane. "Seriously?"

"What?" He seemed perplexed.

"Are you telling me you have never helped her set the table or put the dishes away?"

"You've met my mom. The kitchen is her private domain. She likes to do that herself. I'm surprised she gave in so easily tonight—though I have my suspicions why." At Gina's raised eyebrow, he explained. "She likes the idea of us spending domestic time together. She's got a bit of matchmaker in her." He paused as he opened a cabinet, checked the contents, and then closed the door. "You know this entire dinner was a setup, right?"

"What? No. I ran into your mom this morning at the park, quite by accident."

He shook his head in sympathy. "I don't think so. You think she made that pecan pie this morning so she could enjoy it alone? No. I called her this morning and mentioned that you were upset with me. She insisted I come over tonight for dinner; precisely at six." He opened up a cabinet door and then closed it when it was obvious the pots didn't go there. "If she hadn't run into you in town, she would have called you. I guarantee it."

"Well, when you put it like that."

"Don't get me wrong. I'm glad she went to the trouble."

Gina smiled. "Me, too." They still needed to talk about the elephant in the room, but she was feeling like everything would turn out all right. She pointed to a lower cabinet by the stove. "Try looking in there."

Walking over, he pulled open the cabinet door and looked inside. "What do you know?" He placed the pot inside, shut the door and returned to the dishwasher. "How'd you know that's where it went?"

"Lucky guess." She didn't see any reason to explain kitchen logic to him.

He returned to the dishwasher and pulled out several plates. Then, holding the stack, he surveyed the kitchen.

Gina pointed to the upper cabinet behind him, from which Sarah had taken the plates earlier. "There."

"Maybe we should switch?" He suggested, putting the plates away. "I'll clean off the dirty dishes while you put the clean ones away."

They switched and worked in companionable silence while the show Sarah watched on the television provided background noise. Fifteen minutes later, the clean dishes had been put away, the dirty dishes had been loaded into the dishwasher, the counters had all been wiped down and the few dishes that hadn't fit into the dishwasher had been washed by hand, dried and put away.

Gina looked around the kitchen, filled with a sense of contentment that had nothing to do with the housework. She'd enjoyed spending time with Dane. It was that simple.

They joined Sarah in the family room, where she was watching television. She sat at one end of the couch, so Gina sat at the opposite end, leaving the recliner for Dane.

"Oh, no, honey, you can't sit there," Sarah said when he moved toward it. "That thing is broken."

Dane eyed the offending recliner speculatively. "Since when?"

"Since the other day, when a screw or something fell out of it." She patted the narrow space on the couch beside her. "You can look at it this weekend, but for now, sit here with us. There's plenty of room."

Gina suspected this was another ploy in Sarah's matchmaking attempt because the "broken" recliner had seemed solid enough when she'd sat in it earlier that afternoon while Sarah had gone to dig old photos out of her bedroom closet. Gina had already returned to the craft room by the time Sarah returned.

Dane, she was glad to see, made no move to argue with his mother and started for the couch.

"Before you sit down, would you mind turning off the kitchen light? It's throwing a nasty glare on the TV screen."

"Won't it be too dark to see?" he asked.

"You can leave the light on over the sink."

Dane complied with his mother's request and then joined them on the couch. The dimly lit room definitely had a cozier feel; Gina had to give Sarah props for setting the mood.

"What are we watching?" Dane asked his mother.

"Oh, this is a classic," she replied. "Gina, have you seen Friday the 13th?"

A scary movie? *Good move, Sarah.* "No, I don't believe I have."

"You'll enjoy this one," she replied.

"Mom, maybe Gina doesn't like scary movies."

No, Gina definitely did not like scary movies, so she lied. "This is fine."

"Hush, you two. A good part is coming up."

Dane leaned close to Gina and whispered, "It's really not that scary."

Maybe for him. She was tense just watching a couple of teenagers on the screen dash through the rain. A few minutes later, when an arrow suddenly shot up through the bed to stab a young Kevin Bacon in the throat, Gina jumped and grabbed Dane's arm.

He chuckled at her reaction and, gently extracting his wrist from her death grip, draped his arm across her shoulders and pulled her closer.

She not only felt much safer, but forgot about the movie completely as every thought now centered on the feeling of being pressed against such a solid, male body. The woodsy scent of his cologne was heady, and she breathed it in, trying to create an olfactory memory so she'd never forget this moment.

She glanced up at him and found him already watching her. Their gazes locked and she couldn't look away; didn't want to look away. The smile on his face faded as his gaze turned smoldering. Sarah and the rest of the room faded from existence; it was only the two of them.

Gina's breathing sped up. She wanted Dane to kiss her so badly she felt sure he could see the yearning written on her face. Almost imperceptibly, his head dipped toward hers.

The sound of Sarah clearing her throat shattered the moment. Before Gina even had time to feel embarrassed, Sarah stood and feigned a yawn.

"I'm sorry, you two. I'm so tired, I don't think I can stay awake any longer—even to watch Jason wreaking havoc at the campground. No, no, don't get up. Stay and watch the rest of the movie. Gina, it was wonderful seeing you again. Let's plan to do this again, shall we?" She didn't wait for an answer but headed for the entrance to the hallway. "Dane, be sure to lock up when you leave."

If exiting a room was an Olympic speed event, Sarah could have headed up the US team. One moment, she was wishing them goodnight and the next, she had disappeared down the hall and into her bedroom.

"Subtle, she's not," Dane said softly, lowering his head to hers. "Now, where were we? Oh yeah, I remember."

Then he kissed her. There was no hesitancy this time. He pressed her against the back of the couch and took possession of her lips; her mind; her very soul. She gave herself up completely to the moment; lost in a myriad of sensations. Dane's lips were against hers; his solid body pressed against hers.

The sound of a door opening broke the moment, and they pulled apart just as his mother walked back into the room.

"I forgot to take my pills," she explained apologetically, heading for the kitchen.

Gina heard items being moved around on a shelf, followed by the sound of the water running. When Sarah was done, she walked past them, pointing at the television.

"Oh, that's a good part."

Then she disappeared down the hallway. Neither Gina nor Dane said anything until they heard her bedroom door closing. Then they exchanged looks and Gina giggled.

Dane, whose arm was still around Gina's shoulder, gave her a squeeze.

"Maybe here is not the best place for this."

Gina nodded in agreement. If he kissed her again, there's no telling where it might lead and she didn't think she'd care if his mother heard them or not.

"What do you say we get out of here?" Dane asked.

"Sounds good," she agreed, hoping the evening wasn't over, but then wondering just how far she wanted to let things go. She wasn't ready to say goodnight, but what if he asked her to spend the night with him? A thrill ran through her, immediately squelched by the small voice in her head that reminded her they still needed to talk, and she had not yet decided whether to tell Dane the truth about herself.

He used the remote to turn off the television. Then, taking her by the hand, he pulled her to her feet. He didn't let go as he walked around the living room, flipping off the lights and checking to make sure the back door was locked. Gina liked that he was so protective of his mother's safety. As they headed for the front door, they paused in the hallway leading to the bedrooms.

"Mom, we're heading out." He didn't speak very loud and even if his mother hadn't fallen asleep, Gina wasn't sure his voice would carry that far.

She needn't have worried.

"You kids have a good night," Sarah hollered from her bedroom.

"Come lock the deadbolt after we leave," Dane called back. "Love you."

"Thank you again for dinner, Sarah," Gina called out, not wanting to leave without making sure Sarah knew she'd appreciated it. "And for everything else," she added.

Outside, Dane led her to his truck and opened the door for her while she climbed in.

"Does she really enjoy watching those scary movies?" Gina asked once Dane was sitting behind the wheel.

"Yeah, crazy, right? Although, I don't think her movie choice tonight had anything to do with her appreciation for a cult classic."

Gina smiled. "So, where are we going?"

He sighed and then, as if he'd read her mind earlier, said, "As much as I'd like to take you to my place and continue what we started inside, we probably need to talk. Maybe over a drink?"

"Sounds good to me."

"Great. I know just the place."

CHAPTER TWENTY-TWO

AFTER PARKING HIS TRUCK next to several others in the middle of an empty lot on the outskirts of town, Dane turned to Gina and said, "I think you'll like this place." She stepped out of the truck, looking around with a sense of unease. She had thought they were going to a restaurant or bar for drinks and conversation, but despite the number of cars suggesting otherwise, there didn't seem to be any such place nearby.

For a moment, Gina's worried mind entertained the thought of the town gathering to decide her fate after learning she could be a threat. Lynchings were still against the law, right?

Then Dane reached for her hand and smiled down at her, dispelling those fears.

Most of them, anyway.

When they walked towards an abandoned building, Gina couldn't help but feel uneasy. She recognized this two-story brick building from her frequent drives back and forth from the Bed and Breakfast. In the daylight, it showed signs of neglect—aged bricks and black-painted windows preventing any curious onlookers from peeking inside. And the metal sign reading "Condemned" nailed to the front door only added to its foreboding appearance.

So when Dane pulled open the door and gestured for her to enter, Gina hesitated. "What is this place?"

"Contrary to what you discovered this morning," he emphasized each word, "this is the town's best-kept secret."

As Gina stepped through the door, she couldn't help but feel like she was crossing into a different world. The short foyer led to another closed door, teasing her with the faint sound of music drifting from inside. Her curiosity piqued, she followed Dane as he opened the inner door and revealed a bustling room filled with people and noise.

Her eyes widened in amazement as she took in the scene before her. The room had the rustic charm of an old west saloon, with a long wooden bar running along one wall and cozy booths lining the other. Wooden tables and chairs of varying sizes filled the remaining space, while in the back, three pool tables were in use. To the left of them, two groups were throwing darts against the wall and to the right, a lively game of cornhole was in progress.

Moving further into the room, Gina was taken with other details about the space: the sawdust and peanut shells covering the worn wooden floor and the old west knick-knacks such as spurs, bridles, cattle brands, and a saddle mounted on the walls.

Servers hurried between tables, balancing trays of food and drinks as they took orders from eager customers while a blend of country and rock music blared from speakers. Gina watched one server disappear through a side door and then reappear moments later with a tray full of steaming plates.

Her mind reeled at the thought that none of this bustling bar and grill could be seen from the outside.

"Do tourists even know about this place?" Gina asked incredulously.

"No," Dane replied with a smirk. "This is our little secret spot where we can escape from all the tourists."

She thought the business was missing out on an opportunity to make additional money, but then again, judging from the number of patrons in the bar, it seemed to do well enough.

Dane's hand on her arm interrupted her thoughts, and she let him steer her towards a secluded booth in the back of the bar. A small candle and a vase of wildflowers adorned the wooden table, adding a touch of charm to the otherwise simple setting.

As soon as they were settled, a friendly server appeared at their table. "Hey, Dane. How's it going?" Her smile was warm and welcoming. "What can I get you folks tonight?"

"Hey, Mindy," Dane greeted her. "I'll have whatever's on draft. What would you like?" he asked, looking at Gina.

She ordered a margarita on the rocks with salt and after Mindy left, they exchanged pleasantries while they waited for their drinks, both avoiding the inevitable conversation that loomed ahead of them.

Their drinks arrived in frosty glasses, accompanied by a basket of peanuts still in their shells. Gina took a long sip of her margarita, feeling the cool liquid calm her nerves. She knew she would need every ounce of courage to get through this conversation.

Finally, Gina broke the silence. "So," she began slowly, drawing out the word. "Why does the town have teenagers pretending to be ghosts?"

Dane's expression was serious as he turned to face her. "Jumping right to the heart of the matter?" he asked, his voice low and measured. He let out a sigh before continuing. "Let me see if I can explain. Las Palomas has a long history, dating back to the 1800s." As he spoke, his eyes grew distant, as if he could see the events in his mind's eye.

"In 1850, there was a notorious rustler by the name of Vidal who made the fatal mistake of stealing a horse belonging to Texas Ranger "Big Foot" Wallace's friend and fellow Ranger, Creed Taylor. So, Wallace did what any Ranger would do—he took justice into his own hands." A grim smile crossed his face. "Legend has it that Wallace cut off Vidal's head and secured the headless body to the saddle of his horse and attached his head with a piece of latigo to his saddle horn." His hands mimicked the actions as he spoke, cutting off an invisible head and tying it to an imaginary saddle. "He then sent the horse racing across the pasture as a warning to other horse thieves. A short time later, on nights of the full moon, people started seeing a headless horseman riding across the open pasture of what is now the Double R Ranch. They called him *El Muerto*."

Dane paused for dramatic effect, taking a sip of his beer before continuing.

"Not long after that," Dane continued, his voice dropping even lower. "A beautiful, young Mexican woman fell in love with a handsome man and, in the years after they married, they had two sons. The young woman worked hard to make sure they had a happy home, but time took its toll, robbing her of youth and beauty. Her husband seemed to lose interest in her and gave all his affection to his sons—and other women. One evening, as the wife walked along the banks of the river with her two sons, her husband drove by in a carriage with an exquisite woman by his side. He stopped long enough to greet his sons, but completely ignored his wife. This filled the wife with such jealousy and resentment toward her children that she fell into a terrible rage. Taking her two young sons, she threw them into the river. Only as they disappeared downstream did she realize what she'd done. Her cries of anguish and despair filled the night as she raced along the bank, searching the water for signs of her children. For endless days and nights, she searched, never stopping for food or drink; never finding her children. Eventually, she collapsed beside the river and died, but here in Las Palomas, her spirit continues to search."

"*Llorona*," Gina said, remembering the legend she'd heard growing up.

Dane nodded. "Yes, and those two weren't the only ghosts being seen in Las Palomas," Dane said, his tone now more matter-of-fact. "It soon became apparent that this town is not like any other. Whether it's because of ley lines, like the witches claim, or some other reason, Las Palomas has an unusual number of ghost sightings."

He took another drink of his beer, and Gina used the time to quiet her racing heart. Ghost stories had always fascinated her, but to hear there were actual ghosts in this town was both thrilling and unnerving.

"Ghost hunting has become increasingly popular thanks to television," he continued, "but people have been coming to Las Palomas for decades hoping to glimpse these spirits. However, seeing an actual ghost is hit or miss. Sometimes they appear, and sometimes they don't. So recently, the town council started its understudy program."

"Understudy?" Gina echoed, trying to wrap her head around it all.

Dane's smile was warm and inviting. "That's how we think of it," he said with a small chuckle. "When the ghosts aren't able to make an appearance, we fill in for them. That's the reason for the vibrant costumes and paints you found. The calendars show which performer is playing understudy for each ghost. We only do it when the moon is full," he explained, giving a nonchalant shrug. "Mostly because we need the moonlight to make the glow-in-the-dark paint, you know, glow. And the understudy only goes on if the real ghost doesn't show up, which only happens occasionally. Because that's the thing about Las Palomas. It's actually haunted." Dane gestured around at their surroundings with a wry smile. "Las Palomas may be off the beaten path, but we still attract visitors who are seeking a paranormal experience."

Gina furrowed her brow, feeling uncertain about everything she was hearing. "So those teenagers..."

Dane nodded solemnly. "Sadly, most of our understudies are high school students eager for some spooky fun. However, they weren't supposed to be out there last night.

The town council put a moratorium on any impersonations while you're here, because our problem with *Llorona* is legitimate." His expression turned serious as he continued. "The actual ghost has been terrorizing visitors at the RV park, and we need to make her stop. That's why we hired you—to communicate with her and find out why she's behaving this way."

Gina nodded, which Dane seemed to take as understanding. Instead, shock was keeping her from speaking. The ghosts in Las Palomas might be legitimate, but she was not. Should she tell Dane the truth now?

No, not yet. She needed to talk to Uncle Victor first and come up with a plan.

"I'll take you out there tonight," he offered with a friendly smile. "Or if you prefer, tomorrow night. Then you can see for yourself what we're dealing with."

"Maybe tomorrow night," she quickly suggested.

The sound of a deep, gravelly voice calling out Dane's name echoed through the bar, drawing their attention to the back of the room. A tall, lean man around Dane's age stood confidently at a pool table, his muscular arms effortlessly holding a cue upright as he chalked the tip. He flashed them a charming smile and waved them over. At the other end of the table, another man was carefully racking balls for the next game.

"I think we've been invited for a game of pool," Dane remarked. "We don't have to accept."

Gina smiled. "No, it sounds like fun."

Dane's eyebrows raised in surprise. "Alright then, shall we?"

She nodded eagerly. "Lead the way."

With their drinks in hand, they made their way towards the back of the room. His friends were standing beside one of the pool tables, waiting for them.

"Gina, this is Chad Lucero and Steve Guilbert," Dane introduced them with a sweeping gesture of his hand. "Both fellow officers and two of my closest friends." He placed a reassuring hand on her lower back. "And this is Gina Castillo."

She smiled warmly and shook each man's hand. "It's a pleasure to meet you both."

"I see now why Dane's been keeping you all to himself," Chad said. "If you get tired of this guy, give me a call."

"Ignore him," Dane said.

"Do you know how to play?" Steve asked, raising his cue stick by way of explanation.

"I do," Gina replied confidently.

"Excellent," he nodded approvingly. "You can set your drinks down over there." He pointed to a pub table off to the side where an open bottle of beer and what looked like a glass of Coke already sat.

"Here, let me take that," Dane offered, reaching for her glass. She took one last sip of her tequila-lime drink before handing it over.

"You must be special," Chad said as Dane walked away.

"Why is that?" she asked, curious.

"I can't remember the last time Dane's been on a date." His gaze grew sharp, and she could practically hear his unspoken message: don't mess with my friend.

Appreciating his loyalty to Dane, she simply said, "I think he's a good guy."

Apparently satisfied with her answer, Chad passed her his cue stick. "Take this. Feldman hasn't replaced the sticks probably since the place first opened, so a lot of them are warped. This is one of the better ones."

"Thanks." She accepted it gratefully, relieved when Dane rejoined the group.

As they all gathered around the pool table, Dane picked up two cue sticks and handed one to Chad. "What're we playing?" he asked as they stepped to the side of the table.

"Eight ball," Steve replied, lifting the frame off the racked balls. "We'll let you break."

Dane turned to her with a teasing glint in his eye. "You want to break?"

She shook her head with a laugh. "That's okay. You do it."

Dane took his shot, and the balls broke apart in a satisfying spread, but none fell into a pocket. Steve went next and expertly sank the "2" ball, but his follow-up shot missed and bounced off the rail.

It was finally her turn.

Walking around the table, she studied the pattern of balls closely.

Dane's voice was warm and inviting as he offered, "I could show you how to hit the ball if you're not sure."

Gina couldn't help but consider his offer for a moment. The thought of his muscular arms guiding her through a shot was tempting, but then she noticed the smirks on the other men's faces. It amused her that they assumed she didn't know how to play.

"Thanks, but I think I've got it figured out. You just hit the white ball into one of the others, so it rolls into a pocket, right? Does it matter which ball I hit?"

"Since Steve hit in a solid, we want to only aim for the stripes," Dane explained.

Gina nodded confidently. "Got it."

While he spoke, she studied the table with a determined focus, just like Uncle Victor and his friends had taught her. She visualized her shot until she found the perfect angle. Bending over the table, she ran her fingers along the smooth wood of her cue stick, getting a feel for its weight and balance.

With precision and skill, Gina sent the "11" ball plunging into the corner pocket, exactly where she had intended. In her mind, she was back in Uncle Victor's favorite bar, surrounded by the usual crowd of hustlers.

Moving around the table gracefully, Gina lined up her next shot. Flicking her wrist just right, she added a bit of English to the cue ball's spin and watched as it effortlessly sank the "15". The men stood in stunned silence, their expressions slowly morphing into surprise.

Gina confidently sank a third ball before intentionally missing a shot. Back when she played with Uncle Victor, they would bet money on games to cover their rent and expenses. But tonight, she was simply playing for fun.

Dane let out an awestruck exclamation as she stepped back to join him. "I feel a little silly now, having offered to help you," he admitted. "Where on earth did you learn how to play like that?"

"Uncle Victor wasn't exactly prepared to become a parent after my mother died," she explained. Memories came flooding back, of late nights spent in seedy pool halls with men whose names sounded like they belonged in a mob movie. "It never occurred to him that a pool hall wasn't the place you take an under-aged teen. I learned how to play from guys with names like Eight-ball Eddie and Rail Runner Ronnie."

She watched his expression and then chuckled. "Okay, those weren't their real names, but they could have been. When it came to playing pool, they were excellent instructors."

She braced herself for judgment, but Dane only nodded and grinned. "Chad, you're up bro'. Try not to embarrass yourself." He turned to her with a playful smile and winked. She couldn't help but relax and smile back.

It turned out that Chad was no slouch at pool either, effortlessly sinking four balls into pockets during his turn. When it was Dane's turn again, he made up for his mediocre break by expertly sinking the remaining stripes. And then, he smoothly sank the 8-ball in the exact pocket he had called. Game over.

They played another game, and this time, Chad and Steve emerged victorious. With Steve needing to leave and others waiting to play, Chad, Dane and Gina found an open table and ordered another round of drinks.

No sooner had their drinks arrived than a man and woman, appearing to be in their late twenties, came over.

"You have room for two more?" the man asked.

"Hey, buddy. Of course," Dane exclaimed, rising from his chair, as Chad had, to shake hands with the newcomer. To Gina, he looked like the *Desperado* version of Antonio Banderas, exuding an air of rugged charm and confidence. His physique was lean and muscular, his dark hair swept back and tied in a ponytail. Each man turned to the woman and gave her a warm hug.

"Gina, this is Diego and Elise Juarez," Dane introduced them. "They are the proud owners and operators of the Double R Ranch." He gestured towards Gina with a smile. "I'd like you to meet Gina Castillo. She's here to help us with *Llorona*."

"Oh, right," Elise exclaimed, sounding friendly. "You're the ghost whisperer." Gina braced herself for ridicule or condescension, but was pleasantly surprised when none came. "We're so glad you're here."

Elise was tall and slender, with sun-kissed skin and blonde hair pulled back into a ponytail. Her beauty was natural and effortless, with no makeup or flashy accessories. Despite wanting to dislike her for being perfect, Gina couldn't help but feel drawn to her warm demeanor and genuine smile. She instantly liked her.

Diego pulled out a nearby chair for Elise to sit in before catching the attention of a passing server.

"What would you like?" he asked his wife.

After casting a glance at Gina's margarita, Elise replied with a smile. "That looks good. I'll have one of those."

Diego relayed their order to the server before pulling over an empty chair from a nearby table to join the group.

"What've you two been up to?" Chad asked, his curiosity clear in the way he leaned forward in his seat.

Elise looked down at her dust-covered jeans and T-shirt with a faint smile. "We've been working on the new meeting hall, over on the Drake's old property. It's taking shape, but we needed a break, so we came into town for a bit."

"Hey, Teresa," Chad suddenly called out, standing and waving his hand enthusiastically. Then, sitting back down, he explained to the group, "I hope you don't mind. I bumped into Teresa earlier at the hardware store and told her Steve and I would be here tonight if she wanted to stop by."

The pretty brunette making her way over to their table gave them a slight smile. Chad offered her his seat before going off to find another empty chair.

"Hi, everyone," Teresa said as she settled into her seat with a weary sigh.

The rest of the group greeted her warmly before Dane gestured towards Gina. "Teresa, this is Gina Castillo. She's the ghost whisperer we hired to talk to *Llorona*. Gina, this is Teresa Thacker. We all went to high school together."

Teresa reached across the table to shake Gina's hand with a warm smile. "It's nice to meet you."

"You, too," Gina replied with equal warmth.

"How's work on the house coming along?" Dane asked Teresa, clearly interested. To Gina, he added, "Teresa just moved back to Las Palomas and is turning her family home into a B&B."

"Not great," Teresa admitted with a tired shrug. "Someone broke in last night."

"What?" Dane was immediately on alert, his brow furrowing in concern. He turned to Chad with a questioning look. "Why wasn't I informed about this?"

Chad held up his hands in a calming gesture. "Relax, man. Teresa called me and I went out there. Thankfully, nothing was taken, but there was some damage."

"How bad?" Elise asked, her tone reflecting genuine concern.

"It could have been much worse," Teresa responded with a brave smile. "They punched holes in some walls, but they might have done more if Uncle Bill hadn't scared them off."

Gina's mind immediately raced to the image of her Uncle Victor, bruised and beaten, after his recent confrontation with Frankie's men. "Is your uncle okay? The vandals didn't hurt him, did they?"

Teresa's expression shifted from surprise to a warm smile. "Uncle Bill is more like my great-great-uncle. He passed away years ago, but his spirit still haunts the house. Normally he's a quiet presence, but if someone crosses him, watch out. I'm guessing the vandals didn't expect the house to be haunted."

Gina was only a little surprised by Teresa's revelation, which made her wonder if she was getting used to the paranormal oddities of Las Palomas. She noticed that the other people at the table didn't even bat an eye.

"It was probably just some kids," Teresa continued with a sigh. "You know how they are. They see an empty house under construction and think it would be fun to cause mischief. But the repairs are becoming costly. I'm thinking of moving back into the house, even though it's not quite finished, just so it won't stand empty."

A brief pause followed as the server arrived with their drinks.

Dane turned to Chad with concern in his voice. "Did you let Steve know to swing by Teresa's place a few times tonight during his patrol?"

Chad nodded. "I made sure everyone was aware. It won't be a problem. We're already doing extra rounds through the neighborhoods."

To look for a child predator. The thought sent chills down Gina's spine as she took a sip of her drink.

Chapter Twenty-Three

The conversation flowed effortlessly, filling the evening with laughter and easy banter. Gina found herself completely at ease, enjoying every moment of their impromptu gathering at the local bar. As the night wore on, she lost track of time until someone announced that it was nearly midnight, and they should call it a night.

Everyone said goodbye, then Gina and Dane walked hand-in-hand to his truck, their feet crunching on the gravel driveway.

She'd noticed that Dane had switched from alcohol to soda midway through the evening, showing responsible behavior. It spoke volumes about his character. He wouldn't be the kind of person, for instance, to gamble away a loved one's entire savings.

As they drove towards Ruby Mae's Bed and Breakfast, Gina couldn't stop smiling. "I had such a great time tonight," she told him sincerely.

"Me too," he replied, glancing over at her with a soft smile. "Thanks for putting up with my crazy friends."

She laughed. "I like your friends," she assured him.

"I could tell they liked you, too," he replied.

She stole glances at him as they drove, admiring his strong profile and easy confidence. He caught her staring once and returned her gaze with an affectionate glint in his eyes.

All too soon, they pulled into the driveway of the Bed and Breakfast. Gina felt a pang of disappointment because she wasn't ready for the evening to end. Maybe, like her, he'd want to sit in the truck for a while and chat—or something. Her hand wandered to the center console, which thwarted her fantasies of making out in the front seat.

Dane parked the truck and, before she could even thank him again for the wonderful evening, got out. A twinge of disappointment shot through her, but then he surprised her by coming around the truck to open her door and, reaching out his hand, helped her out of the truck.

As they stood facing each other in the moonlit driveway, Gina couldn't help but hope that their night wasn't over just yet. But then, still holding her hand, Dane started up the front walkway.

When they reached the first porch step, he pulled her to a stop. She looked up at him, once again feeling confused.

"I'd rather say goodnight here," he stated, breaking the silence between them.

Gina nodded in agreement, trying not to let her disappointment show. Then, Dane took her by surprise and pulled her towards a large oak tree in the front yard. The branches above cast shadows around them, making it feel like they had entered their own private world.

Without hesitation, he wrapped his arms around her and pulled her into a passionate embrace. "I didn't want to do this with the porch lights shining on us like a big ol' spotlight," he whispered against her ear. "Ruby Mae may be everybody's idea of the perfect grandmother, but she's also the town's biggest gossip. Worse even than Peg, if you can believe it."

Then slowly, giving her plenty of time to pull away, he lowered his head and pressed his lips against hers. A surge of heat rushed through Gina's body as she eagerly responded to his kiss. His tongue traced along the seam of her lips and she opened up for him without hesitation.

"You taste like margaritas," he whispered against her mouth. "I love margaritas." And with that, he deepened their kiss while one hand tangled in her hair and the other held her close to him. It was a moment filled with passion and desire, making Gina forget all about her earlier doubts.

Gina's fingers traced the hard lines of Dane's back, her touch seeming to ignite a fire within him matching the one raging inside her. Tasting his lips and feeling his arms wrapped around her, she knew that if she kissed a thousand men, the sensation of kissing Dane would surpass them all.

Their lips moved in perfect unison, tongues tasting and exploring each other until both were breathless. With a swift motion, Dane turned them until Gina's back pressed against the rough bark of the oak tree. He pinned her there as he continued to ravish her mouth with his tongue, sending shivers down her spine.

She felt the undeniable evidence of his arousal pressed against her stomach, and it only fueled her desire for him. Clinging to him for support, Gina felt her knees weaken and threaten to give out at any moment.

Dane's hand slipped beneath her shirt, his calloused palm leaving a trail of goosebumps along her waist as he explored every inch of her skin. "God, you feel so good," he breathed against her neck, his warm breath sending chills down her spine as he peppered kisses along her throat.

Gina was like a ticking bomb about to explode with desire. Desperate for more contact, she pulled at his shirt until it came free from his jeans. Then she slipped her hands beneath it so she could run them over the hard planes of his chest.

"We should have gone to my place," he moaned against her skin as his mouth trailed lower. This time, she felt his hot breath across the tops of her breasts and realized that at some point, he had undone the top buttons of her shirt.

"My bedroom is just upstairs," she gasped.

"Ruby Mae be damned," he muttered, grabbing her hand and pulling her along. They had only taken two steps toward the front door when he stopped abruptly, looking down at her.

"We can't go in like this." His fingers fumbled with the buttons on her shirt, trying to fix her disheveled appearance, but she swatted his hand away.

"I'll get these," she said, pushing his hand away. "You worry about your clothes." She let her eyes wander to his crotch.

A sly grin appeared on his face. "Yeah, about that. Afraid it's not going anywhere."

She couldn't help but smile at his playful banter. In fact, she had plans for that particular piece of his anatomy once they reached the safety of her bedroom.

They finished climbing the steps of the front porch in unison, Dane practically glued to her side. Just as she reached for the doorknob, his phone rang loudly.

"Damn it," he muttered, reaching into his pocket to retrieve it.

She wished he would ignore it, but then her own phone started ringing.

"She's with me," she heard Dane say as she quickly dug her phone out of her pocket, the name "Uncle Victor" flashing on the screen.

"Hello?" she said, trying to sound calm despite the pounding in her chest.

"Where are you?" Uncle Victor's voice boomed over the sound of muffled footsteps coming from the other side of the front door.

"I'm at the B&B. Why?"

"You are?" he sounded surprised.

Just then, the front door swung open and Uncle Victor would have slammed into her if Dane hadn't smoothly reached over and pulled her aside. Uncle Victor's abrupt stop caused Sylvia, who was following close behind, to stumble and nearly crash into his back. Gina saw Sylvia had her phone pressed to her ear and realized she must be talking to Dane.

The four of them stood on the front porch in disheveled clothes, looking surprised and slightly comical, with their phones pressed to their ears as they frantically talked over each other. Gina might have laughed if she weren't so irritated that the night of wild, passionate sex she had been anticipating with Dane seemed less and less likely now.

"What is happening?" She demanded; her tone laced with sexual frustration.

"It's *Llorona*!" Sylvia gasped breathlessly, as if she were announcing the second coming of Christ.

"What about her?" Dane snarled, his frustration clear in his voice.

"She's here," Sylvia announced eagerly.

What?! "Where?" Gina frantically scanned their surroundings, not seeing any sign of the infamous ghost.

"Not here," Uncle Victor clarified with exasperation. "At the RV Park."

Sylvia clapped her hands together in delight. "This is so thrilling! I'll finally get to watch you at work."

Gina rolled her eyes at Sylvia's enthusiasm and turned to Uncle Victor for reassurance. To her annoyance, he only smiled at her knowingly.

"I'll drive," Dane declared, pulling his keys out of his pocket and leading Gina by the hand towards his truck, with Uncle Victor and Sylvia following close behind.

As Dane's truck rumbled along the winding road leading to the RV park, Gina couldn't shake the creeping chill that crawled up her spine. The dense shadows on either side of the road seemed to grow darker and more foreboding with every mile they covered, like gnarled fingers reaching out to grab unsuspecting travelers.

She stole a glance at Dane, his profile illuminated by the soft glow of the dashboard lights. His jaw was set in determination, his eyes focused on the road ahead. He expected her to perform tonight; to confront the spirit of *Llorona* and unravel why she was terrorizing people. It dawned on Gina, for the first time, just how terrifying it might be to come face-to-face with an actual ghost. It was almost as terrifying as the prospect of owning up to being a fraud.

As they approached the entrance to the RV park, Gina knew it was too late to pray for a miracle. Dane turned into the entrance and drove along the winding road to the picnic area. The darkness seemed to press closer as he pulled into a parking space in an otherwise empty lot. When he shut off the truck's engine, no one spoke and Gina was sure Dane would hear how hard her heart was beating. Whatever happened in the next fifteen minutes was bound to be catastrophic.

She gave him a weak smile before nearly jumping out of her seat as a figure suddenly appeared outside Dane's window. Dane calmly turned and, upon seeing the man, opened his door and got out.

"Evening, Bill," he said in greeting. "Is she still there?" His tone held a hint of urgency.

"I-I don't know," Bill stammered, his voice trembling. "That crazy ghost started flying toward me, screaming to all hell. Let me tell you, it scared the bejesus out of me. I high tailed it to the office to call Sylvia."

Dane's brow furrowed in concern. "Was anyone else out there?"

"I don't think so," Bill replied, taking a deep breath to calm himself. "I only have three guest trailers here. The artist and his wife are parked over yonder." He pointed towards the side of the park closest to the thick, looming woods. "And I have two trailers over there." He gestured to the two trailers furthest from the river. "There's an older couple in one and a family—parents and two teens—in the other. They're all traveling together; taking the long scenic route to Big Bend National Park. I told them to steer clear of the river at night, so as far as I know, everyone's in their trailer."

Dane nodded, grateful for the information. "Thanks. If you notice anyone headed our way, please suggest they return to their trailer."

"Sure thing," Bill said with a nod. "If you need me, I'll be in my trailer." He pointed towards a small but cozy trailer that served as the main office before shaking hands with Dane and walking away.

"That was Bill Murphy," Dane explained as he stuck his head through the open truck door to talk to Gina. "He owns the RV park." He paused. "I guess we should head over to the river and see if *Llorona* is there?"

Gina nodded, trying to ignore the buzzing in her head. She needed a plan, but it was like her brain was on lock-down; incapable of generating a single idea.

Slowly, she climbed out of the truck and walked to the back, where the others joined her. She cast a glance at Uncle Victor, who gave her a weak smile and slight nod of the head, as much as saying, *You've got this. Right?*

No, she wanted to say. *I don't got this.*

The group crossed the empty parking lot, their footsteps echoing off the pavement. As they neared the river, Gina tried to focus her senses on her surroundings—the aroma of water filling the air, the gentle touch of a warm breeze across her skin—anything to help clear her mind.

"We're too late," Sylvia's voice broke through Gina's thoughts, disappointment clear in her tone as she scanned the bank of the river. "*Llorona* is gone."

Gina couldn't help but feel a surge of hope at this news—maybe there was still time to find a way out of this situation.

"Maybe you can call out to her?" Sylvia suggested hopefully.

Really? Gina fought back resentment. Sylvia was only trying to be helpful. With a sigh, Gina glanced over at Uncle Victor, hoping he'd thought of a way to postpone this charade.

His grim look told her he hadn't. Now, she had no other option—she would have to summon a ghost. The first time hadn't gone so well. She had little hope this time would be any better, yet she had to try. At least now she knew enough not to pretend a ghost was here when it wasn't.

Pulling her phone from her pocket, she flipped the ringer to vibrate and then handed it to Uncle Victor. The last thing she needed was her friend Carla calling her in the middle of a ghost whispering session. Then, taking a deep breath, she stepped away from the group and pretended to center herself, using some of her yoga deep-breathing techniques.

Show time.

A chill sliced through the air, settling like an icy blanket over Gina's skin. The hairs on her neck prickled with unease as if a frozen hand caressed the back of her neck. Her eyes flew open in alarm, only to meet the frigid darkness of the night. She spun around, instinctively taking a step back as her breath escaped in a white puff of steam in the suddenly frigid night air.

The river beside her began to churn and boil as a thick fog rose, coalescing into the ghostly form of a woman with long hair and a flowing gown that fluttered in a phantom breeze. Gina froze in fear as the specter hovered just inches away, its piercing gaze fixed upon her.

Oh. My. God.

Paralyzed with fear, Gina could only watch as the apparition drew closer, its hollow gaze fixed on her with unsettling intensity. When the ghost opened her mouth, a sound, like nails scraping against a chalkboard, pierced the quiet stillness, sending chills down Gina's spine and washing over her with raw emotion.

Then, suddenly, gnarled hands appeared, reaching out for her. She stumbled back in terror; the world spinning around her. Then, she was falling... falling...

CHAPTER TWENTY-FOUR

DANE'S HEART RACED AS he watched Gina, his concern mounting with each passing moment. He had no experience dealing with ghosts, but in all his years living in Las Palomas, he had never seen *Llorona* or any other spirit completely envelop a living person. This couldn't be normal, could it? Was this how Gina communicated with the dead?

His eyes darted to Victor Castillo for reassurance but got none. Victor's horrified gaze probably mirrored his own, which only added to Dane's growing panic.

Should he intervene? Gina would be furious if he interfered needlessly. But deep down, he knew something was not right.

As he continued to watch, *Llorona's* form faded. She was leaving.

No, he realized a moment later. She wasn't leaving. She was merging into Gina, like water seeping into a sponge. And as *Llorona's* light faded completely, Gina's body crumpled to the ground.

Without hesitation, Dane sprinted towards her, noticing the air got colder the closer he got. When he reached her, the sight before him made his blood run cold. Her head was tilted back, and her eyes rolled back so that only the whites showed.

"Gina! Wake up!" He shook her shoulders desperately and alarm ran through him at the feel of her icy skin.

"Oh, dear." Sylvia's voice rang out behind him, filled with fear and shock. Both she and Victor had joined him now, their faces reflecting the same terror that consumed him.

"What happened to her?" he demanded of Victor, who could do nothing but stare in disbelief. It was Sylvia who offered a tentative explanation.

"I think *Llorona* has taken over her body."

"What? That's insane. Ghosts can't do that." Dane's words carried a note of desperation, hoping to convince himself more than anyone else. But when he looked at Gina's face, there was no sign of recognition or awareness. Panic rose within him.

"What do we do?" He turned to Victor, searching for guidance, but the older man could only shake his head in disbelief. Dane then looked to Sylvia, who wore an uneasy expression.

"Call someone, damn it. Call Zelda." Dane's voice cracked with emotion as he grasped at straws for a solution. He had never felt so helpless in his life.

Sylvia stepped away from the group and frantically placed the call. Meanwhile, Victor stepped closer to Gina's side.

"I've never seen anything like this," he admitted, his voice trembling with fear.

"Gina, can you hear me?" Dane pleaded, taking her hand in his and squeezing it gently. "Please, just give us some sign that you're still here." Several feet away, Sylvia could be heard talking on the phone.

Then he felt it. A faint pressure against his hand that made his heart skip a beat. "She's still there," he said, not sure if he was trying to convince himself or Victor.

Sylvia ran back to them, waving her phone in her hand excitedly. "Zelda suggests dunking Gina in the river."

"Are you serious?" He spat out.

"She thinks *Llorona* might have an aversion to water," she said, shrugging helplessly.

"It's worth a shot," Victor said. "I'll help you carry her."

Dane nodded. "Grab her legs," he told Victor, moving to stand behind her head so he could grab her shoulders.

The instant the men took hold of her, Gina began to buck and kick violently, her piercing screams filling the night. Victor grappled with her legs, trying to keep a firm grip, but it was a losing battle as she kicked and clawed ferociously.

The men half-carried, half-dragged Gina to the river's edge. His heart pounding with fear and desperation, Dane knew they had to act fast or risk losing her to the clutches of *Llorona*. With little time to spare, he turned to Sylvia, his voice shaking with urgency.

"Take my gun and phone. I can't risk getting them wet."

Sylvia hesitated, clearly uneasy about handling a weapon. Fortunately, Victor had no such qualms. Releasing Gina's legs, he pulled Dane's phone from his pocket and handed it to Sylvia. Then he removed Dane's weapon from its holster.

Still clutching Gina under the arms, Dane stepped backwards into the freezing water. The icy cold had no effect on him; his sole focus was on the writhing woman in his grasp.

Gina's resistance intensified as they reached the deepest point. With limited options left, Dane made a split-second decision. Wrapping his arms around her, he fell backwards, plunging them both beneath the surface.

Icy cold water enveloped them both as they sank deeper into the murky depths. Dane could feel Gina's frantic attempts to break free from his grip as he struggled against the current that threatened to sweep them both down river.

He held them under water for as long as he dared, but when he came up for air, his boots slipped. As they went under again, he lost his hold on Gina and watched helplessly as the current tugged her downward.

He had to act fast if they were going to make it out alive. Using every ounce of his strength, Dane managed to find solid ground beneath him and stand. Then he reached out and grabbed Gina's collar, the only part of her he could easily reach, and hauled her up to the surface with all his might. Her eyes were closed and her skin had taken on a sickly pale bluish tint.

Dane hadn't thought he could be any more frightened, but as he hauled Gina's body out of the river, he was terrified. Admonishments raced through his head. He should have gotten her into the water sooner. He shouldn't have held her so long beneath the water.

He pushed his thoughts aside as he stumbled from the river and laid her down. He held his finger below her nose but could detect no breath. Blowing hot air into his cupped hands, he quickly rubbed them together, trying to warm them. Then he placed two fingers against the side of her neck, feeling for a pulse.

Oh, God. There wasn't one.

"Is she... dead?" Victor asked, his voice sounding hoarse.

"I can't feel a pulse and I don't think she's breathing," Dane muttered.

"I'll call Doc Niven," Sylvia said, but Dane knew the doctor would never arrive in time. He had to do something now.

"I'm starting CPR," he said, mostly to himself, but loud enough for Victor to hear. He'd never had to do this before, but every year, the entire police force took a course, just in case. He hoped he remembered enough of it.

Tilting Gina's head back slightly, he pinched her nose and, making sure her mouth was open, sealed his mouth around hers and blew in a breath. Out of the corner of his eyes, he saw her chest rise slightly, telling him he'd done it correctly.

Next, he placed one hand on top of the other, interlaced the fingers, and began chest compressions, counting them off in his head. After he reached thirty, he stopped to breathe into her mouth again. Then he started the chest compressions again. He repeated the process several times before—

Gina's body jerked as she sucked in a breath on her own. Then she was gasping and coughing, her arms flailing about so wildly, she clocked him in the eye.

"Gina, it's okay," he shouted, trying to get her attention.

At the sound of his voice, she seemed to calm.

"Dane?" Her voice was weak as she called out his name, and Dane couldn't believe how much relief flooded through him at hearing her. He helped her when she tried to sit up and then pulled her into his arms, offering stability and comfort as she cried softly against his chest. They stayed like that for what felt like an eternity until Gina's sobs quieted and Dane knew it was safe to move.

"It's okay, baby," he soothed, stroking her back. "Just take it easy."

"Doc's on his way," Sylvia said from behind him.

"Call him back and ask him to meet us at the B&B," Dane told her. He'd noticed Gina shivering, and draping his arm around her shoulders, pulled her close again. It was as much to share his body heat with her as to reassure himself she was okay. "Let's head back to the truck. I'll turn the heater on, which will have to do until we can get you into dry clothes. Doc can check you over at Ruby Mae's. And I don't know about the rest of you, but I could use a drink. Maybe Ruby Mae will break out some of her private stash of bourbon for us."

CHAPTER TWENTY-FIVE

Thirty minutes later, Dane had reached the end of the second story hallway of Ruby Mae's Bed and Breakfast and turned. He'd never been prone to nervous pacing, but—damn! What had happened to Gina had scared the hell out of him. He was still trying to figure out what that damn ghost had done to her. Psychic possession? He hadn't realized it was possible.

He reached the opposite end of the hallway and stopped, turning to face Victor, who, like Dane, had been kicked out of the room by Doc Niven as he examined Gina. Sylvia and Ruby Mae had stayed long enough to help Gina change into dry clothes but were now downstairs, puttering around in the kitchen.

"Damn it. This is all my fault," he muttered. "She could have died tonight."

Victor looked over at him, his expression carefully masked not to show emotion. "It wasn't your fault. In fact, you likely saved her."

"I almost drowned her." He couldn't help thinking there might have been a better way to handle the situation if he hadn't panicked.

Victor stepped forward and stopped Dane when he would have started down the hallway again. "None of us knew what to do and you have to admit, the water broke *Llorona's* hold on her. That's thanks to you. Neither Sylvia nor I had the strength to carry Gina into that river and hold on to her. And you're the one who knew enough to start CPR. She's alive because of you."

Dane wanted to believe what he said was true but was having a hard time with it.

At that moment, the door opened and Doc Niven stepped out, a confused expression on his face. Both Dane and Victor turned to him expectantly.

"As far as I can tell, she's fine," he said, shrugging his shoulders. "When you did CPR on her and she came to, did she throw up any water?"

Dane and Victor exchanged glances as Dane thought back to that moment. The details were fuzzy because of the state of mind he'd been in. "A little, but not much," he said, glancing at Victor, who shook his head. "Why?"

"I don't think her heart stopped because she drowned," he told them. "There's no evidence of water in her lungs as far as I can tell. Other than being shaken by what happened to her tonight, she seems otherwise fine."

"You're sure?" Victor asked.

"I'd feel better if she'd let me transport her to the nearest hospital for a thorough exam, but she's refusing to go and I can't very well make her."

"What do you recommend we do for her now?" Dane asked.

"I gave her something to help her sleep, just in case she has trouble relaxing after what happened. I can't do much more for her medically. As far as dealing with the effects of ghostly possession? That's way outside my wheelhouse. I've never had a case of ghostly possession before. Is this the first time Gina's been possessed?" he asked Victor.

Victor nodded gravely, making Dane feel even worse.

"Victor, I never would have agreed to let her confront *Llorona* if I'd known this would happen," Dane said.

Victor placed a supportive hand on his shoulder. "You and me, both, son. You're not to blame. We couldn't have known this would happen."

"I'm headed back home now," Doc told them. "I think she'll be fine, but if something comes up, call me."

Footsteps coming up the stairs had the group of men turning just as Ruby Mae reached the top. Her gazed narrowed on Dane.

"Dane Wolfe, I hope you aren't dripping water all over my carpet. Follow me. I'm sure I can find a pair of sweatpants and a T-shirt you can wear while I dry your clothes."

Dane shook his head and gestured toward the bedroom. "I want to check on Gina."

Ruby Mae shook her head right back and pointed down the stairs. "You can check on her as soon as you change out of those wet clothes."

Dane opened his mouth to protest but quickly closed it again. He'd known Ruby Mae a long time. No one ever won an argument against her. Besides, the towel he'd wrapped around himself as he waited for Doc to finish with Gina had helped, but now that the crisis was over, he was ready to get out of his damp clothes. So, as Ruby Mae started back down the stairs, Dane followed her.

Inside the bedroom, sitting in bed with the covers pulled up around her and the pill the doctor had given her kicking in, Gina was finally relaxing. She couldn't remember a time she'd been so frightened. What the hell had happened? If that was what an actual ghost encounter was like, she wanted no part of it.

A light knock at the door sounded before it opened, and Sylvia stuck her head in. "Can I get you anything? Maybe you'd like another pillow behind your back?"

"No, thank you, Sylvia. I'm good." What she needed was to talk to Uncle Victor before the pill made her too sleepy to think straight. "Is my uncle around?"

"He and Dane are outside waiting to see you," Sylvia told her. "I don't know how much longer I'll be able to keep them out. Do you mind if I let them in?" Sylvia smiled when Gina raised a hand to her still wet hair. "You look fine, but even if you didn't, I don't think he'd notice."

"Who? Uncle Victor?"

Sylvia gave a soft laugh. "I'm sure he wouldn't notice either, but I was talking about Dane."

Gina felt her face heat. She was about to deny it when Sylvia said, "It's pretty obvious that he likes you, too." She winked. "Now, if I don't let them in soon so they can see for themselves that you're okay, they're likely to break down the door."

Sylvia pushed open the door and stepped aside. "You can come in now."

Dane and Uncle Victor both came into the room, their attention immediately focused on Gina. She read twin expressions of concern and worry, which she immediately tried to ease.

"I'm fine. Really."

Dane, she noticed, was now wearing a T-shirt and pair of sweatpants that were both too small for him, leaving little to the imagination. She felt her face heat all over again as her thoughts took a lusty detour. The sound of someone clearing their throat jerked her back to reality and belatedly she realized where her gaze was focused.

She looked up to meet Dane's amused gaze and was desperately trying to think of something witty to say to cover her embarrassment when she noticed the darkening skin around his right eye.

"What happened to your eye?"

"You happened," he said, but he didn't sound upset. "That's a mean left hook you have."

"I did that? I'm so sorry."

"It's okay," he assured her, taking a seat on the edge her bed so he could hold her hand. "I'm more worried about you. How are you doing?"

"I'm fine now, thanks to you." She gave each of them a look. "Thanks to all of you. I don't know what happened out there."

Uncle Victor took a seat on the opposite side of the bed and laid his hand on her lower leg, a reassuring pressure through the blankets. "Do you remember anything?"

"A little," she admitted, her mind taking her back to that moment beside the river when *Llorona* appeared. "I didn't really expect *Llorona* to come when I summoned her." Truer words were never spoken. "Then there she was, standing close enough to touch me. Suddenly, my head was filled with these images. Not pleasant images, either. Some of them were really scary." She brushed a strand of hair from her face. "I don't even want to think about them. When I tried to move away from her, it was like I was no longer in control of my body. Then everything went black." She shivered. "I was so frightened. Then suddenly, I was underwater and couldn't breathe. I panicked." She paused. "I thought I heard someone speaking Spanish, but maybe I just imagined it."

"*Llorona*," Sylvia said, confidently. "Do you remember what she said?"

Gina tried to think back. "*Lo siento*, maybe? That means I'm sorry, doesn't it? And maybe *mee-ho*."

"*Mi hijo*," Dane clarified. "It means my child."

Gina sighed. "Considering she drowned her children and then died from regret, I guess that makes sense."

"Do you remember anything else?" Uncle Victor asked.

"No," she said around a yawn, feeling tired.

"It's okay," Dane said, squeezing her hand. "The important thing is that you're okay. You should get some rest."

Ruby Mae walked in at that moment carrying a tray on which sat a bottle of bourbon and several ice-filled whiskey glasses. "I thought a touch of my cure-all might be just the thing to calm the nerves." She set the tray down and poured a small shot into a glass and offered it to Gina, who shook her head.

"I'd better not. I can already feel the pill Doc gave me working," she said, hiding a yawn behind her free hand.

Ruby Mae filled glasses and handed them out to everyone else, including one for herself.

"While I wasn't there to share the experience," she said, "I would be remiss if I let my friends drink alone." She raised her glass in a silent toast to the others before taking a drink.

Dane finished his drink in one big swallow and wiped his mouth with the back of his hand. When Ruby Mae offered to refill his glass, he shook his head, handing her his empty glass. "Thanks, but I'll wait until I get home to have more. Now that I know Gina's okay, I guess I should leave and let her sleep." He stood and leaned down to whisper in Gina's ear. "I don't want to call you too early and wake you up, so you call me, okay?"

The quick kiss he gave her left her feeling warmer than the thick quilt covering her.

"I'll go check on my clothes. Sylvia, I'll take you home whenever you're ready."

"I'll be down shortly," Sylvia said, holding her now empty glass out to Ruby Mae. "If you're driving, then there's no reason I can't have another." Ruby Mae refilled her glass and then topped off Uncle Victor's drink when he held out his glass.

"I'd better make sure your clothes are dry," Ruby Mae said Dane. Then she turned to Gina. "You holler if you need anything, okay?"

"Thank you," Gina replied.

The two of them left the room, leaving Gina alone with Uncle Victor and Sylvia.

"I suppose I should go as well," Sylvia said, sounding apologetic after she finished her second glass of whiskey. She glanced at Uncle Victor.

"I'm going to stay here with Gina tonight," he told her.

She nodded in understanding. "I think that's best. I'll see you tomorrow?"

"Absolutely," he said, walking over to her. While Gina didn't like thinking of her uncle as a sexual dynamo, the kiss he gave Sylvia was nothing short of fiery.

Oh, my.

A few minutes later, Gina and Uncle Victor were alone in her room.

"How are you doing—really?" he asked her.

She looked at him; her fear and dismay nicely dulled by the effects of the pill. "I'm okay, now, but..." She paused, struggling to find the right words. "That... thing... that showed up tonight. That was a ghost! A real, freaking ghost!" He didn't try to deny it. "I've never been so afraid in my life," she admitted.

"Me, too."

She heard the truth of his words in his tone. She hadn't been the only one afraid she wouldn't survive the night.

"Uncle Victor, what are we going to do?" She stared at her lap, shaking her head. "I never want to go through that again."

"You don't have to."

She looked over at him. "What about the money?"

He shook his head. "Screw the money. We'll get it some other way. I'll ask Frankie for more time."

At the mention of the loan shark's name, she remembered the car she'd seen earlier that day. "Did you see the men I told you about?"

His brows furrowed for a second, like he was confused, but then he shook his head. "No, but it's not Frankie's men. He's not sending his guys down here for a measly fifty thousand dollars."

The lethargy in her body was seeping into her thoughts, and it took a moment for his words to register. "Fifty thousand. I thought you said you owed him ten thousand dollars?"

"Did I?" He sounded distracted. "I mean, I did. Sorry, I don't know what I'm saying. I guess I'm more rattled by your experience than I thought."

She stared at him, trying to decide if he was telling her the truth or not.

"There was something else you wanted to tell me, wasn't there?" he asked.

She thought back and then remembered. "I found out more about those teens from last night," she said, lowering her voice.

She told him about spotting the teens in the park and following them to the school; from finding the costumes and make-up in the temporary building to her confrontation with Dane.

"I don't like it but I can hardly condemn the town for the deception," she finished. "Since we're doing essentially the same thing. I just found the whole thing ironic." She yawned. "By the way. I promised not to tell anyone, so please don't let on that I told you."

Uncle Victor was silent for so long after she'd finished that she nearly dozed off.

"You should get some sleep," he finally said.

She struggled to keep her eyes open. "What about the money?"

He sighed and then patted her knee. "Don't worry about it. These things have a way of working out."

"Okay." She scooted down in the bed until she could stretch out, head on the pillow. "Wake me for breakfast tomorrow?"

"Of course." He sounded distracted as he laid his hand on her head and began running his fingers through her hair, just as he'd done when she was a child.

"Don't worry about a thing. It'll all work out. You'll see."

She hoped he was right. He began humming softly and soon the gentle motion of his fingers through her hair worked their magic. Gina's thoughts and worries quieted and her eyelids grew too heavy to keep open.

The comforting warm press of his lips against her temple swept away the last tendrils of thought and she fell into a dreamless sleep.

Chapter Twenty-Six

Gina woke the next morning feeling oddly refreshed. The events from the night before seemed distant; less devastating. Maybe there was some truth to the adage that things looked better after a good night's rest. She hadn't awakened with the answers to her problems but she was feeling less grim about their future.

Finally, noticing how bright her room seemed, she found her phone on the bedside table and checked the time.

Holy cow! She'd slept until almost noon. No wonder she felt rested. She wondered if Uncle Victor had even tried to wake her?

Checking her messages, she saw he'd texted her an hour ago to tell her that, after her harrowing experience, he let her sleep in, but he would meet her for lunch at Kathy's Café at noon.

She texted him back to let him know she'd overslept and would be late, but to please wait for her. Then she hurried to the bathroom to take a shower.

Forty minutes later, showered and dressed in capris with a light-weight shirt, Gina was ready to leave. She checked her phone, but there was no new text from Uncle Victor.

Outside, a quick inspection of the parking lot confirmed that he had taken the car, so she would have to walk into town. That was okay with her. Even though the temperature was already in the high 80s, it was one of those rare, low-humidity days when one could be outside and not feel like they were standing in a steam room.

As she walked, her thoughts turned to Dane and a thrill ran through her. She'd had relationships before, but this felt different. She was looking forward to seeing him again and wondered if he'd have time to join them for lunch. Pulling out her phone, she gave him a quick call.

He answered on the second ring. "Hello?" His tone was terse, and it was hard to hear him over the sound of raised voices in the background.

"Hi. Is this a bad time?"

"What do you want?"

His abrupt tone caught her off guard, but maybe he hadn't recognized her voice.

"Um, it's Gina."

A heavy sigh. "What do you want, Gina?"

Okaaaay. Not the reaction she'd hoped for, but perhaps she was being too sensitive. After all, from all the shouting she could hear in the background, something big was going on. Maybe this was how he sounded when he was distracted. Deciding to give him the benefit of the doubt and not wanting to keep him too long on the phone, she hurried on.

"I'm headed to the café to meet Uncle Victor for lunch. Any chance you could join us?"

There was a pause before he spoke. "You have got to be kidding."

Again, not the reaction she'd expected. Maybe the child predator had succeeded in kidnapping a child. If that were the case, then it was understandable that he wouldn't have time for a leisurely lunch. These thoughts flashed through her mind in an instant. "Yeah, of course. You're busy. I get it. Will I see you later?"

"I don't think so." There was a sharp edge to his tone.

Ouch. What was going on? She stopped walking as she waited for him to say something more, but when he didn't, she finally asked, "Dane, did I do something wrong?"

"No, I did." The sound of shouting got louder in the background. "I have to go." He disconnected the call without even saying goodbye.

Gina's shock was palpable. What the hell had just happened? Feeling upset, she naturally reached out to Uncle Victor and then felt irritated when he didn't answer his phone.

She didn't bother leaving a message. She would see him soon enough and started walking again.

Ten minutes later, Gina was approaching the café's entrance when the door opened, and Nita Garcia stepped out. Remembering how gracious the woman had been to her the other night at the VFW hall, Gina smiled in greeting. Nita, however, did not smile back. In fact, Gina thought the woman might have frowned and, before Gina could draw close enough to exchange greetings with her, Nita walked off in the opposite direction.

Gina felt her smile falter. What the hell was wrong with people this morning? First, Dane and now Nita. It was like she was in an alternate universe.

Blowing off the woman's rude behavior, Gina stepped through the café door. She stopped just inside and searched the booths and tables for Uncle Victor.

He wasn't there. Maybe he was with Sylvia and, after getting her message, had taken advantage of her delay and was now, himself, running late.

Disappointed, she found an empty booth and sat. It didn't seem that crowded, yet she sat for a full ten minutes before Kathy headed over with a cup of coffee.

"Hi," Gina greeted her, glad to see a friendly face. "Have you seen my uncle this morning? I'm supposed to be meeting him."

"No, he hasn't been in. You want to order something?"

Was there a chill in Kathy's tone? No. She was being hyper-sensitive. Still, Kathy wasn't as talkative as she normally was.

What were the odds that Dane, Nita, and Kathy were all, coincidentally, in bad moods today?

Astronomical. Something was going on. Gina only wished she knew what. Her appetite withered and died as worry turned her stomach sour.

"I'll take a toasted bagel and cream cheese, please."

Kathy didn't bother to write down her order, nor did she utter a word before walking off. Gina's feeling of discomfort increased.

As she waited, she looked around the room. Was it her imagination, or were people stealing glances at her?

Kathy hadn't brought her sweetener or creamer pod, but spotting extra of both on a nearby empty table, she retrieved them and doctored her coffee. Raising her cup to her lips, she took a drink and then quickly lowered her cup in disgust. The coffee was tepid and Gina couldn't help but think that wasn't accidental.

A moment later, Kathy did a drive-by, pausing only long enough to drop off Gina's order and the check. She was gone before Gina could thank her.

Gina stared at the check. Hadn't she told Kathy she was waiting for Uncle Victor to join her? Why close out her tab now?

Unless this was Kathy's way of suggesting she leave.

Feeling more than a little hurt, Gina tried to convince herself none of this—Dane's rudeness on the phone, being shunned by Nita outside and the poor service she was getting from Kathy—was personal.

The problem was that it felt very personal.

Was this because she'd failed to deal with *Llorona* and stop her from terrorizing guests? If so, it was a little harsh, wasn't it? Considering the ghost had almost killed her.

She looked around the room, studying the faces of the other diners. Most of them were focused on eating their food and not looking at her, but occasionally, she caught sight of someone glancing her way. More than one wore an expression so glacial, Gina was afraid she'd get frostbite.

Then her gaze fell on a woman standing in the corner of the room watching her, a look of sympathy on her face.

Gina thought she looked a little odd in her vintage clothing and out-of-date hairstyle, but when their gazes met, Gina offered her a small smile.

A look of surprise crossed the woman's face, no doubt from being caught staring, but then she smiled back.

Feeling marginally better that not everyone in town was being a jerk, Gina returned her focus to her food.

Picking up the cream cheese packet, she noticed it felt warm. Giving the packet a test squeeze, she found it too malleable. She tore off the corner of the packet and squeezed some of the contents onto her bagel. What came out was a soupy-white substance.

Gross.

Hoping it would taste better than it looked, she spread the cheese across her bagel. That's when she noticed how hard the bread was. Setting the knife aside, she picked the bagel up with her fingers and squeezed. At least she tried to squeeze. The bagel was rock hard. She let it fall to her plate with a clatter.

Enough.

She was done with this place. She was done with these people. Hell, she was done with this town. As soon as she found Uncle Victor, they would pack up their things and drive back to Houston. She would call Carla and sell her house, then use the money to pay off Uncle Victor's debt. With the leftover money, they could put down a deposit on a small apartment. Problem solved.

She turned over the check, half expecting to find a threatening message scrawled on the other side. There wasn't one. Just the amount owed.

The meal wasn't worth paying for, but Gina wasn't about to be accused of doing a runner on the check. She pulled a five-dollar bill out of her pocket—and because she was feeling rebuffed and petty—she laid it on top of the bagel, pressing it down into the cream cheese.

Then, she headed for the door, not bothering to glance Kathy's way.

Once outside, she remembered the shop two doors up sold bottled drinks and snacks, so she headed that way. Even if the shop owner was rude, she doubted he'd refuse to take her money.

Fortunately, a kid who didn't seem afflicted with rudeness was running the cash register. She gave Gina a warm smile as Gina entered the store. Walking along the snack aisle, Gina picked up a pack of peanut butter on cheese crackers. About to walk off, she hesitated. There weren't that many places to eat in town. What if they all acted the same way Kathy had? It wasn't like she was made of money and could keep paying for inedible food. She quickly grabbed several more packages of the sandwich crackers plus a couple bottles of water.

After paying for everything—this time using her credit card—she carried her bag of food over to the park and sat on a bench. She called Uncle Victor, but once again got his voice mail.

"I'm across the street from the café," she said. "I'll wait for you in the park. Call me, please."

She pulled out a packet of peanut butter and cheese crackers and started eating, keeping an eye out for Uncle Victor.

She had just finished her third cracker when she noticed a couple of people on the walking path, headed her way. She didn't recognize the man and woman walking together, but she recognized the woman walking several yards in front of them. It was the woman from the café; the one whose clothing was a bit out-of-fashion. She paused when she reached the bench where Gina sat.

"May I join you?" she asked.

Surprised, Gina looked up at her. "Of course." She scooted over to make room for her.

"I wasn't sure if you saw me inside the café," the woman said. "But you did, didn't you?"

Gina nodded. "You kind of stood out as the only person not giving me a cold shoulder or the evil eye."

The woman nodded. "That's the way these tiny towns can be. You're one of them or you're an outsider."

"You're not one of them?"

She shook her head, looking a little sad, Gina thought. "Not for a long time now."

Gina couldn't imagine what that must feel like; to live in a town where no one talked to you. "Why do you stick around, then?"

She shrugged. "I don't know. I guess I'm afraid of what I might find if I left."

It was Gina's turn to nod in understanding. "I get that," she said. "By the way, I'm Gina."

The woman smiled. "It's nice to meet you. I'm Meredith."

"It's nice to meet you, too," Gina said.

At that moment, Gina realized the couple that had been walking along the path behind Meredith were now passing in front of them, giving her a strange look. So rude, she thought. Equally frustrated and disappointed with this town's behavior, Gina ignored them and held her crackers out to Meredith. "Would you like one? I went to the café to eat, but the food they served me was inedible."

Meredith looked surprised at her offer but then shook her head. "No, thanks."

By now, the couple had moved on. "I'm surprised you're willing to be seen with me," Gina commented.

"What do you mean?"

"Well, yesterday, everything was great. People were friendly. Now, it's like everyone's in a bad mood," she quickly added. "I just don't get it."

"Nobody really talks to me, so I can't tell you why they're acting that way," Meredith admitted. "But I overheard snippets of conversation while I was in the café."

"About me?" Gina asked.

Meredith nodded. "They said you had blackmailed the town."

At first, Gina was sure she'd misunderstood. Then the pieces fell into place.

Last night, Uncle Victor had told her not to worry about the money. Was that because he'd found another way to get it? By blackmailing the town in exchange for keeping their fake hauntings a secret?

Oh, crap.

Gina stood up. "Meredith, would you excuse me? I need to make a call."

"Of course," Meredith said.

"It was really nice meeting you. I hope I see you again before I leave town." Gina didn't wait for a response. She walked off, calling her uncle once more.

When the call rolled to voice mail, she couldn't hide her irritation.

"Uncle Victor. What did you do?" she demanded before ending the call.

Next, she called Dane back, praying he answered. When he didn't, she wanted to cry. Things had sure gone to hell in a handbasket.

She sent Dane a text.

> *Whatever my uncle did, he did it without my knowledge or consent. Please, call me.*

She sent the text and then waited.

To her surprise, and relief, her phone rang.

"Is it true?" She asked Dane by way of greeting. "Uncle Victor blackmailed the town?"

"First thing this morning." His tone was cool.

"Oh, my God. This is unbelievable." She took a breath. "I'm so sorry. I didn't know he was going to do that."

Dane sighed. "I want to believe you, Gina. I really do, but it's a little hard to be understanding when the town just paid your uncle fifty thousand dollars in hush money, leaving zero funds to hire another ghost whisperer to deal with *Llorona* who, not coincidentally, is still terrorizing the tourists. If your goal was to ruin the town, you might have succeeded."

She was sure she'd misheard. "Fifty thousand dollars? Are you serious?"

"As a heart attack."

"I'll get the money back," she promised.

"If you do, that's great, but your uncle has worn out his welcome and I'm afraid, by extension—innocent or not—so have you. The mayor's all over my ass to run you both out of town. The only reason I haven't is… well, it doesn't matter. It might be best if you just left town. As soon as possible."

The call ended, but Gina hardly noticed. Leave town? Dane's words were a gut punch, and she struggled past the pain to catch her breath.

She turned back to the park bench where she'd left Meredith and noticed the woman was gone. Feeling more alone than ever, she sank back onto the bench, replaying the conversation with Dane in her head. Pain morphed into anger, directed in part, at Dane, for not believing her, but mostly at Uncle Victor, for pulling this stunt. How could he have done this to her? Maybe he thought he was protecting her from *Llorona*, but he had to know that blackmailing the town wasn't the answer. And for fifty thousand dollars? That hadn't been a slip of the tongue. It had been another lie her uncle had told her.

When she saw him again, he wouldn't have to worry about Frankie getting to him because she was going to kill him herself.

CHAPTER TWENTY-SEVEN

First, she had to find him.

Where was he likely to be?

Would he have gone back to the Bed and Breakfast? Or would he be with Sylvia? She wondered if Sylvia would even speak to him after learning what he'd done.

She dialed the number to the Bed and Breakfast and waited for Ruby Mae to answer, praying the woman would talk to her after seeing who was calling.

"Hello?" Ruby Mae answered.

"Hi, Ruby Mae. It's Gina." She paused, hyper-alert to any negative change in Ruby Mae's tone.

"Yes, dear. What can I do for you?" Her tone, as warm and friendly as always, made Gina want to cry in gratitude.

"I'm looking for my uncle. He was gone when I woke up this morning and I was supposed to meet him for lunch at the café, but he never showed up. I was wondering if he was there?"

"No, dear. I've not seen him since he left this morning and I've been in the front parlor all day. I would have seen him if he'd come back."

Gina sighed. "Okay. Thank you. Maybe he's with Sylvia. Would you have her phone number?"

"Certainly. Let me get it for you."

A minute later, Gina was calling Sylvia's cell phone. The older woman answered after several rings.

"Hello?"

"Sylvia, it's Gina Castillo. Please don't hang up."

There was a pause. "Hello, Gina. I must say that I certainly didn't expect something this vile from you or Victor."

"Uncle Victor acted on his own. I didn't even know he was thinking of this, or I would have stopped him. I hope you can believe me."

There was an audible sigh. "Actually, I do."

Gina was momentarily speechless. "You do?"

"Yes. You don't spend as much time as Victor and I have together and not get to know a little something about the other person. He admitted to me he had some money problems, though he didn't get into specifics. He said that was one of the reasons for taking the job here in Las Palomas. Plus, I know he's impulsive. I saw it when we were alone, and I imagine he's that way in all aspects of his life. What happened to you last night frightened him; frightened us all. I can well believe that he would rather blackmail the town than let you risk talking to *Llorona* again."

"I love my uncle dearly, and I wish I could tell you he's not like that, but you're right about him. Thank you for believing

I wasn't involved. I wish more people believed I wouldn't do something like this."

"Dane?" she asked, her tone understanding.

Gina sighed. "Yeah. He reacted like everyone else in town, letting me know I'm *persona non grata*. He suggested Uncle Victor and I leave town as soon as possible, which is maybe for the best. Only I can't find Uncle Victor. I've been calling him since noon, but he's not answering his phone. I thought he might be with you?"

"I haven't seen him since this morning. We met for breakfast. He wanted to say goodbye. I thought it was because he wanted to get you away from *Llorona* after what happened last night. He said nothing to me about his plans to blackmail the town. Likely, he knew I would try to talk sense into him. I had to hear it from Nita. She and the mayor are most upset."

"I know. I saw Nita this morning. She was pretty obvious about walking the other way to avoid me."

"Victor didn't tell me where he was going when he left my place. I assumed it was back to Ruby Mae's, so he would be there when you woke up." She paused. "I'm sorry, dear. I'm not much help to you."

"That's okay. Thank you for being so understanding. If Uncle Victor should call you, would you let me know?"

"Of course, dear."

They said their goodbyes and ended the call. What now?

A flutter of movement out of the corner of her eye caught her attention, and Gina turned to see a little boy, who'd been sitting near the wall mural, suddenly jump to his feet. With a quick glance toward the street, he raced off in the opposite direction.

On the street, a dusty truck was pulling into a parking space along the curb. When the door opened, a thin blonde woman in a plaid shirt and jeans climbed out. With a blond ponytail hanging from out of the back of a ball cap, she looked to be in her mid-thirties. From the passenger side of her truck, she withdrew a picnic basket and carried it over to where the artist was working.

When the two started talking, Gina wondered if perhaps this was the artist's wife. Who else would bring him a picnic basket?

She studied the couple with unabashed curiosity as the artist put his spray can down and walked over to join the woman. Theirs must be an interesting life, she thought. "Interesting" as in "unusual," she mentally amended. What was it like to live in a travel trailer, constantly moving from town to town? Never staying in one place long enough to call it "home"?

She saw the woman point to a patch of grass under a nearby tree, clearly showing where she wanted to spread their blanket. It was romantic, Gina thought, watching the woman set the basket down and pull from it a blanket, which she shook out. Gina hoped that one day, she too would find someone to share a picnic lunch with.

The image of Dane's smiling face flashed into her thoughts before she could stop it.

Not likely. Not now.

When the artist jerked the blanket from his wife's hands and started speaking loudly, Gina was startled from her reverie. She couldn't hear what he was saying, but he sounded angry, though she couldn't imagine why. Instead of arguing back, the wife stood there silently, head bowed.

Like someone who was so used to being verbally abused, they no longer fought back.

Gina felt herself growing angry on the wife's behalf, especially when she saw the woman wince when something especially mean or hurtful must have been said. When he finished yelling, the artist spread out the blanket and the two sat on it. It was hard to read the wife's expression from this distance, but Gina could well imagine the hurt she must be feeling. Still aching from Dane's recent rejection, Gina felt an emotional connection to the woman. Here they were; two women spurned by the men they loved.

Love? Is that how she really felt about Dane?

She shied away from the question and focused on her current problem. Finding Uncle Victor was her problem. So where in the hell was he?

She understood why he might want to dodge her calls, but he'd have to talk to her eventually, if for no other reason than they eventually needed to leave town together.

For the briefest of moments, she wondered if he'd left without her, but squelched the thought. He wouldn't do that.

At least, she hoped he wouldn't. At this moment, she wasn't certain about anything in her life.

Feeling too antsy to remain seated, she got up and started walking. Action was always better than inaction, she thought, crossing the street so she could peer through the store-front windows as she passed them. There was always a chance he was inside shopping. When she'd walked all the way around town square, she started over again, only this time walking one block out.

Thirty minutes later, nearing the finish of her second circuit around town, this one leading her through the alleys between the buildings, she spotted it. Her Acadia. It was parked behind the café where she would have expected it to be if Uncle Victor were meeting her inside.

She hurried toward the car and glanced inside, confirming it was empty. Assuming that meant her uncle was waiting for her inside, she went in through the back entrance that led past the kitchen and restrooms. She went as far into the café as necessary to see all the tables and booths. Uncle Victor was not sitting at any of them. Her anxiety growing, Gina went back outside.

Standing beside the car, she pulled out her phone, and once again tried to call him. From inside the car, she heard the muffled sound of Beethoven's Fifth Symphony. That was her uncle's ringtone. Letting the phone continue to ring, she stepped closer to the car window and peered inside. There was no sign of his phone, but the ringing was definitely coming from inside the car.

On impulse, she tried the driver's side door handle, with little hope of finding it unlocked. To her surprise, it was.

She tried not to read anything into that. In a large city, like Houston, people who didn't lock their car doors soon found themselves without a car. But this was Las Palomas. Maybe Uncle Victor was taking a walk on the wild side; bucking decades of his door-locking habit while in a small town.

Pulling the door open, she leaned inside to search for the phone. That's when she saw what was sitting in the bottom of the cup holder in the center console. Pulling out the key fob, she felt a cold chill race along her spine.

Even if there might be some legitimate reason that her uncle would leave his car door unlocked, there was no way he'd walk away from the car without taking the keys.

What the hell was going on?

She needed to find that phone. Maybe he'd received a call or text message that would shed some light on where he was now. Pulling her phone out, she once again called her uncle and tracked the ringing to beneath the driver's seat.

Finding the phone was troubling. It was completely unlike him to leave his phone behind. It was possible that it had fallen out of his pocket, between the center console and the seat, without his realizing it.

Tapping the screen to activate the phone, she entered his passcode when prompted. All of her texts, including the one telling him she would be late, showed as "unread."

If he hadn't known she'd be late, then presumably, he'd arrived at the café at noon as originally planned.

And then what? He'd walked away from the car without his phone and car keys?

Irritation with her uncle was rapidly giving way to worry. The urge to call Dane was nearly overwhelming, but she resisted it. He'd made it clear that he wanted nothing more to do with her.

No, she was on her own.

Unsure what to do next, she climbed into the car. With no better plan in mind than to drive up and down the streets hoping to spot her uncle, she started the car, put it in gear, and drove slowly down the alley.

Chapter Twenty-Eight

IT WAS 4:00 P.M. when Dane got the call about the missing little girl. Six-year-old Ariel Lund had been playing in Town Park on the jungle gym. Her mother had stepped to the other side of the dividing wall to watch Ariel's older brother perform a couple of jumps on the skateboard ramps and when she'd returned to the other side to check on her daughter, the girl was missing.

Ariel's mother was late reporting the crime because, at first, she'd assumed her daughter had gotten bored and returned home since the Lunds only lived two blocks from Town Park. She hadn't panicked until she'd gone home and found her daughter wasn't there.

He and his officers had spent a couple of hours talking to neighbors and shop owners. On his third round of questioning, Mrs. Lund had remembered that the graffiti artist and his wife had been finishing a late picnic lunch when they'd first arrived but, in her haste to get home to see if Ariel was there, she hadn't thought to ask them if they'd seen the little girl.

It was now close to 7:00 p.m. and while his men were out canvassing the neighborhoods, Dane was driving down Main Street, headed out to the trailer park to question the artist and his wife.

When he reached the stop sign at the end of the block, he felt a rush of excitement when he recognized the Acadia in front of him. The excitement quickly turned into a brush of annoyance. He'd told Gina that she and her uncle needed to leave town. Today.

So, what were they still doing here?

He resisted the urge to call her and demand an explanation. He would go over to Ruby Mae's in the morning. If they were still there, he'd escort them out of town.

He waited a long moment, expecting the Acadia to pull forward, but it didn't.

What the hell, he wondered? Had they recognized him and were purposely being annoying by not driving on?

Dane placed the palm of his hand against the center of the steering wheel, ready to sound the horn, but then hesitated. The situation with the Castillos was bad enough. He didn't need to aggravate it by blaring his horn at them.

Time passed and still, the car sat.

Fortunately, theirs were the only cars at this intersection, for now. Dane didn't expect that to be the case much longer.

He leaned from one side to the other, trying to see who was driving. From what he could tell, Gina was behind the wheel—and she was alone. Her head was bent forward, face covered by hands that clearly were not on the steering wheel.

What was she doing? Was she ill?

Unbidden, compassion and a sense of protectiveness stole over him. He fought the urge to get out of his truck and go tap on her window, not only because he couldn't leave his truck idling in the intersection without a driver, but he also doubted very much—after their last conversation—that Gina would even want to talk to him.

He did nothing.

That decision lasted all of sixty seconds and then he called her phone. He heard the first ring as the call went through. Then the second ring. He watched her reach for her phone and hold it up to glance at the screen. She put the phone back down without answering it.

Could he blame her?

Now determined to get her attention, he honked his horn, but she didn't even glance in the rearview mirror. In fact, she acted like she hadn't heard him.

Was that possible?

Well, he was sure of one way to get her attention. He turned on his lights and siren.

Gina sat listening to the melody of the song blasting from the car's radio and cried even harder. She was at her wit's end. She'd spent all afternoon looking for her uncle, to no avail. Now, hours later, she was tired beyond belief and starving, having long ago finished the food and water she'd purchased that morning. She'd even driven out to the RV park, willing to risk running into *Llorona* again, on the chance her uncle was there. He wasn't.

She had never felt more worried, lost and alone. When she'd pulled to a stop at the stop sign and Eric Carmen's All By Myself came on the radio, that was all it took to start the waterworks.

She couldn't even stop to answer Dane's call. It was just as well. She couldn't handle hearing more cruel words from him.

How had everything gone so wrong, so fast? Wrapped in her misery, blinded by tears and deaf to everything except the music blaring on the radio, Gina lost track of time. She never noticed the truck pulling up behind her; at least not until she heard the sudden wail of a siren.

Looking in the rearview mirror, she saw Dane in his truck, lights flashing. In a heartbeat, she went from distraught to furious. Was he pulling her over? For sitting in her car?

Hadn't she endured enough already? This was harassment.

Swiping the tears from her eyes, she threw her car into park and climbed out. She took a small amount of glee at seeing his stunned look as she stormed toward him. Reaching his side of the truck, she pounded on the window.

"Dane Wolfe, you'd better put this window down this instant." She glared at him as he complied. "What the hell, Dane?" She bit out as soon as he lowered the window. "It's not enough to order me to leave town, serve me inedible food, publicly shun and humiliate me and treat me like shit? Now you're what? Chasing me out of town? Or arresting me for sitting too long at a stop sign?" She put her hands on her hips. "There are laws, you know. You and the rest of this fucking town are not above them."

She watched him tear off a ticket, which she'd been too busy ranting to notice he was writing. He held it out to her.

"What's this?" She asked.

"A ticket. It's against the law to abandon a running vehicle in the middle of the street."

He was giving her a ticket? Unbelievable.

She snatched it from his hand. "You don't need to follow me out of town. Believe me, I can't wait to leave this place."

"I wasn't following you," he said. "I'm headed to the trailer park, only you're blocking the road."

"So you flash your lights and sound your sirens?"

"Well, I tried to call."

She snapped her mouth shut, knowing he was right. All the fight drained out of her.

"Fine."

She took her ticket and walked back to her car. Just as she was putting it into gear to drive, Dane's voice sounded on the loudspeaker.

"Pull over. Please."

What the... ?

Was he serious? She glanced in her rearview mirror and saw him gesturing to the side. What law had she broken now?

This was like a nightmare that never ended. Driving through the intersection, she pulled over to the curb on the other side. He followed and parked his truck behind her. Then he got out and came over to her driver's side window.

She put the window down and looked up at him.

"What's going on, Gina?" he asked. "I thought you and your uncle would be long gone by now. And what was all that about inedible food and being publicly shunned?"

"Don't act like you don't know," she snapped, not caring that she sounded surly. When he continued to stare at her expectantly, she huffed. "All right. First, I went to the café to meet Uncle Victor for lunch and not only was he a no-show, but Kathy served me a rock-hard bagel with rancid cream cheese." She sniffed. "Most of the people I've run into today are giving me the cold shoulder, and the few who aren't ignoring me have been downright insulting. I haven't done anything. Uncle Victor did. And I plan to correct the situation just as soon as I find him, only I've been looking for him all day. It's like he's vanished off the face of the earth. I found our car, abandoned behind the café It was unlocked, and I found his phone beneath the driver's seat."

Dane didn't like the sound of that. "Have you tried asking around town?"

"Oh, sure," she said with a forced laugh. "Because everyone's so willing to talk to me. If they answer me at all, it's only to let me know how angry they are." She sighed.

"Did you ask over at the café? Maybe Kathy has seen him."

"Yeah, Kathy's not exactly talking to me either, except to let me know I'm not welcome there—a fact she made abundantly clear when I was there earlier for lunch. I tried asking at the Waterin' Hole, but they aren't talking to me either. I was too afraid to go into the Condemned bar. No telling what they'd do to me in there." A tear leaked from the corner of her eye and trailed down her cheek. Dane had to resist the urge to wipe it away. "I'm tired and worried and hungry and I just want to go home, only I can't because I haven't found my uncle."

Her eyes were red from crying and her mascara was mostly streaked down her cheeks. What really got to him, though, was the utter defeat he saw reflected in her eyes. It angered him to learn the people of this town—his people—had treated her so poorly.

Hadn't he treated her just as poorly?

Knowing he had, he felt ashamed of himself. Pulling out his phone, he placed a quick call as she looked on.

He was glad when Kevin Wilson answered the bar phone.

"Hi, was hoping you could do me a favor," he said.

"Sure thing," Kevin replied.

"Can you send a cheeseburger and fries over to Ruby Mae's for me? I'll swing by tomorrow and pay you."

"Not a problem. I'll have it there in about fifteen minutes."

"Thanks."

Dane disconnected the call.

"Go back to the B&B. I'll call Ruby Mae and let her know that the food order is for you. I don't think she'll treat you as poorly as the others."

"No," she agreed. "I've called her several times, thinking my uncle might have returned. She's been very nice, but I can't go back. Not until I find Uncle Victor."

"I'll find him." The words were out of his mouth before he'd even considered what he was promising. If she'd spent the day looking for the man with no luck, what made him think he could do any better?

He had no clue if he could locate Gina's errant uncle, but he couldn't let her continue to wander the city alone at night; not when he doubted if anyone would help her if she got into trouble.

"You will? But I thought you were headed to the trailer park?"

"I am. A little girl—Ariel Lund—has gone missing and I'm looking for her."

"Missing? As in, taken?" she asked, sounding genuinely concerned.

He nodded solemnly. "We think so."

"Larry and Mo—"

He shook his head before she could finish speaking. "I had an officer talk to them as soon as we confirmed Ariel was missing. They aren't our perps."

"But the conversation I overheard in the gift shop—"

"They're gay. And married. What you overheard was them talking about adopting a child."

"Oh." Her face fell. "Okay, well, you need to find the little girl. I'll keep looking for my uncle."

"No," he countered. "You go to the B&B, eat and rest. While I'm at the RV park, I'll look for both Ariel and your uncle. And if I don't find him at the park, there are a few other places I can check. I'll also instruct my men to be on the lookout for him." He held up his hand before she could say anything. "We'll find him, okay?"

She nodded, and her eyes filled with fresh tears. "Thank you."

The urge to open her door and pull her into his arms so he could hold and comfort her was hard to resist.

"Will you be okay driving to Ruby Mae's?" he asked.

She nodded, so Dane stepped away from her car and watched until she'd driven away. Then he went back to his truck. As he started the engine and drove off, he had a feeling it was going to be a long night.

Chapter Twenty-Nine

THE SKY WAS A canvas of deep indigo, speckled with twinkling stars. Shadows danced in the corners of Dane's vision as he navigated the winding road through the trailer park, looking for signs of Ariel Lund or Victor Castillo and coming up empty.

The artist and his wife hadn't been at their trailer and it sat dark on the pad. Having completed an entire circuit around the RV park, he paused when he reached the front parking lot. The faint glow of a campfire flickered in the distance, beckoning him like a mystical beacon from across the river. It was coming from the game preserve, he realized. Intrigued, he left the trailer park and drove across the bridge to the other side of the river.

He turned into the entrance of the game preserve and as he drove deeper into the heart of the preserve, the air grew thick with the earthy scent of damp soil and wild vegetation. With his truck windows down, the sound of crickets and rustling leaves provided a symphony of nature's nighttime music, soothing yet eerie in a way.

Finally, Dane emerged into a small clearing where a parking lot came into view, bathed in the soft glow of moonlight filtering through the tree canopy above. Several cars were parked haphazardly, their shapes looming like slumbering beasts in the night. Dane cut the engine of his truck and stepped out.

He started down the dirt path that would eventually lead to the river, noting how the branches of the trees on either side seemed to reach out like spectral fingers to caress the moonlit sky above.

As he neared the end of the trail, the campfire came into view, its warm light casting an ethereal glow over a small clearing nestled within the embrace of nature. Figures moved around the fire, their silhouettes twisting and turning in a mesmerizing dance.

Dane's heart skipped a beat as he recognized the dancers. They were the Las Palomas witches and these crazy elderly women were reveling in their freedom to dance naked under the moonlight, indulging in wine, pot, and wild abandon. They were harmless, if not a bit eccentric.

Their wiry frames moved with a fluidity that belied their age, their gnarled hands reaching for the stars above as if plucking secrets from the cosmos. The flickering firelight painted their naked bodies in shades of gold and crimson, casting a spellbinding aura around them.

Drawing closer, Dane did his best to avoid looking at their bodies and focused on their faces, recognizing all of them.

Among them was Maggie Parrish, with her silver hair cascading down her back like a waterfall, her eyes alight with mischief. Beside her was Inez, Dane's fifth grade teacher, her hands raised to the sky as she twirled in a graceful pirouette, her voice raised in a wordless song that seemed to resonate with the very heartbeat of the earth.

Grateful to not see his mother in the group, Dane stepped out from the shadows; his footsteps muffled by the soft earth beneath his boots. The crackling of the campfire momentarily masked his approach until he cleared his throat, causing the women to pause their dance and turn towards him, their eyes wide with a mix of surprise and defiance.

"Maggie. Ladies." Dane greeted them, his voice calm yet firm. "I must ask you to put on your robes and leave."

Maggie, the *de facto* leader of the group, stepped forward with a defiant glint in her eyes. "Why? We aren't hurting anyone. We're just celebrating life and the beauty of this world in our own way."

Dane ran a hand through his hair, trying to find the right words. "I know you mean well, but lighting a campfire in the game preserve is both dangerous and against the law, as is smoking pot. I could arrest all of you." As the group of women closed in around him, he turned his gaze upward, praying for patience. "Ladies, please. Put on your robes."

He waited until, with a grumble, they complied. He continued to keep his gaze averted until he was sure they'd all had time to cover themselves, then he turned his attention back to Maggie. "Sam told me the next time I found you out here, I was to arrest you."

"That's fine, officer," Inez piped up. "You do what you have to. It won't be the first time we've spent a night in jail."

Dane sighed. "I don't have time to arrest you and haul you to jail. Ariel Lund and Victor Castillo are both missing. Have you seen either of them?"

Maggie's expression turned thoughtful, but then she shook her head. "No, I haven't."

He turned to the other women. "What about the rest of you?" No one had. Another dead end. "Maggie, I really need you ladies to pack up your stuff and go home. I don't think it's safe for you to be out here."

"Which is precisely why we are here," Maggie said, meeting Dane's gaze, her eyes glinting with determination. "We appreciate your concern, but tonight is no ordinary night," she said, her voice carrying a weight of solemnity. "The veil between our world and the spirit realm is thin, and dark forces stir in the shadows. We are here to perform a protection spell for the town, to ward off the evil spirits that threaten to spill into our world."

Dane furrowed his brow, surprised by Maggie's words. He studied the faces of the women gathered around the fire, seeing a fierce determination in their eyes that spoke of a deep-rooted belief in their cause. A chill ran down his spine as he considered the possibility of unseen dangers lurking in the shadows. He was torn between a need to find the missing girl and an obligation to protect these women.

After a moment of contemplation, Dane let out a re-signed sigh. "I understand that tonight holds significance for you, but I can't leave you here unprotected and risk your safety."

Maggie's gaze softened, her eyes holding a mixture of gratitude and understanding. "We appreciate your concern, Dane, but we've been practicing our craft for years and know how to protect ourselves."

He nodded in understanding. "It's not just that I don't feel right leaving you. Sam would kill me if anything happened to you. So I will stay here and wait for you to finish your ceremony. Just please keep in mind that every minute I'm here with you is a minute I'm not out looking for two missing people, one of whom is a child, and no doubt scared."

Maggie frowned at him for a long moment and then gave him a solemn nod. "Fine. We'll leave." She turned to the other women, and with a gesture of her hand, they broke apart. Two of the women picked up buckets and walked to the river to scoop up water. The other women spread out and started picking up the crystals that lay scattered about.

The two women with the buckets poured water onto the campfire, dousing the flame before stirring it with a stick. Darkness immediately enveloped the site, so Dane pulled his flashlight from his belt and used it to provide light for the ladies as they finished gathering up their crystals. Several of the crystals were white, which he was fairly sure had come from Zelda's store. In addition to the white crystals were a handful of darker crystals, ranging in color from light to dark gray and he wondered if these, too, had been "borrowed" from Zelda's shop. He watched the women carefully place the dark crystals into an ornate box and mentally shook his head. What did he know about witchcraft? Nothing, and he preferred it that way.

He turned a blind eye as the women put their wine bottles, some empty and some not, into a cooler along with their baggies of herbs, as he preferred to view it tonight. Then he followed them as they traipsed back to their cars.

He stood by his truck until the women drove away and only then did he get back into his truck to resume his search for Ariel and Victor.

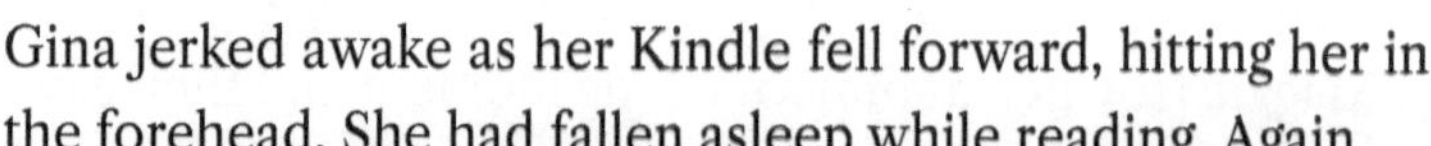

Gina jerked awake as her Kindle fell forward, hitting her in the forehead. She had fallen asleep while reading. Again.

She righted the Kindle and stared at the screen, reading the same paragraph she'd read at least ten times already. Still, her exhausted brain could make no sense of it.

With a sigh, she glanced at the digital clock on the nightstand.

It was after 11:00 p.m. and still no word from either Uncle Victor or Dane. She checked her phone, just in case she'd missed a call or slept through the chirp of an incoming text.

Nothing.

That couldn't be a good sign.

She got up from the bed, needing to stretch her limbs. Thanks to Dane, a burger and fries had been delivered to her at the Bed and Breakfast shortly after she'd arrived. She'd taken the food to her bedroom and despite a stomach churning with worry, she'd eaten all of it. All the while, her brain played out every worst-case scenario of things that could have happened to Uncle Victor.

Finally, she'd opened her Kindle hoping that reading would at least distract her while she waited.

Now, on the off chance that Uncle Victor had returned to the Bed and Breakfast, she slipped out of her room and walked down the hall to knock softly on his door. When there was no answer, she briefly considered calling Dane for an update, but knowing he would have called her if he had one, she returned to her room and once again stretched out on the bed with her Kindle to read.

Two pages in, the words on the screen no longer made sense. When her eyelids felt too heavy to keep up, she let them close. This time, when the Kindle fell forward, she was too sound asleep to notice.

She woke sometime later with a start, wondering what had roused her. She was lying on her side, facing the digital clock on the bedside table.

It was three o'clock in the morning and she wondered what had awakened her.

Grabbing her phone, she raised it and checked the screen. No new texts or missed calls. She set it back down, anxiety welling in the pit of her stomach.

A flutter of movement in her peripheral vision caught her attention and she turned her head, willing her vision to pierce the darkness.

There was something—or someone—standing at the foot of her bed. She lurched upright, into a sitting position, ready to face whoever was there, and then immediately relaxed as Uncle Victor stepped forward.

She stared at him for a long moment, drinking in his appearance. He looked fine. Perfectly fine.

"Do you know how worried I've been?" she growled. "I've been trying to reach you all day. Where have you been?"

As the seconds ticked by in silence, she watched the play of emotions across his face and willed herself to be patient as she waited for his response.

"You can see me," he finally said, his voice gruff with emotion.

"Of course I can. It's not that dark in here," she retorted. "But you haven't answered my question. Where have you been?"

"I'm so sorry, Gina. Things certainly didn't turn out the way I'd planned."

"You blackmailed the town. How'd you expect that would turn out? Now, we're the two most hated people in town."

"I thought blackmailing the town would solve our money problems," he started, then stopped. "Solve *my* money problems," he corrected. "I'd have the money to pay off Frankie and you wouldn't have to face *Llorona* again. Win-win for everyone." He sounded and looked genuinely upset, but she wasn't ready to let him off the hook just yet.

"Not exactly win-win," she countered. "I had something nice starting with Dane. Now he thinks I planned this with you and he can barely stand to talk to me."

"I'm sorry," he said. "I didn't mean for that to happen."

She pursed her lips, fighting to control her temper. "What's done is done, but that doesn't mean I'm going to let you keep that money. You're going to give it back." When he opened his mouth to argue with her, she held up her hand

and shook her head. "It's not a request. Maybe we can avoid going to jail if we give it back." She sighed and muttered. "I doubt we'll be allowed back here, but whatever."

"But Frankie—"

"We'll figure it out," she interrupted him. "We'll sell the house and pay him off."

"I'm just so sorry," he apologized. "Every time I try to do something good, I seem to make things worse."

"You should have talked to me before you blackmailed the town," she scolded. "But what really makes me mad is the way you dodged my calls and texts all damn day. I was worried sick about you. Especially when I found our car with the keys and your phone still in it. What the hell happened?"

She waited for an explanation, wondering if there was anything he could say to make her forget the hours of worry and humiliation she'd suffered today because of his actions. Probably not, but she needed him to offer her something.

He actually looked uncertain. When was the last time he'd acted that way? Not a single occasion came to mind, and she felt an inkling of alarm.

"I can tell you're upset. Maybe you don't know where to start. I can help. I know you saw Sylvia this morning. Then you blackmailed the mayor. At some point, you texted me to meet you for lunch—obviously not realizing just how fast news spreads in this small town if you thought they'd serve us." A thought occurred to her. "Is that what happened? You arrived at the café and some townspeople found you and exacted revenge for blackmailing them?"

"No," he finally spoke. "It wasn't the townspeople. It was those two men you spotted earlier. You were right. Frankie sent them down here to collect his fifty thousand dollars."

"You lied to me about how much you owed." It wasn't a question, and he only nodded. "I see." Actually, she was too furious to truly understand but decided she wanted to hear the rest of his story first. "Go on."

"I arrived at the café, intending to meet you for lunch. They pulled up behind me and before I knew what was happening, they threw a bag over my head and forced me into the trunk of their car."

"Oh, my God." Shock raced down her spine.

"After they took me, we drove for a while. Finally, we stopped, and they hauled me out of the trunk and made me walk. I could tell we were somewhere in the wilderness because I was walking on dirt and there was no traffic or street noise. When we finally stopped, they accused me of skipping town and got a few punches in before I could finally tell them I had Frankie's money on me."

Gina peered at him curiously. "You had fifty-thousand dollars in cash on you?"

"It sounds like a lot but in reality, it's not. Five small bundles of one-hundred Ben Franklins each." Gina tried to imagine five bundles of one-hundred dollars bills stuffed into a pants pocket. He must have sensed the direction of her thoughts because he said, "I had on my sports jacket with the inside pockets. The money fit inside the pockets nicely. It's the only reason I would have worn it on such a hot day."

"What happened after that?"

He shrugged; his expression dour. "I don't really know. One minute, I hear them talking to Frankie on the phone and the next, everything's a blank. They must have hit me over the head or something."

Gina was horrified, hearing what had happened to him. "So Dane found you and brought you back?"

He looked at her in surprise. "Dane?"

"Yeah. When I couldn't find you, Dane offered to look for you. Is he still here?" She looked around the room like she might have missed him standing off to the side.

At that moment, there was a knock on her bedroom door.

"Gina, it's Dane. Are you awake? I need to talk to you. It's important."

Relief ran through her. He hadn't just dropped Uncle Victor off and left. She scooted off the bed to open the door.

"Hey. Come on in." She stepped back so he could step past her into the room. She was about to thank him for finding her uncle when she stopped, noticing his haggard expression. "What's wrong?"

"Gina, about your uncle—" he started, but stopped when she impulsively threw her arms around him to give him a hug.

Then, embarrassed, she stepped back. "Thank you for finding and bringing him back."

He looked confused. "What are you talking about?"

"He was just telling me what happened." She waved her hand, gesturing to her uncle standing quietly on the opposite side of the bed. "How he was kidnapped, hit over the head and left unconscious."

Dane's gaze passed over her uncle before returning to her. "You've been talking to your uncle?"

"Of course." Now she was feeling puzzled by the way he was acting.

"And he told you what happened to him?"

She nodded.

He stood there a moment longer, staring at the floor and shaking his head. "This is a first for me."

"What are you talking about?" she asked, perplexed.

When she thought the silence would go on forever, Dane stepped closer and, taking her gently by the upper arms, steered her back until her legs bumped the edge of the bed and she abruptly sat. He sat beside her, holding her hand between both of his.

"Gina, we found three bodies on the east side of town. All three had been shot." His tone was filled with tenderness. "Gina, one of the victims was your uncle."

"What?" She'd heard the words, but they didn't make sense.

"Your uncle is dead."

"No." She shook her head. "He's standing right there." She gestured emphatically, looking from one man to the other, waiting for one of them to tell her this was part of a sick joke.

Chapter Thirty

Twin expressions of sympathy regarded her, waiting for the truth to pierce her tired brain.

She shook her head. "Stop it. You're not making sense."

Pulling away from Dane's gentle grasp, she stood and rounded the end of the bed. She reached out to touch Uncle Victor, but her hand passed through his arm as if it wasn't there.

Because it wasn't.

Trying to ignore the sudden ringing in her ears, she tried again.

"Uncle Victor?" she pleaded, begging him to deny it. When she reached for him a third time, though, his body shimmered and vanished.

"Oh, God." Her vision started tunneling as the world spun out of control. No longer able to tell up from down, she felt her knees buckle.

Suddenly, Dane was there. "Okay, steady there. I've got you." Strong arms wrapped around her, keeping her from falling, giving her an anchor.

In the next moment, she was lying on the bed and Dane was putting a pillow beneath her feet. Slowly, the dizziness faded, giving way to numbness and shock.

She flinched when Uncle Victor reappeared at the side of her bed.

"How is this possible?" she asked him.

Dane, who, of course, thought she was talking to him, started to respond but she silenced him with a gesture and turned to pin Uncle Victor beneath her gaze. "How?"

He gave her a wan smile. "Your mother's ability to see ghosts was real," he told her. "It seems you inherited her ability, after all, but it's been dormant all these years. I suspect the near-death experience at the river activated those abilities."

She shook her head, not wanting to believe it. "I would have known..." She paused. But she hadn't known he was dead. Now she wondered how many other ghosts she had seen without realizing they weren't living people.

Her gaze traveled to the tule pouch sitting on the nightstand. The one Maggie Parrish had given her.

You mustn't be afraid to be what you are. She had said before giving her the pouch... *just a small spell to help open your third eye...*

Now she wasn't feeling as certain as she had before. She needed time to process everything, but Dane was talking to her, so she turned to him. "I'm sorry. What did you say?"

"Your uncle was shot with a nine-millimeter handgun. We found such a gun on one of the other two victims. They were both shot with a forty caliber, which we couldn't find at the scene, leading me to believe there was a fourth person involved. However, it looks like your uncle was shot first, by one of the two men. Do you know of any reason why they would shoot him?"

No longer feeling faint, but angry, Gina pushed herself up into a sitting position. "They worked for Frankie Goldstein. He's a loan shark in Houston."

Then she told him about Uncle Victor owing money, coming down to Las Palomas hoping to earn enough to pay off Frankie, her uncle's decision to blackmail the town and how Frankie's men had come to Las Palomas and taken her uncle.

"What I don't understand," she finished, "is why they would shoot him after he gave them the money?"

"Because Frankie was sending a message," Uncle Victor replied, "to anyone who thought they could get away with paying late."

It seemed excessive but she believed him. It was consistent with Frankie Goldstein's reputation. She vowed then and there that she would find a way to make Frankie pay for killing her uncle.

"Did you find the money? Uncle Victor said he gave it to Frankie's men right before—"She trailed off.

Right before he was killed.

"Not yet," Dane replied. "I'll take another look when I get back to the crime scene. We're still combing the area for clues."

"I'll go with you."

Dane shook his head. "I don't think that's a good idea."

"I do," she insisted. "First, despite all the evidence, I need to see for myself that my uncle is dead. Besides, don't you need me to ID the body?"

"Yeah," he grudgingly admitted. "But we can do that later, at the morgue."

She wasn't sure why it was so important for her to see where her uncle had died. It just was. "Well, maybe the spirits of the other two men are hanging around their bodies. I could talk to them and see if they saw who shot them."

A small voice in the back of her head started screaming at her, asking if she had lost her damn mind. Until coming to Las Palomas, she'd never encountered an actual ghost. Now, suddenly, she was an expert? So what if Dane assumed she was. She knew better.

She clamped her lips closed before she could withdraw the offer and told the small voice to shut-up.

"I think you'd be better off staying here and getting some rest," Dane suggested. She stared at him in dismay.

"I've just learned that my uncle—my only living relative—is dead. Murdered. I don't think it's possible to fall asleep with that weighing on my mind. I may never sleep again."

The moon hung low in the sky, casting long shadows on the road ahead as Dane gripped the steering wheel. He had agreed to take Gina to the crime scene, albeit reluctantly. Now, the silence in the truck was heavy, suffocating even. He wanted to say something, anything to break it, but how could he? It was his duty as the town's chief of police to investigate a crime, but never had that involved exposing someone like Gina to such a grizzly sight. Yet, with her unique ability to communicate with the deceased, he couldn't afford to ignore the opportunity she might provide in solving this case.

"Where were they found?" Gina's voice was barely above a whisper, her face appearing pale and drawn in the truck's dim lighting.

"About fifteen miles outside of town, on the east side." His gaze briefly flicked over to her before returning to the road. "The land belongs to one of the local ranchers. He's the one who found them."

"This late at night?"

"Poaching has been an issue lately," he explained, his voice taking on a weary quality. "After dark, he was out patrolling the pasture, trying to catch whoever's responsible. That's when he stumbled upon the bodies and called it in."

Gina nodded, her fingers twisting together in her lap. She seemed so fragile.

"Are you sure about this, Gina?" he asked quietly, the concern evident in his voice. "I don't want to put you through anything you're not ready for."

She met his gaze, and despite her obvious fear, a determined spark lit up her eyes. "I have to try," she said firmly. "If there's even a small chance I can help find out who did this, then I need to do it."

Reaching their destination, Dane parked his truck alongside the other police vehicles at the edge of the rancher's pasture. Their feet hit the ground with a thud as they stepped out of the truck and the silence settled around them like a shroud, broken only by the distant hum of insects and the occasional rustle of leaves.

Gina took a deep breath, her heart pounding in her chest as she glanced at Dane, seeking reassurance in his steady presence.

Together, they ducked under the police crime tape that stretched across a section of fencing where the wires had been cut and pulled back, a silent testament to the violence that had occurred just beyond. They continued through the pasture and as they neared the scene, Gina felt an icy shiver run down her spine.

The scene unfolded before her like something from a nightmare. Portable light stands cast stark shadows across the ground, their harsh glare illuminating the lifeless bodies sprawled in the dirt. Several men moved about with grim determination; some were slowly walking around, gazes focused on the ground, while others squatted near the bodies, examining clothing and murmuring to one another.

"Hey, watch where you step," one officer called out, not unkindly. "We don't need you contaminating the evidence."

Gina barely heard the warning, her gaze drawn inexorably to the body of her uncle. The black hood Frankie's men had put over his head lay discarded on the ground beside him. His lifeless eyes, once filled with determination and purpose, now stared vacantly up at the dark expanse of the night sky. The stars twinkled above him, an eerie contrast to the stillness of his body on the ground. The portable light stands cast a harsh glow on his pale skin, emphasizing the deep shadows under the unseeing eyes. He appeared almost frozen in time, as if he had become a part of the hard ground beneath him. Two more bodies lay close by looking equally unreal and gruesome.

Gina shuddered, her stomach churning with a mixture of grief and horror. What was she doing here? She'd needed to see her uncle's body if for no other reason than to prove to herself he was truly dead. But she'd also offered to talk to the ghosts of the other two men. Doubt gnawed at her resolve.

Dane's warm hand on her shoulder grounded her to the reality of the situation. "Are you okay?" he asked, his voice gentle yet firm.

She wasn't, but she swallowed hard and nodded anyway. She couldn't let her distress cripple her now. As if sensing her determination, Uncle Victor's ghost materialized on the other side of her. The anguished expression on his ghostly face made it clear that seeing his own lifeless body was a harrowing experience, to say the least.

A short distance away, two men stood near a tree, watching the police work. Their expressions mirrored Uncle Victor's.

"I need to go over there," Gina said to Dane, gesturing toward the tree, her voice barely above a whisper. She'd recognized the ghosts of the two other victims. Their ethereal forms flickered in the artificial light from the nearby stands, making them appear even more otherworldly than they already were. "You should stay here."

"Alright," Dane relented, stepping back to give her space. "If you need anything, I'll be right here."

As Gina carefully navigated the scene, avoiding treading on any potential evidence, she tried to mentally prepare herself for what she was about to do. She had never spoken to ghosts other than her uncle and initiating a conversation with the deceased seemed like an impossible task. What could she possibly say? 'Hey, sorry you're dead. That's a drag. Any chance you saw who killed you?' No, that wouldn't do. She needed a more tactful approach.

Her shoes crunched softly against the dirt; the sound almost drowned out by the hum of the generator powering the light stands. The ghosts barely acknowledged her presence, their gazes still fixed on their lifeless bodies. She hesitated for a moment, her heart racing as she searched for the right words. It was then that Uncle Victor's ghost joined them, his own face etched with sorrow.

"Not how you expected the night to end, is it?" he said to them, not bothering to hide his disdain.

"Are we dead?" one man asked, his voice trembling. Uncle Victor nodded solemnly.

"No shit?" the other man muttered, bitterness lacing his words. "That's fucked up."

"Who shot us?" the first man asked, his eyes searching Uncle Victor's face for answers.

Uncle Victor shrugged. "I don't know, but I know who shot me." He glowered at them.

The first men had the decency to look contrite. "Yeah. Sorry. Wasn't personal. Just business."

"Whatever," Uncle Victor scoffed. "It felt pretty damn personal to me." Then, perhaps realizing Gina was still hoping for answers, he continued. "So, did you see who shot you?"

"Naw. I watched you fall and then suddenly, I'm waking up..." He gestured to his ghostly form. "Like this."

"What about you?" Uncle Victor asked the other man.

"I turned when Vinnie went down, but the shooter was too far away to see. Then the next thing I know, I'm standing over my body looking down."

Gina's heart sank as she realized they were no closer to finding the killer. She thanked the ghosts and walked back to Dane, relaying the conversation to him. He shook his head, frustration clear in the tense set of his jaw.

"We're not finding much here," he told her. "I doubt those men planned to bring your uncle here, so the shooting wasn't premeditated. Someone was in the right place at the right time."

"But why?" Gina asked, her voice barely above a whisper.

Dane sighed. "If I had to guess, I'd say it was a poacher who happened to see your uncle giving those men the money he got from the town. He, or she, wanted it for themselves so they shot all three men and took it."

"The money's gone?"

Dane nodded. "We've checked all the pockets. It's gone. I'm guessing the killer took it."

The disappointment of not finding the money weighed heavily on her heart, because she'd wanted to return it. Dane's warm hand found its way to the center of her back, startling her out of her melancholy thoughts.

"I hate to ask, but while you're here, would you mind making a positive ID of your uncle? And if the ghosts told you their names, that would be helpful since there's no ID on them."

"Of course," Gina murmured, swallowing the lump that had formed in her throat. With Dane by her side, she walked over to her uncle's body and looked down. Tears welled in her eyes, nearly blinding her, but there was no mistaking who it was.

"That's my uncle," she whispered, her voice cracking. She then glanced over to where Uncle Victor's ghost was talking to the two other ghosts. As he relayed their names to her, she passed the information on to Dane, feeling a strange sense of closure as she did so.

With nothing more they could do at the crime scene, they headed back to Dane's truck. A few minutes later, when he pulled into Ruby Mae's driveway, Gina made no move to get out.

"Are you okay?" he asked.

She turned to him, feeling distraught. "I don't think I can go inside," she admitted. Her room was filled with the memory of the hours of worry followed by news of her uncle's death and then realizing she was talking to his ghost. Staying in her uncle's room was absolutely out of the question. She struggled with how to explain it to Dane, but he seemed to understand because he simply nodded, put the truck into gear and backed out of the driveway.

"Where are we going?" she asked.

"My place."

The truck's engine hummed softly in the darkness as Dane navigated the neighborhood roads, his hands steady on the wheel. Gina glanced over at him, her heart fluttering with a mixture of excitement and uncertainty. His strong profile was illuminated by the dim glow of the dashboard, and she couldn't help but feel drawn to him. Yet, the thought of entering his home for the first time left her feeling exposed and vulnerable.

Gina shifted in her seat, her fingers nervously twisting the edge of her shirt as they neared their destination. After the emotional turmoil of learning about her uncle's death, she craved the comfort and safety of another person—but what if Dane didn't share her feelings? Her mind raced with doubts and questions, but the warmth of his presence beside her was undeniable.

"Here we are," he announced as they pulled into the driveway of a modest one-story house. The darkness made it difficult for Gina to make out any details, but it seemed welcoming and well-maintained.

Dane climbed out of the truck and walked around to open the passenger door for her. She smiled gratefully, allowing him to take her hand and help her out of the vehicle. His touch sent a shiver down her spine, and she held onto him as they crossed the front yard together.

At the door, Dane released her hand to fumble through his keys. Gina's pulse quickened as she watched him, her anxiety mounting.

With a soft click, he unlocked the door and stepped back, gesturing for her to enter. She took a deep breath, gathering her courage, and stepped over the threshold into the unknown.

The soft glow of the living room lamp cast shadows on the walls, making Dane's home feel both warm and inviting. She stood in the dimly lit space, acutely aware of his presence.

"Let me show you the guest room," he said, his voice sounding rough. He swallowed audibly, the simple act betraying his own nervousness. With a nod, Gina followed him down the hallway.

The guest bedroom was cozy, adorned with soft colors and plush pillows. As Gina stepped inside, Dane hesitated for a moment before disappearing down the hallway. When he returned, he handed her one of his T-shirts.

"I thought you might be more comfortable sleeping in this," he explained.

She took it from him and smiled. "Thanks." They stood for a moment longer and then Dane stepped back into the open doorway.

"Well, good night," he said awkwardly, avoiding eye contact. "I'll be right next door if you need anything."

"Thank you, Dane," she replied softly, gripping the shirt tightly. As he turned to leave, something within her snapped. "Dane, wait. I don't think I can handle being alone right now. Will you stay with me?"

He stopped in his tracks, his eyes filled with longing as he looked at her. "That's probably not a great idea," he admitted, his voice heavy with emotion. "I'm not sure I can be that close to you and not want to touch you."

"Okay," Gina answered, her voice barely audible. But as he began to walk away, she found herself calling out to him once more. "No, I mean, I'm okay if you want to touch me." Her eyes pleaded with him, silently begging for the comfort of his embrace.

For a moment, they simply stared at each other, their connection undeniable. Then, as if propelled by an unseen force, Dane crossed the room in a heartbeat. He pulled her into his arms, their lips meeting in a passionate kiss that seemed to make everything else fall away.

The gentle press of their lips sparked a flame in Gina, her heart swelling with every beat as Dane's hands lovingly slid under her shirt. The sensation of his warm palms against her bare skin sent tingles throughout her body as he continued to shower her with tender kisses. She longed for his touch, but at the same time, a nagging thought gnawed at the back of her mind.

As Dane lifted her shirt over her head, Gina abruptly stepped back, breaking their embrace. She clutched the shirt against her chest, her breaths coming in ragged gasps. Dane's eyes widened with concern as he stammered an apology, "I'm sorry, I must have misread the signals."

She shook her head, struggling to find her voice amidst the whirlwind of emotions. "No, you didn't misread them," she admitted, her eyes searching his. "But I can't make love to you knowing there's still a lie between us."

"Wh-what lie?" Dane asked, confusion written all over his face. "I've told you everything."

Gina hesitated for a moment before blurting out, "It's not your lie, it's mine. I'm a fraud. I'm not a real ghost whisperer. Before coming here, I'd never even seen a real ghost. I only pretended to see and talk to ghosts." Her words tumbled out in a rush, the weight of her secret finally being revealed. "I'm so sorry. I only took this assignment because we needed the money so badly."

Dane furrowed his brows, trying to process her confession. "But earlier tonight, you were talking to your dead uncle and those other victims," he pointed out. "Or was that fake, too?"

"No," Gina replied, her voice trembling. "That was real. It turns out nearly dying myself gave me the ability to see and speak to ghosts."

"Let me get this straight," he said slowly, his eyes never leaving hers. "You were a fake ghost whisperer, but now you're not a fake?"

Gina managed a rueful smile. "Yeah, that pretty much sums it up."

She looked at Dane, afraid of rejection; hoping for some kind of understanding. The longer he remained silent, the greater her anxiety grew.

Then he shrugged, his gaze softening. "Okay." His casual acceptance took her by surprise.

"You're not mad?" she asked, her voice barely a whisper.

He shook his head. "You had your reasons, just like I had reasons not to tell you the truth about the town's hauntings." He stepped closer to her, his hand reaching up to brush a stray strand of hair from her face, tucking it gently behind her ear. "We both lied and we're both sorry. Let's not waste any more time being mad or sorry when there are better things we could be doing."

Gina hesitated, searching his eyes for any hint of doubt or anger. "You're sure?"

A slow, warm smile spread across his face. "Oh, yeah," he replied, and before she knew it, his arms were around her again, pulling her close for a deep, tender kiss that reignited the fire within her.

As their lips met, Gina felt herself surrendering to the moment, letting go of the lingering guilt and doubts that had threatened to overwhelm her. She wrapped her arms around Dane's neck, feeling her body respond eagerly to his touch.

A frenzy of hands and limbs ensued as they fumbled with buttons and zippers, eager to remove the barriers between them. In the process, two cell phones fell out of Gina's jeans pockets onto the floor. Dane paused to pick them up, raising an eyebrow at her.

"One's mine, and the other belonged to Uncle Victor," she quickly explained. "I found his in the car earlier."

Dane nodded and set the phones on the nightstand, and then their lips found each other once more. The last of their clothes were discarded, leaving them vulnerable and exposed in each other's arms.

As they fell into bed together, Gina couldn't help but feel a sense of relief and belonging. For the first time since her world had been turned upside down, she was allowing herself to accept love and comfort, with no lies left between her and Dane to keep them apart. They made love passionately, letting their bodies express what words could not.

Much later, feeling both exhausted and sated, they drifted off to sleep, tangled together beneath the sheets. Despite the weight of the lies and secrets that had brought them together, in that moment before sleep took her, Gina felt a profound sense of peace and contentment.

CHAPTER THIRTY-ONE

DANE CAME AWAKE SUDDENLY, his ears straining against the invasive trill of a ringing phone. Aware that it was daytime, due to the sunlight peeking past the curtains, he followed the sound to the bedside table, where Victor Castillo's phone vibrated with urgency. He glanced at Gina's peaceful face, wondering if she would awaken. When she remained still, he snatched the phone from the table, intending to silence it, but stopped when he saw the caller ID: Frankie Goldstein. A chill ran down his spine as he recognized the loan shark's name. The two other men who had been shot presumably worked for him. Swallowing hard, Dane answered the call. "Hello?"

"Victor?" The voice on the line sounded startled, but quickly recovered.

"No, this isn't Victor."

"Who is this?" Frankie demanded.

"Dane. I'm a friend of the family," Dane said, trying to keep his voice steady. "Victor isn't available right now. Can I take a message?"

Frankie grumbled on the other end, obviously displeased. "This is Frankie Goldstein. It's imperative that I speak to him."

"I'm afraid that won't be possible," Dane replied calmly. "He's dead. Shot and killed last night."

"Hmmm, that is most unfortunate," Frankie said, not sounding the least surprised or upset.

"Yeah, well, Victor wasn't the only victim last night. There were two others." He rattled off the names of the other two men and waited. On the other end of the call, he heard a sharp intake of breath. "Know them?"

"Nooooo," Frankie said the word slowly as if he was giving the matter great thought. "Those names don't sound familiar." There was a long pause. "Victor's niece. How's she doing?"

"Fine," Dane replied cautiously, glancing at Gina, who was now awake, sitting beside him. "Why do you ask?"

"I'd like to offer my condolences. Would she be up for a call?" Frankie's voice was smooth and insistent, like oil over gravel.

Dane hesitated, then muted the phone and looked at Gina. "It's Frankie Goldstein. He wants to talk to you." As fear flickered across her eyes, he added, "You don't have to talk to him."

Gina considered her options before silently taking the phone from Dane. She was about to unmute it when she paused, her fingers flying across the screen to find the recording app. She showed the app to Dane, who smiled and nodded in approval. It was a smart move. In Texas, only one party needed to know a call was being recorded.

Then, she unmuted the call and raised the phone to her ear. "Hello?"

The dialogue that followed was like a dance, each word chosen carefully and deliberately.

"Gina, my dear. This is Frankie Goldstein. Do you know who I am?"

Ice flooded her veins as she clutched the phone tighter. "I know who you are," she replied, trying in vain to keep her voice steady.

"Good." He paused for a moment, letting the silence build before continuing. "Your uncle owed me a considerable sum, and since he's no longer around to honor his debt, that responsibility falls to you. And every day the debt remains unpaid, interest is compounding."

"My uncle paid his debt, the night you had him killed. I don't owe you anything," Gina said.

"I'm afraid I disagree and while I can be a reasonable man, I do have my limits. As your uncle unfortunately discovered. Do yourself a favor and pay off his debt, before something unfortunate happens to you."

"Are you threatening me?"

There was a moment's pause. "I must be losing my touch if you have to ask."

The call disconnected abruptly, leaving Gina gasping for breath as if she'd been submerged underwater. Then, with trembling fingers, she ended the recording.

"Everything alright?" Dane asked, concern etched across his face.

She hesitated, then handed him the phone. "Listen to this."

As Dane played back the recording, Gina watched the emotions flicker across his face—shock, anger, determination. When it finished, he looked up at her, his jaw set.

"I'm going to hang onto this for a bit," he told her.

"Okay."

"I hate to leave you, but it's almost one o'clock and I really need to get back to work. I've got state guys coming to look at the crime scene where your uncle was killed and the Lund girl is still missing. I've had guys out looking for her all night and morning."

"Of course. I understand."

"You don't have to leave," he said when she started to get out of bed. "Feel free to stay as long as you want. Make yourself at home."

"Are you sure?" She appreciated the offer because she wasn't ready to go back to the Bed and Breakfast just yet.

"Of course. Try to get some more sleep. I have to run to the next town, but maybe we can do dinner when I get back."

She smiled. "That sounds good."

"Okay, then. If you do decide to leave, Ruby Mae's is only a couple of blocks up." He pointed out the direction and she nodded her understanding. Then, he smiled and, leaning over, kissed her. Then he kissed her again. "I could get used to this," he told her, his voice sounding husky.

"Me, too," she agreed.

He gave her one final kiss and then, with a groan, climbed out of bed. Gina watched him dress with unabashed interest.

When he was finished, he picked up Uncle Victor's phone and slipped it into his pocket.

The reminder of her uncle and Frankie Goldstein had her smile fading. "What am I going to do about Frankie?"

Dane's eyes met hers, his gaze resolute. "Don't worry about him," he said, a hint of steel in his voice. "I've got an idea."

As Dane left the room, a fragile hope took root within her. For the first time since her world had shattered, she dared to believe that maybe, just maybe, she wouldn't have to face this nightmare alone.

CHAPTER THIRTY-TWO

GINA WOKE SEVERAL HOURS later, not realizing she'd fallen back asleep. The bed seemed to swallow her as she lay there, the emptiness beside her a reminder of Dane's departure. She was tracing the imprint he'd left on the pillow, wishing she could bring him back with a simple touch, when the sudden appearance of Uncle Victor's ghost at the foot of the bed startled her.

"Uncle Victor," she breathed, not quite believing her eyes. "What are you doing here?"

"I came to check on you, of course. How are you?"

She made a face. "I've been better. How about you?"

"Same." He offered her a wry smile. "I've been talking to Sylvia, through Henri, if you can believe that."

Gina felt a pang of sadness for her uncle; his relationship with Sylvia had ended far too soon. Yet she couldn't help but feel a thread of happiness for him, knowing he had found some way to communicate with the woman.

"So, you and Dane, huh?" he asked, a teasing look in his eye. She blushed and then a horrible thought occurred to her. "You weren't here earlier, spying on me, were you?"

He snorted. "Like I want to see you and the police chief fooling around. Please. Give me credit for some discretion."

She wasn't sure she believed him but didn't press. Instead, she changed the topic.

"Frankie called. He expects me to pay off your debt."

Uncle Victor's face darkened, and he muttered a curse under his breath. "Gina, I'm so sorry for bringing all this trouble on you."

She shook her head, trying to quell her unease. "I know. Dane said he has an idea of how to deal with Frankie."

"Good, good..." Uncle Victor nodded, though his expression remained troubled. Then he looked around the room before his gaze returned to her. "Why are you in bed?"

"It was kind of a rough night," she said with a touch of anger. "I was tired, so I slept in."

"What I mean is, Dane is gone so why are you STILL in bed?"

This time, her tone came out meeker. "I told you; I was tired."

"It's not good for you to say here. Go into town. Get some fresh air."

She rolled her eyes. "Why? So everyone can shun me again? No thanks."

"Gina Castillo! I did not raise you to be spineless. Stand tall. Don't let them get to you," he admonished. "Besides, I don't think you'll be shunned."

She gazed at him questioningly. "How do you know?"

He shrugged. "I might have been following Dane around earlier this afternoon and overheard him ordering people to be nice to you because you're special to him."

A faint smile tugged at her lips as she imagined Dane defending her honor. Before she could dwell on it too long, Uncle Victor started to fade.

"Where are you going?" she asked, alarmed.

"It's okay. I'll be around," he assured her before disappearing completely.

With a deep breath, Gina threw back the covers and climbed out of bed. Uncle Victor was right. She couldn't stay here, hiding in Dane's house, forever. She would drive into town. Maybe, she would even get out of her car.

The sun cast a warm golden glow over Town Park as Gina drove past an hour later. She'd walked to the Bed and Breakfast, taken a shower and changed clothes. Then she'd driven her car into town.

Her heart raced, but she took a deep breath and reminded herself of Uncle Victor's encouragement. When she spotted Meredith sitting on a park bench, she pulled her car into a parking space and got out.

"Hi, Meredith," Gina greeted her, approaching the woman with cautious optimism. "Do you remember me?"

"Hello, Gina," Meredith smiled warmly, her eyes genuinely kind. "I heard about your uncle. I'm so sorry for your loss."

"Thank you," Gina replied, touched by Meredith's sincerity.

"He's quite a character," Meredith chuckled fondly.

"You knew my uncle?"

Meredith nodded. "We met recently."

As they reminisced, several passersby shot them strange looks, causing Gina's chest to tighten. The familiar sting of being shunned threatened to overwhelm her, but before she could sink into despair, Sarah appeared, carrying a shopping bag.

"Hey, Gina," Sarah called out, stopping near the bench. "I thought I saw you over here." Her gaze flickered between Gina and Meredith, brows furrowed. "Who are you talking to?"

"Oh, I'm sorry. Sarah, this is Meredith," Gina stammered. "Meredith, this is Sarah. She's Dane's mother." She assumed Meredith would know Dane.

Neither woman spoke and Gina wondered if there was a history between them. Then Sarah asked, hesitantly, "Is Meredith... a ghost?"

Gina turned to look at Meredith, who nodded solemnly before excusing herself and fading away. For a long moment, Gina was too shocked to speak. "Wow... yeah. Sorry about that," she finally said.

Sarah smiled. "Hazard of being a ghost whisperer, I suppose."

Of course, Sarah would assume this happened to Gina all the time. Gina didn't bother to correct her. "She's gone now, if you'd like to sit?"

"Thank you," Sarah said and offered her condolences. "How are you holding up?"

As they talked, Gina couldn't help but see that the little boy she'd noticed earlier in the park was now back, lingering near the graffiti artist, watching intently as the artist put the finishing touches on his mural depicting *Llorona, El Muerto* and other ghosts.

"Why don't you come over to the house," Sarah said. "I've got a doctor's appointment this afternoon, but you could come for dinner. Say six-thirty?"

"I'd like that," Gina said.

"Speaking of, what time is it now?" Sarah glanced at her watch. "Oh, no. Is it really almost four?" she asked, her voice laced with urgency. "I'm late. I promised Dane I'd drop these shirts I bought him off at the station, but I guess it'll have to wait."

"I can drop them off for you," Gina offered, sensing Sarah's distress.

"Really? That would be great; if you don't mind. Thank you so much." Relief washed over Sarah's features as she handed over the shopping bag. With a grateful nod and a quick goodbye, Sarah hurried off.

Gina watched her friend disappear around a corner and then, with shopping bag in hand, she headed across the street.

Pushing open the heavy glass door of the police station, she stepped inside. The low hum of the AC system filled her ears and a faint scent of stale coffee lingered in the air.

"Can I help you?" a woman called from behind the front desk. Her fingers flew across the keyboard of her computer as she typed. "You won't find many people here today. Everyone's out working either on the kidnapping or the murder case. It's been ages since we've had this much crime in Las Palomas."

"I was looking for Dane," Gina admitted, glancing around the eerily empty room. "His mom asked if I'd drop this off for him." She held the shopping bag up for the woman to see.

The woman paused her typing to look up, giving Gina a curious look. "You're Gina Castillo, right? The ghost whisperer?"

Gina nodded, bracing for trouble.

"It's nice to meet you," the woman said, surprising her. "I'm Bev, the dispatcher. I'm sorry for your loss."

"Thank you," Gina replied.

Just then, the front desk phone rang, its shrill tone cutting through the silence. "Sorry, gotta take this," Bev said, reaching for the phone. "Dane's still out of town, but you can leave the bag in his office." She pointed to an open doorway across the room.

"Thanks," Gina said, and made her way across the bullpen.

As she entered the small room, she took in the cluttered desk and the plaques lining the walls. All bore the name of Samantha Hunter on them and Gina realized this wasn't actually Dane's office. He was merely using it until the actual police chief returned to duty.

Unsure where to place the bag of clothes, she decided the office chair was her best bet. As she set the bag down, a sheet of paper on top of the desk caught her eye. It was a picture of a young girl with a cherubic face and blond hair. The name "Ariel Lund" was printed below it.

This was the young girl Dane was looking for, she realized. She picked up the picture to take a closer look. That's when her gaze fell to the sheet below it. It was another photo and the boy in the picture looked familiar, but she couldn't quite place him. She furrowed her brows, studying the boy's face. Then it hit her—he was the boy she'd seen in the park, watching the artist.

"Wait a minute..." Gina whispered to herself, her heart pounding in her chest. She knew she shouldn't snoop, but curiosity gnawed at her.

Her gaze darted to the open doorway, ensuring Bev was still preoccupied at the front desk, then she picked up the page, studying the photo and the information printed below it. The boy's name was Josh Tyler, reported missing six months ago from Austin.

She scanned the remaining text on the page, stopping at a handwritten note at the bottom: "Body found in Hebbronville, east of Laredo"—one week ago!

The realization hit her then. The boy was a ghost.

Her fingers tightened around the edges of the paper, her breaths coming in shallow gasps. What did it mean? A knot of uneasiness settled in her stomach, refusing to budge. Carefully, she placed the pages back on Dane's desk.

The memory of the conversation with Peggy Olson resurfaced. Peggy claimed the artist's wife told her they had a son and his name was "Josh." Why would the wife make that up? Peggy had told them the artist had been in Austin before going to San Antonio. Had they been there at the time Josh had been taken?

A horrible scenario was forming in Gina's head. What if the artist had taken Josh in Austin and then something happened, resulting in the boy's death. They couldn't report the boy's death. Not if they'd kidnapped him. And not if they'd killed him. They'd also need to get rid of the body and Hebbronville was between San Antonio and Las Palomas. Suddenly, Gina needed to find Josh Tyler's ghost and talk to him.

"Thanks, Bev!" she called, trying to sound casual as she hurriedly left the office and headed for the door.

Once outside, she crossed the street to Town Park and walked along the sidewalk at a crisp pace. Josh's ghost was where she'd last seen him; standing near the artist as he worked. Needing to get the boy's attention without attracting the artist's attention, Gina walked past the artist until she could duck behind the wall dividing the grassy side of the park from the skating ramps.

She inched along the wall until she reached the end of it and then ducked her head around the corner until she could see Josh. Then she started waving her arm in the air, trying to get his attention.

"Is everything okay?" a soft voice asked, Meredith suddenly materializing beside her.

"Actually, no," Gina replied, once she caught her breath. "I need to talk to Josh, that boy over there." She pointed the boy out to Meredith.

Meredith nodded knowingly. "I'll bring him to you. Wait here."

"Wait!" Gina hissed before Meredith could move off. "Can you bring him to my car? Over there." She pointed it out to

Meredith. "It'll be easier to talk to him there than out here." The last thing she needed was to draw more attention to herself by being seen talking to herself in public.

"Of course," Meredith said with a smile and then moved off.

Gina hurried to her car and got in. Because it was hot, she started the engine and turned on the AC. As she waited, the engine idling softly, she stared at the dashboard clock, watching the minutes tick by with agonizing slowness.

"Come on, Meredith," she whispered under her breath, feeling a blend of impatience and apprehension.

Suddenly, the air inside the car seemed to shift, and she felt an icy chill wrap around her like a shroud. She shivered involuntarily, her eyes darting from one corner of the vehicle to the other. And then, just as abruptly, both Meredith and Josh materialized before her, the boy sitting rigid and pale in the passenger seat while Meredith perched gracefully in the back.

"Hello, Josh," Gina spoke tentatively, not wanting to startle him. "My name is Gina. Do you know what happened to you?"

The ghostly child nodded his head slowly, his eyes wide and sad. "Yes," he whispered, his voice barely audible. "I'm dead."

"That's right." Gina kept her tone tender. "Can you tell me how you died?"

Josh hesitated for a moment, his gaze drifting to the park beyond the car's windows. Then, with a deep, shaky breath, he recounted his story. "I was playing in my front yard when a man in a car stopped and asked me to help find his lost puppy. I got in to help him, but then something bit me and I fell asleep. When I woke up, I was inside one of those homes you can drive around in with that man," he pointed to the artist, "and his wife. They said they were my new parents, but I didn't want them to be my new parents. I wanted to be with my old parents."

Gina's heart clenched at the sorrow and confusion in the boy's voice. "What happened then?"

"They moved the house to a new place so my parents wouldn't find me," he said, sounding miserable. "I tried to get away, because I wanted to go home. But then I got really sick. The lady gave me medicine. She said it was supposed to make me feel better, but it didn't work. One night, I fell asleep... and woke up like this."

As the boy's words echoed in her mind, Gina felt a potent mix of anger and determination surge through her veins.

"Thank you for telling me, Josh," she breathed, her voice resolute.

Josh looked sad. "I thought if I stayed close, then he might take me back to my house. I miss my mom and dad."

Gina's heart felt like it was breaking, and she cast a glance back at Meredith.

"I'll take care of him," Meredith said, laying her spectral hand reassuringly on the boy's shoulder.

"Thank you, Meredith," Gina said, her gaze moving between the two ghosts. "I appreciate your help. Josh, you stay with Meredith now, okay?"

He nodded and then they vanished, leaving Gina alone in her car. Her pulse raced as the weight of Josh's story settled on her shoulders. Best case, the artist was a child predator.

Worst case, he was a murderer. Ariel's disappearance was too much of a coincidence. Could it be that the artist had taken Ariel to replace Josh?

Gina fumbled for her phone and dialed Dane's number, her fingers trembling. She needed to tell him her suspicions, to alert someone who could act on this information.

"Hey, it's Dane. Leave a message," his voicemail greeting played through her speaker.

"Damn it, Dane, where are you?" she muttered before taking a deep breath to steady herself. "Dane, it's Gina. I need to talk to you right away. It's about the artist and Ariel. Please call me back as soon as you get this." She ended the call, her heart pounding.

Her eyes darted around the park, searching for answers that weren't there. She felt restless, useless just waiting for Dane to call back. As she drummed her fingers on the steering wheel, *Llorona* suddenly appeared in front of her car, making her jump.

Llorona's spectral image was both frightening and beautiful, and her presence sent a shiver down Gina's spine. She half-expected *Llorona* to come into the car and try to possess her again, but *Llorona* made no move toward her. Instead, she stared at Gina with fierce determination and a silent demand for immediate action.

Then she heard *Llorona's* voice resonating inside her head. *"Ándale! Ándale!"*

Gina didn't speak Spanish, but the ghost's message was clear—she needed Gina to follow her now. Swallowing her fear and hesitation, Gina put the car in gear and followed *Llorona* as the ghost led her away from town.

CHAPTER THIRTY-THREE

GINA'S HEART POUNDED IN her ears as she trailed behind the ghostly figure of *Llorona*. The absurdity of following a ghost threatened to bubble up into laughter, but she swallowed it down because something told her *Llorona's* purpose in summoning her was serious.

Nerves sent shivers running up Gina's spine as *Llorona* led her to the outskirts of town. When they reached the RV park, the pale specter stopped abruptly before the entrance. That's when Gina knew with certainty—Ariel's disappearance, Josh's kidnapping and death, the artist, and *Llorona*'s sudden attacks were all connected.

"Is this where I'll find Ariel?" Gina asked through the open window, her voice barely audible above the pulse pounding in her head. *Llorona* nodded solemnly and pointed into the park before fading away.

Gina's thoughts raced as she pulled into the park and surveyed the only trailer present—the graffiti artist's RV. She remembered the day she saw him arguing with his wife at the park, his shouts and angry gestures directed towards the trembling woman. Gina suspected then that he was an abusive spouse. She hadn't known he was also a child predator—and possibly a killer.

Her fingers drummed nervously on the steering wheel; her eyes fixed on the RV. She couldn't shake the sinking feeling that Ariel and the wife were both in danger, trapped by the same monster. Though she had limited sympathy for the wife because it was hard to feel sorry for anyone who would allow their husband to kidnap and hurt innocent children. Which raised another question. Would the wife even go with Gina? What if she fought to stay at the trailer? Or worse, fought to prevent Gina from saving Ariel?

She knew she probably should call the police for help, so, with a sigh, she dialed Dane's number again, hoping for an answer this time. Just like before, his phone went straight to voicemail, adding to her frustration.

"Damn it, Dane," she whispered under her breath, disconnecting the call without leaving another message. "Where are you when I need you?"

Ten agonizing minutes ticked by as Gina sat in her car, watching for any signs of activity in or near the trailer. Her mind raced with various scenarios, each one more terrifying than the last. It was only when the RV door opened that Gina's focus snapped back to reality.

Her heart skipped a beat as the artist's wife emerged, clutching a basket of laundry close to her chest. The woman quickly closed the trailer door behind her and hurried off toward the Guest Services building. With the wife out of the picture, this was Gina's chance, and she knew she had to act fast.

Stay calm.. You can do this.

Exciting her car, she resisted the urge to glance around and, instead, strode purposefully toward the trailer. Every fiber of her being screamed at her to turn around, but she knew she couldn't let fear hold her back. Ariel's life might be on the line.

And if she was wrong and the artist was innocent? Well, she'd cross that bridge when she came to it.

Pulse quickening as she approached the trailer, she glanced over at the Guest Services building to confirm the wife was still out of sight. Taking a deep breath to steady herself, she reached for the door handle and found it locked.

She studied the door. It was only the outer screen door that was locked. The inner door behind it stood open. Quickly extracting her driver's license, Gina set to work, acutely aware of time passing. After several failed attempts, she finally got the door unlocked.

"Here goes nothing," she muttered, pulling the door open and stepping inside.

As the door clicked shut behind her, the tension in her body ratcheted up another notch. Her senses sharpened, alert to every creak and rustle. If she got caught... No, she couldn't afford to think about that now. Focus on Ariel, she reminded herself.

Wow, she thought, taking in the surprisingly luxurious interior of the trailer. The artist must have done well for himself with his work. She scanned the space for any sign of

Ariel. Plenty of cabinets lined the walls, yet none appeared large enough to hide a child. The bedroom seemed the most likely place to find her.

Come on, Ariel, please be in here, Gina silently pleaded as she tiptoed toward the bedroom. Passing a window, she instinctively ducked down, peeking out to ensure the wife wasn't returning. All clear. For now.

"Okay, just a few more steps," she told herself, her heart pounding in her ears as she reached the closed pocket door leading to the bedroom. She tried to open it, but it wouldn't move. That's when she noticed the heavy-duty hook and eye latches at the top and bottom; locks designed to keep someone in the bedroom, not out of it. That realization sent a chill down her spine.

Her fingers trembled as they closed around the cold metal of the latches, swiftly undoing them. The door slid open with a whispered hush to reveal a dimly lit bedroom. Thin rays of sunlight filtered through the curtains, casting ghostly shadows on the sleeping form of a young girl. The same girl, she quickly saw, whose picture was on Dane's desk.

"Ariel!" Gina called out, her voice urgent but hushed. She moved closer, the soft rustle of her clothes barely audible above her pounding heart.

No response. Panic clawed at her throat as she studied the child for signs of life. Was she too late?

"Please be alive," she pleaded, her breath hitching. Tentatively, she placed a finger under Ariel's nose, nearly sobbing with relief when she felt the faint warmth of the child's breath.

"Thank God," she whispered, shaking the girl gently. "Ariel, wake up."

Still, Ariel remained unresponsive, and Gina deduced she had been drugged. Time was running out; she had to get Ariel out of here.

"Sorry, sweetheart," she murmured, scooping the limp child into her arms. Her legs quivered beneath her, adrenaline fueling her determination as she navigated the path back toward the trailer door. Just a few more steps...

The sudden sound of the door handle lifting brought her world to a screeching halt. The artist's wife was back!

Gina froze and a bead of sweat trickled down her forehead as she clutched the unconscious child more tightly in her arms. Her heart pounded with both fear and adrenaline as she waited in trepidation for the artist's wife to step into the trailer and confront her.

"Gina Castillo! What are you doing?"

Peggy Olson stepped into the trailer, her gaze darting between Gina and the view out the kitchen window.

"Jesus, Peggy," Gina breathed out, her heartbeat beginning to slow. "You scared me half to death."

"What's going on here?" Peggy countered, trying to keep her voice steady. "Who is that?"

Gina hesitated for only a moment before lifting the limp girl in her arms slightly, the wisp of her blonde hair falling over her pale face. "This is Ariel, the missing girl the police have been searching for."

"Missing girl?" Peggy asked, her confusion obvious as she studied the slight form. "What missing girl?"

"Ariel Lund. She disappeared yesterday—or maybe it was the day before. My days are all mixed up." She shook her head to clear it. "Never mind. What's important is that I found her and we have to get her out of here before Miles or his wife returns."

Peggy shook her head. "I'm sure there's a perfectly reasonable explanation—"

Gina didn't give her time to finish. "There is. Miles is a child predator, and they kidnapped her. Now, if you won't help me, then get out of my way."

Peggy's gaze narrowed on her. "How do you know this isn't Miles' daughter?"

For a second, doubt crept in and Gina glanced down at the sleeping child. No, not sleeping, she mentally corrected. Drugged. Because if she was sleeping, she would have awakened by now. Besides... "You remember when you first introduced me to Miles Davis? He was adamant that he had no children."

Gina could tell Peggy remembered the incident by the way she pursed her lips. She hadn't liked Miles correcting her. "He denied having a son when I know perfectly well his wife said they did," she said. "He never said he didn't have a daughter."

Gina bent slightly so she could peek out the kitchen window to see if Miles' wife was returning. There was still no sign of her.

"Peggy, I don't have time to argue with you, but I promise I'll explain everything later. Right now, I need you to trust me when I say we need to get Ariel away from here and to a doctor."

"Why does she need a doctor?" Peggy inquired, turning her attention to the child.

"I think they drugged her," Gina explained, her stomach churning at the thought. "Wait minute. What are you doing here?"

"Mile finished his mural. I have to pay him and he asked me to bring his check to the trailer." She looked around. "Where is he?"

"Not here. At least, not yet. We need to hurry and get Ariel to Doc Niven right away." Gina had the horrible sense that time was running out on them. "Better yet," she shoved the unconscious girl into Peggy's arms. "You take her."

"Wait," Peggy said, her eyes going wide as she took the child. "Why me?"

"Because I don't think Ariel is their first victim and I want to search the trailer for evidence," she said, nudging Peggy towards the door. "Hurry. Take Ariel to the doctor and then call the police."

Fortunately, Peggy didn't argue further and hurried off. Gina watched long enough to make sure Peggy made it to her car safely, then breathed a sigh of relief when it drove away, kicking up dust in its wake. Turning back to the trailer, she focused on her two objectives: finding evidence of Miles' involvement in kidnapping children and convincing his wife to report him.

The interior of the trailer was dimly lit, shadows playing tricks on Gina's senses as she sifted through drawers and cabinets. Frustration bubbled to the surface as she found only kitchen utensils, food and art supplies, but no concrete evidence of any kidnappings. A feeling of urgency gnawed at her; time was running out.

She hurried into the bedroom and opened the closet door. Some clothes hung from a rod, while others sat folded neatly on a shelf. Shoes littered the floor, which is why the shoe box sitting on the top shelf of the closet, beside the navy ball cap, caught her attention.

She took it down, opened the lid and froze. Inside the box was a picture of Ariel. She was sleeping on the bed, wrapped in the same blanket in which Gina had found her. Gina lifted the picture to study it, but her gaze fell on the picture below it. It was a picture of Josh. Gina sifted through the other pictures. There was easily a dozen, all of a different child; some sleeping, some crying. Had Miles Davis kidnapped all of these children? Gina felt sick.

"What are you doing in my trailer?" a sharp voice demanded.

Gina's heart leaped into her throat at the sound. Before stepping back, she shoved the box onto the nearest shelf. Then she turned to face the artist's wife standing in the bedroom doorway. Her expression was hard to read. Almost as if choreographed, their gazes turned to the now-empty bed where Ariel had lain unconscious.

Knowing she needed to tread carefully, Gina's thoughts raced for an explanation that wouldn't betray what she knew. "I'm so sorry. I was thinking about buying a trailer like this one, and when I saw the door standing open, I couldn't resist taking a peek inside."

"You shouldn't be in here." The wife's voice dripped with censure, but Gina detected something else there—fear, perhaps? She couldn't be sure.

"Look, I'm really sorry," she blurted, her hands raised in a placating gesture. "I didn't mean any harm. I'll just go now."

"Wait." The wife hesitated, her gaze darting between Gina and the empty bed. "You said the door was open?"

Gina nodded. "I called out, hoping someone was inside, but no one answered."

"You didn't see anyone else around?"

When Gina shook her head, the wife's face drained of color, causing the mole on the side of her nose to stand out in sharp contrast.

"Is everything okay?" Gina asked, half-fearing the woman was about to faint.

She suspected the wife was terrified about what her husband would do when he discovered Ariel missing—and, perhaps more urgently, what he might do to her. As if to confirm her thoughts, Mrs. Davis seemed to forget Gina was there and started muttering to herself.

"What do I do now? He's going to be so mad when he finds out."

"Mrs. Davis, are you in danger?" Gina asked kindly.

The woman's gaze snapped to hers. "How do you know my name?"

"I saw you in the park the other day. You and your husband were having a picnic lunch." She hesitated. "I saw the way he treated you. I'd like to help you, if you'll let me."

For a long moment, Mrs. Davis stared open-mouthed. Then she gave a bark of laughter that sounded out-of-place. "You think he abuses me?"

She wasn't a therapist, but Gina had read enough to know that denial was usually the first defense mechanism employed by abused spouses. She decided then that the best way to help the woman and earn her trust was to tell her everything.

"Listen, I lied about why I was here. I know your husband took Ariel. I found her here."

Mrs. Davis' gaze turned sharply to her. "Where is she now?"

"Safe. On her way to the doctor to be checked out. The police have also been notified." At least, she hoped Peggy had called the police.

Mrs. Davis stared at her for a long moment and Gina felt a pang of sympathy for her, but the clock was ticking. If what Peggy said was true, Miles had finished his mural.

"Mrs. Davis. We should go. I believe your husband is on his way back. He could show up at any moment. I'll take you someplace safe; where he won't be able to find you. You can tell the police everything you know."

Her eyes grew round with surprise. "Miles is on his way back?"

Gina nodded. "We should hurry."

The woman ran into the kitchen, presumably to glance out the window. Gina heard a drawer open and shut. "He's coming!"

Then the wife hurried back into the bedroom and pointed to the closet. "There's a shoe box on the top shelf. Can you get it?"

"Of course." Gina turned around, silently commending Mrs. Davis for taking an extra couple of seconds to grab the evidence that would incriminate her husband.

Then she felt a sharp prick of pain on her shoulder blade. Whirling around, she saw Mrs. Davis standing behind her, clutching an empty hypodermic needle like a knife. Confusion flashed through Gina, but it was the enraged, insane gleam in the other woman's eyes that terrified her.

She tried to push past the woman, but her legs felt like they had heavy weights strapped around the ankles and she succeeded only in stumbling forward a few steps.

The realization that she'd been drugged terrified her. She knew panic would only cause the drug to metabolize more quickly, but she couldn't seem to control her emotions.

Seemingly from a great distance, she heard footsteps, and the wife turned toward the front of the trailer.

"About damn time you got back," she growled.

"What's going on?" a man's voice demanded.

Like watching a slow-motion movie, Gina saw the wife turn and point at her. Then the artist was in the bedroom with his wife. In a moment of clarity, Gina saw his expression and realized he looked frightened. Then the moment was gone.

She thought maybe the artist's wife was shouting, but couldn't understand the words. Then the bed was floating off the floor. Beneath the bed was a large wooden box that was mostly empty, except for a scruffy stuffed bunny. The sight was so odd and captivating, Gina could only stare at it, momentarily forgetting where she was.

Then she was pushed and fell forward, landing in a graceless heap in the storage area beneath the bed. A moment later, the bed was lowered, and Gina was trapped in a space so tight that every attempt to move was thwarted by the unforgiving sides of the wooden box.

She lay there, her mind numb to everything except fear—and a deep penetrating sadness that she'd never see Dane again.

Chapter Thirty-Four

DANE WAS STILL TEN miles outside of Las Palomas when he re-entered a cell phone service area and his phone began squawking like an angry goose as it registered missed calls and text messages. He dialed into his voice mail to listen.

The first message was from his mother inviting him to dinner.

The next was from Chad letting him know the photos from County had arrived—five of them—and he was putting them on Dane's desk.

The third message was from Gina, asking him to call her.

The fourth was another call from Chad.

"Dane. Think you better get here ASAP. I'm at Doc Niven's office. Peggy Olson showed up about ten minutes ago with Ariel Lund. She and Gina Castillo found her in that graffiti artist's trailer. They drugged that little girl!" From his tone, Dane knew Chad was upset. "Doc's with her now and says she'll be okay. Her parents are on the way over now." There was a pause. "Peg says the artist finished his mural and was planning to leave town. I checked Town Park, and it looks like he's already packed up his stuff and gone. Peg says Gina stayed behind at the trailer. Unless she's called you, no one's seen or heard from her in a while."

A feeling of dread crept over him and he drove a little faster. He called Chad back.

"Meet me at Murphy's," he said as soon as Chad answered. Then he disconnected and called Gina.

There was no answer. When it rolled to voice mail, he left a brief message. "Gina. It's Dane. Call me as soon as you get this message. And for God's sake, don't do anything until I get there. I'm on my way."

Swearing under his breath, he disconnected the call and pressed the button on his dash. With lights flashing and siren blaring, he floored the accelerator like the devil himself was on his tail.

Fifteen minutes later, as he neared the RV park, Dane turned off his lights and siren. He didn't know what kind of situation he was walking into. There was no chatter coming over his radio to indicate anything was going down.

He pulled into the entrance of the RV park, heading for the public parking lot. Gina's Acadia was parked in the lot and there was a truck backed up to the artist's RV like the artist was preparing to hitch up his trailer and leave. As he got closer to the main office, he spotted Chad's truck parked next to the building.

Good thinking. Parked behind the main building, Chad's truck couldn't be seen from the trailer. Dane considered parking next to him, but then noticed the way the blinds over the trailer's window were parted, like someone was looking out. They'd seen him pull in.

Quickly, he dialed Chad.

"What's the status?" he asked when Chad answered.

"We've been here about five minutes," Chad replied. "No sign of Gina, but Miles has been busy hooking his trailer to his truck."

Dane pulled into a parking space and glanced over at the trailer. "Where is he now?"

"Inside," Chad replied.

"Okay. I'll go talk to them."

"What do you want me to do?" Chad asked.

"For now, nothing. Just keep your eyes and ears open."

He knew from the way Chad hesitated he didn't like that plan, but all he said was, "Be careful."

They disconnected the call and after shutting off his truck, he got out and walked toward the trailer, every fiber alert for the first sign of danger. He tried to tell himself that there could be a logical explanation for why Miles Davis and his wife had Ariel Lund in their trailer. His gut told him otherwise.

He was nearly to the trailer door when he heard a woman cry out. It had come from inside the trailer and his first thought was that Gina was in trouble. Hurrying up the trailer's steps, he knocked on the door.

From inside, he heard shouting.

"...no, stop! You're hurting me," a woman's voice cried.

He was about to break the screen door window to access the lock when it occurred to him to first try the knob.

It was unlocked, and Dane didn't hesitate to pull the door open.

Inside, the artist, his back to Dane, was bent over a woman and it looked like he was choking her.

Gina!

Dane had never felt such anger or fear. His primal instincts kicked in and he grabbed the artist by the shoulders and jerked him back. Swinging the man around, Dane slammed his fist into the man's jaw, knocking him back a step. Dane followed him, hitting him again and again. When someone tried to grab his arm, he shook them off.

Then someone looped their arm around his, preventing him from hitting the artist again. Dane whirled around to see who would dare stop him.

Chad immediately released him and stepped back, his hands raised in the air. "Easy, man. He's down and he's not going anywhere."

Chad's voice snapped him out of his blind rage, and he took a breath. When he turned back to the artist, the man was bent over and bleeding.

"Get him out of here," Dane growled.

He waited only until Chad had cuffed the artist before hurrying back to check on Gina.

However, the woman sitting at the dinette, still rubbing her throat, wasn't Gina.

"Thank you," the artist's wife said, her voice sounding hoarse.

Dane nodded, feeling slightly stunned. He'd been so sure it had been Gina.

"Are you alright?" he asked, stepping closer to the wife.

Her lips trembled as she attempted to put on a brave face. "Yes, thank you."

He nodded. "Do you feel up to coming down to the station to press charges?" he asked her.

She looked horrified at the suggestion. "Oh, no. I could never do that."

"Fortunately, in Texas, I can press them for you. He's going to jail."

She scrambled up from the dinette bench with a speed that surprised him and grabbed his arm, looking beseechingly up at him.

"Please, you can't do that. We have to leave. He's been commissioned to do another piece in New Orleans that starts in two days."

"I'm afraid you're not going to make it," he said, patting the hand that still clutched his arm. "I'm also charging your husband with child abduction, administering drugs to a minor and anything else I can think of. We know he took Ariel Lund and drugged her."

"I... I don't..." She stopped talking, sank down onto the bench seat and seemed to collapse in upon herself. "I begged him not to take that little girl. I wanted to help her, but he threatened to kill me if I did."

Dane sighed. "Unfortunately, because you didn't report him, you'll likely be charged as an accessory. However, there will be a full investigation and if the DA knows you were coerced, he might go easy on you."

Dane could tell she was in shock and gave her a few minutes to collect herself.

"Mrs. Davis, was Gina Castillo here earlier?"

"I'm sorry. I don't know who that is, but I haven't seen anyone. Although, I stepped out for a bit to do laundry. When I got back to the trailer, the door was standing open. That's when I noticed the little girl was gone. I thought maybe the drugs had worn off, and she'd run away. Then Miles came home. When he realized the girl was gone, he was furious and, well, you know the rest."

Disappointed, Dane nodded thoughtfully. He couldn't shake the feeling of unease settling over him. Without asking permission, he walked to the back of the trailer, to the bedroom, and looked around. The space was small and the closet door stood open. The room was obviously empty. Not sure what he'd hoped to find, he walked back to the front where Mrs. Davis was sitting.

"I'll need to take you to the station."

She shook her head. "No."

"Mrs. Davis, that wasn't a request."

She looked like she wanted to argue with him, so he was relieved when she didn't. Instead, she stood and then looked down at her clothes before meeting his gaze.

"Would you mind if I change first?"

For the first time, Dane noticed her ripped sleeve and drops of blood on the front of her shirt. Not hers, he thought, seeing no cuts or scratches on her. She must have scratched her husband while fighting him off. Dane didn't waste a moment's sympathy on the man.

"Sure. I'll wait here."

She shook her head. "The bedroom door won't close and there's not enough room to change in the bathroom. Would you mind waiting outside?"

Reluctantly, he nodded and headed outside.

He walked the short distance to the end of the trailer where he took out his phone and dialed Gina.

At the sound of the first ring, he felt his nerves tense in anticipation, and he counted the rings.

Two.

Every sense became more acute. He was aware of the sound of his own breathing—and a muffled ringing.

Three.

Four.

Five.

"Hi, this is Gina Castillo. You've reached my voice mail—"

He disconnected the call without leaving a message. The trailer park had grown silent, with only muffled sounds coming from inside the trailer. Even the muffled ringing had stopped.

His breath hitched as he realized the direction of his thoughts.

He called Gina's number again, but this time held the phone away from his ear.

The ringing started again. He focused on the sound, trying to locate the direction from which it was coming. The call rolled to voice mail before he could be certain. Impatiently, he disconnected the call and redialed the number.

This time, when it started ringing, he retraced his steps slowly until—

Yes, he was certain now. It was coming from inside the trailer!

Then he heard a loud thumping noise. A door closing?

Or worse, the sound of a body falling?

What was going on inside the trailer?

"Mrs. Davis?" he called, heading for the still open doorway. When he reached it, he caught the acrid scent of something burning. He lifted his head, trying to get another whiff. From the corner seam of the trailer's window, a wisp of gray smoke escaped, so thin he wondered at first if he was seeing correctly.

Fearing the worst, he stepped inside and saw that the fire hadn't spread to the front yet. Visibility was still good, and he quickly scanned the front section for Mrs. Davis.

Not seeing her, he made his way towards the back of the trailer. When he reached the end of the short hallway, he was confused. The supposedly broken bedroom door was now closed, and thin tendrils of smoke seeped out from underneath it. He tried to slide it open, but it was locked.

"Mrs. Davis, open the door!" he shouted, hoping for a response.

The only sound he received in return was that of breaking glass.

With his thoughts racing, Dane focused on one thing: getting the bedroom door open. Despite his best efforts to tug at it, the door wouldn't budge. He needed something to pry it open with. In a hurry, he searched through drawers in the kitchen until he found a knife. With shaking hands, he slipped it between the door edge and the jamb just above the lock and pushed with all his strength.

Amidst a loud creak and the sound of splintering wood, the door finally gave way.

A wall of flames stopped him from entering. The bed was fully engulfed in fire and thick smoke filled the room.

Instinctively, he pulled his shirt collar up over his nose and mouth for protection, as he frantically scanned the room for Mrs. Davis.

She wasn't on the bed or anywhere else in sight. His eyes fell upon a large broken window on the far side of the room. It was big enough for someone to escape through. For a moment, he felt relieved. Mrs. Davis must have escaped through the window to safety. Now he needed to get out of there as well.

A shrill cry from outside the trailer snapped Dane's attention away from the rapidly spreading fire. Through the shattered window, he saw Mrs. Davis standing just a few feet away. She looked relatively unharmed except that one hand was bleeding, blood dripping to the ground. In her other hand, she held a shard of glass. Dane realized that the scream he'd heard must have been when she'd pulled it out.

A flicker of recognition passed between them before Mrs. Davis tossed the shard aside and bolted off into the woods. It was then that Dane realized she had set the fire as a distraction while she escaped.

A surge of disgust washed over him for having trusted her.

With thick black smoke filling the upper part of the room, Dane dropped to his hands and knees, and started crawling towards the door. As he struggled through the suffocating heat and fumes, he felt something slip out of his pocket—his phone.

He remembered putting it there when he'd broken into the bedroom earlier.

Grabbing it, he noticed the still-active call to Gina and remembered the ringing he'd heard earlier. Quickly disconnecting the call, he redialed. This time, the ringing sounded nearby, and he traced its origin to the bed.

When he leaned down to search for Gina's phone, though, he realized it couldn't be there. The bed sat on a wooden pedestal, making it impossible for anything to be hidden under it.

As the flames roared around him, Dane prepared to make a run for the door. It wasn't worth risking his life just for a phone, but as he tried to convince himself, horrifying possibilities raced through his head. What if Gina had her phone on her and she was trapped under this bed somehow? She would burn alive.

His heart pounding in his chest, he desperately searched for a way to access the source of the ringing before it was too late.

Then suddenly, memories of a YouTube video he'd watched about travel trailers flashed through his mind. He hurried to the foot of the burning bed and, with all his strength, lifted the frame until it rose into the air, revealing the storage area underneath. And there, curled up, eyes closed and unmoving, was Gina.

Fear, as he'd never felt before, nearly crippled him at the sight of Gina's lifeless body crammed into the small rectangular space.

"Gina!"

With flames roaring all around them, there was no time to assess her injuries or even check for a pulse. Without hesitation, he grabbed her wrist and hoisted her up onto his shoulders in a fireman's carry.

A quick glance at the door revealed their only escape route was now blocked by a raging inferno. Embers from the fire had ignited the front window drapes when he'd lifted the mattress, causing the blaze to spread rapidly along the wall. Their only hope now lay in following Mrs. Davis' path of escape through the back window.

Though the distance to the back window was short, Gina's weight slowed his progress. Every movement had to be calculated and precise—one wrong move could spell disaster.

Finally reaching the window, Dane grabbed the nearest object, a shoe from the closet, and used it to knock out the shards of glass still stuck in the frame. A gust of fresh air rushed in, filling him with renewed vigor.

"I'm sorry, baby," he muttered, shoving Gina through the opening. He held onto her, controlling her fall to the ground as best he could. Then he followed her.

Once outside, he cradled her in his arms and carried her towards the parking lot where emergency responders were just arriving. He met them halfway, but it took all their strength to pry her from his grasp so they could begin treating her.

As Gina lay motionless on the ground, Dane stood rooted in place; his mind numb with shock. It wasn't until he went to wipe the sudden moisture from his eyes that he noticed the blood. It covered his hands, arms and shirt.

He staggered back, his mind reeling as he stared down at the crimson staining his skin. Panic clawed at his chest, threatening to overwhelm him.

In his haste to save Gina from the fire, he hadn't noticed her wound. Now, confronted with the undeniable evidence, he felt a sickening dread coil in his stomach. So much blood could only mean she'd been stabbed or shot.

His gaze returned to where she lay; so still; too still. The EMTS were making no effort to resuscitate her. That could only mean one thing. It was too late.

His heart plummeted to depths he never knew existed. The world around him blurred as the reality sank in. Gina was dead. His Gina, whom he now realized he loved, was gone. The flames crackled and roared in the background, a cruel backdrop to the horror unfolding before him.

CHAPTER THIRTY-FIVE

DANE COULDN'T TEAR HIS gaze away from Gina's still form.

"I need to take a look at your arms," an EMT said to him, her voice gentle but firm. He heard the words but shock kept him from understanding them. She seemed to sense his confusion and pointed to his hands. "You cut yourself up pretty good getting out of that trailer."

She guided him toward the back of the ambulance, where she began cleaning the blood away with gauze. Her touch was light, almost soothing. "What you did was heroic," she said, looking into his eyes.

Heroic. The word echoed in his head, hollow and meaningless. He didn't feel heroic—he felt sick. He had been too late. "I'm no hero," he muttered, more to himself than to the EMT.

She furrowed her brow. "I don't know about that," she said, her voice earnest.

"I do," he muttered. "I was too late. So much blood."

The EMT cleaning his arms paused; her face softening. "This isn't her blood. It's yours. She's not dead," she told him kindly. "She's groggy because she was drugged, and she's got a few cuts from being shoved out a broken window. But she's going to be fine."

Dane's heart hammered in his chest like a wild animal desperate for escape, the world around him reduced to a blur of motion and noise. Before he knew what he was doing, he was on his feet, pushing past the EMTs, their protests barely registering. His attention was solely on Gina. Her eyes fluttered open just as he reached her side, and for a moment, time seemed to stand still.

Their eyes locked, and in that instant, the chaos surrounding them fell away. All that mattered was the two of them, bound by a connection deeper than words.

"Dane," she murmured, surprise etching her features as she tried to sit up.

He sank to his knees beside her, relief flooding through him. "I thought I'd lost you," he whispered before pulling her into his arms. She clung to him as if he were her anchor in a storm-tossed sea, and he held her with equal fervor, unwilling to let her go.

"I was so scared," she confessed, her voice still raspy from the smoke. "Thank you," she murmured, barely audible above the commotion of the EMTs and the roar of the burning trailer. "For finding me... for saving me." She paused before continuing, her worried gaze searching his face. "When I thought I wouldn't make it out, I realized something."

"What?" he asked, holding onto her tightly but leaning away so he could look into her eyes.

"I love you," she declared, her expression full of both fear and hope.

"Damn it," he swore softly, but there was nothing but adoration in his tone. "I wanted to be the first one to say it." He smiled at her, savoring every moment of this precious reunion. "I love you, Gina."

Her eyes crinkled at the corners as her worried frown transformed into a wide grin. She gave a choked giggle before breaking into a fit of coughing.

"Tell me how," Gina rasped once her coughing subsided, needing to know the details of his search for her. "How did you find me?"

Dane quickly explained about getting Chad's call, his confrontation with Miles Davis and his wife, his frantic search for her that ended with following the sound of her phone to the storage unit beneath the bed. As he spoke, Gina marveled at his determination and resourcefulness.

"Is Ariel okay?" she asked, feeling concerned.

"Yes," Dane assured her. "Doc Niven is with her now, making sure she's alright."

She felt relief wash over her, but it was tinged with guilt. "I should've been able to save her sooner," she confessed, her gaze drifting to the ground. "I recognized the boy hanging around the artist as the ghost of one of the missing kids whose picture is on your desk. When I went outside to talk to him, he told me the artist had taken him."

She took a shaky breath, gathering herself before continuing. "That's when *Llorona* showed up and led me to the RV park." She told him about finding Ariel and Peggy showing up. "I stayed to convince the wife to leave. I thought she was another one of his victims, but she was the one who injected me with something. When I felt the stab of the needle, I pulled away so the EMTs don't think she was able to inject too much of the drug into me. Just enough to knock me out." A shudder ran through her and she offered him a weak smile. "Lucky me."

Dane tightened his embrace, cradling her head against his chest. His heart ached for her, for the terror she had experienced, and the weight of that lingering fear still etched across her face.

"You're safe now," he soothed, his voice soft but resolute. "I won't let anything happen to you."

She let him hold her for a long moment, then leaned back so she could see his face. She offered him a smile to let him know she was okay.

Her heart lurched when she noticed a blur of motion over his shoulder. Through the haze of smoke and debris, she spotted several young children playing dangerously close to the burning trailer, their laughter mingling with the crackle of the flames.

"Dane, those children shouldn't be playing there. They'll get hurt."

He turned to look. "Where? I don't see any children."

She peered closer and two or three of the faces looked familiar. Then it hit her like a punch to the gut—she'd seen them before, in the photographs of the children in the shoe box.

Even before one of the children stepped into a shaft of sunlight filtering through the trees and his form wavered and became transparent, she understood.

"They're not... they're not living children, Dane. They're ghosts. I think they might be the ghosts of earlier victims. Ariel and Josh weren't the only ones."

Dane nodded his understanding, his expression a mix of sadness and determination.

"We can't let them Miles and his wife away with what they did to those children," she said softly. "We owe it to the children."

"We won't," Dane assured her.

Just then, the sun's rays pierced the canopy above, casting a celestial glow across the forest floor as the ghostly children gravitated toward the light. Josh had joined them but lingered at the edge, his gaze fixed on the others like a sentinel watching over his charges.

As Gina watched, the children joined hands and began circling in a game of ring-around-the-rosy, their translucent forms flickering and shimmering with each rotation. A delicate, haunting melody reached Gina's ears—the sound of their laughter, she realized with amazement. She couldn't help but feel a bittersweet pang in her chest at the sight and sound of their joy.

As the children spun faster in their dance, their forms faded further into the light.

"What are they doing?" Dane asked softly.

Gina blinked away the tears that threatened to spill over. "They're crossing into the light." They were letting go of whatever tethered them to this world. Soon, only Josh remained.

He stood alone, bathed in the gentle radiance, his expression serene yet tinged with sadness.

"Go on," she whispered, her heart swelling with hope. "Find your peace, too."

"Thank you," he mouthed silently, the words both a farewell and an acknowledgment of the understanding they'd shared. With one last, shy wave, he stepped forward into the light, his form dissolving into the golden haze like the other children before him.

The forest grew quiet once more, and the brilliant glow that had illuminated the trees receded, leaving only dappled sunlight and shadows in its wake.

"They're gone," she murmured, her voice heavy with both relief and sorrow. Her hand instinctively reached for his. She felt a strong need to anchor herself to something real, something tangible in the wake of such a surreal experience. Dane's warmth and solid presence provided that reassurance, grounding her once more.

As they sat there, surrounded by the remnants of chaos and loss, Dane's phone suddenly rang. He glanced at the screen. "It's Chad," he said, answering the call and putting it on speaker.

"Hey Dane, you won't believe this," Chad began, his voice tinged with disbelief. "Miles Davis claims he's been a victim of spousal abuse for years. His wife, Lilith, is the real monster. She's the one abducting the kids, drugging them into obedience, or worse... killing them. He said she plays the victim in public, making him look like the bad guy, but she's the one who's really in control. The bastard never turned her in 'cause he was afraid of what she might do to him."

Dane's fingers tightened around his phone. "It didn't look like he was afraid of her when I barged into their trailer and found him choking her."

"Yeah, I asked him about that. He said that one moment she was yelling at him and the next, she started crying and choking. He thought she had something stuck in her throat and was trying to help when you came in and started hitting him."

Dane felt conflicted. "Do you think he's telling the truth?"

"I think he might be," Chad admitted. "He took off his shirt and showed us where his wife beat him. I don't know if it was her or not, but someone beat the crap out of him. He was covered in bruises and not all of them are recent."

"Thanks," Dane said. "Keep me posted." He disconnected the call and turned to Gina. "What do you think?"

Her brow furrowed as she recalled Lilith's wild, almost feverish gaze after injecting her with drugs. "I... I think he might be telling the truth," she admitted, her voice barely above a whisper.

"Then I need to find her," he said, sounding determined.

The thought of letting Lilith escape after everything she'd done was unbearable. "Not without me, you aren't," Gina insisted.

Her expression was a mixture of fear and determination, but Dane could see the fire in her eyes—she wouldn't back down.

"Alright," he agreed, knowing there was no point in arguing. He stood up, then extended his hand out to help her to her feet. With her standing beside him, his gaze scanned the river and woods where Lilith had disappeared. "Last time I saw her, she ran that way."

"Then let's go find her," Gina said.

They headed across the parking lot, their resolve strengthening with each step and guided by the hope that justice would finally be served.

Chapter Thirty-Six

Standing behind the trailer, Gina surveyed the woods. Of course, there was no sign of Lilith. She could be anywhere by now.

The task seemed insurmountable as she considered how much time they'd waste if they started looking for Lilith in the wrong spot. As she gazed off at the river, the air near the riverbank shimmered, and a ghostly figure materialized.

"Uncle Victor!" Her heart leaped in her chest at the sight of him, and without a second thought, she hurried towards him, sensing Dane following close behind.

"You're here!" She exclaimed, stopping before his ethereal form. His gaze, filled with a warmth, met hers.

"Ah, Gina," he said, a smile tugging at the corners of his mouth. "I'm so sorry I couldn't do anything to help you. Please thank Dane for me."

Turning to Dane, who came toward her with a puzzled expression, Gina relayed the message.

Dane's face softened, and he wrapped his arm around her shoulders. "Can he hear me?" he asked her, looking around. She nodded and gestured to Uncle Victor's form so Dane would know where to look. "Rest easy, Mr. Castillo. You did a good job of protecting her while you were alive. If she'll let me, I'll take it from here."

At his declaration, Gina felt moisture gathering in the corner of her eye and rubbed it away before Dane could notice. Now was not the time to get emotional, but she still had to clear her throat before she could speak.

"Uncle Victor. We need to find Lilith. Have you seen her?"

"Indeed, I have," he replied, raising a translucent hand to point. "I saw her running upstream. I'll lead the way."

"Thank you," she whispered, turning to Dane and explaining, "Uncle Victor will show us the way. He saw Lilith running up the river."

"Alright then, let's go," he said, a glint of determination in his eyes.

With the sun dipping low in the sky, casting a golden hue across the river, Gina followed Uncle Victor's ethereal form, Dane following close behind her. Beside them, the river water danced with the waning light, creating mesmerizing patterns that shifted with each step they took. There were several instances where they had no choice but to wade through the chilly current, the alternative being a longer, winding path through the trees. Gina couldn't help but find the experience surreal—chasing after a potential serial killer while guided by her deceased uncle's ghost. It was a scene straight out of a gothic novel, yet here she was, living it.

As time wore on, the landscape morphed into something otherworldly—a place seemingly untouched by modernity, isolated from the rest of the world. The sunlight filtered through the foliage above them, casting dappled shadows that seemed to dance on the water's surface.

"Wait..." Gina whispered, stopping in her tracks. Up ahead, a ghostly figure appeared, drifting a foot above the river. Long hair and flowing skirts billowed around her, stirred by a breeze Gina couldn't feel. It was *Llorona*, her visage imposing and terrifying.

"Can you see her?" Gina asked Dane, her voice shaking.

"Yes," Dane said, his tone full of warning. "What's that in the river below her?"

As they inched closer, the slippery rocks beneath the water's surface seemed to shift with every step, threatening to dislodge Gina and Dane from their precarious balance. Despite their best efforts, a treacherous rock caused Gina to lose her footing. Her heart leaped into her throat as she stumbled, but Dane's quick reflexes kept her from tumbling headlong into the water.

She exhaled a shaky breath, grateful for his support. "Thanks. That was close."

Together, they made their way closer to the mysterious scene before them. When they were close enough, Gina realized that the dark shape at *Llorona's* feet was a body lying face-down in the river. Dane knelt beside it and rolled it over.

Gina's heart clenched with distress. "Is that... ?" she whispered, unable to finish the question. It was Lilith, barely recognizable, with her face battered and a nasty contusion marring her forehead.

Dane pressed his fingers against her neck, searching for a pulse. Moments of tense silence ticked by, and Gina held her breath. When he finally looked up to meet her gaze, his expression was grim.

"She's dead," he confirmed, the weight of the words hanging heavily between them.

An eerie silence fell, interrupted only by the sound of rushing water, the river's current seemingly indifferent to the grim tableau on its banks. Gina watched Dane's jaw clench as he studied Lilith's lifeless form, his brows furrowed with concern. "She must've slipped on these damn rocks and hit her head," he surmised.

"That bitch pushed me!"

At the sound of the accusatory voice, Gina's gaze darted around, finally landing on the ethereal figure of Lilith's ghost, standing off to the side with a venomous glare aimed at *Llorona*. The impossibility of the situation left Gina reeling; it was one thing to see her uncle's spirit, but now the woman they'd been chasing was also present in spectral form.

"Lilith's here," she said to Dane, her voice barely audible above the river's roar. "She says... *Llorona* pushed her."

"Christ," Dane muttered, rubbing a hand over his face. "This just keeps getting weirder." He pulled out his phone, fingers tapping at the screen with practiced precision as he dialed for help. "We need someone down here to help move the body. We can't leave her like this."

As Gina watched Dane make the call, she couldn't shake the surreal feeling that continued to cling to her like a shroud. Here they were, bending over Lilith's dead body while three ghosts—*Llorona*, Lilith and Uncle Victor—stood off to the side bearing not-so-silent witness. Lilith was ranting and raving at *Llorona*, who occasionally answered back in Spanish, while Uncle Victor tried, unsuccessfully, to quiet both women. With them all talking at once, it was hard to understand what any of them were saying.

"Okay," Dane said, pocketing his phone. "Help's on the way. Since you can talk to Lilith, maybe you should ask her why she took those children. What was her motive?"

Gina hesitated, unsure if Lilith would even cooperate, but as she locked eyes with the woman's ghostly figure, *Llorona* and Uncle Victor fell silent. "Why did you kidnap those children?" she asked.

Lilith spoke, her voice bitter. "It's all his fault. Miles." She spat the name out like it was a nasty taste in her mouth. "Years of trying to get pregnant, only guess what? His little swimmers can't swim. So then we tried adoption, but the agency said that living in a travel trailer, moving from town to town, was not the kind of stable home they wanted for their kids." Lilith's eyes grew fiery. "One day, I went to a playground and saw a mother ignoring her child. She didn't deserve to be a mother, so I took the child to care for as my own."

Gina felt a shiver run down her spine, imagining the twisted logic that had driven Lilith to such lengths.

"But the ungrateful child wouldn't stop crying," Lilith continued, her voice growing harsh. "I had to sedate her, but she was weak and died, so I had to take another child—a stronger one." She paused, muttering under her breath, her words becoming unintelligible.

Gina shared her words with Dane, who shook his head in disgust. "Psychotic bitch. Too bad she's not still alive to be put in prison."

Before Gina could respond, an eerie stillness settled over the scene, chilling her to the bone. She glanced at Dane, who seemed just as unnerved by the sudden silence. Her gaze turned to Uncle Victor, his spectral expression alarmed.

"Gina, I have to go," he said urgently, before fading away without another word.

Gina's heart raced as she noticed *Llorona's* ghost rising higher in the air, her eyes locked onto something unseen below her. A silent command to move back from the body emanated from her ethereal form. Without hesitation, Gina grabbed Dane's arm, pulling him back several feet.

"What's going on?" he asked, confusion clouding his face.

Gina shook her head, her voice barely a whisper. "I don't know, but something's happening." She clung to Dane's arm as she watched Lilith's ghost tremble, her pale spectral eyes growing wide with fear and confusion.

"What's happening?" she demanded, glancing around nervously. "I can't move!"

Gina's gaze was drawn then to the ground surrounding Lilith's ghostly form, where tendrils of black smoke snaked upwards and wrapped around her ankles, anchoring her in place. More smoke seeped up from the ground, coalescing into dark, sinister figures that seemed to embody malevolence itself. The icy chill in the air intensified, turning Gina's and Dane's breaths into white puffs of steam.

Gina couldn't tear her gaze away from the macabre spectacle unfolding before them.

The dark figures crept towards Lilith's ghost, their shadowy limbs reaching out to paw at her. As they made contact, Lilith let out a bone-chilling scream filled with agony and terror. Her cries echoed through the stillness, adding another layer of horror to the scene.

"What's going on?" Dane whispered, his voice tense.

Gina shook her head, too frightened to speak. Horrified, she watched the dark figures drag Lilith's ghost to the ground, pinning her beneath their weight. Her screams continued, growing more desperate, as the black mound of darkness slowly sank into the earth. With each passing moment, Lilith's wails grew fainter until, at last, Lilith and the dark figures vanished entirely, leaving behind an almost suffocating silence.

Gina felt her breath catch in her throat, her body trembling with a mixture of relief and lingering dread. She glanced over at *Llorona's* ghost, which now descended gently towards the water, hovering just above the surface. The once-fierce countenance had transformed into an expression of serenity and peace. When she met Gina's gaze, Gina felt a sense of understanding pass between them.

"*¿Ella ahora está en el infierno donde pertenece. Se ha hecho justicia,*" *Llorona* said softly, her voice devoid of malice. The Spanish words echoed in Gina's mind, translating themselves into English: "She is now in Hell, where she belongs. Justice has been done."

A shudder rippled through Gina, but she couldn't deny the truth of those words. She exchanged a glance with Dane, his eyes filled with questions she wasn't sure she could answer.

CHAPTER THIRTY-SEVEN

THE COLD CONDENSATION FROM the soda can dampened Gina's fingers as she sat on the hardwood floor, surrounded by the echoing emptiness of the house. It had been a month since she and Dane had found Lilith's body, and even now, the memory sent a chill down her spine.

"Hey, what happened after you guys found the wife's body?" Carla asked, her voice breaking into Gina's reverie.

Gina hesitated for a moment, unsure of how much to reveal. There were parts of the story that she knew Carla wouldn't believe—parts about ghosts and demons that even she had trouble wrapping her head around. "Well, the local doctor did an autopsy," she began carefully. "He confirmed Lilith died from severe head trauma caused when she fell and hit her head on the river rocks." She shrugged. "They couldn't very well blame it on *Llorona*, so they ruled it an accident," she concluded, taking a sip of her soda. The sweet taste couldn't wash away the sour feeling in her stomach.

Her friend's eyes widened. "That's awful." She paused before asking, "And what about Miles Davis? Did he confess?"

"He tried to blame it on his wife," she replied, her grip tightening around the can. "He claimed she was the real monster."

"Wow," Carla breathed out. "Do you think he's telling the truth?"

Her mind raced with the events of the past month, the faces of the ghosts she'd encountered, and the horrifying truth they'd uncovered. "Yeah, I do," she admitted, heart heavy. "But he never tried to stop her, which, in my mind, makes him as much of a monster as Lilith. Hopefully, when his case goes to trial, the courts will see it the same way. For now, they're both off the street."

"Thank God for that," Carla said, nodding her head solemnly. "And did *Llorona* stop terrorizing people at the RV park?" she asked, obviously curious.

Gina exhaled slowly, remembering the ghostly figure's haunting cries. "She did. After all the commotion died down, I went back to the river and talked to *Llorona*, with Uncle Victor's help."

"Wait, you actually talked to her?" Carla's eyes widened in disbelief.

"Yeah," she said, a hint of a smile playing on her lips. "It turned out that *Llorona* wasn't so scary after all. She even apologized for trying to possess me."

"Wow." Carla shook her head in amazement. "So why was she doing all that?"

"Turns out *Llorona* felt terrible about killing her own kids hundreds of years ago," she explained, tracing the rim of the soda can with her finger. "She'd taken it upon herself to safeguard the children of Las Palomas. When she realized a child predator had come to town, she raised the alarm in the only way she knew how."

Carla let out a low whistle, clearly impressed. They each took a swallow of their drinks. For Gina, the fizzy bubbles provided a brief distraction from the heavy conversation.

Setting down her can, her gaze wandered around the nearly empty family room. The walls seemed to echo with memories of Uncle Victor; his laughter and their shared moments together. A pang of melancholy settled in her chest.

Just then, her phone chirped with an incoming text. Glancing at the screen, she couldn't help but smile. "I guess it's time," she said, getting to her feet.

Carla stood up as well, and they tossed their empty cans into the trash before heading for the door. Gina couldn't shake the feeling that she was leaving behind more than just an empty house, but life, like the river in Las Palomas, continued to flow forward—and so would she.

Sunlight glinted off the rented U-Haul, casting playful shadows across the driveway as the women stepped outside. Gina's Acadia rested on a towbar hooked to the van, ready for the journey ahead.

"You still haven't told me what happened with the loan shark," Carla complained, her arms folded across her chest.

Gina gave her a small smile. "Well," she began, brushing a strand of hair from her face. "Dane sent the recorded phone call with Frankie Goldstein to a friend of his in the Houston PD. They added it to the case they were building against him and finally had enough to arrest him. He'll be going away for a long time. As for who shot his two men, we may never know."

A flicker of relief passed over Carla's features, but her mischievous grin quickly returned. "And what about Dane?" she asked, wiggling her eyebrows up and down suggestively. "Is he still in the picture?"

Gina's cheeks flushed as a taxi pulled to a stop at the end of the driveway. Both women turned to watch as Dane emerged, his tall frame unfolding gracefully from the back seat. He smiled and waved, then paid off the taxi so it could leave.

"Most definitely," Gina said, her heart swelling with affection as he walked over to join them.

"Hey," he murmured, leaning in for a long, smoldering kiss that left her breathless.

When they finally broke apart, both turned to face Carla, Dane's arm still draped around Gina's waist. Trying to regain her composure, Gina introduced them. "Carla, this is Dane. Dane, meet my friend and Realtor, Carla."

"Nice to meet you," Dane said, extending his free hand for a shake.

Carla grinned and shook his hand. "I've heard all about you." Then she turned her attention back to Gina. "Don't worry about the house. I'll take care of everything."

"Thank you, Carla," she said, gratefully.

Dane glanced at her; his eyes filled with warmth. "Are you ready to leave?"

She nodded, feeling a sense of certainty settle over her like a warm blanket. Handing him the keys to the van, she watched him climb behind the wheel, giving her time to say goodbye.

Carla looped her arm through Gina's, guiding her around the van toward the passenger side. The air buzzed with that bittersweet feeling of endings and beginnings.

"You still going to do ghost whispering?" Carla asked.

"Every day, as part of my new job."

"What new job?"

Gina smiled. "You're looking at the tour guide for the newly established Las Palomas Haunted Tours program."

Carla chuckled. "They couldn't have selected anyone more perfect for the job."

"That's exactly what I told the Town Council when I was down there two weeks ago." They'd reached the passenger door of the van. Gina stopped and pulled Carla into a hug. "Promise me you'll come visit soon," she said, her voice thick with emotion. "You can stay with us. Dane's house has a guest bedroom."

"Just try to keep me away," Carla said, returning her hug.

Drawing back, Carla brushed a tear from her cheek, her gaze drifting to the van's open passenger window where Dane could be seen inside, patiently waiting. "Are you sure about this? I mean, what's Las Palomas got that Houston doesn't?"

Gina glanced at Dane, his steady presence behind the wheel anchoring her in more ways than one. Turning back to Carla, she smiled through her own tears. "It has everything I want or need."

With a last embrace, Gina climbed into the van. The door closed with a soft thud, sealing her and Dane in their own little world. As he shifted the vehicle into gear, she waved goodbye to Carla, watching her grow smaller in the side-view mirror until she vanished completely.

"Ready for the next adventure?" Dane asked, his hand finding hers.

"As long as we're together," she said, knowing deep down that Las Palomas held the promise of her future. Whatever lay ahead, she was ready to face it—with Dane by her side.

BOOKS BY ROBIN T. POPP

TEXAS AFTER DARK SERIES
Death at the Double R
The Ghost Whisperer's Gambit

NIGHT SLAYER SERIES
Out of the Night
Seduced by the Night
Tempted in the Night
Lord of the Night

THE IMMORTALS SERIES
Immortals: The Darkening
Immortals: The Haunting
Immortals: The Reckoning
Beyond the Mist

SUN SERIES
Too Close to the Sun
Dark Side of the Sun